THE ARMADA LEGACY

13/10

Scott Mariani grew up ... ... es in the wilds of Wales. *The Armada Legacy* is the eighth book in the *Sunday Times* and Kindle bestselling series featuring ex-SAS hero and former theology scholar Ben Hope, translated into over twenty languages worldwide. For further information please visit: www.scottmariani.com

By the same author

SCOTT MARIANI

The Armada Legacy

AVON

This novel is entirely a work of fiction.
The names, characters and incidents portrayed in it are
the work of the author's imagination. Any resemblance to
actual persons, living or dead, events or localities is
entirely coincidental.

AVON

A division of HarperCollins*Publishers*
77–85 Fulham Palace Road,
London W6 8JB

www.harpercollins.co.uk

A Paperback Original 2013
1

Copyright © Scott Mariani 2013

Scott Mariani asserts the moral right to
be identified as the author of this work

A catalogue record for this book is
available from the British Library

ISBN 978-0-00-739843-0

Set in Minion by Palimpsest Book Production Limited,
Falkirk, Stirlingshire

Printed and bound in Great Britain by
Clays Ltd, St Ives plc

Find

That's my last Duchess painted on the wall,
Looking as if she were alive. I call
That piece a wonder, now: Frà Pandolf's hands
Worked busily a day, and there she stands.
Will't please you sit and look at her?

Robert Browning, *My Last Duchess*

Chapter One

Just after ten, on a clear, cold night in late February, and the moon-glow over the Donegal Atlantic coast cast a speckled diamond glimmer across the dark sea. High above the shoreline, a solitary car was weaving its way along the twisty coastal road, leaving behind the distant lights of the Castlebane Country Club and heading inland towards Rinclevan on the far side of New Lake.

The chauffeur of the black Jaguar XF was a square-shouldered former Grenadier Guard called Wally Lander. He kept his eyes on the winding road and drove in silence, studiously detached from the conversation of his passengers: his employer Sir Roger Forsyte, Forsyte's personal assistant Samantha, Sam for short, and an auburn-haired woman Wally had never seen before. Attractive, he could tell from the couple of discreet rearward glances he'd snatched at her – very attractive in fact, wearing a tight-fitting black dress that he frustratingly couldn't see enough of in the driver's mirror. He presumed she must have attended that evening's Neptune Marine Exploration media event and was now coming along as a guest to this private party, which would probably last well into the wee small hours. Maybe something to do with Sir Roger's latest caper, Wally mused. If she was alone, that meant she was almost certainly single. Definitely worth a crack at it. There was a chance he'd get to chat to her at the party, find out more about her.

Wally couldn't know it yet – none of them could know it – but that would never happen. Because Wally didn't have very long to live.

Nor would Wally ever know the mystery woman's name. It was Brooke Marcel, or *Dr* Brooke Marcel, when she was in her professional capacity as an expert consultant in hostage psychology and former visiting lecturer at the Le Val Tactical Training Centre in Normandy, France. Tonight, though, she was just here as a guest of her friend Sam, who was sitting between Brooke and Sir Roger, all clipped efficiency with a tiny netbook resting across her knees and its screen reflected in her glasses as they ran through some NME business details together. Sir Roger had loosened the tie he'd put on for the presentation and was leaning comfortably back against the Jaguar's cream-coloured leather.

As Sam started detailing the plans for the following day, Brooke tuned out and drifted back to the thoughts that preoccupied her so much of the time, with the same mixture of emotions that always came flooding back whenever Ben was on her mind.

She wished he could have been here. He loved Ireland, would have been completely in his element here on the Donegal coast. Maybe she'd been wrong in coming without him – but the fact was, she'd been plain too nervous to ask him. The wrong signals, she'd worried. Moving too fast, trying to force things prematurely. Or something like that. She didn't know any more. For a gifted and highly trained psychologist, it struck her how little she understood her own feelings.

Ben Hope. What an enigmatic, complex man he was. Even before they'd got together she'd been aware he had ghosts in

2

his past, stuff you could never ask him about and which he kept fiercely private; so closed, and yet he could be so open, so warm and tender. Sometimes she felt as if he'd been there all her life; sometimes as if she'd never known him at all.

As she gazed out of the window at the rocky landscape flashing by in the car's lights, Brooke wondered whether her troubled relationship with Ben would ever recover. It had started so blissfully, only to crash and burn so senselessly just when it was beginning to look as though it could last forever.

The crash had come in September. The autumn months had been a forlorn, empty time, drowning herself in her work; the Christmas holiday without him had been almost unbearably miserable. Then, slowly, slowly, over the last couple of months had dawned the prospect of a possible reconciliation. The phone conversations between her home in London and his in France were growing longer and more frequent. Sometimes he even called her.

It was still fragile, though, still just a tiny candle flame that might be snuffed out at any time. There were moments when Brooke thought he was holding something back from her; times when she could sense the tension between them, ready to flare up all over again. In their separate ways, they'd both been equally to blame for the split. *What a couple of hotheads we are*, she thought wryly to herself as she recalled the awful quarrel that had bust them apart. The worst thing was that, in the end, it had all been about nothing. Just a stupid, horrible misunderstanding.

'The chopper will pick us up at the house and take us over to Derry Airport first thing in the morning,' Sam was saying to her employer. 'We arrive at Gatwick just after ten-thirty, then on to Málaga in plenty of time to make your meeting with Cabeza.'

Forsyte pursed his lips and gave a grunt of assent. Drifting momentarily back to the present, Brooke noticed the way he kept fingering the handle of the attaché case secured to his wrist by a steel cuff and a slim chain, and she briefly wondered what was inside that must be so valuable; but her curiosity waned rapidly as she turned back towards the dark window and resumed her own private thoughts.

A flash of white light caught Brooke's eye. The road behind was no longer empty: the bright headlights of a car were coming up fast. No, she thought, twisting round to peer out of the rear window – not a car, but a van of some kind. Going somewhere in a real hurry, too.

Forsyte glanced back as the van's main-beam headlights loomed close enough to fill the inside of the Jaguar with their glare. 'Just some idiot,' he said nonchalantly. 'Pull in a little and let him past, will you, Wally?'

Wally shook his head in exasperation, then flipped on his indicator, slowed to just over thirty and steered towards the side of the narrow road to let the van by. The large vehicle noisily overtook them – a plain white Renault Master panel van, scuffed and spattered with road dirt – then cut in tightly at an angle and screeched to a halt, blocking the road.

Wally hit the brakes and the rear passengers were thrown forwards, except for Brooke who'd braced herself against the front passenger seat a fraction of a second before the emergency stop. Sam let out a little cry as her netbook went flying. 'What the hell—?' Forsyte shouted.

'Fucking arsehole!' Wally thrust the automatic gearbox into park and left the engine running as he climbed out of the car. 'What's your game, you bloody prick?' he yelled, slamming his door shut and storming up to the stationary van.

The Renault Master's doors burst open simultaneously. Wally stopped dead in his tracks and went quiet as two men jumped out and strode aggressively towards him. They were both wearing black balaclavas, and not because of the biting February wind.

Brooke's blood turned icy at the sight of the weapons in the men's hands: identical compact submachine guns, black and brutal with long tubular sound moderators attached to their muzzles. She'd seen weapons like those before.

So had Wally Lander, once upon a time, but his nine years out of the army had blunted his senses and all he could do was gape.

'Oh, my God!' Sam gasped. Forsyte stared in speechless horror, clutching his attaché case.

Neither of the masked men spoke a word. Instead, almost casually, they turned their weapons towards Wally and opened fire. From inside the car, the silenced gunfire seemed like no more than a rapid string of muffled thumps. Wally's legs folded under him, then he collapsed lifelessly at the roadside. His blood was bright in the beams of the Jaguar's headlights. Sam screamed in panic and clung onto Forsyte. 'What do they want with us, Roger? Oh Jesus, they're going to kill us!'

Brooke hesitated, but for no more than a second before she launched herself at the gap between the front seats and scrambled in behind the wheel. She wrenched the stick into drive, stamped the heel of her Italian designer party shoe on the gas and held it all the way down.

The Jaguar took off with a roar and a rasp of tyres. Clenching the wheel, Brooke had no choice but to drive grimly over Wally's dead body with a sickening *bump-bump*.

The masked men hurled themselves out of the way. There was a jarring impact as the car slammed into the angled side of the van; a rumpling of plastic and the screech of metal grinding on metal as she forced her way through the gap, the

Jaguar's wheels spinning wildly and revs soaring to drown out Sam's screams and Forsyte's indistinct roar of fury. Then, suddenly, the way was clear and Brooke could see the open road stretching ahead in the headlight beams. She'd made it.

But then the strobing muzzle flashes lit up the rear-view mirror and she felt the steering wheel go heavy in her hands as a flurry of gunfire blew out the back tyres. There was nothing she could do to prevent the car skidding out of control and veering across the road. Brooke caught a glimpse of a large grey rock looming in front of the car – then a crunching collision, and the airbag exploded in her face, dazing her.

Running footsteps. Voices. The next Brooke knew, the Jaguar's doors were opening and there was a gun at her head. She turned to face her attacker. His eyes were cold and hard in the slits of the balaclava.

'Get out, bitch,' he said.

Chapter Two

Three days earlier

'I'm telling you, Brooke, it's going to be great,' Sam insisted for about the fifth time in twenty minutes. 'You can't possibly miss it. Seriously.'

That was Samantha Sheldrake all over. She'd always been the pushy one, ever since their university days. It was easy to see how she'd managed to land the position of PA to one of Europe's most dynamic multi-millionaire entrepreneurs, the head of the Southampton-based company Neptune Marine Exploration.

'I don't know,' Brooke replied, stretching out on the rug and wiggling her bare toes in the warmth of the open fire as she cupped the phone between shoulder and ear. The remains of a TV dinner for one were cooling on a tray nearby. Another solitary end to another dull day, with just an unexpected phone call from the northwest coast of Ireland to raise her spirits a little. 'Seems a long way to go for a party,' she said. 'And you said yourself it's for company personnel.'

'Rog—' Sam caught herself, ' – Sir Roger won't mind if I invite a guest. Get you out of London. It's so grey and dismal there at the moment.'

It had only been a minor slip, but Brooke had picked up on it and wondered whether Sam's relationship with her boss might be a little closer than she liked to let on. Brooke kept her observation to herself, and said, 'Get me out of London for what? So I can come and see the grey ocean instead?'

'Hey, we're talking about Donegal,' Sam insisted. 'Even the drizzle is beautiful. I should know, I've spent most of the last few months here. Besides, I told you, this is no ordinary party. First there's going to be this brilliant media event at a *very* swish country club – you'll be blown away – more than three hundred delegates – all arranged by yours truly.'

'Naturally.'

'Naturally. And then we're all heading back to the house, where the fun starts for real. Sir Roger's sparing no expense. You should see the manor house he's rented – it's like a chateau, and the party's going to take over a whole wing. You've never seen so much champagne in your life, I kid you not.'

'Remind me again what we're celebrating?'

'Does the "we" mean you're coming?'

'I didn't say that.'

'Well, it's only the grand unveiling of one of the most important historic sunken treasure salvage operations of the last twenty years,' Sam said, with only a trace of smugness. 'The recovery of the sixteenth-century Spanish warship the *Santa Teresa* has been Neptune Marine Exploration's biggest coup since Sir Roger founded the company.'

Brooke smiled into the phone. 'Now you sound like one of your own public relations blurbs. What's the wreck of a Spanish warship doing off the Irish coast, anyway?'

'Did I not tell you all about this when we were in Austria?'

Sam and Brooke had spent a few days in Vienna before Christmas. Brooke had been too preoccupied by her troubles with Ben to enjoy the short break very much. 'Maybe you did,' Brooke said. 'Refresh my memory.'

'Come to Donegal and you'll learn all about it.'

'I have to tell you, Sam, mouldy old boats are not exactly the most fascinating thing in my life right now.'

'Oh, come on.' Sam paused, and Brooke could tell from the momentary silence that she was hatching some new plan. 'Why don't you bring a friend along?' Sam went on slyly. 'As in, a very *special* friend? You know who I mean. That's if things are, you know, back on an even keel.'

'Ben?' Brooke hesitated, a little thrown by the suggestion. 'That might not be such a great idea. Things are still a bit . . .' Her words trailed off uncertainly.

'I knew it. He's treated you like shit, really. When was the last time you set eyes on him?'

Brooke said nothing. She reached up to finger the slender gold chain she wore around her neck. Ben had bought it for her in Paris soon after they'd got together. She'd been wearing it nearly constantly ever since, although she sometimes wondered why she was so attached to it now that their relationship was meant to be finished.

'I'll tell you when it was,' Sam went on. 'It was when he came to pick up that horrid little mongrel he left you with. Am I right?'

'Scruffy's not horrid,' Brooke protested lamely.

'There you go again. Being nice. You're too good for that guy. He's using you, can't you see it?'

'Let's not go there, all right? It's complicated.'

Sam was undeterred. 'All right, so maybe it's not a good idea. Then why don't you invite that dishy upstairs neighbour of yours I met once? The novelist guy?'

'You mean Amal?'

'That's the one. Between you and me, I don't know how you can keep your hands off him.'

'Oh, come on. We're not all like you.'

9

'What's that supposed to mean?' Sam said, in mock indignation.

'Amal and I are just friends. And he's a playwright, not a novelist.'

'Hmm. You can't stay single forever, darling, waiting for that Ben to make up his mind. You'll end up a dried-out old spinster, like Miss Havisham.'

'Watch it, I'm only thirty-six,' Brooke protested. 'And four months younger than you, I might add. Besides which, I don't see you heading to the altar with anyone. Miss Havisham, indeed.'

'Well, whatever. The point is, are you coming to Donegal or not? Won't cost you a penny, you know. Neptune Marine will pick up the tab, first class all the way and back again.'

'I'm thinking about it.' Brooke wasn't usually so quick to let herself get swept up in Sam's enthusiastic schemes, but she was beginning to warm to it. 'Maybe it'd be good for Amal. He's had a bit of a letdown recently. A change of scenery might cheer him up.'

'Then it's settled,' Sam said briskly. 'Now, there's a very nice guesthouse not far from the country club. Not the Ritz, as you'd imagine, but it's cosy and comfortable. I'll take care of everything. All you two have to do is turn up. I'll text you the details.'

'Hold on—' Brooke began. But before she could say any more, Sam interrupted her. 'Oh, listen, Sir Roger's on the other line. I'd better take this. See you on Saturday, darling. *Pronto.*'

Brooke sighed, holding a dead phone. Typical Sam. Once she got a notion into her head, there wasn't a force on earth that could stop her.

*

'I've never been to Ireland before,' Amal mused over coffee later that evening when Brooke trotted upstairs to put the idea to him.

He'd answered his door looking morose, unusually dishevelled and clutching a Jean-Paul Sartre novel guaranteed to cast a pall over the most optimistic soul – but brightened up visibly at the sight of her, and invited her eagerly inside. It never ceased to amaze Brooke how beautifully decorated the inside of his flat was. Not bad for a struggling playwright still not thirty, whose first play had just tanked spectacularly and drawn unanimously abysmal reviews from all the critics.

'I thought it'd be nice for you to get away for a couple of days,' she said. 'I know you've been a bit down lately.'

'It's true,' he sighed. 'Though maybe I've taken it harder than I should have. I mean, it can't have been the first utter disaster in the history of theatre, can it? And not everyone walked out. Did they?' he added, hopefully.

On the night, Brooke had counted twenty-six hardy survivors out of an initially well-packed house, but hadn't had the heart to reveal it to him. 'You make it sound a lot worse than it was,' she said, smiling. 'The play's great. I just think its appeal is, you know, selective.'

'I don't know, perhaps people just don't want to see a three-act tragedy about toxic waste,' he muttered, shaking his head glumly. 'It's all about bums on seats at the end of the day. Now, if I'd written about . . . say, the Vietnam War as seen from the viewpoint of a mule, or something, now *that* would've . . .'

Brooke could see that she needed to get back on topic. 'So, what do you think about Ireland, then?' she cut in. 'A breath of sea air, a bit of partying, a few glasses of champagne . . . ?'

Amal gazed into his coffee for a moment, then set the cup firmly down on the table and forced his face into a broad, white grin. 'Screw it, why not? I haven't been out of this bloody flat for days. Sitting here moping all the time like a big self-indulgent baby.'

'That's the spirit, Amal. You won't regret it, I promise you.'

Chapter Three

Saturday evening, and the vehicles were arriving in droves through the gates of the grand-looking Castlebane Country Club. Brooke and Amal got out of the taxi that had brought them from the guesthouse, and joined the stream of smartly-dressed people filtering towards the illuminated main entrance.

The night air was sharp and cold. Brooke could smell the sea and hear the whisper of the waves in the distance. It was clear from all the press IDs on display and the prevalence of cameras everywhere around her that Sam had done a fine job of whipping up media interest in the event. A paunchy white-haired man who appeared to be the local mayor, judging by the gaudy chain and badge of office that dangled like a cowbell from his neck, was stepping out of a car and straightening his jacket, flanked by official minions.

'This ought to be interesting,' Amal said without any great conviction as they approached the gold-lit facade of the building. But if he'd been having second thoughts about abandoning his Richmond sanctuary for the wintry wilds of Donegal, he was far too polite to show it. As always, he was fastidiously groomed, and had swapped his travelling clothes for an elegant grey suit that looked tailor-made.

It had been a while since Brooke had been to any kind

of party, and she'd had to dig deep in her wardrobe back in London to search out the knee-length black cashmere dress for the occasion, which she was wearing over fine black silk leggings and cinched around her waist with a wide belt. Her only jewellery was the little gold neck chain, Ben's gift. The shoes were Italian – a pair of her sister Phoebe's cast-offs – with heels that made her feel perched ridiculously high. They were strictly not for walking more than a few yards in unless you were some kind of masochist. Just covering the distance from the guesthouse to the taxi, then from the taxi to the foyer of the country club, had been enough to raise a blister on her heel.

Why did women insist on inflicting this kind of bondage on themselves, she wondered as she tottered over to the desk to give her and Amal's names to the receptionist. They were checked against the guest list, then waved through a doorway with a smile and a warm 'enjoy the show', and found themselves in a gigantic ballroom that echoed to the buzz of a three-hundred-strong crowd.

Sam hadn't been kidding about the place being swish. At the far end of the room, a podium stood on a low stage in front of a big screen; to its left, an area had been curtained off. A gleaming dance floor separated the stage from forty or fifty tables, each surrounded by red velvet chairs. For the moment, though, most of the attention was centred on the bar, around which a couple of hundred people were bustling to grab their free drinks. The catering staff couldn't hand out the complimentary canapés and dainty little sandwiches fast enough.

Over the background muzak came a piercing squeal from across the room. Brooke would have known that voice anywhere. She turned to see Sam running over, or trying to run, her stiletto heels clattering on the floor. She'd dyed her hair a couple of shades blonder since the brief break the two of them had taken in Vienna before Christmas. Her crimson strapless dress appeared to be in some danger of slipping down, but Sam didn't seem to care too much, and the assorted men ogling her with varying degrees of discretion certainly had no objections either.

'You made it!' Sam beamed.

'You left me very little choice,' Brooke said as Sam pecked her on both cheeks with a pronounced '*mwah – mwah*', something she'd taken to doing now that she moved in higher social circles.

'I'm so pleased.'

Of course you are: it was your idea, Brooke said inwardly. Out loud she said, 'You know my friend Amal Ray,' putting a subtle emphasis on the word 'friend' that only Sam would be able to detect.

'Of course, the playwright,' Sam cooed, ignoring the warning look that Brooke shot at her. 'Amal, that's a lovely name. Tell me, are you *very* famous?'

'You might say I've recently shot to notoriety in certain quarters,' Amal said graciously. 'But we won't talk about that.'

That's a relief, Brooke thought.

'Come and meet Sir Roger.' Sam motioned for them to follow, and led them through the throng. At the heart of a large cluster of people in the middle of the room, a tall, stately silver-haired man in a sombre suit and navy tie was doing the grip'n'grin routine with the mayor and the other local officials for the benefit of the photographers.

'It's such a boost for the local economy,' Sam whispered in Brooke's ear. When the cameras stopped flashing, she did the introductions: '*Dr* Brooke Marcel; Amal Ray the award-winning playwright: my boss, and the CEO of Neptune Marine Exploration, Sir Roger Forsyte.' She made it sound as though

Brooke had found the cure for cancer and Amal had a Pulitzer Prize for literature in his pocket. Brooke noticed Amal's sharp wince.

Forsyte was about sixty, though he was in better shape than many men half his age. His manner was smooth and dignified, if a little cool. He welcomed Sam's guests, expressed his pleasure that they'd be attending the private party afterwards, and insisted they should help themselves to drinks and snacks before the presentation began. 'Speaking of which,' he said, glancing at his well-worn Submariner watch, 'I have a few things to attend to before we kick off, so if you'll excuse me . . .'

Sam shot a grin back at Brooke as she followed her employer towards a door marked PRIVATE. 'You heard the man,' Amal said. 'Let's grab something before this lot drink the bar dry.' They pressed their way through the swarm and had to shout their orders to be heard by the harried bar staff.

'I didn't know you were a gin and tonic type of guy,' Brooke said, once they'd escaped the chaos and found a quieter spot on the far side of the ballroom.

'I've decided to become that type of guy,' Amal replied, knocking back a slug of it, ice clinking in his glass. 'Starting right here, right now.'

She touched his arm. 'You're okay, aren't you?'

Amal swallowed a handful of peanuts, washed them down with another long swig, then gave a shrug. 'I'm not about to go hurling myself madly off the cliffs, if that's what you mean. What's a bit of salt rubbed into the wound, between friends? Award-winning playwright,' he added in a sullen undertone. 'Like I really needed that.'

These artists. She wished he didn't have to be so sensitive. 'Sam didn't mean to hurt your feelings. It's just her way.'

The crowd was rapidly drifting away from the bar to gather

at the foot of the stage. People were checking their watches in anticipation of the start of the show. The mayor and his little entourage had positioned themselves right at the front, where a photographer took a few more half-hearted snaps of them for the local news. There was a stirring behind the curtain to the left of the stage, as if someone was putting the finishing touches to whatever exhibits lay behind it.

Sam reappeared through the door marked PRIVATE, spotted Brooke and bustled over to join her, diverting her attention for a few minutes with her animated chatter. When Brooke was able to tear herself away for an instant, she saw that she'd lost Amal in the crowd. Peering through the milling bodies she caught a glimpse of his back as he slunk over towards the bar for a refill. He didn't look very happy. *Shit*, she thought. Maybe this whole thing had been a bad idea.

'It's so great you're here for this,' Sam was babbling happily for the twentieth time, clutching her champagne. 'Should be starting any moment now . . . yes! There he is. Here we go. Shush, everyone.'

To enthusiastic applause, Sir Roger appeared under the lights, stepped up to the podium and launched into his speech as the glittering Neptune Marine Exploration corporate logo flashed up on the big screen behind him.

Chapter Four

'It's no secret,' Sir Roger began, 'how in July of last year, after many months of exhaustive mapping and researching possible locations over countless square miles of the Atlantic Ocean, Neptune Marine Exploration, the world leader in historic marine salvage, succeeded in locating one of the greatest finds of the last several decades.' He waved at the screen, and right on cue there flashed up an underwater image that Brooke had to peer hard at to make out. Against a murky, greenish sea bed was the shape of a decayed hulk barely recognisable as a sailing ship. Its masts had long since vanished, leaving just the crumbling ruin of its hull, scattered in fragments and half buried under countless tons of sand and shingle.

Marvellous, Brooke thought, thoroughly unimpressed. She glanced over in the direction of the bar. Amal had his back to the rest of the room, sitting hunched over his second gin and tonic. Or maybe his third by now.

'The previously undiscovered wreck of the Spanish warship *Santa Teresa*,' Forsyte announced proudly. 'Sunk in 1588 off Toraigh Island near the Donegal coast after the Spanish Armada, repelled by the Royal Navy following their abortive invasion of England, were chased northwards and headed for Ireland in the hope of finding a friendly port and refuge among their Catholic allies, only to have the remnants of their fleet devastated by freak Atlantic storms.'

He turned to gaze lovingly at the screen. 'I know, she's not much to look at after sitting at the bottom of the ocean for over four hundred and twenty years. But thanks to the unique 3D underwater scanning technology developed by Neptune's own computer engineers, we are now able to reconstruct in perfect detail the splendour of this once magnificent warship. Ladies and gentlemen, I give you the *Santa Teresa*.'

Forsyte motioned grandly at the screen, and an appreciative murmur rippled through the crowd as the computer reconstruction of the ancient vessel appeared in all her former glory – a vast spread of pearly-white sails billowing against the blue ocean, her majestic bow splitting the water in a white crest, the sun glinting off the dozens of bronze cannon muzzles protruding from her open gun ports, crewmen swarming up and down her rigging, files of brightly-armoured troops lining the deck. Even Brooke had to raise an eyebrow at the impressive sight.

Amal still had his back to the room.

'I'm proud to say that the salvage of the *Santa Teresa* has turned out to be one of the most successful projects ever undertaken by Neptune Marine Exploration,' Forsyte said with a grin. 'This incredible achievement would not have been possible without the dedication, determination and diligence of our salvage crew and dive team. Nobody will contradict me when I say the man most directly responsible for this triumphant success is Neptune's incomparable dive team manager. He's been with us since the humble beginnings of the company back in 1994 and I'm proud to call him my friend. Ladies and gentlemen: Mr Simon Butler.'

More applause as a slightly-built man with sandy hair

appeared on the stage and stepped up to the podium. Forsyte clapped him warmly on the shoulder, then moved aside to give him the mike.

Once the applause had died down, it was immediately apparent that Butler lacked Sir Roger's flair for public speaking. He stumbled his way, red-faced, through a speech of thanks that consisted solely of cramming as many of the names of his team members as possible into a couple of minutes. The audience was soon shifting about restlessly and losing interest. Butler was visibly relieved when Forsyte returned to the podium.

Forsyte went on, and almost instantly regained the interest of the crowd. 'As he launched the Armada to its fate, King Philip II of Spain spoke these words: *"We are quite aware of the risk that is incurred by sending a major fleet in winter through the Channel without a safe harbour, but . . . since it is all for His cause, God will send good weather".*' He gave a dark smile. 'Sadly for him, and perhaps fortunately for England, it didn't quite work out that way. And just as the fleeing Armada had to face the most challenging and perilous conditions that Mother Nature could unleash, even a highly skilled and expert outfit like Neptune Marine Exploration, with the most cutting-edge modern technology at its disposal, has faced sometimes appalling conditions and enormous difficulties to restore this historic treasure to the world. All through autumn and winter our salvage vessel *Trident* was battered by the same severe storms faced by the Spanish sailors all those centuries ago.'

'That's true,' Sam whispered to Brooke. 'I was seasick like you wouldn't believe.'

'We learned first-hand about the force of nature that drove the *Santa Teresa* onto the rocks off Toraigh Island and sent every one of the six hundred souls aboard to a watery grave,'

Forsyte continued. 'But thanks to the heroic struggle of our entire team against all the wrath of the elements, we can now reveal for the very first time the extent and magnificence of the treasures that this lost wreck has yielded up for posterity.'

'He's a great speaker, isn't he?' Sam whispered to Brooke.

'A little on the florid side,' Brooke said, 'but he makes his point.'

Forsyte motioned towards the curtains to his left, and as if by magic they glided open to reveal the screened-off area of the ballroom. This was the moment the audience had all been waiting for, and they surged eagerly forwards, the buzz of chatter rising to fever pitch as they took in the awesome splendour of Neptune Marine Exploration's haul.

Arranged like a museum exhibit were racks and units covered in a dizzying array of gold and silver plates, goblets, candlesticks, trinkets. Open caskets piled high with coins and jewels. Entire dinner sets of fine porcelain. Then there was the weaponry – row on row of pikes, swords and armour, all gleaming under the lights. Mounted on an enormous plinth, a set of bronze cannons, polished to a dazzle. At the centre of it all was the warship's salvaged figurehead, badly pitted with age but somehow brought to the surface intact.

Nothing could get a crowd excited like incredible wealth. There were whistles and exclamations. One of the journalists gasped 'Fuck my boots' loudly enough to be heard by the mayor, who turned and shot him a filthy look. A scrum of photographers jostled for the best shot. Everyone was thinking the same thing, even Brooke.

'How many millions must this stuff be worth?' she asked Sam, who beamed with pleasure.

'Enough to have already sparked quite a nasty little war between the British government and the Spanish treasury officials claiming ownership of the wreck and its contents. It'll rage on for months. But however it's all divided up in the end, Sir Roger will get his forty per cent share. Look at him. I've never seen him this chuffed with himself.'

Brooke could see the security men positioned discreetly at the rear of the exhibit, at least eight of them, all extremely serious-looking. She wouldn't have been surprised if they'd been government agents. There must be an army of them backstage, she thought, and a convoy of trucks waiting to whisk the priceless treasures away to a bank vault somewhere.

Remembering Amal, she looked back over towards the bar. He was still sitting slumped over his drink, mountains of gold coins, emeralds and rubies the last thing on his mind. She thought about going over to him, then decided he probably wanted to be left alone.

'Now, it was by no means uncommon through history for regular line-of-battle warships of any nation to carry all manner of splendid artefacts,' Sir Roger went on from the podium as the cameras carried on flashing in a frenzy. 'But let's remember that the Spanish Armada was no ordinary naval fleet. This was a full-blown invasion force, whose commanders were quite assured would make short work of the English defences, sweep rapidly inland and within weeks, perhaps even days, establish a new Spanish territory upon English soil. In fact, they were so confident in the overwhelming force of this massive fleet that its officers, many of them noblemen of the highest position, loaded their ships with a wealth of luxury goods, artwork and other finery – not just to enjoy on the voyage, but with which the country's new Spanish rulers would have refurnished the palaces and stately homes of Tudor England. And of course if you want to set up a new government, you're going to need money. Lots and lots of it. Aboard the *Santa Teresa* were scores of wax-sealed casks, stuffed with greater quantities of coin, gold bars, jewellery and precious stones than have ever previously been salvaged from a warship wreck. What you see here is only a sample.'

Perhaps sensing that many of the audience were too busy goggling at the treasure to pay him much attention, Forsyte quickly brought his speech to an end and invited questions from the media people. A forest of hands instantly shot up. 'Yes?' he said, picking out the prettiest of the journalists.

'Sir Roger, Neptune Marine Exploration is famous for the amount of preliminary research it does before starting an excavation project. You must have been aware of what you'd find down there. But were there any surprises among the treasure?'

Sam leaned close to Brooke's ear. 'That girl's a plant,' she whispered.

'What do you mean?'

'Just listen.'

Forsyte chuckled. 'Apart from the sheer quantity and value of it?' he said, and the crowd joined in his laughter. More seriously, he added, 'Well, in fact, we did make one highly unexpected discovery.' He paused for effect. 'It's not on display yet, and I'm afraid you'll have to wait for me to reveal it.'

There were groans and calls of 'Give us a clue' and 'Come on, Sir Roger'. Forsyte held up his palms. 'All in good time, my friends. I don't think you'll be disappointed when we eventually make it public.'

What a showman, Brooke thought. Forsyte certainly knew how to bait his hook. 'What's the big surprise?' she asked Sam.

Sam shrugged. 'You think he'd tell me? I only run most of the company for him.'

'Now, enough talk,' Forsyte said. 'Please feel free to wander among the displays, and of course there's still plenty more food and champagne to come. Enjoy.' To a final thunderous roar of applause he stepped down from the podium and slipped away among a sea of arms reaching out to pat him on the back and shake his hand.

Sam turned to Brooke and tapped her watch. 'Now that's over, it's party time.' She seemed to notice for the first time that Amal was missing. 'Where's your friend?'

'He's . . . ah . . .'

'Best go and get him, eh? Wally's coming round with the car. We'll be out of here in a few minutes.'

At the bar, Brooke laid her hand on Amal's shoulder and said, 'You okay?' She knew the answer even before she'd asked the question. There were four empty glasses lined up on the bar in front of him and he was hard at work on the fifth. That many gin and tonics wouldn't have put too big a dent in Ben Hope's sobriety – but that was just one of the ways Amal differed greatly from Ben. His eyes were unfocused and his jaw was slack.

'I'm fine,' he slurred. 'Fresh as a daisy.' He slid down off his bar stool, walked three steps and had to prop himself against a wall for support. 'Christ,' he mumbled, clasping his head. 'I want to be in bed.'

'Oh, Amal, what have you done to yourself?'

'The car's waiting,' Sam announced, materialising out of the crowd and pointing at a side exit. She was holding a laptop case and had slipped on a green cardigan over her dress. 'You two ready?'

'Amal's not feeling well,' Brooke told her. 'I don't think we can make it to the party.'

'You're kidding,' Sam said, reeling as if all her plans were crumbling.

'No, no,' Amal protested. Making an effort to speak coherently, he said very carefully, 'I don't want to be responsible for spoiling your evening. You go.'

'Hurry up and decide, guys,' Sam said irritably, and headed towards the exit with a glance at her watch.

Brooke sighed. 'What about you?'

'Don't worry about me. I'm still sober enough to call a cab.'

'Are you sure? I've got no problem going back to the guesthouse with you. The party doesn't mean that much to me.'

He wagged a finger at her. 'You came here to have a good time. Now go. I . . . I command it.'

Sam was waving at them from the open doorway, mouthing 'come on' and gesticulating at the waiting Jaguar outside.

'You're quite sure?' Brooke asked Amal.

'Go and have fun,' he muttered with a sickly smile. 'Go. *Go*.'

She made her decision. 'Oh, what the hell. I'll see you for breakfast, then,' she said. 'Sleep well, and take care, all right?'

Amal watched as she left the building. The Jag's engine was purring gently, its exhaust billowing in the cold night air. He couldn't make out the face of the driver, but recognised Sir Roger Forsyte in the back seat. Sam opened the rear door of the Jag, climbed in and slid along to the middle to make room for Brooke. With a final glance back at Amal, Brooke climbed in after her and closed the door.

The Jaguar took off towards the gates.

That was the last he saw of her.

Chapter Five

The pale light of the Sunday morning sun hauled Amal up from the dark, dreamless depths, and with consciousness came the first rush of nausea. 'Oh God,' he groaned.

He lay miserably curled up under the covers for a while, nursing his throbbing headache and cursing himself for having drunk so much. What the hell had possessed him? A vision of a tall, frosted glass kept appearing in his mind, making his stomach threaten to flip. He realised he was fully clothed under the duvet. 'Oh, God,' he repeated. 'Why? Why?'

Gradually, the scattered pieces of his memory fitted themselves back together to form a coherent picture of the previous night. He remembered calling the taxi from the country club – nothing at all about the car coming to pick him up, or the journey to the guesthouse. Only the vaguest recollection of letting himself in the door and managing to stagger up to bed.

Once he was fairly certain that the slightest movement wasn't going to trigger off a violent spate of vomiting, Amal gingerly hauled himself out of bed. He kicked off his shoes and left a trail of scattered clothing on the way to the bathroom. Showered, changed and feeling marginally more human, he left his room. It was twenty past eight. Brooke's door across the landing was shut. He tapped lightly on it and murmured her name. When he got no reply, he figured she must either be downstairs or had come back so late last night that she was still sleeping.

Amal tramped heavily downstairs. The frying grease smell that wafted up to meet him was almost more than he could bear, but he managed not to puke as he wandered into the breakfast room.

No Brooke. No anybody, except for the landlady, Mrs Sheenan, who was in the adjoining kitchen frying up a mound of eggs and bacon that would have fattened the Irish Army.

Mrs Sheenan didn't appear to notice his presence, or hear his mumbled 'Good morning'. That was partly due to the fact that she was half deaf – something he and Brooke had discovered when they'd checked in to the place the day before – and partly due to the blaring TV in the kitchen, which was turned up to full volume.

Amal dragged himself over to a table by the window, where Mrs Sheenan would be bound to notice him sooner or later. He couldn't stomach food, but yearned for a comforting mug of hot, sugary tea. He sat there for a few moments, gazing towards the misty bay and thinking how strangely out of his element he felt in this place, and then felt suddenly angry with himself for being so ungrateful towards as generous and warm-hearted a friend as Brooke. He started brooding once again over the way he'd let her down by going and getting wasted. What a prat. He could only hope it hadn't totally ruined her evening.

Eight twenty-five. Amal was lucid enough by now to remember that they'd have to check out in about an hour and forty minutes' time to catch their flight back to London. If Brooke wasn't awake soon he'd have to go and rouse her. Then again, he thought, she might have been up for hours and be about to return any moment, rosy-cheeked and tousle-haired from a brisk walk or a run on the windy beach. That was more her style.

Amal's thoughts were punctured by Mrs Sheenan, who had suddenly registered his presence and begun fussing over him, frying pan in hand, screeching in a voice that pierced through his skull. Yes, he'd slept fine, thank you. Yes, the room was lovely and warm. But her broad, toothy smile vanished as, averting his eyes from the pool of grease swilling in the pan, he informed her as politely as he could that he didn't want any bacon.

'Oh,' she said, scanning his face and then pursing her lips in extreme disapproval. 'You must be one of them Muslins.'

'I'm just not hungry . . . really, a cup of tea would be fine.'

'Just tea, is it.' Mrs Sheenan sighed loudly and returned to the kitchen to dump her frying pan with a crash on the stove.

'You haven't seen my friend Brooke this morning, have you?' Amal called after her through the open door. He had to make an effort to raise his voice over the din of the television. The kitchen was now reverberating to the opening theme of the local RTÉ news.

'Eh?' Mrs Sheenan screwed up her face with a hand cupped behind her ear, then glanced back at the television. 'Shall I turn it down?' she bawled, making a move for the remote control. 'You've an awful quiet voice.'

'I was asking—' Amal began.

He stopped mid-sentence as he realised what had just come on TV. He burst out of his chair and hurried towards the kitchen, his hangover suddenly forgotten. 'No!' he yelled. 'Don't turn it down!'

Too late: Mrs Sheenan had pressed the mute button. Amal stopped in the doorway and gaped at the screen.

The soundless television picture was of a wrecked car on

a winding country road, in the middle of a rugged, empty landscape that looked shockingly familiar to Amal.

The black Jaguar had skidded into the opposite verge and smashed into a huge rock. Wreckage was scattered across the road. Teams of police were milling around the vehicle, blue lights swirling in the early morning mist.

As Amal went on staring in increasing horror, he saw a team of paramedics loading a bagged-up body on a gurney into the back of an ambulance. A close-up of the car showed what were unmistakably bullet holes punched through the black bodywork. The rear window was shattered and the rear wheels shredded, the tyres clearly blown out by the gunfire.

'No, no, no, this can't be happening,' Amal murmured. He blinked his eyes tightly shut and then opened them again.

It *was* happening.

Mrs Sheenan gave a derisory snort. 'There you go. Another eejit gone and killed himself.'

The silent picture changed to a shot of Sir Roger Forsyte, followed by one of Sam Sheldrake. 'Turn the sound on!' Amal yelled. Flustered, Mrs Sheenan fumbled with the remote. Now the picture showed the face of a stocky-looking man in his forties whom Amal didn't recognise.

At that moment, Mrs Sheenan managed to get the sound back on.

'. . . *found a short distance from the vehicle, has been identified as Wallace Lander, forty-two, a former British soldier employed as a driver by Sir Roger. Early reports suggest that Mr Lander was gunned down by at least two automatic weapons, killing him instantly. Police sources have confirmed that both Sir Roger and Miss Sheldrake remain missing, presumed kidnapped by the attackers.*'

Amal slumped in a kitchen chair and numbly absorbed what he could. It barely seemed real to him. The empty, bullet-riddled car wreck had been discovered before dawn that morning by a night shift worker returning home from a local packing plant. Police had traced the Jaguar to a luxury car hire firm in Derry, and confirmed that the vehicle had been leased to Sir Roger Forsyte's company, Neptune Marine Exploration. Forsyte was known to have been en route from Castlebane Country Club to nearby Carrick Manor, his temporary base in the area, when the attack took place. Witnesses had reported seeing the Jaguar leave the country club shortly before ten o'clock that evening; it was estimated that the incident had occurred at approximately 10.05 p.m.

Amal's breath was coming in short gasps as he anticipated the mention of a third passenger. Any moment now, Brooke's face would be on the screen, with the news that she'd been found dead like the car's driver, or snatched by the kidnappers. But there was nothing at all.

An idea came to him, like a flash of white light. Maybe Brooke had changed her mind at the last minute – maybe she hadn't gone off to the party at all, but had got out of the car and taken a taxi back to the guesthouse, assumed he was already in bed and not wanted to disturb him? The wild notion suddenly seemed utterly convincing. Headache and nausea forgotten, he leaped to his feet, ran upstairs and hammered on her door. 'Brooke? Are you there?' She had to be. Come on, Brooke. Be there. *Come on.*

Silence. Amal burst into the room and saw it was empty: the bed neatly made, unslept in, Brooke's clothes folded on top of the sheet, her travel bag sitting on the rug nearby, the novel she'd been reading propped open on the bedside table. Amal dashed into the ensuite bathroom, but all there was of Brooke were her toothbrush and hairbrush by the sink, her little wash-bag and shower cap on the shelf.

His head was spinning as he thundered back downstairs.

'You're sure you didn't see her this morning?' he quizzed Mrs Sheenan.

'Who?'

'My friend! Brooke! The woman I was here with.' With some effort, he managed to drag it out of Mrs Sheenan that he was definitely the only guest who'd come down to breakfast that day.

That was when the panic set in for real. Amal began to tremble violently, first his hands, then his whole body, feeling weak and jittery as though his knees might buckle under him. His brow was damp with cold sweat.

'I have to call the police,' he said.

Chapter Six

Ben Hope hauled the Explorer sea kayak onto the little tongue of shingle, wiped his hands on his wetsuit and gazed up at the towering white cliff. The saltiness of the cold air was on his lips. Circling gulls screeched overhead. 'All right,' he said, as much to himself as to the cliff, 'let's see what you're made of.'

Sunday morning, and the relaxed pace of life in the little corner of rural France Ben now called home was going on much as it always had. He could hear a church bell chiming from a kilometre or so away inland, summoning to Mass those locals who weren't enjoying a late breakfast, pottering about their homes, feeding their chickens or still lazing in their beds.

Ben Hope's way of relaxing was a little different from most people's. The stretch of shoreline he'd driven the ancient Land Rover to that morning with his kayak lashed to the roof was known locally as the Côte D'Albâtre, the Alabaster Coast, for the chalky whiteness of its sheer, gale-battered cliffs. Nineteenth-century painters had travelled here to depict them; writers and poets had been inspired by them – today he was going to climb them.

Partly just because they were there, and because Ben's idea of pleasure was to set himself challenges that normal folks would have done anything to avoid, and also partly because doing this kind of thing helped him to forget all the churning thoughts that otherwise tended to crowd his mind these days.

After securing the kayak and warming up his muscles with some bends and stretches, he pulled on his rock-climbing shoes and gloves, strapped the lightweight waist pack around his middle, then walked up to the foot of the cliff and reached for his first handhold. He paused as a jolt of pain ran up his arm.

The two bullet wounds sustained on Christmas Day were well healed now. They'd both come from the same small calibre handgun, but even a .25 could do terrible damage at close range. Ben had been lucky. The first shot had glanced off his ribs and passed on through; only the second, lodged in his shoulder, had caused any difficulty to the surgeon who'd pulled it out. Now there was just a little stiffness, some pain from time to time and another couple of scars to add to the collection of war wounds Ben had accumulated over the last twenty years. The man holding the gun had come off very much worse.

Ben waited for the twinge to pass, then launched himself upwards.

The rock face was sheer. As he made his way higher and higher, the wind whistled around him and the hiss of the surf on the rocks below grew fainter. The summit approached, inch by careful inch. Hand over hand, the pain only served to drive him on, energy exploding inside him and a kind of fierce joy filling his heart.

But even suspended from his fingers and toes halfway up a high vertical slope with a dizzy drop beneath him, he found he couldn't shut out his thoughts completely. Which wasn't entirely a surprise, considering that he'd recently come through just about the most tumultuous episode of a life that nobody could have called boring. Few things could shock Ben any longer, but the discovery just before Christmas that he had a grown-up son he'd never known about had hit him like an express train. He'd been reeling from it ever since.

He hadn't told Brooke about it – hadn't been able to bring himself to, though he'd been on the verge of telling her a dozen times over the phone during the last few weeks. Now that they were speaking again and there seemed to be a faint hope of reconciliation, Ben was extremely wary of complicating matters and placing an added strain on their slowly-mending relationship. The right time would come.

Ben's son's name was Jude Arundel, and until the age of twenty he'd taken for granted that his parents were Simeon and Michaela, the vicar and vicar's wife of the Oxfordshire village of Little Denton. In reality, Simeon had raised Jude as his own son despite knowing full well that the boy had been the product of a brief romance between Ben and Michaela, back when they'd all been students together at Oxford.

It hadn't been an easy transition. Jude had only learned the truth in the devastating wake of Simeon and Michaela's deaths in a car smash. Just as Ben was finding it alien and awkward coming to terms with sudden parenthood, not to mention the loss of his friends, Jude had had a difficult time adapting to the knowledge that his whole upbringing had been a lie, and that the man he'd called his father for most of his life hadn't been at all. He'd gone through every shade of emotion, from outright denial and disbelief, to furious resentment, to simmering rage and finally a brooding acceptance.

But out of all the friction, a fledgling relationship was slowly developing between Ben and Jude – not so much that of a father and a son, but more like two friends, or even two brothers, one of whom just happened to be twenty years older than the other. The fact that Ben had recently rescued Jude from the hands of a secretive and ruthless government agency called the Trimble Group, who were blackmailing Ben into acting as their gun-for-hire, had helped more than anything to forge their friendship.

When Jude had visited Ben's French home and place of business, an old farm called Le Val, in mid-January while Ben was still convalescing from his injuries, the two of them had had their first real chance to sit down and talk. Among other things, they'd discussed Jude's growing disenchantment with his Marine Biology degree course at Portsmouth University. Ben, who'd cut his own Theology studies short twenty years earlier and often wished he hadn't, had encouraged him to see it through to the end.

Jude wasn't so sure where his future lay. There were times when Ben could see in his newfound son the same restlessness of spirit that had driven him in his own headstrong, sometimes foolhardy younger days, and wished the boy had taken more after Michaela than himself.

Those worries aside, Ben had deeply enjoyed Jude's visit. When it was over and he'd driven him back to the ferry port at Cherbourg, he'd suddenly realised how much he was going to miss Jude's company until the next time they'd meet.

Then it had been back to business. The Le Val Tactical Training Centre was still overbooked with people wanting to acquire the specialised skills it had to offer, skills that only men like Ben, his business partner, ex-SBS commando Jeff Dekker and their team of instructors were qualified to teach. The training schedule at Le Val had never been so busy, which made a Sunday morning getaway like this one all the more welcome.

With a final heave, Ben hauled himself up onto the cliff's summit. He knelt in the grass, dusted his hands and looked down. The moored kayak was a tiny red sliver far below.

'There, that wasn't so difficult,' he murmured to himself. His heart rate was steady and he wasn't out of breath. Not in disgraceful shape for an old man, he thought. He mightn't have bet on still being able to fly through 'sickeners', the gruelling SAS selection tests he'd endured long ago, but he was pretty sure that he'd give young squaddies half his age or less a decent run for their money.

Ben stood up, unzipped a compartment of his waist pack and took out a small bottle of mineral water. He cracked the seal and drank, then spent a few moments gazing out to sea, the breeze ruffling his thick blond hair, as he considered whether to take the long, easy footpath back down to the shore or descend the way he'd come.

The phone buzzed inside his waist pack before he could decide. He answered, expecting the call to be from Jeff Dekker with some work-related query or other.

It wasn't Jeff.

'Am I talking to Ben Hope?' someone said on the other end.

A man's voice, shaky, uncertain. Ben was certain he'd heard the voice before; but where?

'Who is this?' Very few people had this number.

'My name's Amal,' the voice replied. 'Amal Ray. We met once, around Christmas time. Brooke's upstairs neighbour.'

Ben remembered him perfectly well, and if it hadn't been for the tension and anxiety he could hear in the guy's voice, he might have responded with something like, 'Hi, Amal, it's a pleasure to hear from you.' Instead he frowned and stayed silent.

'Something's happened to Brooke,' Amal said. 'Something terrible.'

Chapter Seven

A constant thin drizzle was slanting down out of the dark afternoon sky as the Ryanair flight from London Stansted touched down at City of Derry Airport, a few miles east of the border between Ulster and the Irish Republic.

There was a hard set to Ben's face as he strode from the plane. Outwardly, he was calm, but a violent storm was raging inside and he fought to contain his impatience going through passport control and customs. His only luggage was the battered and well-travelled old green canvas army bag into which he'd thrown a few things before dashing away from Le Val, leaving everything in the hands of Jeff Dekker.

Jeff had been as shocked as Ben to hear the news of Brooke's disappearance. 'Just call if you need me,' he'd said. 'I'll be there.'

Amal was waiting nervously for Ben near the airport entrance. His eyes were red-rimmed and he looked several years older than when Ben had last seen him.

There was no time for greetings. 'Anything new?' Ben asked, and Amal morosely shook his head. They left the terminal in silence and went outside into the gathering dusk. The drizzle had intensified, and Ben turned up the collar of his scuffed leather jacket. He motioned at the smattering of vehicles in the car parking area. 'Which is ours?' His final instruction to Amal over the phone earlier that day had been to hire the fastest car he could find locally.

'That one,' Amal said, and bleeped a key at a dark blue BMW saloon. 'Hope it's okay. It was the best I could get.'

Ben tossed his bag into the back of the car. 'I'll drive,' he said, taking the keys. Amal didn't argue, and climbed into the passenger side. Before he'd shut his door, Ben was already gunning the car backwards out of its parking space. The tyres squealed on the damp concrete as they took off for the exit. Ben aimed the car westwards, heading for the N13. 'Now tell me everything,' he said.

Amal closed his eyes and let out a sigh. 'What more is there to say? I already told you everything on the phone.'

'Let's go through it again. Starting from the beginning.'

Amal miserably recounted the whole thing: Brooke's idea for getting him out of London; the media event at Castlebane Country Club; how he'd got too drunk to go on to the party afterwards and she'd reluctantly gone off without him; how that had been the last he'd seen of her. Ben listened and pushed the BMW on hard and fast as Amal talked, overtaking traffic and keeping an eye on the mirror, on the lookout for police. He didn't want anyone slowing him down.

'It's all about this Forsyte guy, isn't it?' Amal said, interrupting himself. 'Surely it must have been him they were after?'

Ben had used every moment of his journey from France to plough through all he could find online about Sir Roger Forsyte, the company he'd founded, Neptune Marine Exploration, and its various highly lucrative exploits over the years salvaging sunken treasures around the world's oceans. Despite the wealth of material available, from reams of newspaper articles to spreads and interviews in *National Geographic* and other publications, Ben had noticed that the details of Forsyte's past career, prior to NME's founding in 1994, seemed just a little hazy. As his flight had crossed westwards over England, he'd wondered why that might be.

He'd also been pondering over where he'd heard the name Roger Forsyte before. The bell it was ringing in his mind was distant and faint, but it was ringing nonetheless and he was frustrated that he couldn't make more of it.

'Seems that way,' he replied to Amal's question. 'Successful businessman, just made a killing and splashing it all over the media. He's the primary target for a kidnap and ransom job. The others just happened to be there. Wrong place at the wrong time.'

'It's a nightmare,' Amal said, on the edge of panic. 'Oh, God, it's a nightmare. It isn't really happening. Tell me it isn't happening.'

'It's happening. Take a breath. Focus, keep talking.'

Amal took several deep breaths to compose himself. 'What more is there to say? I got up this morning, saw the news and realised Brooke hadn't come back, so I called the cops. They call them the Garda here.'

'Yeah, I know that. Go on.'

'It took ages for them to send a car out. When they finally got there, they gathered some of Brooke's personal things and sealed them in these plastic pouches . . .'

'For DNA sampling.'

'I can't believe they even have that kind of technology in this backwater.'

'They probably have to send them to Dublin. Go on.'

'Well, then they put me in the police car and drove me miles to the nearest proper town, a place called Letter-something . . .'

'Letterkenny.'

'They took me into this tiny room with no windows. I spent over an hour there giving my statement to this angry, racist little bastard who's in charge of the case. Felt like I was being interrogated.'

Border signs flashed by as the speeding BMW passed from Northern Ireland into the Republic. When Ben had first known the place as a young soldier the border had been thick with heavily-armed checkpoints, and vehicles passed through under the stern eye of a British Army GPMG gunner with his finger on the trigger. Those days were all but over now, but the memories of the Troubles were soaked like blood into the land.

'What's the name of the detective in charge?' Ben asked.

'Hanratty. Detective Inspector Hanratty. Real charmer. Needless to say, they'd never heard of Brooke being in the car until I told them. At first, I reckon they thought I was some kind of crank. Next thing you know they're grilling me as if it was me who was under investigation. Anyway, when I finally managed to get away from the police station I wandered up the road and found this café where you can *actually go online.* That's when I thought about looking you up. Brooke's told me a little about what you used to do for a living, and the business you run now in France. God knows how I remembered the name of it. I called and spoke to a guy named Jeff who gave me your mobile number.' Amal shrugged wearily. 'That's it. We should never have come to this bloody place. It's all because of me and that stupid play . . .'

'Never mind the stupid play,' Ben said. 'What else can you tell me?'

'Only what I've seen on TV. When Forsyte's car didn't turn up for the party last night, the people waiting for him at the big house just assumed at first that he'd been delayed by the media, or whatever. Then more time went by, no sign of him, and they started making phone calls. It wasn't until

41

the middle of the night that anyone called the cops. Even then, the police didn't lift a finger until after the car'd been found by some guy on his way home from work early this morning.' Amal glanced anxiously at Ben. 'They'll be looking for them, won't they? I mean, surely they'll be doing everything they can . . .'

'There are standard procedures,' Ben said, cautiously. 'First priority is to establish contact with the kidnappers. Forsyte's been divorced for years. No siblings, no children, so the ransom demand will probably be made to the company itself. Meanwhile, it's a question of combing over the crime scene to see what they can dig up, fingerprinting everything in sight, bringing in the sniffer dogs, taking any evidence back to the lab for analysis. They'll want to talk to staff at the country club for anyone who might have seen anything, and check out CCTV footage. Round up every photographer who was at the media event, and check through all their images for anything suspicious – someone hanging around, looking out of place. Go through the records of local vehicle rental companies during the last week or so for anything paid in cash. Liaise with the Coastguard and check the registers of any boats in and out of local harbours, as well as spot-checks on vessels. Call out the air support unit to scout for possible safehouses, empty farm buildings, disused industrial units, where kidnappers might try to hide a victim.'

'Sounds pretty thorough,' Amal said, sounding marginally more optimistic.

Ben agreed, in principle. But the caution in his tone was because he also knew that this particular crime had occurred in one of the sleepiest parts of rural Ireland, even more slothlike in its ways than Galway, where he'd lived for a number of years. The place was so neglected by the authorities that it had come to be known as 'the forgotten county'.

Even at the height of the Troubles in the seventies and eighties, when the occasional IRA incident would take place on the Republic side of the border, there had been comparatively little for the Garda to deal with – hence they had even less experience of this kind of contingency than the most parochial police force in England. The local cops would most likely have had to send out to faraway Dublin for a forensic investigation team equipped and specialised enough for the job.

In short, Ben would have been extremely surprised if Detective Inspector Hanratty had got his thumb out of his arse to do half the things he'd just described to Amal.

'Lastly,' he said, 'they should be talking to all the Neptune Marine Exploration employees, checking phone records and finding out if anyone's been unfairly dismissed recently or might have any kind of grudge against Forsyte. In a case like this they'll study the victim's background and history for significant enemies, and to check whether Forsyte might have any financial problems of his own, like gambling debts, dangerous and expensive habits, the kind of thing that might cause someone to stage their own kidnap for ransom.'

'What?'

'It's not unheard of.' The speedometer needle climbed above the ninety mark as Ben urged the powerful BMW past a slow-moving truck.

'I can't believe that,' Amal said. 'But then, nothing makes sense to me. Like, for instance, if someone kidnapped Forsyte for ransom, why did they take Brooke and Sam? They're not rich like Forsyte. Nobody can pay millions to get them back. Is it because they were witnesses?'

Ben shook his head. 'No. You can shoot a witness, like they shot Forsyte's driver. It's more than that. From a kidnapper's point of view, female hostages give you better leverage,

43

more bargaining power. Nobody wants to see them get hurt, so ransoms get paid faster.' His voice sounded detached, but speaking those words cost him a lot of pain. The moment he'd said them, he wished he'd kept his innermost thoughts bottled up more tightly.

'*Leverage?* Oh, Jesus.' The horror in Amal's eyes reflected what was in Ben's own mind. Images of severed body parts sent in the mail. Torture. Or worse. 'They won't harm them, will they? Will they? Answer me. They won't do anything to Brooke, will they? Ben?'

Ben's fists clenched around the steering wheel. He was silent for a beat, swallowing back the rising tide of crazed anxiety that made him want to scream and pound the dashboard to pieces.

Then he said quietly, 'I'll get her back.'

And the voice inside his head replied: *if she's still alive.*

Chapter Eight

Evening had fallen like a black shroud and their conversation had lapsed into a heavy silence by the time Ben stopped the car. He cut the engine but left the headlights on, spilling a broad pool of white light across the road and carving through the slowly-drifting fog of drizzle.

Amal looked up from his lap as if emerging from a trance, and saw that Ben was checking his phone. 'You expecting a call?' he asked.

'From a guy called Starkey,' Ben muttered, frowning at the phone.

'Who's that?' Amal asked, but Ben was too preoccupied to answer. There had been no call. He tutted and shoved the phone back in his pocket.

'What is this place?' Amal said, peering through the glass.

Ben said nothing. He got out of the car. The night felt damp. He could hear the whisper of the Atlantic in the distance, and smell the salt tang in the air.

'This is where they were taken, isn't it?' Amal said ominously, climbing out of the passenger side and hugging his coat tightly around him.

Ben just nodded grimly. He wanted to break into a run, but forced himself to walk calmly towards the lights and activity he could see up ahead. As he made his way up the road he glanced left and right, up and down, drinking in details.

He hadn't walked far when he paused in his stride. Faintly discernible on the glistening wet road surface by the glow of the BMW's headlamps were the traces of heavy skid marks where a car had pulled to an emergency stop. He considered them for a moment and then continued a few steps further, before pausing again and turning to look to his left, where a small section of the roadside verge had been cordoned off with markers and police tape.

A short distance further up the road was a second set of tyre marks. The vehicle that had made them had a wider wheel track than the first, and judging by the curve of the marks it had overtaken at speed and then swerved across the road from right to left, screeching to a stop. What was odd about the second set of tyre marks was the additional smudge of rubber that seemed to indicate that the vehicle had been shunted sideways after coming to a halt. He pictured it in his mind.

Ben knelt down and pressed a fingertip against the cold, wet road. Lifting it back up, he examined the tiny flake of paint stuck to it. It was white on one side, blue on the other.

He flicked it away, stood up and walked on again. Some thirty yards ahead on the right-hand side of the road, a large area of the verge and the ground beyond was barricaded off and illuminated by blazing halogen floodlights perched up on tall masts, haloed by drifting moisture. Rows of cones and a temporary traffic control had been set up to filter what few vehicles might pass by through the narrowed gap. Three Garda Land Rovers were parked off-road, casting their flashing blue glow over the rugged ground.

Tucked in in single file behind the row of cones sat an empty Toyota Avensis patrol car, an ageing unmarked Vauxhall

46

Vectra and a van that Ben guessed belonged to the forensic team he could see combing the large field to the right of the road, their reflective vests shining yellow in the distance. The van's number plate bore the county identifier D for Dublin: his guess about the forensics guys having to come all the way from the Garda HQ in the capital had been correct. That didn't make him feel any better.

He wasn't hugely surprised either to see that, some twenty hours or so after the fact, the cops were only now getting themselves organised to conduct a proper search and remove the crashed Jaguar XF from the scene. A pair of uniformed officers were standing back watching as the vehicle was winched up onto a flatbed lorry. All that would be left behind were the skid marks and the pieces of debris littering the verge at the foot of the large roadside rock that Ben could make out in the glow of the recovery vehicle's swirling orange light. The Jaguar's front end was badly crumpled and it was obvious it had hit the rock at some speed after skidding violently to the right.

Even more noticeable were the bullet holes that had chewed up the Jaguar's rear bodywork and shredded its back tyres.

Ben swallowed. The particular kind of hole made by a nine-millimetre full metal jacket round as it punched through thin sheet steel was a very familiar sight to him. He'd seen enough bullet-riddled vehicles in enough war zones all over the world to tell at a glance that this kind of damage was the work of fully-automatic weapons. Whoever had carried out the attack, they were disturbingly well equipped and not afraid to use it.

Ben sensed a presence next to him and turned to see that Amal was standing at his shoulder.

'Oh, my God, look at the state it's in,' Amal groaned as the recovery crew started securing the Jaguar to the lorry's flatbed. 'It looks even worse than it did on TV. How could anyone—?'

Survive that, Ben knew Amal had been about to say. And under normal circumstances, Amal would have been right. Nothing could walk away from that kind of firepower.

Unless . . .

'See where most of the damage is?' Ben asked him, pointing. 'The mass of the gunfire was concentrated on the car's undercarriage, not the bodywork at passenger height.'

'So what does that mean?'

'That the gunmen were aiming to disable and stop it, not to kill everyone inside. If they'd wanted to do that, it would have been easy for them.'

Amal nodded, but didn't seem much reassured.

Ben couldn't feel entirely reassured either. He didn't want to think about the amount of lead that had been sprayed into the car with Brooke inside, or the fact that a stray bullet could easily have ripped a path through enough layers of thin steel and plastic and leather to find its mark. But the thought wouldn't go away. He kept seeing Brooke's face in his mind, and he wondered with an icy chill whether he'd ever see it again for real. His hands felt shaky and he was breathing fast.

But there was no time for sentimentality here, he reminded himself with an effort. He had to keep his wits about him or he'd be about as much use to her as the police.

'What are we doing here?' Amal asked. The cold and damp were getting to him, making him shiver.

'I wanted to see it for myself.'

'So you've seen it. What happens now?'

'I need a moment,' Ben said. He left Amal hovering uncertainly as he walked a few yards closer to the crime scene. Among the sparse grass of the verge near the cordon was a tall flat rock, wet and glistening under the floodlights and the blue swirl from the police vehicles. Ben leaned against the rock and reached into his jacket's hip pocket for his crumpled pack of Gauloises and his Zippo lighter. He fished out a cigarette and lit it, but after a few seconds the drizzle had made the paper soggy and his heart wasn't in it anyway. He tossed the fizzling cigarette down into the grass at his feet, and was mechanically crushing it into the dirt with the heel of his boot when he felt something under his sole and looked down.

It wasn't a pebble. He dropped into a crouch and poked around in the wet grass. When he found the small object, he held it up to the light to examine it closely.

'What've you found?' Amal asked him, walking across.

Ben didn't reply. Clasping the object in his palm he stepped over the police tape to look for more.

An angry yell made him turn to see a short, stout figure in a flapping raincoat marching rapidly towards them from the direction of the Land Rovers.

'Hoi! You! This is a police crime scene!' As the man approached, shouting and gesticulating at them, Ben could see in the glare of the overhead floodlights that it was a plain-clothes detective, a stockily-built guy in his mid fifties or thereabouts.

'That's him,' Amal said in a low voice. 'Hanratty, the one I told you about.'

Chapter Nine

Detective Inspector Hanratty stormed up to them, scowling. A slick of carrot-red hair was plastered across his puckered brow. He had mud spattered over his shoes and the bottoms of his trouser legs were sodden. But Ben guessed that spending hours out here in the shit weather wasn't the sole reason for the sour grimace on Hanratty's face. It looked permanently etched into his ruddy features. Ben's first impression was of a chronically malcontented guy who, when he'd finished harrying and persecuting his work colleagues for the day, bullied his wife and kicked the dog.

'This is a police crime scene,' Hanratty repeated loudly. 'Get out.'

Following a few yards behind was a female officer. Like her colleague, she was in plain clothes – a detective sergeant, was Ben's guess. She was petite, elfin in her looks, with dark shoulder-length hair that had gone limp from the drizzle. She was visibly tired, but in contrast to the dogged stupidity in Hanratty's eyes, hers were quick and sharp.

'My name's Hope,' Ben said. 'I'm a close friend of one of the victims, Brooke Marcel.' He reached for his wallet and took out the little photo of her that he carried inside. The picture had been taken in France during summer. She was smiling and the sun was in her hair. He couldn't bring himself to look at it.

Hanratty gave it only a cursory glance. 'See that police tape there?' he blustered. 'Know what that means? It means keep your nose out of where it doesn't belong, understand?' He turned his sour gaze on Amal, and his eyes narrowed with recognition. 'Ah, Mr . . . Ray, wasn't it? What are you doing poking around here with him? We've taken your statement already, so now you can—'

Ben looked at him. 'Listen, I came to help, not to argue with you, okay?'

Hanratty flushed and was about to fire an angry reply, but his colleague got in first. 'Mr Hope, I'm Detective Sergeant Lynch,' she said calmly. 'We do have the situation under control, thank you, so if you'd like to return to your vehicle . . .'

Ben opened his clenched palm and tossed them the small object he'd found in the grass. Hanratty caught it in his fist, peered down at it and then stared up at Ben in surprise and indignation. Lynch stepped closer to her colleague to see what it was.

'It was lying over there by the roadside,' Ben said. 'Thought it might be useful. It's a nine-millimetre shell casing.'

Hanratty's features twisted into a sardonic leer. 'How helpful of you, sir. It happens we've already recovered a number of these.'

'Then I imagine you've learned something from them,' Den said.

Lynch took the small steel casing from Hanratty's hand and examined it. 'Who the hell do you think you are?' Hanratty growled. 'Get out of here before I—'

'Learn what?' Lynch said. 'We already know shots were fired at the car.'

Ben pointed at the cartridge in her fingers. Her nails were trimmed short and practical. 'Thin steel, not brass,' he said. 'Plus, two small flash holes in the primer socket instead of the more usual single larger hole means the cartridge was designed to take a Berdan type primer. That's unusual. You don't normally see them, except with milsurp ordnance. That's military surplus,' he added for the benefit of Hanratty, who was glaring at him with widening eyes and turning mottled under the floodlights. 'Secondly—'

'Secondly?' Lynch said. She was listening closely, her head cocked slightly to one side.

'See where the case mouth is dented from the weapon's ejector port, where it spins and smashes against the receiver on its way out? That denting is typical of the way the Heckler & Koch MP5 submachine gun mashes its spent shells. Expensive weapon, and this one was brand new.'

'How the hell can you tell that?' Hanratty snapped impatiently.

'Scrape marks on the side of the casing, from loading,' Ben said. 'The magazine isn't fully broken in yet, follower spring's a little stiff. It's normal for the first few hundred rounds. So your perpetrators are using milsurp ammo, hard to come by without the right contacts, and they're very professionally equipped.'

Lynch arched an eyebrow. 'Is there more?'

'Just that the placement of the empty casings you've already found, and the others that're probably still scattered in the grass, should allow you to figure out by the distance and the angle of ejection more or less where the gunmen were standing, how they moved,' Ben said. 'Might help you to find footprints, determine the exact number of shooters, little things like that. If it were me, I'd have the team searching over here instead of out there in the field.' He smiled a thin, humourless smile. 'But then, who am I to tell you your job?'

'What did you say your name was?' Hanratty demanded.

'Forget it,' Ben said. 'I don't have time to waste talking to idiots. Come on, Amal, let's go.'

'Hey!' Hanratty yelled as they headed back towards the car. 'Don't you walk away from me. Who're you calling an idiot?'

Ben kept walking. Amal followed along nervously.

'Hold on a minute,' Lynch called out, trotting after them. 'Mr Hope, wait.'

'I've seen all I need to see here,' Ben said without turning round. He was nearly at the car when she caught up with him and gently grasped his arm.

He wheeled round to face her. 'I've dealt with a thousand Hanrattys in my time,' he said. 'He's a fool, and he's totally out of his depth.'

A long-suffering little smile played at the corners of Lynch's mouth, as if she'd be only too happy to agree with him if she were free to. 'You're not dealing with him now,' she said calmly. 'You're dealing with me, DS Kay Lynch. Let's talk, Mr Hope. Please.' There was no hostility in her expression, no suspicion, just earnestness and fatigue.

'No offence, Kay, but I think someone like Tommy Logan at the ERU in Dublin should be handling this.' The Garda's Emergency Response Unit was the nearest thing the Irish police had to SCO19. One or two of their units had undergone hostage extraction training with the SAS during Ben's time, and Commander Tommy Logan had sent a team for instruction under Ben and Jeff Dekker's tutelage last year.

Lynch frowned. 'Who *are* you?'

'I told you who I am. I'm a friend of Brooke Marcel who was in that car.'

'No, I mean, who are you really? You've got experience at this kind of thing, haven't you?'

'More than your friend there, for sure,' Ben said, with a dismissive gesture at the distant figure of Hanratty, who was marching back over to the Land Rovers and barking orders at the forensic team.

Ben had had enough of this place. He was about to turn back towards the car, but the expression in Lynch's eyes made him hesitate. He slipped his wallet and a ballpoint from his inside pocket and pulled out one of his business cards, slightly crumpled. It bore the name Le Val Tactical Training Centre in bold letters, with his name below. For the sake of appearances, it showed his former military rank – something Ben had never liked but which Jeff Dekker had persuaded him would impress clients.

Ben scribbled his mobile number on the back of the card and handed it to Lynch. 'The web address is there too, if you want to check me out,' he told her. 'It'll give you an idea of my background and what I do.' In fact, the information about him on the website had been trimmed and edited down to the barest possible minimum. Little of what he'd done in his life, both during and since his military days, could be stuck up online for all to see.

But the card alone was enough. Lynch glanced at it and raised an eyebrow. 'All right, I'm impressed. Do I call you Major Hope?'

'It's just Ben now,' he said.

'So what did you mean when you said you came here to help, Ben?'

'I came here to find Brooke. That's what I'm going to do.'

'This is a police investigation. We don't normally invite civilians to come on board.'

'I didn't ask to be invited. I'll do this with you or without you.'

'I have to caution you to stay out of it. For your own sake as well as hers, and that of the other victims.'

'Of course. The last thing you need is a crazy guy like me messing the whole thing up.'

Lynch looked at him. 'I understand that this a very difficult time for you. You're upset and frightened. The police have a victim support counselling service . . .'

'What frightens me the most is that prick Hanratty,' Ben said.

'I'm serious,' she warned. 'You can't go meddling in this on your own. I don't want to have to arrest you.'

'No,' he said. 'You don't.'

Her eyes narrowed for an instant as she sensed the quiet menace in his voice. Then she seemed to soften. 'Look. There's nothing you can do here.'

'You're still waiting for the ransom demand, correct?' he said after a pause.

Lynch hesitated to reply. 'There has been no contact as yet, no. They're still up at Carrick Manor.'

'Carrick Manor?'

'That's where the party was supposed to take place,' Amal put in. 'The big house.'

'Forsyte's land base during the salvage project,' Lynch said, 'while he wasn't supervising the operation from on board his ship. They're expecting the ransom demand call either to come through there, or to the company's main offices in Southampton.'

Ben pointed past Lynch's shoulder. 'Now, that cordoned area on the left side of the road. What's that?'

Lynch didn't need to look round to know which area he was talking about. She pursed her lips. 'You think I can't see what you're doing, trying to prise information out of me? I told you, you can't get invol—'

'It's where the body of the driver, Lander, was found, isn't it?' Ben cut across her.

She rolled her eyes, nodded reluctantly.

'Thirty yards back from the crash site,' Ben said. 'Ideas?'

'You're pretty damn persistent, aren't you, Mr Hope?'

'Just Ben. And yes, I can be. Tell me something, Kay. Lander's body. Apart from the gunshots, what other injuries did he have?'

She looked at him.

'Crush injuries, for instance? Like he'd been run over?'

'Y-yes,' she blurted, her eyes opening wider. 'There were tyre marks on the body that matched the tread pattern of the Jaguar. But how . . . ?'

'Indicating that the car was driven over the top of him after he'd been shot. I thought so. And I'm guessing that there are traces of paint on the front right wing of the car. White or blue?'

'White,' Lynch said, staring at him.

Ben nodded. 'So it was blue before. It was an overspray,' he explained. 'Figures.'

'How do you know all this?'

'Just from looking around,' he said. 'This is how I see it. The car was coming along this road when it was overtaken and forced to stop by a white van. A Ford Transit, maybe, or a Fiat Ducato, something like that, bought cheap and repainted in a hurry.' His eyes were fixed on the scene, as if he were watching the events unfold in front of him in real time. 'Lander, the driver, gets out of the Jaguar to have it out with the van's occupants, who have already stepped out of their vehicle. I'd say two of them, at least. He's got no idea of their intentions, not until it's too late. They open fire on him from near the van, shooting in this direction. Just a short burst, three rounds apiece. The empty cases are ejected into the left-side verge.'

'We found half a dozen of them there,' Lynch muttered.

'Lander goes down at the side of the road. Brooke, Forsyte and his PA must have seen it all happen right in front of them. It's at this point that someone inside the Jaguar takes charge of the situation and gets behind the wheel.'

'That's more or less what we figured out, too,' Lynch said, still stupefied but struggling to hide it. 'One of them tried to make a break for it. Probably Forsyte. That's what the DI says, at any rate.'

Ben was certain it had been Brooke. He knew the way she responded in a tight spot, and this was exactly what she'd have done here. The stab of proud admiration he felt was quickly swallowed up by a fresh surge of grief and anxiety. He reined in his emotions and pressed on.

'Now whoever's taken the wheel of the Jaguar needs to get out of there by the most direct route. They've got the van in front of them partially blocking the way, and Lander's body in between. But there's no other way round, no choice but to aim straight ahead. That's what I'd have done. The car goes right over Lander's body and rams into the left wing of the van from an angle, shunting it far enough aside to the right to create a gap. Hence the traces of white paint on the car's wing, and the sideways tyre marks on the road. The gunmen must have had to jump out of the way as the Jaguar forced its way through. But as the car accelerates up the road, they open fire on it. Now they're shooting in the opposite direction and the empty cases are flying this way, bouncing off the tarmac into the right-side verge. There'll be a lot more there besides the one I found. They take out the tyres and the car loses control.'

Lynch finished for him. 'The victims are moved out of the car and transferred into the van, leaving Lander's body behind. That pretty much sums it up. Well, you've certainly put this together, haven't you?'

'You'd have to confirm it with your genius friend Hanratty,' Ben said. 'But that's how I see it happening.'

'And now what?' Amal said restlessly. 'What's being done?'

'All that can be done,' Lynch told him. 'You need to believe that. And you,' she said, facing Ben, 'need to go home, sit tight and get some rest.'

Ben shook his head. 'What I need is to be kept informed. I can't be left on the outside. If there are developments I don't want to be seeing them on the TV along with the rest of the public half a day later.'

Lynch said nothing.

'Will you do that for me, Kay? Please. I'm not asking for a lot.'

'Hanratty—'

'Doesn't need to know. He's been ignorant all his life. A little more can't hurt him.'

Lynch held up Ben's business card. 'It's this tactical stuff that concerns me. You're not going to do anything silly, are you?'

'If I promise not to do anything silly, will you help me?'

'I'll do what I can,' Lynch replied after a beat.

Chapter Ten

'So where to now?' Amal asked, slumping heavily into the passenger seat.

'Castlebane Country Club,' Ben replied. He twisted the key in the ignition. The BMW's engine roared into life, the tyres rasped and the car reversed hard down the road until he stamped on the brake and slewed round to face the direction they'd come from.

Ben didn't need to ask Amal the way. He'd already studied the map and found the same winding coastal route the Jaguar had taken the night before – besides which, he had precious little trust in his companion's navigational skills. He glanced in the rear-view mirror at the retreating figure of Kay Lynch, who was walking back to rejoin Hanratty, then put his foot down.

Amal was getting the hang of Ben's driving by now. He gripped his door handle tightly, braced himself for the acceleration and closed his eyes as they hurtled into the first set of bends.

Not long afterwards, the BMW was one of the steady procession of vehicles entering the country club's illuminated gateway and filling up the car park. The drizzle had finally petered out and the clouds were breaking up to reveal a clear and starry sky. There were no police vehicles anywhere to be seen outside the country club, but then Ben hardly expected any. He looked at his watch and saw that it had taken twelve minutes to cover the distance between here and the scene of the kidnapping. Assuming that Wally Lander had made similar time in the Jaguar, that pretty much tallied with the official estimate of when the attack had taken place.

It was now quarter to eight. Brooke had been missing for twenty-one hours and forty minutes.

With Amal silently in tow he walked up to the building, climbed the steps and pushed through the heavy door into the foyer.

Ben took in his surroundings. The carpet was red and lush. Faux olde-worlde decor designed to impress the nouveau-riche golfing and tennis crowd. Glossy oak panelling. Display cabinets filled with polished silver trophies. Whirring overhead fans that mimicked the colonial era. Artificial foliage spilling out from reproduction antique urns. A stream of mostly middle-aged and elderly couples was filtering into the foyer behind him, heading towards the busy restaurant area he could see through an open doorway to the right of the reception desk and being greeted by a solemn-looking maitre d'. It was clearly business as usual at the Castlebane Country Club. The events of the night before seemed to have left barely a ripple.

The smell of food from the restaurant reached Ben's nostrils; it occurred to him that he'd eaten nothing at all since leaving France. He shoved the thought to the back of his mind and wandered deeper inside the foyer. A young woman looked up at him with a frown from behind the reception desk. He glanced at the arriving diners in their suits and ties and dresses and pearls, then at Amal in his silk polo-neck and expensive designer coat. Catching a glimpse of himself in a mirror, he saw an unshaven and tousle-haired character in a scuffed old leather jacket, faded denim shirt, well-worn jeans and combat boots who didn't exactly fit with the place's dress code. That was tough shit. He returned the woman's gaze with a cold glare and she averted her eyes.

'I'm pretty sure that's where we were last night,' Amal whispered, pointing at a gleaming double doorway off to the left. 'It's a ballroom, or something. I don't remember it so well.'

Then it was time to refresh Amal's memory, Ben thought. He headed for the doorway. The woman at reception threw him another glance, but nobody tried to stop him. The doors glided open. Ben walked through, Amal followed, and they found themselves inside a vast room, empty except for the stacks of tables and velvet-backed chairs that lined the far wall.

'This is it,' Amal said, gazing around, slowly remembering. 'At least, I think it is. It all looks so different.'

'Is it or isn't it?' Ben said testily. Impatience flared up inside him for a moment, then subsided as he told himself to go easy. Amal was just as upset as he was.

'It is, definitely. But they've cleared everything away. It's weird, as if none of these things had happened. Shouldn't the police have made them keep the place the way it was? For evidence, or whatever?'

'Hanratty,' Ben grunted. 'Never mind him for now.'

'It's coming back to me,' Amal muttered, narrowing his eyes to slits and cocking his head to one side as though that would help him visualise the scene more clearly. He turned to motion at a large expanse of empty floor in the corner nearest the door. 'That's where the bar was.' He grimaced as if to say, *the less said about that the better*. 'Over there was a curtain, with all the exhibits and stuff behind it. To the left of it was the stage, with a speaking podium and a big screen. That's where Forsyte and that other guy gave their speeches.'

'What other guy was that?'

'One of the company employees. I only got a quick glimpse of him when I turned round at some point to see where Brooke was.'

'This is while you were sitting at the bar?'

Amal sighed and nodded.

'With your back to the room.'

Amal sighed and nodded again. 'I remember . . . I remember that he was a younger guy than Forsyte. Quite small, sandy hair. Forsyte introduced him as . . . as some kind of manager. Dive team manager, something like that. His name was . . . I don't know. Baxter? Baker?'

'Butler,' Ben said, remembering the name from the Neptune Marine Exploration website. 'Simon Butler. But I'm not so interested in him right now. Take a minute, look around and see if anything else jogs your memory. Anything at all that might have seemed unusual at the time, or maybe has struck you since as odd. Anyone hanging around Forsyte, for example, or acting out of the ordinary.' As he said it, he was painfully aware that the kind of things a trained eye could pick out would go quite unnoticed by an ordinary observer. Especially one who'd made a point of hitting the bar.

Amal looked anxiously around him for a few moments. 'I don't know. The place was full of people. Journalists firing questions, photographers everywhere. I've never been to anything like that before. I wouldn't know what was strange and what wasn't. Anyway,' he admitted miserably, 'I wasn't even paying a lot of attention. I was too busy drowning my pathetic little sorrows in bloody gin and tonic. And Brooke – poor Brooke – what's happened to her? It's all my fault . . .'

He ran quaking fingers through his hair, dug the balls of his thumbs into his eyes. His breathing was ragged, as though he was about to burst into tears.

'Nobody's blaming you,' Ben said. 'Lay that idea aside. Get a grip, Amal. You're no use to me otherwise.' He was conscious of the harshness in his tone. In a softer voice he asked, 'You want to go into the lounge bar for a drink? You look like you could use one.'

Amal shook his head vigorously. 'No way. Never again. I swear.'

Ben fought back his own desire to drain the place dry of every drop of liquor they had. Anything to slow his mind down, dull the thoughts that kept spinning round and round inside his head, threatening to drive him crazy. 'All right,' he said, taking the BMW key from his pocket. 'Let's get out of here.'

'Are we going back to the guesthouse?' Amal asked as they headed outside towards the car.

Ben's jaw tightened. He wanted, needed, to keep moving. 'Not yet.' He bleeped the central locking open and slid behind the wheel. 'There are some people I'd like to talk to.'

'People?'

'At Carrick Manor.'

'But how do we find the place?'

'There's something called Google Maps nowadays. I thought you writers knew these things.'

'I'm not really that kind of . . . never mind.' Amal closed his door and Ben fired the car up again.

They were three or four miles from Castlebane Country Club and speeding inland when Ben's phone buzzed in his pocket. He dug it out urgently and answered without slackening his pressure on the gas. 'Thanks for calling back, Mike.'

'No problem, mate,' said the raspy voice on the other end.

'Gather you've got a bit of trouble. Sorry to hear it. Anyway, I've dug up the info you asked for. Not a word to anyone, mind, or it's my arse. It's only because it's you.'

'Appreciated,' Ben said. 'Fire away.'

'All right. Neptune Marine Exploration took out a comprehensive K&R policy four years ago with Rochester and Saunders. Apparently they'd had a near miss with Somali pirates in the Gulf of Aden while hauling up some shipwreck or other, and got jumpy in case they were less lucky the next time. Deal was brokered by that greedy bastard Ronnie Galloway.'

'I don't know him. What's the coverage?'

'Twelve million. That's pretty much all I can tell you.'

'It's plenty. I owe you one, Mike.'

'Or two. Good luck, mate.'

Ben ended the call. He knew the name Rochester and Saunders well. Operating from a glittering glass tower in central London, they were one of the top players in their field and provided kidnap and ransom insurance services to high-risk corporate employees, VIPs and other potential kidnap targets all over the globe.

As Ben had known all too well for too many years, kidnap and ransom was a booming industry, not just for those who did it but also for those who could claim to offer protection from it. Long before he'd given up active field work to move to France and set up Le Val, he'd now and then been hired as a freelance negotiator by the insurance companies, to maintain contact with kidnappers, obtain the crucial proof of life, smooth along the negotiations and do everything humanly possible to ensure the early release, unharmed, of the hostages.

Occasionally, other ways and means – more or less peaceable, more or less legitimate – became necessary to get them out.

In those cases, the insurance companies were no longer involved. Nobody was, not officially. Those contingencies, and the direct action needed to resolve them, had been Ben's particular area of expertise.

A lot of K&R operatives had come from a military background – some, like Ben, from 22 SAS and other Special Forces units; Mike Starkey had been a twenty-year veteran of the London Met before switching careers. Many of the guys knew each other well, and because their work tended to take them to the world's concentrated kidnap and ransom hotspots, their paths often crossed, frequently in the seedier bars and nightclubs where criminal informants and other undesirables tended to hang out. Theirs was a strange, closed and often clandestine community, made more so by the fact that in some countries getting paid to help secure the release of kidnap victims was considered tantamount to profiting from the kidnap itself. Some negotiators burned out from the stress, some ended up on the wrong side of the rails completely, or dead, or kidnap targets themselves. Some simply got tired of the life and ended up behind a desk.

Mike Starkey had been one of those. Nowadays he filled a cushy, safe little niche as a broker in London, the world's K&R capital, acting as middleman between the clients desperate for kidnap protection insurance and the underwriters who collectively raked in over £150 million a year in return and were extremely reluctant ever, ever to part with a penny of it in the not-uncommon event of a claim. Business was soaring year on year and guys like Starkey were happily surfing the wave.

Some critics partly blamed the meteoric rise in the popularity of K&R insurance for the terrifying worldwide growth of the trade in human misery, on the grounds that the insurers were only fuelling potential kidnappers with greater financial incentives than they'd ever enjoyed before. It was a point of view Ben privately couldn't disagree with.

'Was that the call you were expecting?' Amal asked as Ben put the phone away.

Ben nodded. 'A contact in London.'

Amal waited for more, and when it wasn't forthcoming he said, 'Are you always this talkative and open with people?'

'Yup, I'm a regular chatterbox,' Ben said, and drove faster.

Chapter Eleven

It was 8.27 p.m. when Ben and Amal rolled up on the crunching gravel outside Carrick Manor. The huge, imposing house was sequestered in its own sweeping grounds at the end of a long private road. A golden glow of light illuminated the entrance and the cluster of vehicles parked outside it.

As Ben stepped out of the BMW he noticed the same unmarked Garda Vauxhall Vectra that had been at the crime scene earlier that evening. He brushed his fingers along the bonnet as he walked by and felt the warmth from the still-ticking engine.

'Hanratty,' he said to Amal.

'I'd a feeling we hadn't seen the last of him,' Amal groaned.

The manor house's front door wasn't locked and the huge entrance hall was empty. Ben paused, listening. From an open doorway at the far end of the hall came the distant sound of voices. Crossing the hall, he followed the sound down a long corridor, Amal tagging along behind him. The sound of voices grew louder and finally led them to another door. Ben peered in.

It was a dining room, or had been before it had been turned into a makeshift operations room by the crowd of police personnel and the fifteen or so other people inside. The room was uncomfortably warm and smelled of stale coffee, sweat and fear. The atmosphere was fraught. Everyone was too busy pacing up and down, looking extremely nervous or shouting at one another to notice Ben slip through the door, followed by Amal.

At the centre of the hubbub was a telephone, sitting silently on the gleaming surface of the long dining room table under the fixed eye of half a dozen men and women in suits.

Ben recognised a number of faces from the Neptune Marine Exploration website: the company had clearly flown out most of its chief executives to Ireland. One of them was the big, broad, balding man in the grey suit, Justin Maxwell, who until yesterday had been Sir Roger Forsyte's second-in-command and now found himself apparently Neptune's most senior executive, a responsibility that he wore gravely. He was leaning over the table, staring down at the phone as if trying by sheer force of will to make it ring.

Ben ran his eye over the monitoring equipment. An ordinary splitter cable was plugged into the wall socket and hooked up to a digital recording device with headphone outputs so that the police could listen in live to calls. Nearby stood a pair of laptops, one to trace the origin of any call online, whether via the GPS tracking system of a prepaid mobile phone or to a landline, and one to pick up any emails the kidnappers might send, complete with video clips of hooded hostages with guns at their heads. It was a pretty minimal setup, but that wasn't the problem.

In fact there were two problems Ben could see, which were of a more fundamental nature. One was that, based on their behaviour so far, these kidnappers didn't seem the kind of people who'd let themselves be so easily traced. Only an idiot nowadays would use a landline to make a ransom demand call, or hold on to a mobile phone they'd used for that purpose. It was just too easy to pinpoint the call's origin, which was why a common trick kidnappers played was to toss the phone onto the back of a long-distance freight lorry after use, to lead the police far off the trail. Other times, they simply burned them.

The second problem was much more worrying. It had to do with timing. Ben looked at his watch.

It was almost eight-thirty. Not good.

A third laptop stood open on another table, surrounded by a small group of people. Onscreen was the BBC News website, showing the unfolding story in all its colourful drama: images of the bullet-riddled Jaguar; a shot of Castlebane Country Club; of NME's ship *Trident*; and of each of the victims in order of newsworthiness – Forsyte's was the most prominent, then Wally Lander, then Samantha Sheldrake. Brooke's had now been added to the bottom. The cops had dug up the same photo of her that she'd given Ben to use on the Le Val site. He'd often caught himself gazing at it when they were apart. He couldn't look at it now.

Hanratty and Kay Lynch were standing on the far side of the room. Neither had seen Ben and Amal come in; their attention was fully occupied by the slightly-built, sandy-haired man who was yelling at them. Ben recognised him as Neptune Marine's dive team manager, Simon Butler. The man looked completely destroyed from stress – his face pale and moist, eyes rimmed with red, his hair and shirt damp with sweat. His voice was slurred, as if he'd been hitting the sherry. 'Surely Scotland Yard should have been flown out here by now?' he was demanding. 'I mean, what is being *done*?'

Hanratty was protesting vigorously that it was his job to liaise with the English police, that everything was in hand, that he knew what he was doing. Lynch was saying nothing, looking down at her feet.

'Ben? Ben Hope?' said a voice. Ben turned round to see a much-changed but still familiar face peering at him out of the crowd.

'Hello, Matt.'

Matt Webster had been one of the regulars on the hostage negotiator circuit when Ben had still been active. He obviously hadn't opted for life behind a desk yet, though he looked as if he should before too long. What little hair he had left had turned grey.

They shook hands, and Ben briefly introduced him to Amal. 'It's been a long time,' Webster said. 'Six years?'

'Seven,' Ben said. 'Lahore.'

'Lahore. Christ, who could forget that one?' Webster shook his head at the memory. Seven years earlier, a wealthy Kent-based private doctor named Shehzad, who had some time before taken out a kidnap and ransom insurance policy with a leading firm, had been violently abducted by an armed gang while visiting family in Pakistan. The ransom demand had been quickly followed up by a severed toe thrown from a passing car; when the toe had been verified as indeed belonging to Dr Shehzad, the insurance underwriters had panicked and sent in a whole team of negotiators. Both Ben and Webster were on it.

The negotiations had been looking reasonably positive until the Pakistani police had managed to trace the phone used by the idiotic kidnappers and taken it upon themselves to storm their hideout in a pre-dawn raid using two armoured personnel carriers. In the ensuing gun battle several officers had been shot to pieces, as well as the entire gang of kidnappers and the doctor himself. The episode had been just one of the instances that had made Ben extremely wary of police involvement in kidnap cases, in any country.

'So Rochester and Saunders sent you up here,' Ben said.

Webster motioned across the room to a colleague who had his back turned to them. 'Me and Dave Hughes there.' He paused and looked puzzled. 'So what are you . . . ? I heard you were doing your own thing now.'

Ben nodded. 'You heard right. My involvement in this is private. I'm here because of Brooke Marcel. She and I . . .' He didn't finish the sentence.

'God, I had no idea,' Webster said, blanching. 'I'm so sorry.'

'What's the situation, Matt? There's been no contact, has there?' Even as he asked the question, he already knew the answer. Just one glance at the haggard faces around the room had told him what he'd come to Carrick Manor to find out.

Webster shook his head. 'Zilch. Not a squeak.'

Ben could have asked Webster if he was thinking the same thing he was, but there was no need. He could see it in his eyes.

He said nothing. It was eight thirty-two. He glanced across at the silent phone. Justin Maxwell was still staring at it fixedly, barely blinking.

At that moment Detective Inspector Hanratty, managing to get away from the angry Simon Butler, spotted Ben and Amal across the room. 'Here comes trouble,' Amal muttered as Hanratty battled his way round the long table and strutted up to them with his fists clenched.

'Not you again,' he growled. 'Did I not tell you to stay out of this, Hope? There's the door.'

'Why don't you fuck off, Hanratty?' Ben said quietly, looking him directly in the eye.

Hanratty blanched. 'What did you just say to me?'

'You heard me,' Ben said more loudly. 'You've three seconds to get out of my face before I put you through that window.'

Kay Lynch was watching Ben from across the room with an expression that said, 'See, this is what I meant by you being silly'.

The buzz of noise dropped to a murmur. People looked around. Hanratty's eyes bulged. Two seconds went by, then three. Hanratty swallowed and took a step back from Ben. Before he could muster up a riposte, Justin Maxwell spoke up.

'Will someone please tell me who this gentleman is?'

'I know him,' Matt Webster cut in. 'I can totally vouch for him.'

Hanratty exploded in protest.

'Let me put it this way, pal,' Webster said, giving him a cold glower. 'If you were kidnapped, this is the guy you'd want on your side.'

'With respect, sir,' Lynch said to Hanratty, 'I think he can be of some use to us. He's got more experience in this kind of situation than the rest of us put together.'

'Then perhaps he should introduce himself,' Maxwell said, silencing Hanratty's objections with a raised hand and looking expectantly at Ben.

Ben disliked talking about himself or his background, but there were times when it was to his advantage to reveal a little more than usual. 'My name's Ben Hope. I served as a Major in the British Special Air Service before becoming a freelance crisis response consultant. In that capacity I've been involved in over a hundred hostage rescue situations. Sometimes as a negotiator, sometimes more directly. I'm here because of Dr Brooke Marcel.'

'I see,' Maxwell said. 'May I ask what is your relationship to Dr Marcel?'

'That's none of your business,' Ben said. 'What does concern all of us here is that the clock's ticking. It's eight thirty-three. Approximately twenty-two and a half hours since the snatch. In my experience, that's a hell of a long time to wait for first contact.'

'Meaning what exactly?'

'Meaning that you people can stand here staring at that phone all you like, but I don't think it's going to ring anytime soon, if ever.'

Maxwell looked long and hard at Ben. His eyes were wide-set and penetrating. 'Couldn't the delay be a deliberate strategy?' he asked. 'The longer we stew, the greater the kidnappers' psychological advantage over us and the more likely we are to acquiesce to their demands. Although we'd do anything to secure Sir Roger's and Miss Sheldrake's release. And that of Dr Marcel, naturally,' he added quickly.

'Kidnappers like to play mind games,' Ben said. 'That's true enough. We call it The Wait, and it's a nightmare for negotiators, victims' families and everyone concerned except the insurers, who're happy to hang onto their money for as long as they can. The kidnappers will often go quiet for days, months, sometimes years, to soften you up like putty so that you'll cave in to whatever terms they throw at you. But not,' he emphasised, 'before making that initial contact. It's crucial to them to approach you and identify themselves as the real kidnappers. This story's already all over the internet by now – it's only a question of time before a hundred opportunists start coming out of the woodwork making phoney demands. Kidnappers generally just want money, and they want it as quickly as possible. Especially when there's an eight-figure sum on the table, you wouldn't expect them to hang around.'

Maxwell narrowed his eyes. 'Who said anything about an eight-figure sum!'

'Let's not mess about,' Ben said. 'I know that your company's insured for ransom claims of up to twelve million with Rochester and Saunders. And if I know it, rest assured the kidnappers will know it. You're not dealing with amateurs, that much is clear.'

'Where did you get that information?' one of the other Neptune executives demanded.

'Ronnie Galloway told me,' Ben said.

The executive shook his head in outrage. 'That little—' he began. Maxwell quieted him with a stern gesture.

'Which strongly suggests to me that the time for a ransom demand has been and gone,' Ben went on. 'Believe me, I don't like it any more than you do.'

Maxwell's brow furrowed into deep creases. He looked at Simon Butler, then at Matt Webster and his colleague from R&S. Butler was chewing his fingernails in agitation. Webster's face was taut.

'Matt will agree with me,' Ben said.

'Is that the case, Mr Webster?'

Webster sighed. 'It's getting pretty damn late in the day,' he admitted. 'I'd have expected to hear something by now. Frankly, I'm more than a little concerned that every passing hour makes it less likely we'll hear anything at all.'

'I don't understand,' Maxwell said. 'Where does this leave us? I'd assumed . . . I mean, if it's not about ransom . . . what's going on?'

'I think you might need to re-evaluate the whole situation,' Ben said. 'You might want to consider other reasons why someone would want to snatch your man.'

'Such as?'

'I'd imagine the treasure recovered from the *Santa Teresa*'s worth a good deal more than twelve million,' Ben said.

'You're suggesting what? That they'd use force against Sir Roger to make him give them access?'

'Unless he's in on it,' Ben said.

There was a shocked silence in the room. After a few seconds, Maxwell said, 'That's absolutely out of the question and totally impossible. Besides, not even Roger could have access. Every single item recovered from that vessel is under secure lock and key.'

'Then maybe there's something else,' Ben said. 'Something we don't know about, but which Forsyte does.'

'But that's just a guess,' Maxwell said.

'At this moment, guesswork is pretty much all we have,' Ben replied. 'All we know for sure is that while we stand around here staring at that phone, whoever did this is somewhere far away, laughing.'

'And?'

'And so it's going to have to be done the hard way,' Ben said. 'They're going to have to be found, and caught. That was meant to be Hanratty's job. Whether he's up to it is another question.'

'I'm not having some outsider come into this investigation to cause trouble and make wild allegations like this,' Hanratty burst out, pointing at Ben. 'And you count yourself lucky, Hope, that I don't charge you with threatening a police officer and obstructing the course of justice. Sergeant, get him out of my sight.'

Lynch hesitated, but she couldn't refuse a direct order from her superior. She stepped towards Ben with a veiled look of apology in her eyes.

'Hold on,' Maxwell said. 'This property is under lease to Neptune Marine Exploration. It's not a crime scene and I don't think you have the authority to expel anyone, Inspector. Mr Hope is welcome to stay and I appreciate any help he can offer us in this terrible situation.' He looked at Ben. 'Mr Hope, I'd be extremely grateful if you'd allow me to formally enlist your services.'

Ben shook his head. 'Thanks, but I'm not interested in being on your company payroll. Like I told you, I'm here for my own reasons.'

Maxwell shrugged. 'I'm sorry to hear that. Here's my number, in case you change your mind.'

Ben pocketed the card. 'No need to see me out, Sergeant,' he said to Lynch. 'I was leaving anyway.'

'What are we going to do now?' Amal asked as they headed back towards the car.

'I don't know, Amal,' Ben said. 'Right now, I really don't know what to do.'

Chapter Twelve

There was nothing more to say on the drive back to the guest-house. When they arrived, Ben took his bag from the back seat of the car and followed Amal up the steps to the door. Amal had gone very quiet and was visibly upset as he let them inside. Mrs Sheenan was nowhere to be seen, but there was a TV blasting from somewhere upstairs. Ben was grateful not to have to speak to anyone.

Amal led him to the first floor, showed him Brooke's room and announced in a shaky murmur that he needed to be alone for a while. Shuffling like an old man, he disappeared into his own room.

Ben stood for a long time outside Brooke's door before he eventually reached out and grasped the handle. He slowly opened the door, summoned up his strength and walked in.

She had never been one to wear a lot of perfume, but the subtle, fresh scent in the air was so familiar that for a weird, disorientated moment or two he fully expected to find her sitting there on the bed. She wasn't.

Of course she wasn't. Sickening reality closed back in on him. He shut the door, feeling numb and utterly deflated and more tired than he could remember having felt for many, many years.

Where are you, Brooke?

He wanted to scream it, but at that moment he would barely have had the energy to raise his voice above a whisper.

He unslung his bag from his shoulder and laid it down with his leather jacket, then gazed around him at the room. Brooke's travel holdall was sitting next to an armchair, unzipped. The slender reading glasses she sometimes wore at night, and a novel by an author he knew she liked, were sitting on the bedside table. Lying neatly folded on the pillow were the lightweight jogging bottoms she wore in bed, along with her favourite faded old pyjama top.

They suddenly seemed so much more a part of her now that she wasn't here. He reached down and stroked them with his fingertips. Closed his eyes a moment, then moved away from the bed and walked into her little ensuite bathroom. On the tiled surface by the sink were some of her things that the police hadn't taken away: her wash bag, her little jar of face cream, and several other of those familiar little items he remembered seeing in the bathroom at Le Val and at her place in Richmond, that signalled the warmth of her presence close by and made him feel happy to be alive.

Now there was only emptiness.

He couldn't stop seeing her face in his mind, thinking of the last time they'd been together. If only those stupid, senseless arguments between them had never happened. She'd have been with him at Le Val, far away from all this mess. Or maybe it would have been him here with her in Ireland instead of Amal – he might have been there to protect her when it happened.

He had to believe she was alive. It couldn't be any other way.

Mustn't be any other way.

He looked in the oval mirror above the sink. The face that stared back at him was one he barely recognised, gaunt and pale, with a terrible look in its eyes. A sudden gushing torrent of rage welled up inside him. More than rage. Hatred. Hatred for whoever had done this, whoever had taken her like this. If they harmed her . . . if they did anything to her . . . He lashed out with his fist and his reflection distorted into a web of cracks.

Fragments of glass tinkled down into the sink. He gazed at his bloody knuckles. There was no pain; it was as if he'd become completely detached from his physical body.

Where are you, Brooke?

He mopped the blood up with a piece of toilet paper, flushed it away and walked stiffly back into the bedroom. Turned off the main light and clicked on the bedside lamp. Knelt down by his bag, undid the straps, rummaged inside for his whisky flask and shook it, feeling the slosh of the liquid inside. He slumped on the edge of the bed and unscrewed the steel cap. He was about to drain most of the flask's contents in one gulp when he stopped himself.

No. This wasn't the way. This wasn't going to bring her back. He tightened the cap and tossed the flask into his bag.

But then another thought hit him like a kick in the face and almost made him reach for the flask again.

If it's not about ransom, he heard Julian Maxwell's voice say in his mind, *If it's not about ransom, what's going on?*

And then his own reply, coming back to him like a faraway echo: *You might need to re-evaluate the whole situation . . . You might want to consider other reasons . . .*

What if they'd all been getting this horribly, dreadfully wrong – him, the police, the company executives, Amal, everyone? What if their whole basic assumption was flawed, and this wasn't about Roger Forsyte at all? What if he hadn't been the target?

What if the target had been Brooke?

The idea left Ben stunned, winded. It was possible. Off-the-charts crazy, but possible, that this was some kind of reprisal against him. A sick, twisted punishment for something he'd done in his past. A relative of someone he'd killed or had put away, perhaps – had Jack Glass had a brother? – or maybe one of the many other enemies Ben had made over the years who were still out there.

Then wouldn't the kidnapper have wanted Ben to know the truth, just to hurt him even more? Wouldn't they have contacted Le Val?

Maybe they had, it occurred to him. A call could have come after he'd left. The phone could be ringing right this moment in the empty house; an email could be pinging into an unattended inbox.

Get a grip on yourself, he thought angrily. *Jeff's there. Jeff would have told you about it.*

But the thought wouldn't stop haunting him, and neither would the awful visions that kept circling through his head.

'I'm going to find you, Brooke,' he said out loud. 'I'm going to . . .'

His voice trailed off into a croak. He sank his head into Brooke's pillow and clutched her clothes tightly to his face, like a child needing comfort. His vision blurred. His tears moistened the pyjama top. The pain felt like too much to bear.

For the next hour he lay there curled up, staring at the door, praying for it to open and for Brooke to walk through it with a cheery greeting and a smile on her face. But time passed on and on, and the door stayed shut. He turned off the bedside light and went on staring into the darkness for what seemed a lifetime before he eventually slipped away into a shallow and restless state of unconsciousness.

*

When Ben awoke, it was still dark. His phone was thrumming in his jeans pocket. Instantly alert, heart thumping, he turned on the light and grabbed the phone to reply. *This is it*, the voice said in his mind. *This is when you get your payback.*

But there was nobody on the line, no mysterious voice from the past to make his worst nightmare come true. It was a text message alert.

The text was from Kay Lynch. Ben's heart almost stopped when he read its opening words.

Think u need 2 know. Found bodies.

Chapter Thirteen

The location given in the brief message was just a few miles from the abduction spot, deep within the heart of the rugged Glenveagh National Park, in an area of lakes and valleys known as the Poisoned Glen.

Twenty-seven frantic minutes had gone by since Ben had received Lynch's text. Still an hour to go before the first red shards of dawn would come creeping over the hills. Racing towards the scene he saw the blue lights of the Garda vehicles through the darkness and the sheeting rain, and brought the BMW to a slithering halt inches behind them.

On a grassy slope fifty yards from the roadside was the only building in sight, a tumbledown old stone bothy. A century or two ago the tiny primitive structure would have served as a refuge for shepherds – nowadays it was more likely to be used by tramps and drug addicts.

This was the place. Light shone from its only window. There were figures in reflective Garda vests moving in and out of the single entrance. Thick electric cables snaked down the slope, hooked up to the forensic investigation van that had been at the kidnap site the previous evening.

'Brooke's in there, isn't she?' Amal whispered. His eyes were red and puffy.

'We don't know that, Amal,' Ben replied through clenched

teeth. Until the last minute before setting off, he'd been resolved not to wake him up and bring him out here. He regretted his change of mind now.

'It's obvious, isn't it? I can feel it. Oh, God.'

Ben cut the engine and flung open his door. 'Stay in the car.'

'You must be kidding. I'm coming too.'

'I said, *stay in the damn car*.' Whatever was in that building, Ben didn't want Amal to see it. He jumped out of the BMW and sprinted up the steep, slippery path towards the bothy. The building had no door, just a crude stone doorway thick with moss. Ben ran inside. The earth floor was damp-smelling from the long winter months. That wasn't all he could smell. The place was rank with the stink of death.

The bothy was filled with people and activity and bright lights, but they couldn't have been there more than forty-five minutes or so. Before that it had been empty and silent. Empty, apart from its grisly occupants.

Almost the first person Ben saw as he rushed in was Kay Lynch. She was standing near the entrance, looking drawn and pallid. 'I'm sorry I didn't say much in my text,' she said in a low voice. 'I couldn't get away from Hanratty.'

'Where are they?' Ben said. He was breathless, but not from the fifty-yard sprint up the hill.

'Over there,' she said, motioning towards the far corner, where the forensics team were clustered around something Ben couldn't see.

'It's not a pretty sight. Are you sure you—'

Ben was already pushing past her. With his heart in his mouth he shoved two cops out of the way and saw what the forensics team were attending to under the white glare of their lights.

'They were found by the farmer who lives over the hill,'

Lynch said from behind his shoulder. 'He was looking for a missing sheep when his dog picked up the scent of blood and ran in here. The poor fellow's being treated for shock now.'

Lying sprawled on the floor were the corpses of a man and a woman. The woman was face down in the dirt. She wore a green cardigan over a red dress. Her bare legs were kicked out at unnatural angles and one of her shoes was missing. From the blueish hue of her skin it was clear that she'd been dead for some time. The right side of her head had been blown away at extreme close range by a gunshot. Her blond hair was thickly matted with congealed blood and pulped brains.

'Samantha Sheldrake, Forsyte's PA,' Lynch said.

Ben felt suddenly dizzy and had to lean against the stone wall. He was boiling with anger at Lynch for not having said more in her message. She could have spared him the torture of the last half hour. But he was too overcome by a strange mixture of relief and horror to say anything. After a few moments his breathing had slowed a little and he turned to look at the other corpse.

Roger Forsyte was recognisable from his pictures, although he looked very different in death, especially after such an obviously horrible death. His face was twisted in agony and terror. His pupils had rolled completely under his lids, so that just the ghoulish white eyeballs stared up at the ceiling. There was no gunshot wound. Forsyte had died some other way. Something much worse.

He had no hands. Somebody had chopped his arms off a few inches above the wrist and tossed the severed body parts across the bothy. From the quantity of blood that had sprayed over the rough walls, saturated his clothing and soaked into the floor, it had been done while he was still alive. Corpses didn't bleed this much.

The double amputation looked as though it had been carried out with a heavy blade: an axe or a butcher's cleaver. The shock of such an injury could be fatal, but not always. In his SAS days Ben had seen enough poor limbless survivors of African war atrocities to know that the human body could withstand the most brutal acts of mutilation. No, it wasn't the hacking off of his hands that had killed Sir Roger Forsyte. Ben observed the telltale signs – the leprous pallor of the skin, the grotesque swelling, the tongue protruding from the lips. Extreme pain, then creeping muscle paralysis and eventual asphyxia. Maybe an hour to death, maybe two. Not a good end. Whoever had done this had intended to make Forsyte suffer, and they'd got what they wanted.

'He's been poisoned,' Ben said.

Lynch gave a dark little smile. 'In the Poisoned Glen. Someone's idea of a joke? Looks as if you might have been right, too. There goes our whole kidnap theory.'

And with it had gone any remnant of a chance that getting Brooke back might be as simple as paying over whatever ransom the kidnappers demanded in return for Forsyte. Even if they'd wanted more for the women than the insurance policy could cover, Ben would have happily sold Le Val and reduced himself to a pauper to bring her back.

But that faintest, most tentative shred of hope was dead now. For all he knew, Brooke was dead too, her body dumped elsewhere for another passerby to find, hours, days, weeks from now. Or she might have tried to escape and be lying hurt or dying in a ditch somewhere, anywhere.

Lynch must have been able to read his thoughts from the strain on his face. 'We'll keep searching for her. The Dog Support Unit came up from Dublin during the night. We might turn up evidence that she was here. It's not the end. Not yet.'

Ben didn't reply. The sight of Forsyte's mutilated body had set something jangling deep in his memory. He couldn't bring it into focus; it was like a word on the tip of his tongue that wouldn't come, gnawing at him, teasing him through the mist of fear and stress and confusion that was clouding his mind. *What was it?*

Just when it seemed about to come to him, the sound of an angry voice interrupted his thoughts – a voice that was becoming way too familiar for Ben's liking. Hanratty had spotted him at last.

'I don't believe this! Who let *him* in here? Lynch! Did you tell him about this?'

Ben turned away and stepped out into the rain. It was pouring even harder now, but he could barely feel the cold water running down his face and soaking his hair and clothes. He gritted his teeth and tried to focus on the vague, fleeting memory that still eluded him. What the hell was it that seeing Forsyte's severed hands had triggered in his mind?

From fifty yards away, Amal had seen Ben emerge from the bothy. He swung the BMW's passenger door open. The inside light shone on his worried face. 'Well?' he called out nervously, expecting the worst.

Ben trudged down the muddy path. 'There are two bodies in there,' he said to Amal. 'Brooke's not one of them. It's Forsyte and his PA.'

The tension dropped from Amal's face. He climbed out of the car. The rain began to spot on his expensive coat. 'Then she's alive. I mean, it's awful. For the others, that is . . . but Brooke's alive. Thank God!'

Ben wasn't sure he had anything to thank God for.

'She must be alive, mustn't she?' Amal said, seeing the look in Ben's eyes. 'This is good news, isn't it? Isn't it?'

But Ben couldn't give him that reassurance. They both

turned to look as Kay Lynch came down the path from the bothy and joined them beside the car. 'I'm grateful to you for letting me know about this, Kay,' Ben said sincerely. His anger with her hadn't lasted more than a minute or two.

'I'm sorry it wasn't better news,' she said. 'And I'm afraid there's something else you should know. The Inspector's on the phone to Scotland Yard right now. He's requesting for a search warrant to be issued for your friend Dr Marcel's home in Richmond.'

'What? Why!?' Amal exploded.

Lynch gave a shrug. 'Because he thinks that in the light of this turn of events, her disappearance looks suspicious. He's dispatched a patrol car to Sea View Guest House to collect the rest of her belongings for examination. He says we can't afford to assume she isn't implicated somehow.'

'Implicated?' Amal yelled.

'Don't tell me you agree with Hanratty about this,' Ben said to Lynch.

'He's my superior. I don't have an opinion. Not one that matters, at any rate. And I've already told you far more than I should. I'm sticking my neck right out here.'

'It's insane!' Amal shouted. 'It's absolute cretinous imbecility of the highest order! What kind of utter moron would—?'

Lynch glanced over her shoulder. 'I'd keep my voice down, if I were you. Here he comes.'

Hanratty marched down the muddy slope towards them. 'Well, well. Having a party, are we? Fancy you two just happening to turn up *again*.' He glowered at Lynch, then turned to face Amal and stabbed a stubby finger into his chest. 'You,' he said, blowing spittle, veins standing out on his forehead, 'had better not be thinking of going back to

87

your own country, wherever that is. The situation has changed now, and you're mixed up in it, pal.'

'I happen to be a British citizen, *pal*. England is my country,' Amal shot back in fury. 'And I suppose you think I'm a suspect too? It's outrageous. Brooke and I were here for a bloody party, that's the beginning and end of it. We went through all this yesterday, over and over. Instead of standing here wasting time with these ridiculous allegations, why don't you go and do your job, you colossal great prick?'

'Amal,' Ben said, putting a hand on his arm to quiet him. The cop's eyes were beginning to burn with a dangerous light, and he was quite capable of having Amal dragged away to a cosy little cell if he carried on like this. 'My friend's upset,' Ben said to Hanratty. 'We'll be getting out of your way now.'

'Delighted to hear it,' Hanratty snorted. He was about to say more when his phone rang and he wheeled back towards the bothy to take the call.

'I'm sorry,' Lynch said, seeing the look in Ben's eyes. 'It's not me.'

'I know,' Ben said.

'The moment I hear anything more, I'll call you, okay? But you have to promise me to stay out of this and leave the investigating to us.'

'I promise,' Ben said. Lynch nodded, then turned to follow Hanratty back up the slope.

'It's just unbelievable,' Amal was raging as they got back into the car. 'Brooke a suspect? Based on what?'

'It's time for you to go home,' Ben said.

Amal looked at him with hurt and confusion in his eyes. 'So that's it? No protest, no nothing? How can you just accept this shit from Hanratty, after all the things you said before? I thought you were going to do something. That's why I thought you could help, because you had expertise in this kind of thing.'

'There's nothing more we can do here,' Ben told him. 'It's over.'

Amal boggled at him. 'It's *over*? Are you serious?'

'We'll go back and get your stuff,' Ben said. 'Then I'll take you to the airport.'

Amal stared. His throat gave a quiver. 'You think she's dead, don't you? That's why you're giving up.'

Ben didn't reply. He started the engine and put the car in reverse.

'Why can't you just be straight with me and say so? That's right, just go silent on me again. I can't stand it. I can't stand any of it.' Amal slumped despairingly in his seat as Ben backed the car away from the police vehicles and turned it round in the narrow road.

Arriving back at the guesthouse, they found a Garda patrol car parked outside and two officers loading the rest of Brooke's things into the back of it, sealed up in plastic evidence bags. Mrs Sheenan was watching from the doorway in her curlers, dressing gown and slippers, extremely displeased to have been roused so early from her bed and even more mortified that her establishment had been ransacked by the Garda like it was a den for common criminals. It would be the talk of the village for evermore. Amal tried in vain to mollify her and explain what was happening, then gave it up to go to his room and start packing to leave.

Ben watched the police car disappear down the street before returning inside to check flight times and book Amal a seat on the first plane to London that morning. Minutes later, they were back in the BMW and setting off.

Amal looked deep in thought all the way to Derry Airport, privately chewing over something with a set expression on

89

his face. As they were about to part, he turned to Ben. 'Listen, I, ah, I don't generally go around telling people this, but I do actually have some family connections. Fairly powerful ones, in fact. And I have my own money, a lot of money. I believe that Brooke is alive. I'd do anything – I mean anything – to find her. Whatever it takes. You understand me?'

'I understand you,' Ben said. He thanked him. Left him standing clutching his bags and headed back towards the car.

The truth was, he'd only wanted Amal out of the way. He knew what he had to do next, and that it was something he needed to do alone.

Because as he'd been standing there on the dark, rainswept roadside in the middle of the Poisoned Glen listening to Amal ranting at Lynch and Hanratty, Ben had suddenly remembered.

Chapter Fourteen

With the realisation of what had happened to Forsyte, the situation was suddenly totally altered. Things were about to turn an awful lot uglier than they already were.

Ben also knew now that there was no point in crossing back into the Republic. He was already on the side of the border he needed to be. Sitting behind the wheel of the BMW at Derry Airport, he took out his phone and dialled a number in Italy. After a few rings he heard a familiar, warm voice that would normally have made him smile. '*Pronto?*' she said.

'Hello, Mirella.'

'Ben!' She was delighted to hear from him. 'Are you coming to see us again?'

'Not exactly.'

'What is wrong?' she asked, hearing the tone of his voice.

'I need to talk to Boonzie, Mirella. Is he there?'

'I will call him,' she said anxiously. A muffled clattering on the line as Mirella laid down the phone and went off to fetch her husband. Ben could hear her voice in the background shouting 'Archibald!'. Boonzie would never have tolerated anyone but his beloved wife calling him by his real name. After a few moments, his gruff Scots voice came on the line.

'I don't suppose you've been following the British news,' Ben said.

'What's going on?' Ben could see the grizzled, granite-faced Scot standing there, his eyes narrowing in concern.

'I have a problem, Boonzie.'

Boonzie McCulloch had been a long-serving 22 SAS sergeant, and a mentor and friend of Ben's for many years, before he'd astounded everyone by quitting the army to settle in the south of Italy and set up a smallholding with a vivacious black-haired Neapolitan beauty he'd fallen head over heels in love with while on a few days' leave. The flinty, battle-hardened fifty-nine-year-old had found his own private heaven at last, contentedly working his sun-kissed couple of hectares to produce the basil and tomato crop that Mirella turned into gourmet bottled sauces the local restaurant trade couldn't do without.

But the soft life hadn't got to Boonzie completely. He still had a few aces up his sleeve, like the small arsenal of military weaponry that had got Ben out of a sticky moment in Rome the year before. And because the SAS had always been so much more deeply embroiled in matters of political secrecy and delicacy than other British army regiments, he still carried around with him a headful of the kind of privileged information that the likes of Detective Inspector Hanratty wouldn't have had access to in a thousand years.

'Jesus Christ,' Boonzie muttered when Ben had finished quickly filling him in. 'Need help?' He'd always been the practical type. Ben knew it would take only one word for him to lay down everything and be on the first flight to Ireland.

'I just need to know I'm on the right track. Forsyte. Roger Forsyte. It was before my time, but it's ringing bells.'

'Aye, me too, laddie. Big fuckin' bells. In some ears they havnae stopped ringing since Belfast, 1979.'

Ben nodded, but it wasn't much of a relief to have it confirmed that his hunch had been correct. 'The Liam Doyle incident.'

'Think it was maybe my second stint in that godforsaken hole,' Boonzie said, 'maybe my third, when they found Doyle's body. This shit was happening all the time, but they'd normally just blow your brains oot, not chop both your arms off that way. Nasty.'

'About six inches above the wrist?'

'With a cleaver,' Boonzie said. 'While he was still alive.'

'Just like Forsyte.'

'Then they put a nine-milly between his eyes and dumped the body out in the sticks in County Antrim. It was never confirmed that Doyle was IRA. Neither were the rest of the rumours, like who'd done it. A lot of folks were certain it wisnae the handiwork of the UVF or any of the other Loyalist bunch, though Lord knows some o' those fuckers were even worse than the Republican boys. Let's just say that in certain circles, it wisnae any secret who wiz behind it.'

'And Forsyte?'

'Roger Forsyte,' Boonzie said. 'Hold on a sec. I'm looking him up on the internet.' Ben could hear a tapping of keys. 'Here he is. Oh, aye. Marine Exploration?' Boonzie gave a dark chuckle. 'So that's what former MI5 agents end up doing, digging up sunken treasure? There's a lot of digging up to be done in Northern Ireland too. A lot of dead bodies were put in the ground in those years, and yer man'd know where to find half of them.'

'You're sure? Forsyte was MI5?'

'You can bet your arse on it, Ben. I've seen that face before. These bastards were all over the place. And I heard the name Forsyte mentioned more than a couple of times.'

'I need facts, Boonzie. Not surmises.'

'Trust me. He was mixed up deep in this shite.'

Although it had taken place a decade or so before Ben had joined the army and while he was still a boy, he'd heard enough about that unsavoury chapter in Ulster's history to know of the scandal that had erupted over the Liam Doyle incident. It was later to be overshadowed by the events of Operation Flavius during the Thatcher era, when three unarmed suspected Provisional IRA members had been shot dead in Gibraltar by the SAS amid strong concerns about government cover-ups and misinformation – but at the time the cruel, unusual nature of Liam Doyle's murder and the mass of rumours surrounding it had sparked off a great deal of heat. Many Catholic Republicans had been convinced that the brutal killing had been sanctioned by British Intelligence.

Ben knew all about the ugly, complex backdrop to the incident, too. In those days, Northern Ireland had been the tense staging ground for a hidden war between Britain and America, both of which were illicitly supplying weapons and intelligence to their respective sides of the conflict. On the one hand, interests sympathetic to the Republican cause within the CIA were allegedly arming the Provos with weaponry and information to help them kill their Loyalist enemies. As part of the deal, the FBI had turned a blind eye when IRA members visited America to liaise with their secret allies there. Meanwhile, the British government and MI5 had been doing exactly the same thing to help the opposite side, by providing guns, explosives and intelligence to members of both the Ulster Defence Force and Ulster Volunteer Force against the IRA, with the tacit compliance of Northern Ireland's police force, the Royal Ulster Constabulary. Both sides had been guilty of all manner of atrocities, but few had been so shocking as the mutilation done to Liam Doyle.

'Here's what I heard, strictly off the record,' Boonzie said.

'One of Forsyte's MI5 subordinates was making an under-cover weapons drop-off to a UVF cell when he was nabbed by a bunch of IRA led by Liam Doyle. Never confirmed, mind. The agent's body was dumped the same day from a moving car outside the RUC station in Dungiven. It was soon afterwards that Liam Doyle was kidnapped from his home in the middle of the night and ended up dead in a ditch with his arms hacked off. Word had it that some MI5 chappies got their arses toasted over it, but there was never any official inquiry. Just a lot of extremely pissed-off people who wanted Forsyte dead. One in particular. Liam Doyle's brother, Fergus, swore that he'd get his revenge, no matter if it took him the rest of his life to catch up with the bastards that'd done it.'

'Fergus Doyle.' Ben had heard that name.

'Bad rep,' Boonzie said. 'Made the Shankill Butchers look like a bunch of choirboys. He'd be an auld man now, Ben, but if he's still alive he's an evil bastard. This isnae something you can deal with alone. Talk to the cops, for Christ's sake.'

'No chance. Thanks, Boonzie. Take care.' And before his old friend could say any more, Ben ended the call.

Chapter Fifteen

It wasn't quite true to say that Ben Hope loved Ireland, at least not all of it. And Belfast was somewhere he'd chosen to avoid for a long, long while.

His first ever experience of the place had been during his early twenties, just months after finishing basic training, in his first tour of duty with the British armed forces. Join up and see the world, the recruitment campaign had said, promising everything but the hula-hula girls of the Shankill Road. The last time he'd seen it, some years later, had been as an SAS officer and a very different person from the inexperienced youth sent out with a rifle to patrol those terrifying streets.

With the SAS Ben had witnessed the tail end of the Troubles, an era that had claimed over three thousand Irish lives over four decades, as well as a good number of the British soldiers whose job it had been to try to keep the whole volatile mess under control.

Whether they should have been there at all was a question that Ben had privately asked himself many times over – but when the bullets began to zip about your ears you didn't dwell too long on ethical or political debate, and the air had been thick with them back then. Shortly after Ben had first landed at RAF Aldergrove with his new SAS unit, a British Army Gazelle helicopter had been shot down in flames by an IRA rocket just over the border, killing the pilot and maiming three soldiers. Not long afterwards, two SAS troopers from Ben's company had been cut down in a gun battle with the IRA outside the village of Cappagh, County Tyrone. Then just days later, the army had caught up with the gunmen after a daring but ultimately foolish attack on an RUC station with a stolen heavy machine gun mounted on a lorry. The IRA men had been switching to their getaway vehicle in a Catholic church car park when the SAS unit in pursuit had engaged with them: a bloody little firefight that had left six corpses on the ground and given Ben his first serious bullet wound.

And on it had gone. Right up until the official 1997 ceasefire, the city of Belfast and the surrounding areas had been caught up in a relentlessly violent storm of reprisals, counter-reprisals, bombings and beatings, ambushes and assassinations.

All things considered, it wasn't a part of the world Ben had ever wanted to return to. Yet here he was, speeding towards the city, foot on the floor and overtaking everything in sight with his windscreen wipers working flat out to beat aside the rain. He covered the seventy-mile journey from Derry in just under an hour, stopping only for fuel and to stoke himself up with a coffee and a wolfed-down sandwich at a motorway services.

As he made his way into the rain-slicked streets of Belfast, the marks of a community forever divided by hatred were painfully visible, even after years of official peace. Ben drove along a road that skirted one of the city's 'peace lines', tall reinforced mesh fences and gates erected to segregate the clashing sectarian groups wherever their territories met.

It was Ireland's own version of Apartheid, its own Berlin Wall. Union Jacks hung limply from lampposts and poles in the Protestant Loyalist districts; the Irish green, white and gold tricolour in the Catholic Republican areas. Still that same old atmosphere of cold, brooding fear. All that was missing were the military Land Rovers, the Saracen armoured personnel carriers and the checkpoints that had once been a common feature throughout the city and the surrounding area.

Ben knew the majority of the people were trying to put the past behind them. But some things never really changed, deep down. Some things never really could.

By lunchtime he was parked opposite a pub called The Spinning Jenny in the staunchly Catholic west of the city. He had a reason for being there. In its day, the place had been a watering-hole for some of Belfast's more notorious IRA hardmen. From the look of the place, Ben reckoned it probably hadn't changed a hell of a lot since then either.

Sitting at the wheel, he took out his phone and dialled Amal's number. When there was no reply, he left a brief message to say he had a possible lead and would be in touch again soon. Amal didn't need to know that the lead concerned a stone-cold IRA killer recently sated with the blood of his long-time enemy and most likely capable of just about anything.

After he'd left his message Ben spent a few minutes trawling online for any further information on Fergus Doyle that he hadn't already researched. From what he could put together, it seemed that the man had reached the peak of his ultra-violent career in 1983, five years after the death of his brother. Boonzie had been right: the atrocities committed by the Shankill Butchers, the gang of Loyalist thugs responsible for the wholesale murder and torture of innocent Catholics throughout the better part of the seventies and early eighties, were by no means any worse than the catalogue of carnage and cruelty attributed to Doyle and his followers.

But where the Shankill Butchers had been slow-witted enough to let themselves be hunted down and caught one by one, either shot or imprisoned, Doyle had somehow managed to evade capture all these years. From the turn of the nineties there seemed to be nothing more on him. Even in terrorist circles, everyone had their fifteen minutes of fame before obscurity beckoned.

Ben studied every image he could find of the man until he was confident that he'd recognise that ugly, mean, lopsided face at a glance, even lined and wrinkled with age as it must be today. Fergus Doyle had an evil look in his eye. Ben had seen enough of the dark side of the world to know what some evil men did to women unlucky enough to fall into their hands. Trophies kept for personal amusement, battered and raped until they were finally discarded dead in a ditch; drugged-up into hopeless junkies who would prostitute themselves to anyone for another fix; sold into the international trade in human trafficking.

Fergus Doyle. Ben didn't give a damn how old and wrinkled that face was now. He'd still happily put three bullets through it if he couldn't have Brooke back.

And maybe even if he could.

He put his phone away, clenched his jaw hard and took three deep breaths. Then he flung open the driver's door, got out of the BMW and crossed the road to The Spinning Jenny.

Chapter Sixteen

The pub was dark and drab inside, and almost empty apart from a few drinkers hunched over pints of Guinness around a table at the back. Dirty light filtered in through the windows. The place smelled of stale beer. Stale tobacco smoke too, and there were flecks of cigarette ash on the floorboards – evidently nobody had been too bothered to clean up after last night's after-hours lock-in, when small matters like abiding by the non-smoking regulations became even less important. That was fine by Ben. He sat at the bar and mechanically lit a Gauloise.

The barman, a burly guy of about thirty, paused in the middle of polishing a pint glass, and fixed him with a belligerent eye. 'Can't smoke in here, friend.'

'Right,' Ben said, and took another drag. 'How about a whiskey? Double.'

'Ice?'

'As it comes.'

When the barman slapped the glass on the scarred surface, Ben grabbed it and swallowed the liquor down in one stinging gulp. The alcohol hit his system fast, making him realise how little he'd eaten in the last couple of days. He ordered another, and a bag of crisps to go with it.

'Haven't seen you in here before,' the barman said, not

any friendlier, and not just because of the cigarette. In a place like The Spinning Jenny, Ben's English accent marked him out as the enemy whatever he might spend at the bar. A guy like him walking into a staunchly Republican pub was like a black man walking into a Ku Klux Klan meet. That was why he'd purposely left his bag in the car. Toting such a very obviously ex-military piece of kit with him would have been no less of a red rag to a bull than wearing a beret with the SAS winged dagger on it. Not that Ben was overly concerned about provocation. But he had to get inside the door before he could state his business.

He flicked away the stub of the Gauloise. 'I'm looking for a man called Doyle. Fergus Doyle.'

The barman frowned. The low murmur of conversation from the table at the back suddenly dwindled into silence and a couple of faces turned around to stare coldly.

'What did you say?' the barman asked.

'Fergus Doyle,' Ben repeated. 'I'm looking for him. Thought this establishment of yours would be a good place to start.'

'And why might that be?' the barman said tersely.

'Let's not play games,' Ben said.

'What would you want with Fergus Doyle?'

'I'd like to have a conversation with him,' Ben said.

'A conversation about what?'

'You don't want to know.'

'Nobody by the name of Fergus Doyle drinks here.'

'Then why did you ask me what I wanted him for?'

The barman motioned towards Ben's glass. 'I'd say you'd be best to finish that up and go and look elsewhere for your friend.'

'I didn't say he was a friend,' Ben said. 'And I'll have another drink.'

The barman leaned closer across the bar. His gaze flickered past Ben's shoulder towards the table at the far end of the room, then turned back on Ben with a meaningful look. 'Listen,' he said in a low voice. 'I'm only going to say this once. My advice to you is to leave before you open your mouth too wide.'

'Why would that be?'

'Because opening your mouth too wide can get you in a lot of trouble around here,' the barman said. 'If I was you, I wouldn't hang around.'

'I was just getting comfortable,' Ben said.

'That's my advice. A clever man would take it and a foolish man would ignore it.'

Ben nudged his empty glass across the bar. 'Same again.'

'It's your funeral.' The barman refilled it from the optic and then withdrew to the other end of the bar.

The pub was very quiet now. The drinkers at the back slowly returned to their pints but were saying nothing. As Ben sipped his third whiskey and munched on a crisp he noticed one of them, a scrawny little guy with a greying crew cut, take out a phone and start keying in a text message, head bowed and thumbs twiddling. The conversation resumed around the table. The barman busied himself tidying up more glasses.

Ben was finishing his crisps when the guy who'd sent the text message got up from the table and left with a nod to his mates. Ben noticed the agitation in his step as he headed for the door. Someone else at the table glanced back towards the bar, caught Ben's eye and quickly glanced away again.

It wasn't too long before Ben heard a car pull up outside. Moments later the pub door swung open and the scrawny grey-haired guy came back in. He was accompanied by three other men, all of them much larger than he was and all wearing the same set scowl. The scrawny guy jerked his chin at the bar, as if to say 'that's him'.

'We'll take it from here,' the middle one of the three men said. He was in his fifties, six-two and built like a grizzly, half lard and half muscle with the features of a bare-knuckle boxer who'd lost a few too many fights. 'Scram,' he said to the scrawny guy, jerking his thumb at the door.

The rest of the guys at the table spontaneously drained the dregs of their pints and beat a hasty retreat along with their companion. The barman disappeared into a little office, suddenly absorbed by some paperwork he had to attend to.

The three guys strode purposefully up to the bar and circled Ben. Arms folded. Faces hard. It looked as if he was making progress.

He studied them. There was always a leader, and the big bear with the beaten-up chops was clearly it. His shoes were polished and he was wearing a long black overcoat that didn't do much to hide his bulk. The one on the left in the bike jacket was an orang-utan: cropped ginger hair, heavy brows and arms longer than his legs. Textbook henchman, just waiting for the word to launch into a violent onslaught. The one on the right was wearing a hoodie and had more the look of a hungry wolf, greased-back hair, darting eyes, acne-pitted hollow cheeks and a nervy twitch to his mouth.

'Name's Flanagan,' the leader said, eyeing Ben with a steely expression. 'Frank Flanagan. You might have heard of me.'

'Yeah, you're a comedian, or something,' Ben said.

'That's very funny,' Flanagan said, unsmiling. 'We'll all have a laugh in a minute.' He dug a meaty fist in the pocket of his overcoat and took out a BlackBerry. 'Now, I just received a message on here from my friend, saying there was a fella asking about Fergus Doyle.' He pronounced the name with reverent emphasis, as though it belonged to some hallowed patron saint. 'And he informs me that this fella in question is you.' He pointed a stubby finger at Ben's face.

Flanagan was one of those wise guys who thought he had the gift of the gab and could use it to intimidate. Ben wasn't in the mood to waste time, but he was content to play along for now. 'Top marks to your friend. That's correct.'

'I was afraid you might say that,' Flanagan said. 'For your sakes, that is. So why would a fella like you be in here asking for Mr Doyle?'

'That's between him and me,' Ben said.

Flanagan's crooked smile widened. 'For the moment, I'm acting as his intermediary as you might say.'

Ben calmly returned his stare. 'Well, then let's just say that I think he has something I want, and I have something he might want. I take it you know him pretty well, do you?'

'I know him, aye. But here's the problem. I don't know you.'

'Fucking soldier boy,' said the orang.

'You got that wrong, ape face,' Ben said.

'What did you call me?'

'I can't be the first one to have noticed it,' Ben said.

'We know a fucking soldier boy when we see one,' said the wolf, with a twitch. 'You think we didn't spend enough time watching you bastards when there was a machine gun pointing at every woman and child in Ulster?'

'I'm just a guy who's lost something,' Ben said. 'If Doyle can help me get it back, we can do business.'

'What if Mr Doyle isn't inclined to do business with the likes of you?' Flanagan said.

'Then Mr Doyle is going to have to think again.'

Flanagan recoiled in mock outrage. 'That sounded like a threat to me.' He turned to the orang, who was staring, seething, at Ben. 'That sound like a threat to you, Sean?'

'It did, Frank,' Sean replied, not taking his eyes off Ben.

'I'm very disappointed,' Flanagan said. 'I'd hoped we could resolve this more amicably, but I see now we're going to have to do it the hard way.'

'That's a very regrettable choice,' Ben said.

'Not for us, it isn't. Scalpel, Gary.' Flanagan held out a beefy hand and the wolf instantly reached under his jacket and came out with a knife bayonet. He passed it to Flanagan, who drew it deliberately from its scabbard. Seven inches or so of blackened forged-steel blade, the kind of mass-produced military killing tool that could be procured dirt cheap and disposed of without a second thought when the job was done.

'Now move yer arse,' Flanagan growled, wagging the blade towards the rear exit.

'Are we going somewhere?' Ben said.

Gary gave another twitch and threw a nervy glance at his colleagues. 'Should we not wait for the others, boys?'

'What for?' Flanagan asked coldly.

'John has the gun.'

'We don't need a gun to take care of this piece of shite,' Flanagan growled. He motioned to the other two and they grabbed Ben's arms.

Ben let them. The bayonet looked sharp and its tip was just a few inches from his throat. They yanked him away from the bar and started marching him roughly towards the rear exit.

Chapter Seventeen

The doorway led out onto the alley at the back of the pub. A cold damp wind was funnelling down the narrow passage from the main street to the left, blowing litter and dead leaves. Flanagan shoved Ben to the right, away from the street. 'Walk.'

'The car's that way,' Gary said, motioning back.

'We're not going to the car,' Flanagan said. 'We're taking yer man for a wee scenic stroll, and then he's going to find out what happens to big-mouthed fuckers like him who go around asking too many questions.'

'What do you think about that, soldier boy?' said Sean.

'I think you're making a mistake,' Ben said. 'But you still have time to get out of it.'

'You won't be so cocky with your liver hanging out,' Flanagan said, jabbing the blade at Ben's back. He paused, as if waiting for Ben to dissolve into a gibbering panic. When it didn't happen, he added, 'I'd just as soon have carved you up inside the pub, but why should they have to clean up all the mess?'

'That shows a considerate side,' Ben said. 'Maybe you should consider putting the toothpick away, too. Because it's going to hurt like hell when the doctor's prising it out of your arse later.'

'Would you listen to this fucker?' said Sean.

'I still think we should wait for the others,' Gary muttered.

'They'll be here any minute,' Flanagan said. 'They can help put what's left of this bastard in with the rubbish.' He motioned at a wheelie bin at the side of the alley that was overflowing with garbage bags. Next to it was a row of battered metal dustbins with rusty lids. 'Okay, that's far enough,' he told Ben, grabbing his collar and wheeling him round so his back was against the alley wall. Flanagan's fingers were white on the hilt of the knife bayonet. 'You'll be dead in a couple of seconds, so if you've got anything to say, say it now.'

'Stick him like a pig, Frank,' Sean said excitedly.

Flanagan sucked in a deep breath. Then his eyes flashed as he gathered up his energy and stabbed the knife hard and fast at Ben's chest.

Ben moved faster. There was a metallic screech as the tip of the knife sheared through thin sheet steel instead of human flesh. Flanagan's eyes opened wide to stare at the circular lid Ben had whipped off the nearest dustbin at the last instant and was holding in front of him like a shield by its metal handle. The sharp blade, with two hundred and fifty pounds of bulk thrusting behind it, had punched through right up to the hilt.

Before Flanagan could recover his wits, Ben twisted the dustbin lid violently, wrenched the trapped weapon out of his hand and then drove it straight back at him.

The heavy steel pommel had been designed to attach the bayonet securely to a rifle barrel, but it also made a pretty good impact weapon. It caught Flanagan square in the mouth, ripped through between his lips and kept going about three inches before Ben tore the lid away and the knife with it.

Flanagan let out a howling shriek and staggered backwards, clapping his hands over his mouth. Blood spurted from between his fingers and red and white dental fragments spilled out over the alleyway.

Ben slammed the edge of the bin lid into the bridge of his nose with enough force to knock him flat on his back. 'You were right, Flanagan. Why should the good folks at The Spinning Jenny clean up your mess?'

As Ben expected, Sean didn't hesitate as long as Gary before coming in for the attack. He ripped an extending baton out of his bike jacket and flicked it out to its full length as he rushed in, yelling at the top of his voice. Ben dodged the blow, tripped him and sent him flying headlong with all his weight and momentum into the alley wall. The top of his skull impacted the brickwork with the sound of a lump-hammer crushing a cabbage.

Before Sean's unconscious body had slumped the ground, the sharpened screwdriver in Gary's hand was punching through the air towards Ben's throat. Ben blocked the stab with a blow intended to break bone. There was a crack and a screech as Gary's wrist snapped. The screwdriver fell to the ground. Ben drove an elbow into his sternum, driving the wind out of him, then grabbed a fistful of his greasy hair and used it to drive the guy's face down into a rising kneecap.

After that, Gary wasn't much use to anyone. He flopped down on the ground and Ben stepped over him, walking towards Flanagan, who had managed to clamber halfway to his feet. The big man's mouth was a red hole and there was blood leaking all down his shirt. He staggered upright, turned and began to stagger away up the alley towards the street.

Ben planned to let him go, but not just yet. 'Come back here, Flanagan. Let's have that fancy phone of yours, so your owner can call me on it within the hour and tell me how he's going to give me what I want.'

'Fuck you!' Flanagan screamed over his shoulder, his stagger turning into a run. Ben scooped the bin lid off the ground, yanked the knife bayonet out and flipped the weapon over in his hand so he was holding the tip of the blade lightly between forefinger and thumb. It was an ungainly object with that big steel rifle lug on the end, but when it came to throwing knives, judging the distance and the number of spins through the air was more important than balance.

Ben gauged the throw, then let it fly. The blade flashed through the air and embedded itself deep in Flanagan's left glute. Flanagan crashed to his face and began rolling and howling, clawing to get it out.

Ben stepped up to him and was about to speak when there was the roar of an engine and a screech of brakes as a van skidded to a halt outside the mouth of the alleyway, blocking it.

The van's doors burst open. Three men leaped from the front, three more from the rear, all armed with baseball bats and machetes except one who was waving a semi-automatic pistol. A seventh guy followed them from the back of the van, manhandling a snarling, barking Doberman on the end of a chain.

'Get him!' Flanagan was bawling incoherently through his mangled lips from where he lay with the bayonet hilt protruding from his buttock. 'Kill that fucking bastard!'

Three inept morons with one decent knife between them was one thing. This was another. There'd been a time when a wilder, more reckless Ben might have gone wading into the attack. But he was older and wiser now, and he needed to think of Brooke. If she was still alive, he wasn't going to be of much use to her all smashed and chewed up with a couple of bullets in him. He turned and sprinted down the alleyway, past the bins and the slumped bodies of Sean and Gary. The back doors of houses zipped by as he ran, broken windows and boarded-up entrances covered in graffiti. Racing footsteps and furious shouts echoed down the alley behind him. If they let the dog go, this would be over fast.

He suddenly found himself in a maze of passages that wound in all directions between the houses. Set at intervals in the cracked concrete were iron bollards that he guessed were to stop local kids tearing down the alleys on their motorcycles. A fork opened up in front of him and he took the right turning, then a left a few metres further on, and almost collided with a large yellow builder's skip that blocked most of the passageway. It was piled high with bits of scaffolding, old fence posts and rubble. Beyond the skip to the right was the recessed doorway of a house or flat that was either a squat or unoccupied, with planks nailed across the entrance and weeds growing from the cracked steps.

Ben could hear the thunder of footsteps getting close. It sounded like two, at most three men. His pursuers must have split up to flush out the maze of passages. He couldn't hear the dog; guessed its handler had taken one of the other turnings.

He moved quickly to the skip, then slipped into the doorway and pressed himself flat against the planks.

The two men appeared round the corner, running as fast as they could, darting their eyes left and right into every corner. One held a crude machete, the other had the handgun clenched in his fist. 'Keep moving,' he rasped breathlessly at his younger companion. 'He can't have gone far.' They raced past the skip, running close together side by side in the narrow space.

Neither of them had time to register the blurred object

that suddenly came swinging at them out of nowhere. To a dull clang that resonated all through the alley, all four of their feet left the ground together and kicked up high in the air in a sprawl of limbs before they crashed down on their backs against the concrete.

Ben stepped out of the doorway. The length of heavy iron scaffold pole was still quivering in his hands from the impact. Two days' worth of anguished frustration and pent-up rage had gone into the blow and it had knocked both men out cold. He laid down the pole and picked up the men's fallen weapons. The machete was of no interest, and he tossed it over a wall. The other was an American Colt Government .45 automatic, badly scuffed with most of the finish worn away. If it had been one of the weapons supplied by the CIA back in the heyday of the Troubles, it had seen a lot of use over the years since. It was fully loaded, seven rounds in the magazine and one up the spout. Ben stuffed it in his belt.

'So you must be John,' he said to the gun's unconscious owner, remembering what Gary had said. He reckoned he had about ten seconds before the others appeared. He dragged the two limp bodies to a nearby iron bollard, propped them sitting up back to back either side of it and used a coil of rusty old barbed wire from the builder's skip to lash them together. He did a rough, hasty job of it, but they wouldn't get free without leaving half their flesh on the barbs. Counting down the seconds he ripped strips from their clothing as improvised gags. He dusted his hands and stood over them. 'Don't go anywhere,' he said. 'I'll be right back.'

He drew the Colt from his belt, flipped off the safety and trotted towards the head of the alley just as the remaining four men appeared. They skidded to a halt at the sight of the pistol in his hand. The Doberman reared up when it saw him, fangs bared and straining its chain tight.

Ben stood in the middle of the passage with the .45 in a two-handed Weaver stance and the dog square in his sights. 'You'll be burying Fido tonight if you let him go,' he said.

The four men gaped at him. The handler kept hold of the chain. Ben was glad of that. He was very fond of dogs, even ones that wanted to savagely rip him to pieces. He wouldn't have liked to paint the alley with its brains.

'Where's Fergus Doyle?' he said.

'Who the fuck are you?' one of the men blurted.

Ben didn't think he was going to get a lot out of these guys. If John had had the gun, that meant John was probably the furthest up the hierarchy. And John was currently trussed up ready for interrogation. He'd already wasted enough time on deadbeats and lackeys.

'Fuck it,' Ben said to himself, and resorted to the most effective way of clearing the decks. The Colt boomed and kicked in his hands, and again, and again, aiming off first a little to the left, then a little to the right. The fat .45 bullets ricocheted off the walls either side of the men, clouding the alley with masonry dust. They scattered in panic and fled, the dog handler desperately tugging his Doberman along behind him as he ran.

Ben lowered the gun. Through the ringing in his ears he heard their racing footsteps disappear, then a few moments later the screech of spinning tyres as the van took off up the street at high speed. He turned and walked back to his two captives.

They hadn't gone anywhere. The one called John, who was a slab-faced nondescript guy of about thirty-five, had only just come to. The younger one, a spotty kid of about nineteen, had been awake long enough to start chewing frantically through his gag. They were both struggling against their bonds and rolling their eyes up at him as he stood over them.

He thrust the Colt back in his belt and dropped into a crouch next to his prisoners. 'Now, if you two want to go home today instead of to the morgue, you're going to tell me where I can find Fergus Doyle. Who wants to start? How about you, John?'

He was reaching out to rip away the guy's gag when he felt a sudden pressure against the base of his neck.

The cold, hard touch of a gun muzzle.

Chapter Eighteen

There were two basic possible responses to an unexpected turn of events like this. Ben didn't consider the first one very long, because whipping round to lash the weapon out of the opponent's hands wasn't such a clever idea when he'd just heard the hammer go back with a small, sharp *click-click*. You couldn't quite dodge or deflect a handgun bullet the way you could a knife bayonet in the hands of an idiot.

The second response was just to go very still and hope that nothing terminal was about to happen in the next few moments.

Ben went very still.

'Lose the pistol,' said a woman's voice. It was a young voice, and might have been pleasant-sounding if she'd had something different to say. 'Any tricks, this gun goes off and your frigging head goes off with it.'

Ben slowly moved his hand to his belt, grasped the butt of the Colt between thumb and forefinger, drew it out and tossed it away with a clatter.

'Now get on your feet. Slowly does it.'

The gun muzzle stayed pressed to his neck as he stood. It still didn't seem like a good moment for any sudden moves.

'Now turn round,' she commanded. The pressure disappeared from his neck as she took a couple of steps backwards.

Ben turned cautiously round to face her. She was as youthful as her voice: not much more than twenty-one or twenty-two, willowy with a pretty face and long black hair, tousled, a little gypsyish. Her dark eyes were watching him unblinking down the barrel of the .357 Magnum revolver she was clutching. The gun looked oversized in her hands. Ben could see the jacketed hollowpoint rounds nestling in the mouths of the cylinder chambers. There was no chance she could miss at this range. The expanding bullet would blow a hole in him that a boxer could poke his fist through, glove and all.

'Put your frigging hands up,' she said.

Now that they were face to face there was an edge to her voice that might have been anxiety, and Ben wondered whether she'd ever pointed a loaded gun at anyone before.

'I know how to use this thing,' she said.

'I certainly hope so,' he said. He put his hands up.

'You hope so?' she said. Her brow puckered up in a frown.

'We wouldn't want any accidental discharges. The old Model Nineteen has a light single-action trigger.'

'Who are you?' she demanded. 'What do you want with Fergus Doyle?'

'Like I told those other guys,' Ben said. 'I'm looking for something.'

'Something?'

'Someone. Someone who's missing, whom I care about very much. If Doyle has her, I'd like to discuss business with him, man to man.'

She frowned again, scrutinising him intently. 'What kind of business?' she said suspiciously.

'The ransom kind,' he said. 'Money. If he can give me back what he took from me, I can offer him something in exchange.'

A few months earlier, Ben had had Le Val valued for insurance purposes and the figure that had come back was a shade over 1.9 million euros. It was everything Ben had in the world. He'd already decided that was a small price to pay for Brooke's return, and it was what he intended to put on the table.

The young woman made no reply, just stared at him as if slowly digesting what he'd just said. Before she could speak, from somewhere far away beyond the houses came a wailing of sirens, growing rapidly louder. Ben guessed that the Belfast police weren't so jaded nowadays that they wouldn't respond to the sound of a forty-five being let off in the street.

'What's your name?' he asked her.

'Tara,' she replied after a beat. 'Tara McNatten.'

'If you're going to fire that thing, Tara, you need to do it before the police turn up. It won't suit either of us to be caught standing here.'

She glanced over her shoulder, not quite long enough for Ben to move for the gun. 'Okay,' she said, appearing to make a decision. 'You want to see Fergus Doyle. I'll take you to him. That way.' She motioned with the gun.

'What about your friends here?' he said, looking down at the two captives lashed to the bollard, still struggling wildly to get free and moaning loudly behind their gags.

'Those are no friends of mine,' she said. Ben didn't understand, but there wasn't time to hang around discussing the finer points. The police sirens were getting close.

He started walking the way Tara was pointing. She followed a few steps behind, keeping her revolver aimed steadily between his shoulder blades. The first police vehicle screamed to a halt and they could hear raised voices and the crackle of radios. Tara guided Ben into the entrance of a winding passage that snaked along between grimy houses and rundown fences for a hundred yards before it opened onto another dismal street. Parked a short distance away was a silver Honda SUV. There was nobody else in sight.

'That's my car,' she said. 'You're driving.' She kept the gun carefully trained on him as he opened the driver's door. He could tell she wasn't too experienced at this, but one thing she was was thoughtful. If she'd tossed him the key before he got behind the wheel, he might have been able to get the vehicle fired up and speed away without her; instead she waited until they were both inside, him in front and her behind, and only then did she let him have the key. 'Go easy,' she said. 'Keep to the speed limits. Any tricks and I'll shoot.'

Ben started the car and pulled away. Following her directions he drove through the maze of streets and back out onto the main road, where they passed the police vehicles speeding in the opposite direction towards the scene of the shooting. Cops were like wasps. If you acted unconcerned about their presence, there was generally a pretty good chance they'd leave you alone. Ben drove the Honda at a steady, nonchalant pace and managed to get by the police without getting stopped.

After a few minutes they were heading out of Belfast. A thin rain started up again, slanting out of the grey afternoon sky. Signs for Dromore and Banbridge flashed past. 'Keep going,' Tara's voice said from the back seat. Finally, she said, 'Okay, next right,' and Ben turned off the main road to wind along a few miles of narrow country lanes. 'See that stand of trees up ahead?' she said. 'There's a gate just after them.'

The gate led to a bumpy track and into a farmyard that had seen better days. 'This is it,' she told him. 'Pull up by the barn over there. Stop the engine and give me back the key. Right. Now get out.'

Ben did as he was told, glancing around him as he stepped out onto the hardcore yard. He'd more than half expected to be greeted by a bunch of hard-faced guys toting sawn-off shotguns and pistols – maybe Flanagan among them, if he'd made it to the getaway van, still nursing his punctured glute and mad for revenge.

As it was, there was no sign of life in the place. A heavy silence hung over the dilapidated outbuildings and the old farmhouse. Ben was baffled, but said nothing.

Tara climbed out of the car, holding the .357 more loosely now but still watching him closely. 'Over to the house,' she directed him, and made him stand a few paces away as she unlocked the front door. It swung open with a creak and she motioned for Ben to go in first.

The farmhouse was sparsely furnished and the decor hadn't been refreshed since about 1956, but it smelled clean. Tara walked Ben down a passage to a laminated door, from behind which he could hear the sound of a TV. Beyond the door was a small sitting room, dark with the curtains drawn. Tara waved Ben inside.

Sitting slumped and immobile in a chintzy elbow chair, half silhouetted by the glow of the television screen and the light of a dim table lamp behind him, was the room's only occupant. The old man didn't respond as they walked in. His eyes were closed, his jaw hanging slackly half-open with a trail of drool running down off his chin. His white hair was shaggy and unkempt, and his body looked wasted and withered under his clothes as if he'd been sitting there for years on end.

At first Ben thought he was dead, but then saw the very slow, very shallow rise and fall of his emaciated chest as he slept. The table behind him was almost completely covered with an array of tubs and bottles of medicines.

Tara padded over to the TV and switched it off. With great care and gentleness, she plucked a tissue from a box on the table and used it to clean up the dribble of saliva from the old man's mouth and chin. Then she turned to Ben. 'Here he is,' she said in a low voice. 'Fergus Doyle. My uncle.'

Chapter Nineteen

Ben looked at her and saw she was totally earnest. The revolver was uncocked now, and pointed at the floor rather than at him. He took a step closer to the old man's chair, softly so as not to wake him, and ran his eye over the collection of medicine bottles that littered the table. Among them was a doctor's prescription. He picked it up, held it in the light of the lamp and saw the name on it: Fergus R. Doyle, with his date of birth.

'Satisfied?' Tara asked.

Ben replaced the slip of paper on the table and peered more closely at the old man. Under the mass of wrinkles was the same ugly, mean-looking face he'd studied in the photos earlier that evening. It was Doyle, for sure. He wasn't seventy yet, but he looked well over ninety. Whatever disease had struck him down had caused terrible ravages, and judging from the quantity of painkillers on the table his waking hours must have been filled with agony.

'All right,' Ben said.

'Now you see him,' Tara said. 'You can see how harmless he is. You can see how stupid and impossible it is that he could ever be a threat to anyone any more, and how he couldn't have taken anything from you. You can see it, can't you?'

Behind the old man's chair was a shelving unit crammed

with books. Ben noticed several titles about multiple sclerosis, and another called *Stroke Recovery: A Patient's Guide*. But the majority of Doyle's reading material was composed of evangelical Christian literature. The nearby sideboard was covered with more pamphlets and leaflets, as well as a copy of the Bible so well thumbed that its cover was mostly tape.

'He's peaceful,' Tara said. 'I don't want to wake him.' She motioned towards the door. 'We can talk in the other room.'

The other room was a tiny kitchen. The table was blue Formica and the linoleum was ridged and cracked, but everything was clean and tidy. 'I come here to look after him,' she explained. 'A nurse visits a couple of times a week, but I do the cleaning and stuff, see to it that he eats properly.'

'What happened to him?' Ben asked, still trying to understand.

'The multiple sclerosis was diagnosed more than fifteen years back. Then about six years ago he had his stroke. Since then, he's done little but sit in that chair and watch TV. I don't even think he understands much of what he's seeing any more.'

Ben was silent.

'I know he was a bad man once,' Tara said. 'Like, really really bad. I've heard the stories. But he's not like that now. I was still just a wee girl when he turned his back on violence and found God. Please believe me. He wouldn't harm a fly, even if he could. He's my uncle and I love him.'

'This isn't the kind of story I'd have expected from someone who was just pointing a Smith and Wesson at me,' Ben said.

Tara looked at the gun in her hand, then flipped out the cylinder, dumped the six tarnished hollowpoint cartridges into her left palm and slipped them in the pocket of her jeans.

She set the unloaded revolver on the tabletop with a clunk. 'It was his, from years ago. I found it among his stuff once while I was cleaning. I've always been scared that one day someone would come looking for him. You know, to settle an old score, ancient history that ought to have been laid to rest. That's why I need to protect him. Anyone starts poking around asking about my Uncle Ferg, believe me, I'll hear about it. It was Michael O'Rourke, the barman at the Spinning Jenny, who called me earlier, told me there was someone nosing about asking questions. I went over straight away. Then I heard the shots.'

'Seems you're not the only one protecting your uncle.'

She shrugged. 'If you got yourself in trouble back there, it was nothing to do with me. What did you expect, going into a pub like The Spinning Jenny and stirring folks up with a lot of questions? This is Belfast. The past doesn't die here. These guys think they're still fighting for the cause. Fergus Doyle is a legend to them. They don't see what I see. They don't know him like I do. They're just cowboys. But it's not their fault that there'll never be real, proper peace in Ulster, not for a hundred more years. It's thanks to you lot. Thanks to the English who started this whole frigging mess of shite in the first place.'

'I'm half Irish,' Ben said. 'Just so you know.'

She snorted. 'Well whoopee-doo. You want a medal or something?'

'I'm glad you brought me here, Tara.'

'I could have shot you. I'll kill anyone who tries to harm him.'

'I appreciate that.'

'I still could.'

'I appreciate that too.'

'But it's not what I want,' she said. 'What I want is for all this to be over, for people to understand that Fergus Doyle is just this poor old man who wants to be left alone so he can die in peace. It won't be long before he goes.' A tear began to form in the corner of her eye. 'I wanted you to see him and know how wrong you were.'

Ben said nothing.

'The person you said was missing,' Tara said. 'I think I saw it on TV. Is it anything to do with that sunken treasure guy, Forsythe?'

Ben nodded. 'Forsyte. Roger Forsyte.'

'They said there were women in the car with him. She was one of them, wasn't she? They took her too?'

Ben nodded again.

'You love her a lot, don't you? I can see it in your face. Is she your wife? Girlfriend?'

'She was,' Ben said quietly. 'We split up.'

'I hope you find her. I hope she's okay. I really do mean that.'

'I hope so too,' he said. 'Thanks, Tara. You're the sweetest girl that ever pointed a loaded revolver at me.'

She smiled sadly. 'I don't even know your name.'

'It's not important,' he said.

'S'pose I should give you a lift back into town.'

'If you could take me back to my car. I need to get moving.'

'Where will you go?'

'I don't know that yet,' he admitted. He was only just beginning to realise how lost he felt now that his one and only lead had vapourised before his eyes.

'You won't tell anyone, will you? Where Uncle Fergus is, I mean. In case anyone might . . .'

'Not a living soul.'

By the time Tara drove Ben back to his car, the police had long since disappeared from the scene of the shooting. There would be a few interrogations going on now, but none of the men Ben had left behind him in the alleyways could have any notion of who he was.

Tara left him with a few last words that he barely heard. He climbed into the BMW and watched the Honda vanish into the distance.

Then he was alone again, alone with the pressing knowledge that the trail had gone cold under his feet. He'd never felt so alone; so desolate; so weary.

It was 2.38 p.m. Brooke had been missing for forty hours and thirty-three minutes.

He didn't think he was ever going to see her again.

Chapter Twenty

'Get out, bitch.'

Everything a terrifying whirl of impressions, the man's fingers iron-tight round her arm as he hauled her out of the car. The unwavering gun never more than a few inches from her face. Sam's whimpers and pleas as the three of them were bundled into the back of the van. The slamming of doors; the rocking, juddering journey inside the hard bare metal shell of the van.

'Out. Get out.' More guns. Being prodded and marched roughly away from the road, up a grassy slope to a dark building, echoey inside. The smell of fear and damp earth and the sound of Sam's crying next to her and suddenly, a dazzling floodlight that made her blink. She was aware of men standing all around, just shapes behind the glare.

One in particular. He stood so close to the bright light that Brooke could hardly see more than his tall outline, but she could tell he was watching her curiously; intently.

Then he spoke, not to Brooke but to Forsyte. 'The case, if you please.' His English was clipped, too perfect to be native. What was that accent? Not European.

'I told you before. It isn't for sale.' Forsyte, trying to master his fear and almost succeeding.

Half blinded by the light, Brooke thought she saw the tall

figure motion to one of his men. Sam's cries became shrill and then were obliterated by an explosion that pierced Brooke's eardrums in the enclosed space.

Sam's body sprawling lifelessly to the earth floor. The numb shock of disbelief. More screams now, Forsyte's cries of rage turning to a screech of horror. The men closing on him, grabbing his arms, shoving him down to his knees. The glitter of the blade being drawn from its scabbard. Forsyte shouting wildly out 'No! Please! No!' Then the men holding his right arm down on the floor and the rise and fall of the blade. The awful meaty crunch and the inhuman wail of agony. The hand holding the case rolling away across the floor, the steel cuff still attached to the severed wrist.

Then the same again with the other arm. Forsyte's terrible, animal scream echoing around the walls.

Brooke could feel the pistol at her head and knew it was over for her, too. Waiting . . . waiting . . . for the gunshot that was going to put her down there on the floor with Sam.

Then the voice of the tall man behind the light: 'Not that one. I want her.'

I want her . . .

Brooke awoke with a sharp gasp. She was breathing hard and covered in sweat. She blinked, blinked again, disorientated by the vividness of the nightmare. Except that it had been no dream. The experience was going to stay with her for the rest of her life.

However long that might be.

As her confusion melted away, she realised she was in a bed: a massive four-poster with drapes and a canopy. The sheets felt cool and satiny to the touch. She swept them off her and saw she was wearing a silk nightdress she'd never seen before and certainly wouldn't have worn out of choice.

Someone had undressed her. The thought made her squirm.

She sat up straight in the bed. She felt woozy and there was a bitter taste on her lips. She knew why. Whoever had brought her here, taken off her clothes and put her into this damn nightdress, had drugged her. 'Bastards,' she muttered, then clamped her mouth shut in case someone was listening.

She swung her legs out of the bed and got up. The floor was cool against her bare feet. She could hear the soft whisper of an air conditioning unit, and smell the scent of flowers. On the little bedside table was a glass of water and, neatly coiled up next to it, Brooke's little gold neck-chain that someone had removed. What the hell was happening?

As she ventured away from the bed her legs felt weak and unsteady with the aftereffects of the dope. How long had the bastards kept her under? What had they done to her while she was unconscious? She was filled with helpless fury.

The room was in semi-darkness, just a line of sunlight shining round the edge of the window blinds. Brooke fumbled round for a way of opening them. They were metal and seemed to be electrically operated somehow, but she couldn't find a switch anywhere. She turned on a lamp instead and looked around her.

The bedroom was the biggest she'd ever seen. Flowers were everywhere, orchids and heliconias and other exotic species whose names she could only guess at, spilling from vases and filling the room with their colour and perfume. The furniture was antique, the floor was white marble inlaid with lapis lazuli. On a beautiful ornate table had been left a neat stack of books, together with a collection of the latest fashion magazines and some CDs, all classical.

How thoughtful of her kidnappers to provide entertainment. She furiously dashed the lot on the floor, then overturned the table. The effort made her dizzy.

At each end of the room was a gleaming white door. Forcing herself to walk straight, Brooke stormed over to one of them and wrenched it open. It led to an enormous luxury bathroom that smelled of lavender, shelf upon shelf stocked with an absurd array of beauty products and perfumes. Gold-plated toilet roll holder, she thought. Great.

She slammed that door, crossed the room to the other and stepped through into a living room. Like the bedroom, it was shaded by metallic window blinds with no obvious means of opening them. She turned on a light switch.

The living room looked like something out of the grandest kind of hotel. Plush armchairs and sofas, rich Persian rugs, framed oil paintings on the walls. A bowl of fruit, a variety of gourmet snacks and a carafe of iced lemon water had been left for her on one of the two massive antique sideboards while she was asleep. Her eye was drawn to the ornate clock on the marble mantelpiece. Its hands read eight-forty. In the morning, she supposed. How long had she been here?

There was a set of double doors at the far end of the living room. She tried them: locked, naturally. She pounded on the doors and yelled a few times, but there was no response from outside. She raced to the nearest window and tried once more to find the switch for the blind. Nothing seemed to make them open – nothing, until she grabbed a heavy brass table lamp from one of the sideboards, smashed the shade away, ripped the wire from the wall and used the lamp like a hatchet to strike the blind repeatedly with all her strength until it finally came away from its mountings and crashed to the floor at her feet.

Golden light streamed into the room, making her blink. She shielded her eyes from the glare and looked out.

It wasn't the freshly-painted black iron bars on the other

side of the thick glass of the window that made her gasp. It was the landscape that lay beyond them.

'Oh, my God,' she breathed.

It damn sure wasn't Ireland. And it wasn't London, either. She'd never seen a place like this before, not for real.

Beyond a sweep of white buildings, gardens, hangars and roadways, all contained within the same high stone-walled perimeter, the tropical jungle stretched away to a seemingly infinite and lushly verdant horizon. Large birds more colourful than the flowers in her room wheeled and squawked against the unbroken expanse of pure, deep blue sky.

Brooke watched in amazement as one of them glided down to land on the roof of one the buildings just fifty feet from her window, folded its broad red and yellow wings and strutted along the ridge of terracotta tiles to scrape at a piece of moss with its huge nutcracker beak. It was a macaw.

'I'm in South America,' Brooke murmured to herself.

Chapter Twenty-One

Ben drove. He had nowhere to go, no destination in mind, no longer any plan to work to. He just kept moving because he needed something to do in order to prevent the black despair from swallowing him up.

He'd been so sure he was on the right track. Like a predator steadily closing in on its quarry, that single-minded certainty of purpose had been his only focus, the only thing sustaining him. It seemed ridiculous now, bitterly ridiculous and pathetic.

As he sat there mechanically going through the motions to keep the car on the road, he struggled to get his thoughts in order. But if he was hoping for some miracle of inspiration to strike him out of nowhere, it wasn't happening. Smoking a cigarette often helped him think; he lit a Gauloise, but it tasted bad and felt self-indulgent, as if he no longer deserved such pleasures. After a few shallow puffs he flicked it out of the window.

He'd been driving aimlessly on and on like that for almost an hour when his phone went off. He had to summon up all his energy just to answer it.

'It's Kay Lynch,' said the familiar voice on the line. 'How are you holding up?'

'What do you think?' he muttered.

'You don't sound so good.'

'I'll be doing a lot better if you tell me you've found her.'

'I wish I could do that, Ben. We're still searching.'

'Until Hanratty calls it off,' he said.

'He won't. And even if he did, I won't stop. I can assure you of that.'

'Neither will I,' Ben said.

'Yeah, well, we talked about that, didn't we? Where are you now?'

He didn't even know. 'I'm . . . on a road,' he muttered.

'In France, I hope.'

'No. I'm still in Ireland.'

'You sound exhausted, Ben. There's nothing you can do. Go home. Get some rest before you burn yourself out.'

'Is that why you called me?' he said with a stab of anger. 'To tell me to give it up and go home?'

'Actually,' she said, 'I was calling because I'd promised to keep you updated, and something's come up. Thought you ought to know. It's, well, it's a little unusual.'

Ben was suddenly alert again. 'I'm listening.'

'Strictly between you and me, all right? My job's on the line if you breathe a word of this to Hanratty or anyone else.'

'Strictly between you and me.'

Lynch spoke fast as she filled him in. 'All right. Forsyte's and Samantha Sheldrake's bodies were flown down to Dublin just after dawn this morning for autopsy because we don't have enough facilities here. Top priority – the lab were at work on it by seven this morning. I've been waiting impatiently all day for them to feed back to us. Nothing until just a few minutes ago, when I finally got the reports faxed over. I have them here in front of me.'

Ben heard a rustle of paper over the phone, then Lynch went on: 'No surprises with Sheldrake. It's what it looked

131

like, single large calibre expanding handgun bullet to the head, did a vast amount of damage and she didn't stand a chance. The delay in getting the reports through was down to Forsyte. It's taken them most of the day to figure out what kind of poison killed him. Turns out it was some kind of extremely rare venom. There's a chemical analysis here, a whole list of stuff, like serotonin, 5'-nucleo—' She tutted. 'Sorry, excuse my lack of medical knowledge here, I'm reading this from the page. 5'-nucleotidase, phosphodiesterase, and it goes on. You still there?'

'I'm listening.'

'The first one, the serotonin, causes the victim extreme, unbearable pain. The other two are enzymes responsible for causing tissue breakdowns typical of the kind seen in stingray evenomations. Cause of death was a catastrophic accelerated necrosis of heart tissue, culminating in right ventricular rupture and fatal cardiac tamponade. I had to look that up. It means a massive and sudden accumulation of fluid or blood.'

Ben frowned. 'Hold on. Did you just say that Forsyte was poisoned with the venom from a stingray?'

'As strange as it sounds, yup. I phoned them just now to double-check, talked to the lab guy who did the tests. Thank God for chemistry nerds. He's been working on this for eight straight hours, and he's never seen anything like it either. But he's one hundred per cent certain that's the source. And not just any old stingray, either. He reckons the venom was extracted from a unique freshwater species that only lives in South America. Amazonia, to be precise. That's been checked out with the zoology department at Trinity College, Dublin.'

'Amazonia,' Ben echoed, narrowing his eyes.

'It's weird. I mean, this is Ireland, for Christ's sake,' Lynch said. 'And there's something else, too. The forensic examiner also found a small metal key inside Forsyte's stomach. It hadn't been there long, and lacerations inside his throat suggest that he might have swallowed it down in a hurry sometime not long before his death. We think he did it after the kidnappers struck, while the victims were in transit.'

'What kind of key?'

'Examination shows that it's the key to a set of handcuffs. Not the universal type key you can use to open just about any make of cuffs. Looks like it's some kind of special custom job. We don't know what to make of it.'

Ben's mind was working so furiously hard that he was going to crash the BMW if he didn't pull in. He rolled to a halt on the verge and killed the engine.

Cutting off Forsyte's hands hadn't been a reprisal at all, neither by a former IRA man sworn to revenge, nor by anyone else.

'He had something cuffed to his wrist,' he said. 'A briefcase, maybe. That's what the kidnappers were after, and Forsyte knew it. Must have swallowed the key to try to stop them getting it from him. He obviously didn't reckon on what they were capable of doing to get the cuff off his arm.'

Lynch sounded doubtful. 'That was my initial thought too. But then why chop off both hands, not just the one holding the case or whatever it was?'

The obvious answer was as simple as it was callous. 'To throw us off the mark,' Ben told her. Like ransom extortionists tossing their phones onto the back of a long-distance lorry to lead the cops astray, the ploy had worked beautifully.

'It's highly speculative,' Lynch said. 'For a start, we don't know that Forsyte was carrying anything.'

'If he had it cuffed to him when he left the country club, someone must have noticed.'

'Officers already talked to all the staff who were on duty that night.'

'Every single one?'

'Yes, everyone, and nobody saw Forsyte leave. He must have gone out a back way to avoid the photographers. Secondly, even if we did know he was carrying, say, a briefcase, we'd still be no closer to knowing who did this.'

'Not unless we knew what was inside,' Ben said. 'If it was something worth killing for, it could lead us back to the killers. And maybe to Brooke.'

Lynch must have heard something in his tone. 'You and I had a deal,' she reminded him a little more severely. 'I agreed to keep you in the loop if you agreed to stay out of this. That's a condition I need you to respect. You *are* staying out of this, aren't you, Ben?'

'I'm a law-abiding citizen, Detective Sergeant.'

'I'm glad to hear it. Look, the fact that we have these fresh leads now takes us a step closer to finding her. You need to trust that. Promise me you'll go home.'

'I will go home,' he said.

But he never said when. The instant the call was over he restarted the BMW and slewed it violently round in the road to point back the way he'd come.

'Sorry, Kay,' he said out loud.

Chapter Twenty-Two

South America?

It took a while for the initial shock to pass. Once Brooke's mind had settled enough for her to think more clearly and the lingering effects of the tranquillisers had worn off, she paced the luxurious suite of rooms – her gilded cage – and tried to understand what in the world was happening to her. One minute on a couple of days' break in Donegal, the next whisked halfway round the world for no reason she could imagine.

It was hard to shut out of her mind what those people had done to Roger Forsyte; even harder to stop replaying the sickening memory of what had happened to poor Sam. Her eyes wouldn't stop clouding with tears every time she thought about her dead friend.

Clearly, Forsyte had been the target, for some reason connected to whatever was inside that briefcase attached to his wrist. Sam and Brooke had both been in the wrong place at the wrong time, Sam because of her job and Brooke just from sheer wild chance.

Then why was she here now? Why had these men who'd murdered her friend brought her here to this villa, or whatever the hell it was?

The clothes she'd been wearing when she was kidnapped

had disappeared; the only possession she had left, apart from her own skin, was the little gold chain. She slipped it back around her neck. It made her think of Ben: what he was doing at this moment, where he was, how he was going to react when he heard the news she was missing.

Peeping furtively through the bars of the window whose blind she'd smashed away, she observed her surroundings. Her quarters seemed to be on the first, maybe the second, floor of what was obviously a very large house, almost like a fortress in size. It was hard to tell whether there were any more floors above hers. Outside her barred windows was what looked like a rooftop garden, tastefully laid out with pots of flowers everywhere and surrounded by a stone balustrade. Beyond that she could see the figures of men down below among the complex of buildings that stood clustered around the house.

Even if she'd been able to open the sealed window pane or yell loudly enough to be heard through the thick glass, she quickly realised there was little point in calling to anyone down there for help. The automatic weapons the men wore on their belts or slung round their shoulders as they came and went in twos and threes, attending to their mysterious duties, were enough proof of that. She was being well guarded.

Unable to do much else, Brooke spent a while watching the movements down below and trying to count the number of guards. They were all Hispanic, mostly in their twenties and thirties as far as she could tell from this distance. All were armed, whether with a handgun or a high-capacity military rifle, or both. The men wore no kind of uniforms, but it wasn't hard to see that the place was run with careful organisation and discipline. It made her think of an army base.

Twice she saw a vehicle appear from what she now realised was the main hangar or garage building, making billows of dust as it approached the barred gateway in the wall that seemed to be the only way in and out of the complex. The first vehicle was an open Jeep carrying three men, the second an olive-green military truck with a canvas top. Each time the armed guards opened up the gates, waved the vehicle through and then locked them shut again. Brooke caught only a brief glimpse of what lay beyond the gates – a winding dusty road that soon disappeared into the depths of the dark green forest.

Her head-count of the guards had reached eighteen when she heard a noise outside the door and whirled away from the window. There was the tinkle of a key in the lock, and the sound of a deadbolt being slid back. Brooke held her breath as the handle turned and the door began to open, fully expecting a host of armed men to come swarming into the room. What would happen next was something she didn't want to think about. Her heart began to pound. She looked about her for somewhere to hide. It was too late.

But it wasn't kidnappers with guns who entered the room. It was a pair of women, both olive-skinned and black-haired and dressed in simple, plain maids' outfits. The short one was middle-aged, thick-hipped, somewhat swarthy and carrying a white cardboard box a little larger than a shoebox. The taller one was twenty years younger and rail-thin with enormous brown eyes, but the family resemblance was obvious. Mother and daughter were muttering softly to one another in Portuguese as they came through the door.

Portuguese, Brooke thought. *Was this Brazil?*

The two women fell silent as they saw Brooke standing there in the light from the window, and stared at her for a moment before both gazing in horror at the crumpled metal blind on the floor.

Brooke stared back at them.

'I Consuela,' the elder woman said shyly after a few moments, then, motioning at her daughter, 'This Presentacion.'

Brooke said nothing. Consuela laid down her box on a table and lifted off the lid to reveal rustling paper and something shimmering blue inside. 'You wear,' she told Brooke in hesitant English, and jabbed a finger towards the box's contents.

The women appeared harmless, and a lot more nervous of Brooke than she was of them – especially Presentacion, who seemed transfixed with awe and apparently couldn't take her eyes off her. Brooke stepped a little closer and peered suspiciously into the box. The blue was some kind of satin material. As Consuela lifted it out and laid it across the back of an armchair with extreme care, Brooke saw that it was a very expensive and beautiful dress. There was underwear in the box, as well as a pair of high-heeled shoes the same shade as the dress.

'You wear,' Consuela said again.

Brooke shook her head. 'You must be kidding,' she said emphatically. 'Uh-uh. No way.'

Consuela pointed at Brooke's hair, her face, her nightdress. Brooke felt almost nude in it, and wished she had something to cover herself up with. 'You need get ready,' Consuela said in her stumbling English.

'Ready for what?' Brooke replied in Portuguese. She'd started learning the language when she'd first bought a tiny holiday retreat near Vila Flor, and could manage rudimentary conversation. No reply. She tried a different tack. 'Where am I?'

All she got in return from either of the women was blank

138

stares. It was impossible to tell whether they just hadn't understood her, or whether they were too frightened to answer. Very reluctantly, she allowed them to usher her back into the bedroom, where they sat her down at a dressing table and began clumsily fussing with her hair, speaking to one another in rapid-fire snatches of Portuguese that she couldn't catch. What the hell were they doing to her?

'Não,' she said firmly as Presentacion approached brandishing a tall can of hairspray. '*Por favor*, okay? I don't want it. Get it away from me.'

They kept insisting she put on the dress. Brooke would as soon have ripped it into little blue tatters, but anything was more dignified than the almost translucent nightie, and in the end she relented. 'Fine. Give it here.' She snatched the dress from Presentacion's hands, grabbed the box and carried them angrily into the ensuite bathroom.

'This is the most insane kidnapping ever,' she muttered to herself in the brightly-lit mirror as she slipped off the nightdress. She emerged a few minutes later wearing all but the high heels, which she'd left in the box and dumped on the bed. She drew the line at those.

Mother and daughter smiled and gazed at her in satisfaction, though they seemed concerned that she hadn't put on the shoes. '*Bonita, bonita*,' they said over and over, and then Consuela came out with a stream of rapid Portuguese of which Brooke only caught the name 'Alicia' mentioned at least two or three times.

'Who's Alicia?' she demanded.

The women suddenly looked worried, exchanging nervous glances. Presentacion seemed about to say something, but her mother shot her a look and shook her head, then turned back to Brooke and pointed at the shoes on the bed. 'You must wear,' she said.

'What do I have to wear them for?' Brooke snapped in English. 'I've been brought here against my will and now you want to dress me up like a fucking doll? Why won't you tell me what's going on?'

'You meet El Senhor,' the older woman replied, motioning agitatedly at the shoes. 'Must put on.'

'El Senhor? The master? Your boss, yes?'

'Yes, yes. You come meet now. He want see you.'

'All right, we go meet,' Brooke said. 'I've got a few things to say to this El Senhor of yours.' She grabbed the shoes off the bed and carried them in her hand as the women nervously led her out of the room.

Three guards were waiting in the corridor. They were big, solidly muscular men, and in her bare feet Brooke felt dwarfed by them. One was holding a large black assault rifle with a long, curved magazine; the other two cradled compact submachine guns in their arms. Her impression that the one with the assault rifle was in command was confirmed when he turned to one of the others and, without a word, sharply gestured at him to get rid of the stinking cigar he was smoking.

It figures, she thought. A basic lesson in male psychology. The guy with the biggest gun rules.

The flimsy dress might have been a step up from the nightie, but Brooke still felt so exposed and vulnerable under the eyes of the men that she swallowed back all the furious questions that she was bursting to ask, and kept her mouth shut. They all seemed to keep their distance, though, she noticed, and the glances they threw up and down her figure were careful and oblique, as if to ogle her too openly was off limits to them.

They were clearly under orders to handle her with care. There was something in their eyes. More than just professional discipline. It looked like fear.

Nothing she'd ever learned, or taught to any of her students, about kidnapping and hostage situations could have prepared her for such a situation. Her instinct told her she was in no immediate danger – but another voice in her mind was warning her that her predicament was as uncertain as it was bizarre. Anything could happen at any moment.

The man with the rifle motioned brusquely down a broad passage that was lined with antique chairs and oil paintings in heavy gilt frames. 'This way,' he grunted in thickly-accented English.

She felt like some kind of mascot on parade as she was escorted down the corridor and out onto a broad, galleried landing that looked like something from a movie. More paintings, enough to fill an art exhibition. A gleaming marble staircase swept down to the opulent hallway below.

From behind a doorway came the sound of someone playing the piano. Playing it very well, Brooke couldn't help but notice. The piece was a Bach fugue that she'd heard before. *So kidnappers have culture now?* she grunted to herself.

Brooke could see the deepening apprehension on all the guards' faces as they approached the sound of the piano. The one with the assault rifle knocked on the door. It seemed odd to see such a tough-looking, intimidating guy behave so furtively, almost meekly, like a child sent to see the headmaster. He waited for the music to trickle to a close after a few more bars, then opened the door and showed Brooke in.

Chapter Twenty-Three

Brooke found herself inside a salon that wouldn't have looked out of place in the Palace of Versailles. Near one window, a pair of graceful chairs was drawn up to a small table laid with fine chinaware and a silver coffee pot, a basket filled with croissants. But she had other things on her mind than to admire the furnishings or smell the coffee.

In the middle of the room stood a gleaming black grand piano. Rising up from the keyboard and turning to greet her with a smile was a tall, elegant man in beige slacks and a white silk shirt. His thick black hair was swept back from a face that was handsome and lean, slightly olive in complexion. His eyes were dark. There was no smile in them. The intensity of their gaze made Brooke want to look away, but she wouldn't let herself. As she padded across the polished floor, still barefoot and carrying the high-heeled shoes in her hand, she realised with a chill that this wasn't the first time she'd seen this man.

He was the man in her nightmare. The tall figure behind the light. The killer of Forsyte, and of Sam Sheldrake. Brooke couldn't repress the shiver that ran from the nape of her neck all the way down her back.

The man dismissed the guards with a curt wave. They seemed relieved to go. The door closed, leaving Brooke and the man alone in the magnificent room.

He stepped towards her, his dark eyes still watching her intently. 'My name is Ramon Serrato,' he said, in the same studiously perfect English with that merest hint of an accent she couldn't place. 'It's my pleasure to welcome you to my home, Dr Marcel. Or may I call you Brooke?'

She forced herself to return his unflinching gaze. Working hard to mask the tremor in her voice, she said, 'I see you've been going through the handbag you stole from me. Was that before or after you killed my friend and her employer, you murdering piece of shit?'

Serrato's composure remained unruffled. 'Like many others, you may be ignorant of certain things about Sir Roger Forsyte. He was an evil man, and he surrounded himself with evil people. However, I deeply regret that you were made to witness that unpleasant spectacle. It was not for such beautiful eyes to see.'

He motioned over to the little table. 'Please. I wish to make your stay here as comfortable as possible. Would you care for some breakfast? The coffee is excellent. Actually,' he added with a smile, 'I export the brand myself.'

'No coffee, thanks. How about a fucking explanation instead?'

Serrato sat down at the table, picked up the silver coffee pot and poured himself a cup. 'Explanation?' he asked nonchalantly, tearing a croissant and dunking it into the coffee.

'I *have* been kidnapped, haven't I?'

He looked at her with a wounded expression. 'Have you been chained up in some filthy hole in the ground and been stripped of all human dignity? No. Has anybody made any threat against your person? Harmed you in any way? No. You are a guest.'

'A guest!'

'Yes, a guest. In my home. Are you quite sure you won't

have some breakfast?' He raised the dripping croissant to his mouth and took a bite.

'You're insane. I don't even know who you are! How did I get here?'

Serrato shrugged. 'If it pleases you to know, you were brought from the Irish coast in a fast motor launch. We touched at Brest in northern France, then on to the Spanish port of La Coruña. From there an aircraft took us to Casablanca, where we embarked upon my own private jet for the final leg of the journey. I'm sorry you were unable to appreciate its comfort. You were sleeping very soundly.'

'You mean I was drugged.'

'A very mild sedative. I felt you would benefit from it, after the disagreeable business to which you had been a spectator.'

Brooke balked at the calmness in Serrato's eyes. An image flashed up in her mind of the side of Sam's head disintegrating in a cloud of bloody spray and her body collapsing limply to the ground. She swallowed back the bile and the hatred rising up in her throat. 'So where am I? Brazil?'

He looked at her approvingly. 'You are as clever as you are beautiful. You have rightly observed that your maids speak Portuguese, as they themselves are in fact originally from Brazil. But your deduction is false. Consuela and Presentacion have been in my employ for some time. This is not Brazil.'

'Then where am I?'

Serrato laughed and spread his arms. 'Where else but Paradise?'

'Paradise with armed guards and barred windows. Do you imprison all your guests this way?'

'I will do everything to make you feel at home,' he said. 'And to provide you with everything you could possibly require.'

144

'Good,' Brooke snapped back at him. 'Then I *require* that you put me back on your private jet and take me home. Today. Right now.'

'That is one request I regret I cannot grant you.'

'What's the idea? To hold me here for ransom? Why me, for Christ's sake? I'm a single thirty-something freelance consultant with a savings account containing about twelve and a half grand, an eight-year-old Suzuki Vitara with bald tyres, and a flat that I don't even own and couldn't get a mortgage to buy. Wait a minute,' she added as a new thought suddenly came to her. 'Is this about Marshall Kite?'

'Marshall Kite?' Serrato asked with a look of wry amusement.

She stared at him. Was it possible that he'd figured out her family connection with the wealthy director of Kite Investments Ltd? Her sister Phoebe's husband had already caused Brooke a great deal more trouble than he was worth by thinking he was in love with her and stalking her, leading to the whole breakdown with Ben, who'd been convinced they were having an affair.

'If that's what it is,' she told Serrato, 'you're wasting your time. First of all, Marshall and Phoebe probably don't even know what's happened to me. They've been cruising around in the Bahamas on their boat for the last several weeks, far away from phones and TV and email, and they won't be back for a while yet. Second, Marshall spends every last penny he earns on himself and his toys. He couldn't pay out a ransom for me even if he wanted. So if you were looking to extort money out of someone, you should've kept Roger Forsyte alive. In fact you might as well let me go right this bloody minute, because there's nothing whatever to gain by—'

Serrato interrupted her with an explosion of laughter. His shoulders quaked for a few moments, then he took out a silk handkerchief and dabbed his eyes. 'Such an imagination. Yet I'm afraid you are – what is it you English say? Far off the mark. Further off it than you can possibly imagine.'

His mirth died away abruptly. His penetrating gaze wandered over her face, drinking in and savouring every tiny detail. 'You must be very hungry. Can I not persuade you to eat something? I will have my chef prepare you whatever you desire.'

'Maybe you didn't hear what I said. All I desire at this moment is my freedom. You have no right to keep me here like this.'

He sighed. 'In time, you will see things differently. You will come to understand that you have nothing to fear from me. Nothing at all. Quite the contrary.'

Brooke balked at his words. 'In *time*? What are you talking about? Look, there's some mistake here,' she said desperately. 'Whoever it is you think I am, you're getting it all wrong.'

'There is no mistake,' Serrato replied. 'I know what I can see with my own eyes.' He drained the last of his coffee, dabbed the corners of his mouth with a crisp napkin, and glanced at his watch. 'And now, you must excuse me, but I have some business to attend to.'

The snap of his fingers echoed in the large room. The door opened, and the guards appeared. 'My men will escort you back to your quarters,' Serrato said. 'It was a pleasure to meet you, Brooke. We will meet again very soon.'

Chapter Twenty-Four

One hour and forty-nine minutes after he'd had the call from Kay Lynch, Ben sped in through the gates of the Castlebane Country Club and crunched to a sliding halt on the gravel by the front entrance. He burst inside the busy foyer and crossed the red carpet to the reception desk in three strides.

A different receptionist was on duty, a dark-haired girl who looked up at him in alarm as he demanded to see the manager. Ben was aware that he probably was a slightly alarming sight, haggard and unshaven and somewhat tousled from his encounter with Frank Flanagan and his boys. He guessed that not many of the country club's genteel membership were much given to brawling in alleyways.

The receptionist picked up a phone. 'Mr Church, it's Katrina at reception. There's a . . .' – she glanced anxiously at Ben – 'a Mr Hope here to see you.' Pause. 'No, he didn't say. Just that it was important.' Pause. 'All right, I'll tell him. Mr Church will be with you in a moment,' she said to Ben, putting down the phone.

Ben paced the foyer for six drawn-out minutes, aware of the looks he was getting and the way the staff and clientèle were shying clear of him, until a beaky, officious-looking man in a pressed suit and a bad wig appeared, introduced himself as Aidan Church, the country club's manager, and invited Ben curtly to follow him to his office.

As Ben followed Church down a corridor, they passed a young guy with a wild shock of curly hair who was half-heartedly mopping the tiled floor. Church paused to cast a disapproving eye on his work. 'Do it properly, for heaven's sake. You're meant to clean it, not just get it wet.'

The young guy shot a resentful glance at his manager, splashed the mop into his bucket and redoubled his efforts, muttering under his breath as he scrubbed the tiles. Ben caught the words 'at least I have me own hair, wanker,' and smiled to himself. He didn't think he'd have much liked to work for Mr Church either.

Church marched up to a door with a brass name plaque, swung it open and ushered Ben impatiently into his drab office. He didn't close the door or offer Ben a seat, as if he wasn't expecting the interview to last very long. He glanced at his watch. 'Now,' he said in a haughty tone that instantly rankled Ben. 'I'm taking it that this concerns recent tragic events.'

'Yes, it does,' Ben said.

Church eyed Ben's scuffed jeans and jacket with distaste. 'And I'm also taking it that you, Mr Hope, are not with the police.'

'No, I'm not,' Ben said. 'I'm conducting my own private investigation.'

'Look, I'm a busy man. I can assure you that we are cooperating fully with the authorities and that everything is being done—'

'Not quite everything,' Ben said. 'Some new information has just come to light that I believe could be of huge importance. With your permission I'd like to speak to the staff about it.'

Church balked. 'Speak to the staff? About what?'

'About who might have seen Sir Roger leaving the club. More specifically, about what anyone might have seen him carrying.'

'But everyone has already given their statements to the police.'

'Not about this,' Ben said.

'It's out of the question,' Church replied flatly. 'You obviously have no idea what it takes to keep an establishment of this size running smoothly.'

'Five minutes of their time,' Ben said, feeling his temper rise. 'I'll talk to each in turn, so as not to interrupt the running of your club. It isn't much to ask. This could be a matter of life or death, do you understand?'

Church shook his head. 'Uh-uh. No way.' He glanced at his watch again and gave a sharp wince. The UN General Assembly was waiting. 'I think we're done. I would like you to leave now, Mr Hope, and to stay away from Castlebane Country Club in future. I can't have you coming in here like this and frightening the employees and the customers. I mean, *look* at you. This is a reputable—'

'Listen to me, you beaky little turd,' Ben interrupted. 'The woman I . . . a very close friend of mine is missing. Her life is at stake here. I'm not going to ask you again.'

Church glowered at him in righteous indignation for a second or two, then snatched the phone from his desk and began stabbing keys. Ben heard the dial tone and a voice on the line. 'Put me through to Detective Inspector Hanratty, please,' Church said, with a smirk.

In his mind's eye Ben saw Church somersaulting backwards through the air and crashing headlong into the filing cabinet behind him, the phone spinning away in one direction, the wig flying off in the other – then he collected himself and unballed his fists. That wasn't the only scene he could visualise. He could just as well picture the one with Hanratty taking great delight in bundling him into the back of a police car and making him cool his heels overnight at the cop shop in Letterkenny pending an assault charge.

'Forget it,' Ben said to Church, and walked out of the office leaving him standing there with the phone in his hand.

Outside in the corridor, the young guy with the shock of hair was still mopping the floor. He nodded at Ben with a half-smile. Ben returned the nod, and was about to walk by him and head back towards the foyer when the young guy whispered, 'Psst.'

Ben paused and looked at him. The young guy put down his mop and pointed up the corridor to a fire exit.

'You got something to say to me?' Ben asked.

The young guy nodded, threw a furtive look back at Church's door and motioned for Ben to follow him out of the fire exit. It opened out onto a narrow passage between the buildings. A stack of crates was piled against one wall; a ratty old motorbike leaned against the other with a helmet dangling from its handlebar.

'Name's Billy,' the young guy said. 'Billy Johnson. Heard what you said to that gobshite Church.' He spoke with a pronounced Derry accent; as if by way of explanation he pointed at the motorbike and added, 'I come over the border to work. Cash in hand, you know? Doing the double, like.'

Ben knew what he meant by 'doing the double'. Some benefit scroungers were more enterprising than others.

'Need the extra money for the missus and the weans,' Billy said. 'Can't afford to lose it. That's why I didn't say too much to the cops, in case the fuckers started, you know, asking questions. Anyway, thing is, I was here, so I was.'

Now Ben understood where this was leading. 'The night of the kidnap?'

Billy nodded. 'Your wife that's missing, is it?'

'Close enough.'

'Sorry to hear about that, mister. Hope they get her back, like.'

'Thanks, Billy.'

'She got reddish kind of hair, has she?'

Ben showed him the photo from his wallet. Billy scrutinised it. 'Aye, that's her.'

'You saw her?'

'Saw him, too, what's-his-name.'

'Forsyte?'

Billy nodded. 'Church gave him the staff lounge to use as his dressing room. We were all told not to go near it, like he was the friggin' Pope or something. Door was locked and he had that driver standing guard outside the whole time he was giving his speech.'

'Lander,' Ben said.

'Aye, that was him. Anyway, afterwards auld Church had me lugging empty champagne bottles out to the back when I see this Jag waiting, with Lander at the wheel. Then I see this other guy Forsyte come out of the staff lounge exit, looking like he wanted to make sure none of the photographers were around. The place was hotching with them, so it was. He goes over to the Jag, gets in the back. Then the car drives round to the side entrance over there and I see these two women get in the back with him, this blonde and this other woman in a black outfit, with reddish hair. That's her in the photo, no mistake.'

Ben tucked the picture carefully back into his wallet. 'The man in the back of the car. You're sure it was Forsyte?'

'It was him all right. Saw him on the telly after, and the

151

driver. Saw the blonde, too. Who'd go and shoot a pretty lady like that, eh? Christ, I hope they get the bastards who done it, like.'

'What I need to know,' Ben said, 'is whether he was carrying anything.'

Billy nodded. 'Aye, he was carrying a case, so he was.'

'What kind of a case?'

'About so big. Black, thin, you know, one of them – what do you call them? – attaché cases. Nothing out of the ordinary, like. Wouldn't even have noticed if it hadn't been for the cuffs.'

'Tell me about the cuffs, Billy.'

'Like something out of a movie, you know? Like the dude in Ocean's Eleven. I love that fillum, so I do.' Billy affected a deep Eastern European voice. *'My name is Lyman Zerga.'*

'You're saying he had an attaché case cuffed to his wrist?'

Billy nodded. 'Think it was the right wrist.'

'And you're completely sure about this?'

Billy nodded more emphatically. 'I felt bad afterwards, that I didn't say anything to the cops, in case it was important or something. Just I didn't want any trouble. Under the circumstances, if you know what I mean.'

Ben thanked Billy, assured him that his secret was safe and asked him to show him the way between the buildings to the car park.

The evening was growing chillier and the stars were out. The BMW's clock read 17.42. Brooke had been gone over forty-three and a half hours.

Ben dug Justin Maxwell's business card out of his pocket and dialled his mobile number. After three rings, a tired and morose-sounding voice answered: 'Maxwell'.

'This is Ben Hope. I have a question. What do you know about the briefcase that Sir Roger had with him in the car?'

'I don't understand. No briefcase was found at the murder scene.'

'But he had one when he left the country club.'

'Maybe so. It's not unusual for us all to carry a case around, you know. We're businessmen.'

'Are NME executives in the habit of cuffing their briefcases to their wrists?'

'What are you talking about? Why would Roger do that?'

'The usual reason people do those things. To make it hard for anyone else to get hold of whatever was inside. It was obviously something very important. Not just to him, but to the people who took it from him. The only problem was that he didn't quite realise who he was dealing with.'

'Hold on. You're confusing me,' Maxwell said. 'How do you know all this? The police haven't mentioned anything about it to me.'

'I've just had it confirmed by an eye witness. Plus, Forsyte had the handcuffs key in his stomach. He swallowed it.'

'He *what?*'

'That's why they removed his hands,' Ben said. 'The right one, to free the case from his wrist. The left, just to cover their tracks.'

'I can't believe it. This just gets worse and worse.'

'The question is, what was inside the case that he was so keen on keeping hidden? That's what I need to find out.'

'You think it's connected to the murder?'

'You think it isn't?' Ben said. 'Like you said, the case was gone from the death scene.'

There was a long, appalled silence on the phone while Maxwell struggled to get his thoughts in order. 'What can I say? I . . . I'm aware that in his speech that night Roger alluded to some other discovery from the wreck of the *Santa Teresa* that he wasn't going to make public yet. I can only assume that's what the case contained, or something connected with it. I didn't have access to that information.'

'You're now the company's top executive and you didn't have access to that information?'

'Look, Roger moves . . . oh, Jesus . . . I mean *moved* in mysterious ways. He was a very secretive man at times, but nobody questioned his way of doing things, because he always turned out to be right in his decisions and he'd made this company very wealthy indeed.' Maxwell paused, reflecting. 'If anyone might know more about this business, it's Simon Butler. He was the one most directly involved with handling and itemising the artefacts, and he and Roger were close friends. It's possible that Roger may have said something about it to him.'

'Is Simon Butler still with you at Carrick Manor?'

'Neither of us is at the manor any longer. What's the point of hanging around sitting on our hands in the arsehole of nowhere? I'm back here at the company offices, fielding a million phone calls and trying to cope with this whole nightmare. Simon went home yesterday and I haven't heard from him since. I can give you his address, if it helps. It's his old family place a few miles from Southampton.'

As soon as the call was over, Ben was keying in the number Maxwell had given him for Simon Butler. There was no reply, no answerphone. Ben tried a couple more times before he put the phone away. He sat there in the darkened car, staring at the digital readout of the dashboard clock.

Forty-three hours and thirty-nine minutes since Brooke had been taken.

It didn't take long to decide what he had to do next. He fired up the BMW, sped out of the country club car park and headed once more for the airport.

This time, he was pretty sure he wouldn't be coming back.

Chapter Twenty-Five

It was ten-thirty in the evening by the time Ben's rental Lexus IS F pulled up at the side of a quiet road on the village outskirts. The sky over southern England was cloudy and starless. He turned off the ignition, flipped on the little overhead light and checked the address Justin Maxwell had given him.

This was the place, all right. A nameplate on the wall by the gate read 'Knightsford'. The large stone period house stood in the shadows some distance from the streetlamps, at the end of a long driveway.

Ben noticed the FOR SALE sign planted near the front gate and wondered what kind of mansion Butler must be planning to upgrade to from his old family home. NME obviously must pay well.

He stepped out of the car and breathed in the cold night air. He was wearing a newly-bought pair of black jeans and a black sweater and had cleaned himself up as best he could at the airport. There were fresh scuffs on his leather jacket that he couldn't do much about, but he looked presentable enough for his purpose. He went in the gate and walked up the long driveway towards the house. The lawns were smooth and rolling. Most of the house's windows were dark, but the new Mercedes sports coupé parked outside told him someone might be at home.

Ben rang the front doorbell and stood waiting for a few moments on the doorstep, running through in his mind what he wanted to ask Simon Butler about the contents of Forsyte's briefcase. A minute went by. He rang the doorbell again, more insistently. This time he heard stirring inside the house. A light came on through the dappled glass; a figure appeared and the front door opened.

'Yeah?'

It wasn't Simon Butler, but a skinnier, acne-spangled version of him about twenty-five years younger. The teenager was experimenting with some kind of proto-punk look, lip-stud and nose ring and weird hair. His eyes were a little unfocused, which Ben reckoned might have to do with the smell of marijuana smoke that wafted out of the doorway. It looked as if Mum and Dad weren't home, but Ben introduced himself and asked anyway.

'He's not here,' the teen told him in a laconic drawl. 'They're letting him out tonight. She's gone to fetch him.'

'Letting him out of where?' Ben asked.

'Out of the hospital.'

'Hospital?'

'Yeah. Should be back soon. You want to wait inside? Might as well come on in.'

The house was warm, and even bigger than it looked on the outside. Everything was expensive. The carpets were thick and soft underfoot. Ben had expected to be shown into a living room or maybe the kitchen, but instead the punkish teenager led him through the house to a doorway at the end of a dark passage. The doorway led to a downward flight of steps and a dimly-lit, bare-brick basement. A couple of heavily made-up teenage girls were lounging on a sagging sofa, either side of a chubby kid of about the same age who was in the middle of some anecdote that nobody seemed particularly interested in. A young guy who was obviously the twin brother of Ben's punkish host, but without the facial adornments or the chilled-out demeanour, was firing balls across a billiard table. Marijuana smoke drifted in the glow of the single naked bulb. Empty beer cans were strewn carelessly about and there was an overflowing ashtray perched on the edge of the billiard table. A giant *Lesbian Vampire Killers* poster was peeling off the brickwork. Ben guessed that Mum and Dad probably didn't venture too often into their kids' domain.

The twin at the billiard table glanced up as his brother led Ben down the steps. 'Who's this?'

The punkish one blinked, as if he'd forgotten Ben was even there. 'Uh? Oh, some guy to see Dad. What was your name again?' he said absently to Ben.

'Ben,' Ben repeated.

'Right. I'm Damien. That's my brother Rupe. Never mind that lot of morons.'

'Hey, watch it,' came a slurred protest from one of the girls on the sofa.

Ben sat on a bar stool and picked up the thread of the conversation. The chubby kid was still doing all the talking and seemed set on holding the stage for hours. 'They're out there,' he kept insisting with relish, waving his joint around for emphasis and scattering ash over the girl next to him, who didn't seem to notice. 'Fucking believe it. You can't see 'em yet cause there's not enough of 'em and they're lying low, taking the odd farmer here and there. But pretty soon it'll start to spread geometrically. First we'll see 'em in the villages, then the towns, then the cities. Then everywhere. Full-scale apocalyptic shit.'

It took a couple of moments before Ben realised the kid was fantasising about an impending zombie pandemic. Just as he was thinking of making his way back upstairs and waiting in another room, the twin called Rupe laid down his billiard cue and fixed him with a look of suspicion. 'You a friend of Dad's, then?' He was either an angrier kid generally than his brother, or he was just marginally less stoned out of his wits.

'We're like this,' Ben said, holding up crossed fingers.

'Right. So you're not a fucking debt collector come to, like, break everyone's legs or something. Well that's good news. You want a beer?'

'Anyway, like I was saying about the coming invasion,' the chubby kid said, keen to share more.

'Oh, bollocks to your coming invasion,' Rupe snapped at him.

'I'm fine,' Ben said, waving away the proffered beer. Now his curiosity was piqued. 'Tell me, why would I be a debt collector?'

'Yeah, Rupe, why would he be?' Damien said, squeezing up next to one of the girls on the sofa and putting an arm round her. 'We're not on the hit list any more, remember?'

Rupe pulled a sarcastic face and rolled his eyes. He grabbed a beer can and slurped noisily, then crushed it and tossed it with a clatter into the corner. 'Oh sure. Now that Daddy's rich again for five minutes. Sorry. I lose track of his little ups and downs. So what d'you want to see him for, then?' he added, glancing back at Ben.

'This and that. Boring stuff you don't want to know about,' Ben said. 'Tell me, what was he in hospital for? Nothing serious, I take it?'

Rupe snorted loudly. 'Just a little prefrontal lobotomy. That's what the twat needs, anyway.'

'Give it a rest, Rupe,' Damien muttered. 'Happened last night,' he explained to Ben. 'They kept him in all day for observation.'

Rupe picked up his billiard cue and fired a shot that scattered the balls violently all over the table. 'Next time that arsehole tells me to act more mature, I'll remind him that I'm not the one who swallowed half a bottle of vodka and a pile of sleeping pills and ended up getting carted off in an ambulance to get his stomach pumped. That's a dad to be proud of.'

'S'pose he'll have to go back to that shrink again, or whatever,' Damien said glumly.

'Huh. Like it's ever helped him in the past.'

'At least we don't have to move house now and go off and live in some poxy little close. Wish someone'd come and take that bloody sign away. It's embarrassing.'

'And at least I won't have to share a room with you, you farter.'

'Arse-picker.'

'Twat face.'

The twins' repartee continued to degenerate as Ben reflected in silence. Now he knew why Julian Maxwell hadn't heard from Butler since he'd left Ireland. People tended not to be in contact much when they were bent on ending it all. The question was why Butler had tried to do it in the first place.

As a professional soldier for thirteen years, most of them with the SAS, Ben had lived very much in a world of men. Moreover, it was a world where men under the extreme pressures of military training and conflict tended to form strong bonds with one another only, too often, to see their friends die. Grief for a lost comrade was commonplace, often everlasting – yet Ben had never once known a soldier to kill himself over it. Sure, a man could be heartbroken enough over a lost love, the passing of a beloved wife, that he couldn't go on any more – it happened. But over another man's death?

Ben thought about that. Had the relationship between Butler and Forsyte been closer than they'd outwardly let on? It was certainly possible. But more likely there was another reason.

'Has he ever done anything like this before?' he asked Damien.

The kid shook his head. 'I wish,' Rupe said, and that got them arguing again. Ben went on thinking, about the house that had been put up for sale only for it to be taken back off the market; and about Daddy getting suddenly rich again.

There was a faint rumble of car tyres on the gravel outside, then the sound of a key in the front door. 'Here they come,' Rupe muttered. 'Good old home sweet home again.'

'Won't be long before they're at it like cats and dogs,' Damien said, glancing anxiously up the basement steps. 'I give it thirty seconds.'

Ben made his excuses, climbed the steps and left the basement. It was good to breathe air again. From the end of the dark passage he could see the Butlers taking off their coats and hanging them up in the front hall. Neither of them was aware of their unexpected visitor's presence.

Ben watched them a moment and could immediately sense the tension between husband and wife. They barely spoke to one another. Butler looked even more wrecked than he had in Ireland, and as subdued and shamefaced as any man driven home from hospital after a suicide attempt. His wife, a small birdlike woman with mousy hair, was tight-lipped, tense, and looked like a spouse trying her best to be supportive but coming close to the end of her tether.

Ben stepped towards them. Butler's wife was the first to see the movement out of the corner of her eye. 'Rupert,' she began in an exasperated tone, 'if you think I can't smell what you and your brother have been—' She stopped mid-sentence with a gasp as Ben came closer, and stared at him in alarm.

An instant later Butler saw Ben too, and froze like a statue. The recognition in his eyes was quickly followed by a glimmer of fear that Ben found just as intriguing as the things the twins had been saying a few moments earlier.

'I didn't mean to scare you,' Ben said to Mrs Butler. 'Your son Damien let me in.'

'W-who are you?' she asked, nonplussed.

'Mr Butler knows who I am,' Ben said. 'And I think he knows why I'm here. We need to talk.'

'It's all right, Rachel,' Butler said wearily. 'I do know this man.' To Ben he said, 'Please, I don't want to talk to anyone right now. Just leave me alone, all right?'

'Listen, whoever you are,' Rachel Butler said, rounding on Ben. 'My husband isn't well. This is a very difficult time for us. Please leave at once or I'm afraid I'll have to call the police.'

'It's a lovely home you have here,' Ben said, looking intently at Simon Butler. 'It'd have been a shame to have to sell it. You must have come into some money. That was luck.'

A look of panic flashed across Butler's face at Ben's words. 'It's okay,' he quickly reassured his wife. 'I'll talk to him. We'll go into the study.'

Chapter Twenty-Six

Butler's study was at the other end of the ground floor. The walls were covered with framed pictures, nearly all of them blown-up prints of scenes from various marine salvage expeditions. One showed the Neptune Marine Exploration flagship *Trident* taken from the air; nearby Ben noticed three others of Butler himself, photographed on deck with Roger Forsyte, the two of them surrounded by NME crew members and all grinning like schoolkids over a barnacled hunk of unrecognisable marine salvage that was obviously some fantastically valuable artefact they'd just dredged up from the sea bed.

The Simon Butler in the photos was a far cry from the defeated, pale, shrunken man who threw himself down in a chair by the desk. 'All right. What do you want?'

'I came here to talk about the briefcase that your employer had cuffed to his wrist the night he was kidnapped,' Ben said, sitting on the arm of a couch opposite. 'Nobody seems to know what was inside. I thought maybe you might. And we'll get to that, but now I'm here I see there's more to all this. Isn't there, Butler? Better start talking fast, because I'm not in a patient mood.'

'I . . . I . . .'

'What was it, the horses? Cards? Or just drugs and women?'

Butler just stared. He opened his mouth to speak, then closed it again.

'That's fine,' Ben said. 'Frankly, I don't give a damn what kind of sordid little vice it is that you need your head examined for and almost had to sell your house over. I'm more interested in knowing where all the money came from all of a sudden to pull you up out of the shit.'

'It's . . . an inheritance,' Butler stammered. 'From a wealthy uncle.'

'People normally celebrate a windfall like that with a bottle of champagne,' Ben said. 'You went for vodka and sleeping pills instead. Some people might find that odd.'

'Who the hell do you think you are, coming into my home and prying into my affairs?' Butler rose up out of his chair and started marching towards the door. 'You're going to have to leave now.'

Before he'd made it halfway, Ben stood up and blocked him, grasping a fistful of his shirt collar and propelling him back into his chair. 'Why don't we get Mrs Butler and the twins in here and talk more about this wealthy uncle of yours?'

Butler gaped up at him from the chair.

'The truth,' Ben said. 'All of it, and fast. Or when you leave this room, it'll be another ambulance trip. One way only.'

Butler's face suddenly contorted and he began to weep miserably. 'It wasn't meant to happen like this!' he wailed.

'What way was it meant to happen, Butler? Speak to me.'

Butler did, and Ben sat and listened as it all came out. the usual squalid tale, and with it all the usual excuses. The urge was stronger than him. Nothing, no form of therapy ever invented, not even the terror of total ruin and social and professional disgrace, could rein it in. It had started years ago with a few innocent flutters on the fruit machines, and steadily grown from there into a full-blown addiction to anything and everything that could be gambled on, at the expense of the family's savings and, very nearly, his marriage. Losing the house would have been the last straw.

'You've no idea how deep I was in,' Butler sobbed. 'There was no way out. I was on the verge of losing everything. I had to think of my family. It's what any husband or father would have done. I swear, I didn't know anyone would get hurt. It was just business. Why was I so weak? Oh Christ, why did I . . . ?'

'I'm going to break your neck in the next minute if you don't tell me exactly what happened,' Ben said quietly.

'All right, all right, I'll tell you. Let me start at the beginning.' Butler wiped away tears and looked pitifully up at him. 'It wasn't *all* my fault,' he sniffed. 'I mean, it wasn't as if they hadn't tried to buy it from Roger, fair and square. I knew how pig-headed he could be. They said he'd turned them down flat, wouldn't budge no matter how much they offered him for it.'

'Offered him for what?'

'What he was carrying in the case,' Butler said. 'I'm certain it was what he found inside that casket.'

'Forty seconds,' Ben said.

'Let me explain,' Butler pleaded. 'You see, back in early December, we were pulling up so much stuff from the *Santa Teresa* that the whole staff, including Roger, were mucking in to help bring it aboard *Trident*, clean it up, categorise it and store it. It wasn't usual for Roger to get his hands dirty like that. It was as if he knew in advance that the casket would be there. It was just this iron-bound strongbox with a kind of seal on the lid, not like any of the others, and nothing much to look at compared to some of the incredible pieces we were finding. The moment the crane brought it up, Roger took it away to his office and spent a long time alone with it before locking it up in his private safe.'

'So you've no idea what it was?'

'When I asked him about it, he was evasive. He only told me that it was something incredibly hot. He was acting as if it was worth more than the rest of the stuff put together, would hardly let it out of his sight. Said he didn't want to make it public until he knew more, and then it was going to cause a massive sensation. The morning after the media event he was due to fly down to Spain to talk to this historical consultant about it. That's all I know, I swear.'

'Who are *they*?' Ben demanded. 'These people who approached you?'

'Not long after Roger had got the casket,' Butler explained, 'I got a call from a man who said his name was Smith. I couldn't tell where he was from, but he didn't sound British. Told me he was coming to me because I'd been with the company so long and knew Roger the best. Now I know it was because they must have checked up on my background, had me followed or something, and knew about my . . . my problem.'

Butler heaved a deep sigh, staring into the middle distance as he talked. 'At first I wouldn't speak to him, wouldn't take him seriously. But he seemed to know so much, about the casket, and about NME's business. And when they wired a down payment of fifty grand into my bank account, I knew they were serious. I called the bank and tried to find out where the money had come from. It was from some numbered offshore account that couldn't be traced to anyone. Smith told me there was another half a million in it if—'

'If you helped them to kidnap and murder your friend Roger Forsyte.'

'On my kids' lives, I promise you that it wasn't like that.

They told me they only wanted what was in the case. I knew he'd have it with him when he went back to the manor from the country club that night. My job was to call Smith and tell him when the car was setting off. Once Smith's people had the case, they were meant to take Roger and the others to a safe place, unharmed, and call the cops to come and get them. No guns, no violence. That was agreed.'

Ben looked at him in disgust. His hands were shaking with the urge to slam Butler's head against the desk. Hard. Repeatedly. 'And you believed all that.'

'You can't make me feel any worse than I already do,' Butler said in a flat, empty voice. 'I know I don't deserve a penny of that money. I don't even deserve to live. It wasn't just Roger. Wally and Sam are dead too, thanks to me. And your friend . . . I'm just so very sorry. I don't know what to say.' He buried his face in his hands. 'Rachel hates me, you know. My kids hate me. They're right to hate me. I wish I was dead.'

Ben's face hardened even more. 'You said Forsyte had planned to meet up with a history expert about whatever was inside the case.'

Butler sniffed. 'Yeah. He said Cabeza would help him learn more about it, before going public.'

'Cabeza. Who is he?'

'Juan Fernando Cabeza. He's a history professor. Used to teach at the University of Seville, now he's freelance. Specialises in old manuscripts and documents, stuff like that.'

'Why did Forsyte need to go to Spain to find a historian? There must be fifty thousand of them in London.'

'Because nobody can beat Cabeza in his area of special knowledge,' Butler said. 'It's the Habsburg Empire, the period of Spain's domination of most of Europe and its massive overseas territories during the sixteenth and seventeenth centuries.

So much sunken treasure dates back to that time that we've gone back to Cabeza for help again and again in the past.'

'You said he dealt in old manuscripts and documents?'

'There's other kinds of treasure apart from gold and precious stones,' Butler said. 'Maps. Letters, diaries, memoirs of historical significance. Military orders. Political communiqués. Stuff like that can be of huge value. When important papers were to be carried by ship in those days, they often used to protect them inside waterproof caskets sealed with wax. We've recovered examples that had survived for centuries at the bottom of the ocean.'

'So can we assume that the briefcase contained some kind of old documents that had been taken from the wreck?'

'I suppose so,' Butler said. 'If Cabeza was involved, it seems likely. But I can't say. Like I told you, Roger didn't let me in on it.'

'But he might have revealed more to this Cabeza?'

Butler shrugged. 'Might have. I don't think the guy would have agreed to a meeting otherwise. He's become more and more reclusive over the years. Roger used to gripe about how hard it was to get him on the phone, let alone agree to a face-to-face. Then again, Roger might have just offered to pay him a packet and wasn't going to tell him anything until the meeting.'

Ben considered for a moment. 'Where does Cabeza live?'

'After he quit his university job he went off to live in the mountains near Málaga. Out in the middle of nowhere, Roger said. I couldn't tell you exactly.'

Ben looked at him.

'I swear,' Butler said. 'If I knew, I'd tell you.'

'Then who does? Maxwell?'

'As far as I know, Roger was the only one in touch with him. I suppose he'd have his address.'

'Where?'

'In his business address book.'

'Where?'

'He keeps . . . I mean, kept it in his desk at the office.'

'Get your coat on,' Ben said, standing up. 'We'll go in my car.'

'Now? At this time of night?'

'Now,' Ben said, and Butler didn't argue any more.

Butler gave out reluctant directions and kept a death-grip on the passenger door handle as Ben sped into Southampton. The NME offices were a large steel-and-glass building on the outskirts of the city, overlooking the broad stretch of Southampton Water and the lights of the Fawley oil refinery in the distance.

'Security?' Ben asked as they pulled up outside.

'A guard patrols the building at night,' Butler said nervously. 'What if he asks questions?'

'You can offer to cut him in on your poker winnings,' Ben said.

'That's not funny. Can't this wait until morning?'

'No.'

'What if Roger's office isn't open?'

'Then we'll open it,' Ben said.

'I shouldn't be doing this.'

'Just keep reminding yourself why you are,' Ben told him.

Butler used a scan card to let them into the building. They stepped into a large foyer. Butler was heading automatically for a light switch when Ben stopped him, producing the Mini Maglite he carried in his bag.

'Roger's office is on the first floor,' Butler whispered. Ben darted the thin light beam around the foyer and noticed a fire exit stairway leading upwards. 'That way,' he said.

Ben kept his ear out for the night watchman as they

climbed the stairs and emerged through the fire door onto the first floor. The building was cold, but Butler's face was shiny with sweat in the torchlight. 'Roger's office,' he whispered at the end of a shadowy corridor.

Butler tried the door. 'Just as I thought. It's locked.'

Ben brushed his hand down the door and shone his torch. It looked and felt like solid oak.

'It's no use,' Butler was saying. 'Let's get out of here.'

Ben moved a step back from the door. Took a breath, mustered up his strength, then rushed at it and lashed out with the sole of his boot. The ripping crackle of splintering door frame reverberated down the corridor. Ben felt it give slightly. He kicked it again, and this time the door crashed wide open and smacked hard against the inside wall of Forsyte's office.

'Jesus Christ,' Butler muttered.

'Never mind him,' Ben said, handing him the torch. 'Get me the book.' If Forsyte's desk was locked, he'd have to smash that open too.

'I can't do this.'

Ben gave him a look. Butler quickly scurried into the office while Ben stayed out in the corridor listening for the security guard. He could hear Butler groping about inside. The sound of a drawer sliding open, papers being shuffled about, then a soft cry: 'Got it.'

Butler stumbled his way out of the shadowy room and pressed the hardback address book into Ben's hands. By the thin white beam of the torch Ben quickly flipped through the address book to the letter C. There he was, halfway down the crammed page in Forsyte's jerky, sharp-edged writing: Professor Juan Fernando Cabeza, together with the address in Spain that Ben needed. He tore out the page and tossed the book back inside the office. 'Let's go,' he said to Butler.

Back outside, Butler was about to clamber into the Lexus passenger seat when Ben grasped his arm and wheeled him away from the car. Butler cringed like a beaten dog.

'You're walking home,' Ben said. 'The exercise'll do you good.'

'What are you doing to do?' Butler quavered.

'I'm going to see Cabeza,' Ben said.

'No, I meant, what are you going to do to me?'

'That depends on what I find at the end of this,' Ben said. 'If Brooke's all right, maybe I'll be able to forget that a piece of shit like you exists.' He started walking round to the driver's side. 'But if she isn't all right, then you'd better get some more vodka and pills, and kill yourself properly before I come for you.'

Butler had no reply to make. Ben got into the car, shut the door and started the engine. As the Lexus sped away, Simon Butler shrank to a tiny figure in the rear-view mirror and then disappeared altogether.

Chapter Twenty-Seven

Brooke had interviewed many former kidnap victims during her years as a hostage psychology educator and consultant. One of the key lessons that had come out of those discussions, and which she'd always striven to emphasise in her lectures on the subject, was the vital importance of staying mentally sharp and focused during captivity. Psychological fitness was at least as critical as physical exercise to a hostage's wellbeing – one UN aid worker she'd known who had been abducted by a volatile armed gang in Somalia and held for five months in a dingy cellar, not knowing from day to day whether he was to be released or shot in the head, had managed to survive the ordeal by building a wooden boat in his mind.

Plank by plank, joint by joint, he'd designed and constructed the thing over and over in his imagination as he'd sat there in the rat-infested darkness. As soon as the boat was completed, he would mentally dismantle it piece by piece and then immediately start redesigning an improved version. On his eventual release he'd never wanted to see another boat again in his life, but those months of mental discipline had saved him from going crazy.

How an individual chose to cope was down to them, as long as they found something to keep their mind busy and ward off the soul-destroying fear and stress of captivity. Those who caved in under the terrible pressure might survive the experience physically, but were very often never the same people again.

Brooke didn't know much about boat-building. Instead, using an eyeliner pencil and a page ripped out of one of the vapid women's magazines that had been left for her to read, she busied herself during that afternoon by drawing a plan of her prison.

She started with the house itself, based on the parts of it that she'd seen when the guards had taken her down to see Serrato earlier. She'd returned from her meeting with her 'host' to find that the damaged window blinds had been repaired, but that the unseen workmen had accidentally left a small gap allowing her to peer through and observe the surrounding compound.

She'd traced the shape of the outer wall, or as much of it as was visible to her, and drawn little rectangular shapes to show the positions of the buildings around the main house. The hangar from which vehicles came and went was marked 'garage'; the squat white building from which she'd observed more armed men wandering to and fro in pairs and groups throughout the afternoon was tentatively labelled 'guard house?'. A twisting dotted line represented the roadway from the gates that vanished into the surrounding jungle. Then there were the fortified gates themselves, with tiny matchstick figures showing the guards who constantly manned them.

Brooke spent a long time staring out beyond the gates at the jungle and wondering where that snaking road went. Was there a town nearby, or even a small village where a lone fugitive on foot might be able to get help?

Her secret map wasn't an escape plan, not yet. Another

cardinal rule that she'd always drummed into anyone attending her lectures was that, unless they had a solid strategy and were completely certain they were fully equipped to survive outside the stronghold, a kidnap victim should *never* try to escape. It was a last resort that almost always ended in disaster, death or recapture, entailing punishment and the loss of whatever tiny privileges the hostage might have started out with. But she was determined to find out everything she could about her environment.

The only way Brooke had of telling the time was to go over to the window repeatedly to check the position of the sun over the jungle, which told her that her room faced west. Sometime in the middle of the afternoon, the door was unlocked and Consuela and Presentacion came in with a tray of coffee and little cakes, seeming anxious to tend to her every need.

Room service only made her predicament seem even stranger. Despite the language barrier, Brooke made the older of the Brazilian women understand that she'd like some more comfortable things to wear. Consuela seemed reluctant and anxious at first, but the clothes arrived an hour or so later: a couple of neatly-ironed T-shirts, tracksuit bottoms, a pair of tennis shoes.

Brooke was interested in forming a rapport with Consuela and her daughter, firstly because a hostage's most valuable asset was a friendly face among their kidnappers, and secondly because it was very obvious that the two women weren't to be counted among the bad guys. She could tell that they were almost as scared as she was of their employer.

But what was less clear to Brooke was the odd, continual fascination they seemed to have for her – the way they'd stare at her sometimes, and whisper to one another in

Portuguese. Twice more she'd caught the name 'Alicia' – but like before, when she asked who Alicia was, all she got were timid looks and silence.

Left alone again, Brooke checked her window for any more developments outside. She spotted a figure she recognised: it was the stinky cigar-smoking guard, standing over by the compound wall sneaking a quick puff when he thought nobody was watching. He took a half-smoked stub and a lighter from his breast pocket and started blowing great clouds. Brooke observed him for a moment, then moved back from the window to do some push-ups, sit-ups and running on the spot. She might be trapped in here, but she was determined to stay fit and strong.

The sun was sinking in the west by the time she received another visit: Consuela and Presentacion had returned to prepare her for what she quickly realised was to be another meeting with her host.

'Not again,' she groaned when Consuela revealed the dress she was to wear. It was as delicate and expensive as the first, but this time it was a deep shade of emerald green. Needless to say, the high-heeled sandals matched perfectly. Brooke closed herself in the bathroom and put on the dress and shoes without protest. What was the point? Satisfied and beaming at her, the women departed.

Moments later the door opened again. Two guards had come for her. It was hard to tell which one looked more menacing: the musclebound one with the glossy jet-black hair tied back in a thick ponytail, or the wiry one with the top half of his right ear missing.

'Only two goons this time,' she snapped at them. 'We must be making progress. How about you just give me a key to my door?'

The guards said nothing as they walked her along the

passage, down the staircase and through a maze of corridors and hallways she'd never seen before.

'Slow down,' she told them. 'I can hardly walk in these bloody things.' Whether they understood her or not, they slowed their pace and she was able to take in the layout of the passageways so that she could add them to her map later.

The guards ushered her into an enormous room and shut the door. The walls were adorned with gilt-framed oils and mirrors, and a glittering crystal chandelier shone down on a long dining table covered in a white silk cloth and a gleaming array of silverware and glassware.

Sitting alone at the head of the table was Ramon Serrato, immaculate in a cream-coloured suit. He stood up as Brooke entered the room, and stared at her for a long moment as if stunned by her appearance. Then, seeming to collect his wits, he wished her good evening and pulled out a chair near the top of the table for her.

'I trust you passed a pleasant afternoon?' he asked.

Brooke was about to make an angry reply when another door opened and two white-coated male servants filed into the room. One was carrying an ice bucket on a silver platter, the other wheeling a trolley bearing hors d'oeuvres. Without a word they set everything down on the table, then hurried away again like mice.

'What's the matter?' Serrato said, seeing her expression. 'Are you not hungry? The pâté de foie gras is very good. I recommend eating the toast while it is still warm. And the wine is a Cabernet-Sauvignon, from my own vineyard in Chile.'

Right, she thought to herself. *So we're not in Brazil. And we're not in Chile either.* How many South American countries did that leave to choose from? Too damn many. 'Am I supposed to be impressed with all this?' she said out loud.

'I would have hoped so. There are many people who would never have a meal like this in their lives.'

'That makes me feel so much better. I should be grateful to you, really.'

'Have you ever been poor?' he asked her, reaching for the champagne. 'So poor that you had only stinking rags to wear, so hungry that you would kill a rat with your bare hands and eat it?' he smiled. 'No, I don't think so. You have always been comfortable. Perhaps if you had grown up in poverty as I did, you would appreciate this more.'

Brooke said nothing.

'You don't believe me,' he said. 'And yet it's true. I spent my childhood in the slums of Mexico City. My brothers and I had to beg for food while my mother cleaned toilets and my father picked watermelons for a few pesos a day. Our whole family lived in two rooms that were not fit to keep animals in.'

'I'm overwhelmed with sympathy.'

Serrato looked at her sharply. 'I am sure you would have been, if you could have seen the way we lived. It was a squalid existence. As a boy I would watch the rich men drive past in their big cars and I knew that I was destined for better things. My grandfather used to tell us that for all our poverty and unhappiness, there was noble blood in our veins. Noble blood,' Serrato repeated, 'dating back to the time when the Spanish Empire covered half the world. My mother and father used to laugh and tell us not to listen to an old fool's tales. It was not until I was much older that I learned that my grandfather was right.'

Brooke didn't reply.

Serrato seemed about to continue, then restrained himself. 'But I have no right to bore such a charming companion with stories of my past. Won't you take some foie gras?'

176

'Stick your foie gras. I'm not hungry.'

'Perhaps this will whet your appetite.' Serrato reached behind him and picked up a square, flat jewellery box, which he slid across the table towards her. 'A gift.'

'You think I'd want anything from *you*?'

'Please, I insist.'

Brooke opened the box. Inside was a diamond and emerald necklace that looked as if it must be worth about the same as her flat in Richmond, together with a matching bracelet. 'What the hell are these?'

'They're yours. And I should very much like to see you in them.'

The green dress matched perfectly with the sparkling emeralds: it was clear that Serrato liked to plan every little detail. The way he was looking at her was deeply unsettling, but she met his eye and replied fiercely, 'I'm not your doll, or anyone else's, to be draped in bangles and beads.'

'You're a woman of strong opinions,' Serrato said. 'I have every respect for that.'

'Then why are you dressing me up like this? Is this how you get your kicks, kidnapping women and making them wear this stuff? It's sick.'

'It seems to me that you underestimate your own beauty,' he said. 'Whereas I do not. And you would greatly oblige me by putting the jewels on.'

Brooke saw a strange light in his eye. Something told her she shouldn't push him too far. 'If you insist.' She plucked the bracelet from the box and tried it on.

'As I thought, a perfect fit,' Serrato said admiringly. 'And now the necklace.'

Brooke knew she couldn't refuse. 'Let me take this off first,' she said, and reached behind her neck to undo the clasp of the little gold chain Ben had given her. She removed it with real reluctance, picked the cold, heavy necklace from its velvet liner and slipped it round her neck in its place. The clasp was awkward to fasten.

'Allow me,' Serrato said. Rising from his chair he stepped behind hers, and she felt his fingers delicately touching the back of her neck. 'There, it's done. It looks as wonderful on you as I had thought it would.'

She could see herself in the gilt-framed mirror opposite, and him standing over her, watching her as if she were something in a museum to be admired and gawked at. His hands brushed her shoulders. She twisted away from his touch.

'You have such fine features,' he said, carefully studying her face in the mirror. 'If you were to tie your hair up it would accentuate them even more. Let me show you. There. Like this.'

'Please tell me what's going on. Tell me what I'm doing here.'

'You'll understand in due course,' he said, returning to his chair. In the meantime, there is something I've been meaning to ask you.' Taking a small envelope from the pocket of his blazer, he opened it and produced a tiny photograph. 'Is this the man you mentioned, this Marshall person?'

Brooke instantly recognised the photo of Ben, taken the previous spring at Le Val. Even when it had looked as though their relationship was over forever, she hadn't had the heart to throw it away. Serrato must have found it in her purse.

There was a gleam in his eye as he waited for her reply. It suddenly struck her what his expression was. It was the look of a jealous lover, and it turned her blood cold to think what might happen if she told the truth.

'That's nobody,' she said carefully.

Serrato scrutinised her face for a long moment. 'Are you

quite sure? Not, for example, the man who bought you that?' He pointed at the slim gold chain that Brooke was holding in her hand.

'Forget him,' she said. 'He's not important.'

'I'm pleased to hear it. Is there anyone else . . . *important* in your life?'

She shook her head. 'No. There's nobody.'

Serrato gazed at her a moment longer, then smiled and seemed satisfied she was being truthful. 'What about some wine?'

'Just a little,' she said, and held out her glass for him to fill. She hated playing this game that he seemed to enjoy so much, but she badly needed something to steady her nerves.

'You should eat, as well,' he said, scraping pâté onto a sliver of toast. 'We don't want you becoming too thin.'

Why, then I won't fit your fucking dress collection any more? she wanted to yell at him, but kept her mouth shut. After a few moments she reluctantly began to pick at the food.

'Good, no?'

'Better than I had in my last prison,' she said dryly.

'I love your sense of humour.' Serrato rang a little bell and the two servants instantly filed in to clear away the hors d'oeuvre plates and bring in the main course and more wine before disappearing as quickly as before. Serrato lifted the lid of a silver platter and breathed in the aromatic steam that rose up. 'Salmon poached in fino sherry, with a butter and parsley sauce,' he said with relish. 'It's wonderful together with these sautéed potatoes and steamed asparagus tips.'

'You really must give me the recipe,' she muttered.

He picked up a silver fish slice. 'Let me serve you.'

'I've had enough to eat. I want to leave now.'

'You wish to return to your rooms?'

'I wish to return to my country. To my home, my friends,

the ones you and your thugs haven't murdered. To my life. It's been left kind of interrupted, in case you hadn't noticed.'

'Your life is here with me now,' he said quietly after a pause. 'That is how it was meant to be.'

The words hit her like a slap across the face. She nearly laughed at the surreal absurdity of it. 'I beg your pardon?'

'You'll soon forget your old life,' Serrato told her, delicately laying a slice of salmon on his own plate. 'Believe me when I say that the one I have to offer you is far superior in every way. I have so many plans for us. There's so much we can do together. Once my plans are finalised, the world will truly be ours.' He reached for the vegetables.

'You're mad. Who do you think I am?'

Serrato began eating and made no reply.

'Who's Alicia?' she asked suddenly, breaking the silence.

Serrato put down his knife and fork with such a loud clatter that it made her jump. He looked across the table at her with a hard, wild glare in his eyes. His tanned face had turned almost white. 'What did you say?'

'You heard me. Consuela and Presentacion keep talking about someone called Alicia, and looking at me. Who is she? Do you think I'm her? Because I'm not. You know my name. It's Brooke Marcel. Not Alicia someone-or-other.'

Looking as though he was making a huge effort to control himself, Serrato wiped his mouth with a satin napkin and rose from his seat. He left the dining room without a word.

Brooke sat there alone at the empty table. A minute went by, then another. She carefully pushed the little gold chain into the cup of her bra, for want of a pocket. It was more precious to her than a million emerald necklaces and she didn't want to lose it.

Because a crazy, dangerous, irresistible idea had just come into her mind. She stood up, slipped off her shoes

180

and crept silently across to the door through which the guards had brought her. After listening for sounds outside the door and hearing nothing, she gently opened it a crack and peeked through. There was nobody around.

She swallowed. *You're as mad as he is*, she thought. But the opportunity was too tempting to resist. She stepped out of the dining room and glanced around her. The wide hallway had four other doors, all gleaming walnut with shiny gold handles, any of which could lead to some kind of exit.

Brooke was committed now. She padded furtively across the hallway to the nearest of the doors, pressed her ear to it for a moment and then turned the handle.

The room behind the door was a lounge that looked like something from a gentlemen's club circa 1850: heavily varnished panelling, yet more artwork, a mirror over the fireplace, Chesterfield furniture. Brooke searched the room for a phone. She had no idea what country she was in, let alone what number to call for the police, but if she could make a call to Ben's mobile, she might be able to get through to him. The thought of being able to speak to him made her heart jump.

But there was no phone. Brooke was about to leave the room and try another when the sudden tap of approaching footsteps outside made her back away from the door and press herself against the wall. The footsteps paused outside. Voices: two men, speaking Spanish.

She held her breath. The door was a couple of inches ajar, and leaning forward she could just about make out the two guards in the hallway. Both were armed with pistols. They'd paused so that one could show the other something on his phone, some picture that made them both laugh. Brooke drew away from the door. Would they notice it was hanging open and come inside to check the room? For a terrifying instant she glanced about her for a hiding place, convinced she was about to be caught – but then the guards moved on and she could breathe again.

Their footsteps grew fainter. She counted one – two – three –

And stopped at four.

She stopped because she'd just realised that what she'd taken to be a mirror over the fireplace, framed in ornate gilt wood, was actually a painting.

It was a portrait of a woman. A woman in a shimmering green dress, with long, curling auburn hair that was elegantly swept up to show off the diamonds and emeralds around her neck. The slender hand posed resting on her lap wore the matching bracelet. Her green eyes looked straight into the viewer's, stunningly lifelike and filled with joy and excitement. She was smiling.

Brooke gaped at the painting. It couldn't be . . . was it . . . ?

It was of her.

Chapter Twenty-Eight

Her mind reeling so much she could hardly walk straight, Brooke crossed the room to stare at the painting more closely. It seemed incredible, impossible.

And yet it seemed true. The woman had her face, her hair. The dress in the picture was the exact same one that she was wearing. The jewels were the ones that Serrato had given her at dinner. Brooke couldn't believe what she was seeing.

It was only when she got right up close and stared hard at the detail of the picture that she began to make out subtle differences and realised that the painting was of someone else. The eyes were a slightly different shade, and slightly closer together than hers. The shape of the nose, the ears, the chin. But nonetheless the resemblance was unsettling.

Brooke ran her hand along the bottom of the painting's ornate frame and her fingers found something. She looked at it: a small rectangular plaque sculpted into the golden wood. A plaque that bore, in tiny black script, the name 'Alicia'.

Her thoughts were racing as she left the room and ran up the passage in the opposite direction that the guards had gone, searching left and right for an exit as she went, the marble floor hard and cold under her bare soles. The notion of trying to escape now, dressed as she was, barefoot, totally vulnerable and lost, was insane – it was against everything she'd ever learned or taught. But none of her training or knowledge were of any use to her now. She was no normal hostage; and this Ramon Serrato, whoever the hell he was, was certainly no normal kidnapper.

Alicia. Did Serrato truly believe that Brooke was Alicia? It was hard to grasp what was happening to her. She almost wished he *was* holding her for ransom in a dank cellar, hooded and chained up. Anything was better than this bizarre, fetishistic kind of slavery. She had to get out of here.

Doors; more doors. They passed in a flurry as she ran on, gathering up the hem of the dress to keep it from tangling up her legs. Nothing that looked like an exit, and there could have been a bunch of guards standing right behind any of them. She'd never been inside such a huge house before – it seemed to go on forever and now she was starting to panic, her breath coming in gasps as she thought about what would happen when Serrato returned to the dining room to find it empty. A whole army of his men would go storming through the whole place searching for her. She couldn't possibly evade them for long.

A glimpse of a window as she tore down a passage and went hurrying down a narrow flight of steps told her night had fallen. This part of the house was workmanlike and plain, dimly lit with bare walls and rough concrete floors that chafed on her bare feet as she ran. She hurried round a corner and had to fling herself into a shady alcove for cover as a set of doors swung open and she almost ran right into two men dressed in catering aprons. The place they'd emerged from was a kitchen, but from the pungent aroma of grease, fried beans, tomato and chilli that wafted out of the doors she guessed it catered for Serrato's troops rather than meeting the elevated gastronomic tastes of the man himself. She waited hidden, holding her breath, for the cooks to pass by, then ran on.

She was quite lost now, and becoming more panic-stricken by the second. The passage she was heading down was getting narrower and seemed to be leading nowhere. Brooke was on the verge of turning round to head back the way she'd come or find another route through the house, when she suddenly stopped dead.

She'd heard something. And as she stood there tensed up in the gloomy passage, she heard it again. The sound of a woman's voice not far away. She cocked her head, listening in alarm. No, there were two distinct voices – two women.

And they were both screaming in fear.

Brooke moved along more slowly now, wondering where the terrible keening sound was coming from. She paused at a door, gave it a tentative shove and peered inside as it creaked open. It was a laundry room, with a row of large, squat washing machines along one wall and stacks of laundry baskets along another. Near the ceiling above the machines was a window, thick with dirt and cobwebs. She realised she'd wandered into a basement.

Her escape attempt was forgotten for the moment as she felt herself drawn to the source of the awful, continuous screaming that she now realised was coming from through that high window. A bright white light, like a floodlamp from outside, was glaring through the dirty glass.

Despite the awkward dress Brooke managed to clamber up onto one of the washing machines, so that the window ledge was about eight inches above her head. She reached up to the ledge with both hands and hauled her chin level with the window sill, scrabbling with her bare toes to get a purchase on the wall, then peered through the dirty glass.

The window was a few inches above the ground level of

a brightly-lit concrete yard, about ten metres square and surrounded by a whitewashed block wall. There were six men standing in the yard, one of them just inches from where Brooke was straining to peer through the window, so that the leg of his combat trousers half-blocked the view. But she could see enough.

At the opposite side of the yard, the two guards who'd brought her from her quarters earlier, the muscular ponytailed one and the one with the damaged ear, were violently dragging and shoving the Brazilian maidservants against the wall. Presentacion was clinging desperately to her mother and sobbing hysterically in the glare of the floodlights. Consuela let out another high-pitched scream as the ponytailed guard ripped her daughter away from her and sent her sprawling to the concrete.

Brooke wanted to scream 'Stop it! Leave them alone!' But all she could do was hang there from her fingertips and stare in horror as she realised what was about to happen.

A tall figure in a cream suit stepped into view. He had his back to the basement window, but she knew Serrato well enough now to recognise him instantly even from behind. He appeared quite unfazed by the frantic screams of the two women as he walked over to them. Consuela tore herself from the grip of the guard holding her and threw herself at his feet, clutching at his trouser legs, her face covered in tears, pleading with him in her native Portuguese. Brooke understood every plaintive, sobbing word.

'Don't harm my child, I beg you! I'm to blame, I swear. Punish me, but please don't hurt my baby! Please!'

Serrato's reply was too quiet for Brooke to catch through the glass, but she didn't need to hear to understand. He shook his head, brusquely pushed the weeping mother away with his foot, and took three slow steps back. He reached

186

out his hand. One of the guards unholstered an automatic pistol and passed it to him, butt-first. In no hurry, Serrato checked the weapon over and then aimed it down at Consuela's bowed head.

Presentacion let out a wailing, inhuman shriek. Brooke almost screamed, too. He was going to slaughter the Brazilian maids just the way he'd slaughtered Sam and her employer, and there was nothing anyone could do to stop it.

The gunshot reverberated sharply round the walled yard. Consuela gave a lurch and then slumped over on her side. There was a spatter of blood up the white wall behind her.

Then Serrato turned the pistol on Presentacion. The pony-tailed guard who'd been tightly gripping the screaming girl's arm now let go. Presentacion had nowhere at all to run, but in her desperation she raced for the far wall and almost reached it before the pistol cracked a second time in Serrato's hand.

The shot caught her in the back. She collapsed on her face in a tangle of arms and legs, but she wasn't dead. Brooke went on watching in anguish as the young girl tried to drag herself across the concrete yard. Serrato calmly walked up to her and fired another shot into the back of her head. The blood sprayed a foot across the ground. This time Presentacion stopped moving.

Serrato returned the pistol to his man. 'Dump the bodies in the jungle,' Brooke heard him order the guards in Spanish. Her heart was pounding. She felt numb, barely conscious of the pain in her fingers clinging to the window ledge.

Serrato turned round to walk away from the two dead women. There was nothing in his expression. As he moved closer to Brooke's window she could see the flecks of blood on his suit. He paused to dab at them with a handkerchief, tutted irritably and walked on out of sight, followed by all

187

but two of the men, who stayed behind to take care of the corpses.

Wanting to throw up, Brooke lowered herself back to the floor. She knew that if Serrato returned to the dining room and found her missing, there might be a third woman's body thrown out for the jungle scavengers that night.

She staggered for the door, threw it open and started running frantically back the way she'd come. By a miracle she didn't meet anyone as she retraced her steps; by an even bigger miracle she managed to find the dining room without getting lost in the maze of passageways. Her heart was in her mouth as she opened the dining room door, fully expecting Serrato to be there already waiting for her with a pistol in his hand. But the room was empty. Brooke hurried across to the table, sat down at her place and tried to control the emotions that were making her hands shake.

A few minutes later, Serrato returned. He'd changed out of the cream-coloured suit and into a pair of chinos and a navy blazer. 'I hope you will forgive me for so rudely interrupting our dinner,' he said with a smile. 'I suddenly remembered a matter of business that simply could not wait, not even for you.' He glanced downwards and his smile faded into a frown. 'You have taken off your shoes?'

Brooke had completely forgotten the sandals she'd slipped off and left under the table. 'They're a little tight on me,' she said, thinking fast. She managed to control the tremor in her voice.

'No matter. I will have new ones made to fit,' he replied. 'Now, shall we eat?'

Chapter Twenty-Nine

The address on the ripped-out page from Forsyte's book was in the province of Granada, Andalucía, in the deep south of Spain. When Ben checked out the location, he could see Butler had been right about Juan Fernando Cabeza being reclusive. The historian had chosen a home high up in the Sierra Nevada mountains, some way east of Granada City and just about as remote as anywhere in Europe. His old university still had him listed on their website as a former faculty member, offering a blurb about his various academic achievements, accolades and publications. Cabeza's birth date was 1966. The image of him on the site showed a craggy-faced man with a serious expression and unusually fair hair and pale eyes for a Spaniard. Ben committed the face to memory.

After a few hours' snatched sleep in the car, he boarded the earliest possible flight from Gatwick to Málaga, the airport nearest his destination. Another two hours later he was touching down on Spanish soil, dragging his heels impatiently through customs and hiring a Volkswagen Touareg four-wheel drive. His head was aching badly and he'd barely eaten a thing for two days, but a powerful, furious inner force kept driving him on.

Ten-eighteen, local time. Brooke had now been missing for over fifty-nine hours.

Ben's last time in Spain had been a brief but eventful visit to Salamanca the previous September, when the weather had been hot and sultry. This time round, the dashboard thermometer read minus four and plummeted down two degrees further as he bypassed Granada in the Sierra Nevada foothills, 130 kilometres east of Málaga, and wound his way up and up into the mountains.

The scant traffic thinned out to almost zero the higher the road climbed, and he saw nothing for miles and miles except endless snowy forests of oak and pine. He had to stop frequently to check his bearings. Once he almost collided with a curly-horned mountain goat that burst out from the roadside shrubbery and darted across his path. On and on the road led him, often buried deep in snow and almost impassable in places, climbing ever more steeply until he could see the snowy mountain peaks rearing up above the clouds like something out of a dreamscape.

It was early afternoon by the time Ben caught his first glimpse of the house through the trees, checked his map again and knew he'd come to the right place. By then the road had dwindled into a narrow track that was virtually invisible under a blanket of white. If any other vehicles had made it up here recently, all trace of their passing had been covered in the last snowfall. Judging by the heavy sky, another was due before long.

The final hundred or so yards to the house were blocked by a fallen pine trunk that looked as if it must have come down in a recent winter storm, and drifts too deep even for the 4x4 to negotiate. Ben got out and began trudging through the crisp snow, his legs sinking in knee-high. The cold air was stunning after the warmth of the car. Condensation billowed from his mouth. He dug his hands deep in his jacket pockets.

He paused at the fallen tree to brush away the clumps of snow from his jeans and observe the house. It was a long, low building except for the round, ivy-clad, two-storey tower that dominated one wing. The stonework was as white as the snow that had drifted high up against the foot of the walls. Thick bushes and spreading pine trees had grown in close all around. He could see no sign of a vehicle, but guessed that Cabeza's car or truck must be parked behind the wooden doors of the garage built into the ground floor of the house. Straining an ear over the constant whistle of the cold, biting wind, he was sure he could hear faint music coming from somewhere inside. Someone was at home.

He could hear the music more clearly as he approached the foot of the building. It sounded like Beethoven, being played loudly from one of the rooms within the round tower.

The front entrance to the house was at first-floor level, on a raised terrace skirted by a wrought-iron railing. Ben climbed the slippery steps and tinkled the little bell that hung from an ornate bracket by the door. It didn't surprise him when there was no response. The Beethoven was blaring loudly enough from inside to drown out anything short of a shotgun blast. Maybe Cabeza was deaf, he thought. He tried the door and found it unlocked. Creaking it open a few inches, he peered in and could see the woody interior of a living room with exposed beams and a tall stone fireplace.

'Hello?' he called out in Spanish. 'Anyone here?'

Still no sign of life except for the music. Ben kicked the snow from his boots and stepped inside the house. He looked around him. The scent of freshly-brewed coffee drew his eye to an open doorway to his right, and the kitchen beyond.

He walked in and touched the coffee pot by the stove. It was warm, and so was the half-finished cup sitting on the table next to an open newspaper.

The music was still playing in the background. Ben made his way back through the living room towards the sound. Through another door was a hallway that led to the first floor of the tower, a round library completely encircled with wooden bookcases crammed with thousands of volumes and periodicals. Next to a little reading table was an iron spiral staircase leading upwards to a neat circular hole in the ceiling. Ben climbed the steps and found himself emerging into a hallway on the tower's top floor with a door on either side of him.

The music was coming from the left hand door. Ben knocked lightly, then more firmly. 'Hello? Professor Cabeza?' He waited for a reply, but all he could hear were the strains of Beethoven from behind the glossy wood. If Cabeza was inside the room, he didn't want to scare the man by walking in unannounced – but he couldn't wait out in the hall forever, either. He gently opened the door and stepped inside.

The semicircular room was bright and spacious, lit from above by a large skylight and from the east and west by a sweeping, curved expanse of floor-to-ceiling windows looking out through the pine trees over the snowy forest and the peaks in the distance. Historical prints hung on the walls. More books and papers lay in heaps and piles every-where: on the floor, on a side table and among the clutter of the large desk by the window. But what Ben was looking at was the high-backed leather chair facing away from him, and the man he could see sitting in it.

All that was visible of the chair's occupant were the top

of his head and his zip-up tan leather ankle boots. His fair hair was unkempt. He was completely still and looked from behind as if he were gazing dreamily out of the window, so taken up with the soaring orchestral music that he was oblivious of anything else going on around him.

'Professor Cabeza?' Ben said.

No response.

'Are you Juan Fernando Cabeza?' he asked again, more loudly. Still nothing.

The Beethoven was blaring from a powerful little stereo system in a cabinet. Ben had had enough of it. He stepped across and turned the music abruptly off.

Silence flooded the room like cold water. Ben looked back across at the leather chair, expecting Cabeza to react. What that reaction would be, he'd no idea – outrage, indignation, terror, maybe; as long as the guy didn't keel over with sudden heart failure, Ben was sure he could get him talking with more or less gentle persuasion and find out whether coming all this way was going to prove a wild goose chase or bring him any closer to finding Brooke.

But Cabeza didn't so much as twitch at the sudden stopping of the music. Was he asleep? Comatose from drink or drugs? Dead? Ben edged closer, moving round the chair so that he could see the tip of the man's left shoulder and his legs as well as the top of his head. He was wearing a beige fleece jacket and brown corduroys.

Ben was about to reach out and shake the back of the chair when something moved on Cabeza's desk.

It was only a minute movement, and Ben only registered it for a tiny fraction of a second before he realised what it was and how he needed to respond to it.

The desk lamp was a metal Anglepoise, chrome-plated to a mirror finish. What Ben had seen was a reflection in the lampshade.

The reflection of something behind him, moving fast towards him.

The reflection of a man with a gun.

Chapter Thirty

Ben wheeled round to see the man striding across the room, headed right for him. He'd been hiding behind the door as Ben came in – a powerfully-built man of thirty-five or forty with short dark hair and a look of animal ferocity on his face. He wore black combat trousers and a military-style jacket.

The gun in his hands was one that Ben recognised instantly. It was a SIG SG 553 carbine: stubby, black. Special Forces and tactical law enforcement personnel termed it a primary intervention weapon; everyone else in the world would call it a machine gun. Seven pounds one ounce of lethal Swiss efficiency, mounted with laser and optical sights and handled by someone who seemed to know disconcertingly well what he was doing as he pointed it directly at Ben's chest. He wore the weapon's black nylon tactical sling round his neck and shoulder like a man who'd been trained in combat. The expression in his eye told Ben he wouldn't hesitate to pull the trigger.

A quarter of a second later, Ben was proved right. But by the time the room erupted with deafening gunfire and the flurry of high-velocity 5.56mm bullets was in midair, Ben was already flying over the desk for cover. The windows shattered. Plaster exploded in chunks from the wall, showering Ben with white dust as he crashed to the floor on the other side of the desk, bringing it down with him and colliding hard against the side of the leather chair, knocking it over.

Out of the corner of his eye Ben saw the body of Juan Fernando Cabeza spill out of the fallen chair, his head rolling off his shoulders and falling down separately to split open into a liquid mush on the carpet.

Except that it wasn't a real man – it was a mannequin. The beige fleece jacket and corduroys had been stuffed with towels. The head was an overripe pumpkin topped with a straw-coloured wig. The hems of the trousers had been carefully draped over the empty ankle boots, which stayed where they were as the rest of him fell apart.

Ben wasn't able to gape at the fallen dummy for more than an instant before the man with the gun opened fire again. Bullets thunked into the top of the overturned desk. It wasn't much of a shield against the potent assault weapon. The gunman rattled off another string of fully-automatic fire that whipped up a storm of splinters from the rapidly disintegrating desk.

Ben was aware there could only be one reason why the shooter hadn't just walked right up to him, pointed his weapon over the top of the desk and shot him to pieces. He must think that Ben was armed.

And if that was the case, it wouldn't be long before he sussed out that he wasn't. Which meant Ben had to get out of this trap, and fast. There was only one way he was going to do that. He flung himself out from behind the desk and made a dive for the smashed window.

Broken glass raked his arms and sides as he went crashing through what was left of the window pane. He dropped through empty space for what seemed several seconds, cold air whistling in his ears, arms and legs outflung. Then the impact of the pine branch below the window drove the air out of his body. He let out a grunt of pain, bounced away from the branch, dropped a few more feet and felt another crash into his ribs. His fingers raked twigs and branches but he was falling too fast to get a purchase on anything solid. His vision became a spinning kaleidoscope of green foliage and gnarly bark and the white snow below as he tumbled, ripping and crackling, through the foliage of the tree. The white ground rushed up to meet him. Then suddenly he was buried, blinded, coughing and choking and groping frantically to claw his way out of the deep snowdrift that the wind had piled up at the base of the tower.

Ben burst out of the snow and struggled to his feet, ignoring the crippling pain of dozens of minor cuts and bruises. Looking up, he saw the shooter appear at the smashed window high above. The spent magazine from the SIG dropped into the snow as the man discarded it with professional cool and slammed in another. Before he could release the bolt and resume firing, Ben took off at a stumbling sprint through the snow, heading between the trees in the direction of the car and running in a wild zigzag to make himself a harder target.

The shooter opened fire again. Single shots now, let off in rapid succession with deliberate, surgical precision. A bullet thwacked off a pine trunk just inches from Ben's head.

Who was this guy? A soldier? He acted like one.

Ben sprinted on towards the car, reaching into his pocket as he went for the ignition key, praying it hadn't fallen out during his tumble from the window and muttering a quick thanks when his fingers closed on the cold metal key ring. He'd reached the fallen tree now. He hurdled over the top of it, snow flying in his wake, and hit the ground running. The Volkswagen was just a few yards further.

The shooter wasn't about to let him get there. The car's

windscreen and side windows disintegrated into a thousand fragments. A line of holes punched through the metal of the bonnet. Another burst took out the lights and shattered the front grille. The perforated bonnet flew open. Liquid spewed out of the destroyed radiator. The VW wasn't going anywhere.

Ben veered away and changed course, heading deeper into the forest. The bursts of gunfire were following close behind, and gaining. A snow-laden pine branch exploded into a hail of ice fragments a foot from his head. Then suddenly the terrain was with him as the ground sloped away from the house, putting him out of sight of the shooter.

He kept running. Silence from the house now; the only sound the rasping of his own breath in his ears and the crunch of his boots on the snow. He knew the gunman faced a choice: either to leap out of the smashed window after him and take his chances with the tree and the snowdrift below, or else to run back down the spiral staircase, through the house, out the door and down the steps after him. Ben didn't think the guy would be crazy enough to choose the former. Which gave him a time advantage, albeit a slight one.

A hundred and fifty or so yards from the house, the hillside was sloping more and more steeply downwards. Ben took a diagonal line down the incline, nimbly avoiding jutting tree roots that could hook and break a running man's ankle. He had no idea where he was going. He could only hope that the slope wouldn't lead him to the edge of a sheer drop, cutting off his escape. He leaped over the black, rotted trunk of a fallen pine, misjudged the depth of the snow beyond it, stumbled and fell, his arms disappearing up to the elbow. He cursed, staggered upright and kept moving.

Then he stopped, listening hard, suddenly aware of the buzz of a chainsaw in the distance. There was somebody else in the forest.

Or was it a chainsaw? As the wavering two-stroke engine note grew rapidly louder, he realised that it was coming from the direction of the house. It was the sound of a snowmobile, and it was getting closer very quickly. The shooter was coming after him.

Chapter Thirty-One

Ben ran faster down the wooded hillside, sliding and stumbling through the snow, knowing that one trip would send him tumbling down the slope in a fall that would probably break his neck. He could hear the snowmobile catching up. He glanced over his shoulder and saw it clear the top of the slope, sending up a white spray from its skids, the rider steering wildly with one hand and pointing his machine carbine over the top of the windscreen with the other. Ben caught a glimpse of the shooter's face. His teeth were bared in rage. The eyes behind the plastic goggles were burning with hatred.

Flame crackled from the muzzle of the weapon. Snow flurried up at Ben's feet a fraction of a second before he heard the shot. The shooter let off another round; something went *crack* just a few inches away, bark flew from the trunk of the nearest tree and Ben felt a glancing blow strike his arm. The ricochet had left a deep sear in the sleeve of his jacket. He might not be so lucky next time.

The snowmobile kept coming. It was forty yards behind now, careering crazily down the slope, totally out of control, slamming off trees and exploding through bushes, its engine note screeching. Ben could see the rider clinging on like a berserker.

Ben moved faster. Ducking to avoid another blast of

gunfire, he tripped over a root, lost his footing and felt himself go. He reached out to check his fall by grabbing a nearby branch. It snapped off in his hand.

There was nothing he could do to save himself from tumbling down on his face. He felt himself sliding and rolling helplessly, over and over. A blinding avalanche of snow slid down the hillside with him as he went. Certain that he was about to smash into a tree or a rock at any instant, he braced himself for the bone-crunching impact and tried to plan a way to scramble away to safety, like a wounded animal escaping a predator.

But the impact didn't come. He felt himself slide to a halt. He brushed the snow and dirt out of his eyes and blinked them open to see that he'd reached the bottom of the slope. The ground under him felt strangely hard; as hard and cold as sheet steel.

When he scrambled to his feet, he understood why. At the bottom of the hillside was a frozen lake, and he was standing right on it. The opposite shore was a good hundred yards away, flanked by thick bushes and pines. Just visible through the trees were some buildings – a little chalet or cottage with a barn, offering cover and maybe, just maybe, some kind of improvised weapon that could help even Ben's odds at closer range against his pursuer. Even a rusty pitch-fork or a loose brick were better than nothing. And nothing was exactly what Ben had right now.

All he had to do was make it across a hundred yards of open lake before the shooter caught up with him.

Ben set out across the ice. The surface was smooth and glassy under just a thin layer of powder snow, too slick for the heavily-ribbed soles of his boots to get any purchase. He couldn't run without falling on his face, so he skated, sliding one foot forward and then the other, arms outstretched to keep his balance. It was tough going, but he'd been able to cover about sixty yards by the time he heard the buzzing roar of the snowmobile catching up with him again.

He snatched a glance over his shoulder, lost his balance and fell hard on the ice. He used his elbows rather than his hands to break his fall, because he knew from experience that bare flesh could stick to ice on contact. He didn't feel like leaving half the skin from his palms behind.

Crack. Where his right elbow had struck painfully against the surface, a thin blue fissure had appeared. All that separated him from the freezing depths of the lake were a few inches of fragile ice. He didn't dare move in case the crack spread any further.

He looked up. The snowmobile had somehow managed to reach the bottom of the slope without overturning. Without hesitation, the shooter steered the vehicle straight out onto the lake. Ben saw the man's grin as the engine note soared and the craft accelerated towards him, veering madly from side to side on the slippery surface.

Suddenly much less concerned about the crack in the ice, Ben clambered to his feet and skated onwards with all the strength he could muster. Thirty-five yards to the opposite shore. Thirty. He could see the buildings clearly now. They looked derelict, but he didn't care. All his energy was focused on reaching them.

But it was no good. The snowmobile was gaining too quickly. As it got to within a few paces, the engine note fell and it glided to a halt on the ice. Ben stopped skating. He turned slowly round to face his pursuer, and raised his hands. 'Who are you?' he said.

The shooter made no reply. Keeping the machine carbine pointed steadily at Ben, he tore off his goggles and tossed them into the back of the snowmobile, then climbed off the craft and took a step forwards. His face was hard, his jaw clenched, his eyes stony.

'Where's Cabeza?' Ben demanded, although at this moment he wasn't sure how much it would serve him to know the answer.

Very slowly and deliberately, the man ejected the spent magazine from the gun's receiver and slotted in another from the pouch on his belt, then let the bolt forward with a *clack* and raised the butt to his shoulder.

Ben sighed. He'd come so far, only to get shot. There wasn't much he could do about it. He thought of Brooke, and hung his head.

The shooter took aim. He seemed to be relishing the moment.

Until the first crackling sound came from the ice, and the surface gave a lurch under his feet. Ben felt it, too, and saw the web of blue-grey cracks suddenly appear and spread quickly out from underneath the snowmobile.

The vehicle's weight was too much for the frozen lake to support.

The shooter's aim wavered as he stared down in horror at the widening circle of unstable ice under him.

Too late. There was a slow, ripping groan, then an explosion like the crack of a rifle as the ice gave way.

The snowmobile's front end rose sharply up in the air, then tipped over backwards into the water and was gone. The shooter staggered and let go of his weapon, windmilling his arms for balance and trying to jump towards more solid footing, but he was too slow. He fell with a splash and a cry that became a gurgle as the icy water closed over his head.

It wasn't because Ben had once lost a close friend to an icy lake, and that he knew what a horrible death Oliver had suffered, that he felt impelled to save the man. He had to know what was going on.

The ice was breaking up alarmingly underfoot as he moved towards the edge of the ragged hole. For a moment he thought that the man had already sunk, overwhelmed by the deadly low temperature of the water – but then he saw his fingers gripping the edge of the hole, desperately trying to prevent himself from being drawn away under the ice sheet by the currents.

Ben fell into a crouch and plunged his arms into the freezing water, grasping the man by both wrists and pulling with all his might to haul him out. More cracks rippled outwards from the hole, threatening to break away the thin, unstable ledge Ben was crouching on.

The man's head broke clear of the water, coughing and spluttering. Ben hoisted his shoulders and torso out of the lake, then laid him flat on the ice and dragged him away from the hole by the arms. The cracks were spreading everywhere. The ledge Ben had been crouching on seconds earlier suddenly gave way with a grinding creak.

Whoever this guy was, he was as tenacious as he was reckless. Even as Ben was hauling him away from danger, he was struggling like a trapped animal – but he was too winded and stunned by the shock of the icy water to put up much of a fight, or to realise that the SIG machine carbine was still hanging from his neck by its sling. Ben dragged him the last few yards to the lakeside, grappled him down firmly into the muddy snow, ripped away the weapon and tossed it aside.

'Stop,' he said. 'Give it up.'

The guy wasn't ready to stop. He lashed out wildly with his fists. Ben blocked one blow, but the next caught him across the cheek and made him see stars. He smashed the man hard in the face. Blood spurted from the man's nose and poured down his lips and chin.

'Where is she?' Ben yelled. He drew his bloody fist back for another strike, but he hadn't saved him from the lake to beat him insensible. He held back the blow. 'Where is she?' he repeated.

The man blinked; coughed up a gout of blood; blinked again. The expression on his face was a mixture of animal hatred and blank incomprehension.

Ben snatched up the fallen machine carbine. It was in battery and the safety was off. He thrust the muzzle hard under the man's chin, forcing his head up. The SIG 553's trigger would break at just under eight pounds of pressure. Ben had about six pounds on it right now and could almost feel the first bit of give before it would let go and blast the man's brains all over the snow. It would have been so easy.

'You tell me what you've done with her,' he rasped, 'or you die.'

The man spat red. His eyes blazed with defiance. His face was so numb with cold and his body was shuddering so badly after being soaked in the freezing lake that his voice was nearly incoherent – but not so much so that Ben couldn't make out his words.

'Kill me, then, motherfucker! Then go tell your fucking boss it was me who shot the bitch. Me. Nico Ramirez. You tell him!'

Chapter Thirty-Two

Ben recoiled. For a moment he was dumbstruck. 'What did you say?' he asked. 'Shot who?'

Before Ramirez could answer, Ben had clubbed him over the head with the gun. Ramirez tried to cover his face with his hands. 'What woman did you shoot?' Ben roared, so hard he felt blood rise up in his throat. Terror was gripping his whole body. He felt as if he was on fire.

'I shot Serrato's bitch of a wife!' Ramirez screamed back. 'You tell him it was me who killed Alicia!'

Ben stopped hitting him. Breathing hard and shaking with adrenaline, he kept the gun warily trained on the man and tried to make sense of what he was hearing. He was beginning to realise that he and his attacker, this determined maniac who'd very nearly succeeded in taking him down, and whom he'd been just about to beat to a bloody pulp, were totally at cross purposes. Who the hell was Serrato?

Ben tried to focus his thoughts. The mannequin in Cabeza's study. The music playing in the tower, loud enough to be heard by anyone approaching the house. It had been a lure. This Nico Ramirez – if that was his real name – had set a trap for someone he'd known in advance was coming to see Cabeza. Whoever that someone was, he wasn't coming to consult the historian on a matter of scholarship. And Ramirez obviously believed that he'd caught the would-be assassin.

'Where's Cabeza?' Ben demanded, just a little more gently. 'Is he alive?' But he could see that his prisoner was barely in a state to answer the hundred questions he wanted to ask. Blood was pouring from his nose and forehead, and he was convulsing with cold as the first stages of acute hypothermia began to take hold. Ben's own clothes were wet through from the freezing lake and he could feel his extremities beginning to lose sensation. He slung the machine carbine over his shoulder, reached into his jacket pocket for his whisky flask and fumbled with his numb fingers to unscrew the cap. He took a gulp of the stinging whisky and then thrust the flask at Ramirez. 'Drink some,' he commanded.

Ramirez took a shuddering sip, coughed, drank some more. Ben snatched the flask away and hauled him to his feet. 'Now, hands above your head and move,' he said. 'That way,' and pointed through the trees to the buildings near the lakeside.

Ben marched his shivering captive up the snowy bank towards the largest of the old buildings. As they trudged wearily through the trees he could see the old cottage had been derelict for a long time. 'Inside,' he snapped, shoving Ramirez through the half-collapsed doorway.

The place was littered with junk and debris. Judging from the rusted shotgun casings lying about, it had most recently been used as a hunter's refuge by someone who'd been up here wildfowling on the lake in the summer or autumn, but it looked as though someone had lived here once. There was a crude stone chimney at one end, and the remains of a fire in the soot-blackened hearth. A broken-up rocking chair and a few mossy logs were all that was left of the firewood supply.

Ben made Ramirez sit on an upturned bucket in the corner

with his hands still on his head, found some old newspapers in a box and got to work getting a blaze going. When it was crackling nicely, he let the shivering man move closer to the fire and ordered him to strip off his wet things.

Ramirez willingly obeyed. The shirt he was wearing was military issue, for extreme cold conditions. He'd obviously been prepared to wait up here a long time on the snowy mountain for whomever he intended to trap.

When Ramirez was down to his underwear, Ben tossed him an old blanket he'd found, dirty and mouldy but dry. Ramirez towelled himself vigorously until his skin was pink, then wrung out his wet things and hung them up close to the leaping, crackling flames. As his clothes steamed, he sat down with the blanket wrapped tightly around him and gingerly prodded his bloodied nose and mouth with a wince of pain.

'You'll live,' Ben said. He was keeping the SIG machine carbine pointed at Ramirez with a round in the chamber and the safety off. Given a chance, he'd have liked to dry his own wet clothes by the fire and get warm. But this man was dangerous and there were too many potential weapons lying around to be off his guard with him even for a second.

He moved across to the fireplace, threw more broken pieces of wood and a log into the flames and then began frisking through Ramirez's jacket for some identification. There was a wallet and a dripping wet passport. Ben examined them and saw that Ramirez hadn't been lying about his name. His passport and personal identity card were marked 'REPUBLICA DE COLOMBIA'; their owner Nicolás Ramirez had been born in 1974 in Bogotá. He was carrying a sheaf of fifty-thousand peso banknotes in among his thin supply of euros, as well as a much-creased and well-thumbed photo of a pretty woman with black hair and a white smile.

But the most interesting thing Ben found in the sodden wallet was the faded, tattered ID bearing the green badge of the Policía Nacional de Colombia, showing the rank of sergeant. The ID had expired seven years ago.

'So what do I call you?' Ben said. 'Sergeant Ramirez?'

'People call me Nico,' the Colombian muttered.

'Even people you try to kill?' Ben said.

'Whatever, asshole.'

'All right, Nico,' Ben said. 'Let's start over. My name's Ben Hope. We'll get to what a former Colombian police officer is doing running around the Spanish Sierra Nevada taking pot-shots at people with a machine carbine later. First you're going to tell me where Cabeza is.'

Nico shot him a murderous look. 'You can kill me. But you'll never get him.'

'I don't want to kill you,' Ben said. 'Not unless I have to. But I might have to, if you don't tell me what I want to know. So let's have some answers. I came here to see Juan Fernando Cabeza. Instead I find you. Why?'

Nico spat on the ground between his feet. 'Two words is all I have to say. *Fuck. You.*'

Without another word, Ben pointed the gun and pulled the trigger. The sound of the shot was harsh and painful in the enclosed space. The bullet cracked off the fireplace three inches to the left of Nico's head.

Nico's reaction to the shot was interesting. Ben had seen, and dealt with, a lot of wild and crazy guys in his life – the kind of guys who would snap out a defiant 'fuck you' looking death in the face in the form of a loaded and cocked military rifle. Some of those men genuinely hadn't cared whether they lived or died, but Nico wasn't one of them. Ben had seen something in his eyes as the gun went off. More than just the fear of dying: an infinite sadness that death should have caught up with him now, at this moment, in this place, in this way. Nico Ramirez desperately wanted to stay alive, for a reason that he alone knew very clearly.

'Like I told you, Nico,' Ben said, 'not unless I have to. How this works out is all down to you. Let me ask you again. Where's Cabeza?'

The defiant look was still there, but it was a little more tempered now. 'Somewhere your boss Serrato ain't ever gonna find him. Not if he sends a hundred men or a thousand.'

'You're getting it wrong,' Ben said. 'I don't work for anyone called Serrato. I've never even heard of him. And I didn't come here to hurt Cabeza.'

Nico gave a cynical grunt. 'Sure. You'd tell me that.'

'You could be lying too,' Ben said. 'How do I know Cabeza's alive? Maybe you killed him.'

'He's alive, motherfucker.'

'He'd better be.'

'Alive and safe.'

'So you're protecting him? Why would you do that? Protecting him from whom?'

Nico said nothing.

'Or maybe it's not that you're protecting Cabeza,' Ben said, reading his face. 'Maybe you're just using him as bait. You knew someone was after him.'

Nico remained staunchly silent, but a flicker behind his frozen expression told Ben he was right. Seconds ticked slowly by and still Nico wouldn't talk. Ben felt a molten ball of intermingled emotions rise up inside him, making him want to scream. 'I need you to help me understand what's going on here, Nico,' he said, trying to keep his voice calm but hearing an edge of desperation in it. 'I'm not working for anyone. I'm looking for a friend. More than a friend.

210

They kidnapped her in Ireland, the day Roger Forsyte and his assistant were murdered. Do you know about them?'

'I watch the news,' Nico said. He was watching Ben intently, as if he knew more but was holding it carefully back.

'I think Juan Cabeza might be able to help me find her,' Ben explained. 'I just want to talk to him. I don't want to harm him. Far from it.'

Nico looked at him long and penetratingly.

'Please,' Ben said. 'I have to get her back. She's been missing for over two days. Her name is Brooke. Brooke Marcel. Somehow all this is connected, but I don't know how and I don't know where else to go.'

There was another long silence, during which Nico went on staring curiously at him, still apparently undecided as to whether he could believe him. Eventually he motioned at the weapon in Ben's hands. 'You tell me you need my help. But you're the one holding the gun, amigo.'

Ben looked down at the SIG. Looked back up at Nico and saw the earnestness and the depth of pain in his eyes, and it suddenly struck him that it was like looking into a mirror. Without another thought he flipped the gun round and passed it to Nico, butt first, with the muzzle pointing back at his own chest. 'There. Take it.'

Nico hefted the machine carbine in his hands and looked even more curiously at Ben.

'Now you're the one holding the gun,' Ben said.

Chapter Thirty-Three

Nico Ramirez smiled and shook his head. 'You're a crazy motherfucker.'

'Maybe so,' Ben said.

Nico raised the butt of the weapon to his shoulder and peered through the sights at Ben. He held it there for a long moment. Then he pursed his lips and lowered the gun, letting it rest across his knees. 'But now I guess maybe you're on the level.'

'Right. And so you can tell me what's going on here.'

'You want to know what I was doing in Cabeza's house, man? Simple. I was aiming to kill anyone they sent to kill him. I already got the first guy. I was waiting for the next to come. I thought you were him. Then if they'd sent more, I'd have killed them all, I swear.'

'Who wants to kill Cabeza?'

'The same people that have your woman,' Nico said. 'You want to get her back, huh? Maybe I can help you. Tell me – what's she look like?'

'What the hell is that to you?' Ben said angrily.

'You'll understand, man. Describe her to me. Her hair. What colour?'

'It's not red,' Ben said. 'It's not brown. Somewhere in between.'

'Long? Short? Speak to me.'

'Long.'

'How old? Fat or thin?'

'She's thirty-six. Slim. What the fuck is this about?'

'And real good looking, huh?' Nico said, then saw that Ben was about to launch himself up and punch him again, gun or no gun. 'Hey, hey, cool it, my friend. I'm asking you this shit for a reason, okay?'

Ben stared at him for a moment, then relented. He took out his wallet, pulled out the little photo of Brooke and held it out.

'It's like I thought,' Nico said, studying the picture and shaking his head.

Ben snatched the photo back from him. 'You'd better explain yourself, and fast.'

'Sure I'll explain. First, tell me – you're willing to risk your life for this woman, right?'

'I don't know if she's alive or dead,' Ben said. 'Either way I'll do whatever it takes.'

Nico nodded thoughtfully. 'You'd kill for her too, huh? Prepared to do that?'

'It's not something I choose to do.'

'But you know how and you ain't scared.' Nico touched his injured face and gave a dark smile. 'Who are you, man?'

'I was in the British Army,' Ben said. 'I'm retired now.'

'I knew there was something. You're hard to kill. Some things a man doesn't forget, right? Skills, training, all that stuff. And believe me when I say you're gonna need them all if you want to go up against Ramon Serrato.' A glimmer of hate passed behind Nico's eyes as he spoke the name.

'And why would I want to do that?'

'Oh, you will, man. You will.'

'Sounds like you need to tell me more about this Serrato.'

'You're talking to the right guy. I study Serrato like Einstein studied physics. Born into the slums of Mexico City in 1969. Grew up fighting for scraps as the youngest of four deadbeat punk brothers and the only one who made it past the age of twenty-five. Could have ended up like them, but he pulled himself up out of the barrio by washing pots and serving tables to put himself through law school. Moved to Bogotá, set up in business and became a millionaire by the age of twenty-six. Taught himself the social graces: well read, speaks perfect English, dresses immaculately, excellent classical pianist, appreciates art and sculpture and all that kind of shit. Nowadays he lives in Peru. His business is real estate development and exports: bananas, coffee, wine, you name it.'

Nico paused and looked as if he wanted to spit. 'At least, that's how he likes to appear. But to those of us who hunted the fucker and never caught him, and to the families of the hundreds of people he slaughtered back when he was capo of the biggest, most ruthless goddamn drugs cartel in Bogotá, he was known as the Stingray.'

Stingray, Ben thought. Connections lit up in his mind. 'Roger Forsyte was poisoned with a rare type of venom. Stingray venom, from South America.'

'Serrato's trademark. Legend was, he kept a tank full of rays at his mansion in Bogotá, used to extract the poison from them. It was how he killed his special enemies. The rest he just slaughtered like animals.' The Colombian lowered his eyes. 'Like he did to my little Daniela and Carlos.'

Ben looked at him. 'Your children?'

Nico swallowed. 'Yeah, my beautiful children. Serrato had them butchered, because of me. Because I was the first cop who ever had the balls to get close to catching him. I never did. But I will one day. I don't care if it takes me the rest of my life. I will.'

'So that's what this is, a vendetta?'

'Nobody deserves to die like Serrato deserves to die. If you'd seen the things he's done, you'd want him dead too. The things he did to women, like he hated them all so bad . . .' Nico shook his head in disgust. 'There was a coke dealer in Bogotá called Feliciano Betancourt, flashy, good-looking dude, real ladies' man, who made the mistake of breaking in on Serrato's territory one time. They took him from his house in the middle of the night, along with this pretty girlfriend of his. We found out later she was a waitress at the restaurant he'd been eating in that night. I mean, Betancourt was filth, but the girl didn't even have anything to do with anything. That didn't stop Serrato from getting his guys to work her face over with a blowtorch. After she'd been raped by about twenty of them. We found her body in the Bogotá River the next day.'

Ben looked down at his feet and felt sick. This was the man Nico was saying had Brooke.

'Others were the wives of his enemies, or their daughters. One of those poor bitches he had hung up from a warehouse ceiling and sliced into strips like a fucking kebab. Another one he chained up in a barrel and—'

'All right,' Ben said tersely. 'I get the idea.'

'But he ain't gonna do any of that to your woman,' Nico said emphatically. 'No way.'

As much of a relief as it was to Ben's frazzled nerves to hear it, something about the Colombian's certainty struck him as strange. 'What does that mean?'

'It means she's alive, man,' Nico said. 'I know she's alive.'

The words hit Ben like an electric current wired up to his whole body. He reached out and gripped the Colombian's arm. 'How do you know that? How? Why?'

'I know it, because I don't have a life of my own any

more,' Nico said. 'For three years while I was a cop and for seven years since I quit my job, Ramon Serrato has been my whole life. It's been my fucking mission to know everything about him, everything he does. I know why he had the English guy Forsyte killed, what he took from him. And I know what he wants with—'

'What he wants with Brooke? You have to tell me.'

Nico shook his head. 'It ain't something you can tell. To understand some things, it takes more than words, man.'

'Then show me.'

'Need a cellphone. Mine's full of water.'

Without hesitation, Ben took out his own and handed it over. Nico bent over it for a few moments, pressing keys as he searched online for something. It didn't take him long to find. He grunted, 'There. Look,' and passed the phone back to Ben.

Ben grasped the phone tightly in his hands and stared in complete disbelief at the image on the screen.

The photo was of a woman. She was posing by a pool, pouting seductively for the camera. A golden tropical sunset backlit her auburn curls. Her skimpy green swimsuit matched her eyes and clung wetly to the few parts of her it didn't reveal.

He blinked. It couldn't be. But it was. He was looking at a picture of Brooke.

Chapter Thirty-Four

'That's one beautiful looking woman, no?' Nico said wistfully.

Ben thumbed the phone's tiny keys to zoom closer in, but the picture quickly lost resolution and the focus dissolved into blocks of pixels like a Cubist painting. He zoomed out again and stared hard.

No, wait. It wasn't Brooke. The woman's features were slightly different; the cheekbones higher, the lips fuller, the nose a tiny fraction longer.

They could have been twins.

Ben's mouth had gone dry and his head was spinning. He looked up at Nico in confusion.

'Her name was Alicia Cabrera,' Nico explained. 'She was an actress in Colombia's most popular soap opera and before that, as you can see, she was a model. At the age of twenty-nine she gave up her acting career to become Señora Alicia Serrato.'

'She was Serrato's wife?'

'He was crazy for her. And I mean crazy. He chased after her with flowers and gifts until she said yes. He owned her like some kind of trophy until the day she took a bullet that was meant for him.'

'Fired by you,' Ben said.

'Yeah, fired by me. I tell myself that short of killing the

217

fucker it was the best way I could hurt him. It was a quick death for her, and that's more than he gave to my kids.' Nico paused. 'But an innocent woman died because of my mistake, and that's something I don't forgive myself for. I know God don't forgive me for it either. I'll pay for it all through this life and into the next.'

Ben said nothing. He could see the genuine pain in Nico's eyes.

'But you understand now, right? Why I asked you what your woman looks like?' Nico pointed at the image on the phone. 'This is how I know she's got to be still alive. Serrato could have killed her with the others, but he didn't. Why? Because he wants his Alicia back. He wants things the way they were before. You see now?'

'So Brooke is . . . in *Peru*? With Serrato?'

'Bet your life.'

'That's insane,' Ben said. But the look of absolute sincerity on Nico's face was making him feel very cold.

'Insane, sure. But I know this fucker as well as I know myself. Better. Serrato's a lunatic. A very smart, very devious lunatic. This is his fantasy. He'll never let her go. He'll use all his power to make her his woman.'

'Make her his woman,' Ben repeated.

'You know what I'm talking about,' Nico said, looking Ben in the eye. 'If she lets him have her, he'll just keep her there like a pet. But if she refuses him, and goes on refusing him, then sooner or later he's going to lose patience. And when Ramon Serrato loses patience with you, you're worse than dead, man.'

Ben was silent for a long time. His blood felt like ice water in his veins.

'Trust me. I know this guy. You have to believe what I'm telling you.'

218

As terrifyingly crazy as it sounded, Ben did believe it. The only question now was what to do.

'Give me back the phone,' Nico said. 'I got to check on Cabeza.' The tiny image of Alicia Serrato vanished from the screen as Nico punched out a number. He pressed the phone to his ear, listened and frowned. 'Not answering. Damn it, I told him to stay close to the phone.' After waiting a few more moments he left a message. 'Professor Cabeza, this is Nico. I thought we agreed you'd stay put? Call me back as soon as you get this, okay?'

'Where is he?' Ben asked when Nico gave him back the phone.

'In this cheap holiday place I rented near Granada, in a village called Montefrio. It was somewhere safe for him to lie low while I came back here to wait for the next bastard Serrato sent to kill him. I took care of the guy, made sure he was okay, and now he goes wandering off somewhere like a goddamn fool.' Nico stood up impatiently and went over to the fireplace to check his hanging clothes. Satisfied they were dry, he tossed away his towel and hauled on his black combat trousers, then the military cold-weather shirt.

'I'm trying to put all this together,' Ben said. 'What makes Cabeza a target? What's he done?'

'I'll tell you everything. But not here. I'm worried that he's not returning my call. I gotta go back to Montefrio.'

They didn't speak much as they trekked back across the lake, keeping to the thicker ice and skirting round the hole that the snowmobile had vanished into. Then it was the long, difficult hike back up the steep wooded slope and through the forest back to Cabeza's house. Ben went first, picking the best path and letting Nico follow up behind with the gun.

The snow around the base of Cabeza's walls was puckered with little oblong holes where hot cartridge cases had melted through. The garage doors were wide open and swaying in the wind. 'The snowmobile was his,' Nico explained, walking inside the shadowy space underneath the house. Two cars were parked there, one a shiny Nissan soft-roader that looked exactly like the kind of car a mild-mannered academic would own, and next to it an ancient Subaru four-wheel-drive with all-terrain tyres, a torn canvas soft top, a roll cage and a motor winch mounted on the front. 'That piece of shit there is mine,' Nico said. 'Now let's move. We got no time to waste.'

It was clear enough to see that Nico was operating on a tight budget. As the Colombian drove the dented, rusty Subaru out into the daylight, blue smoke belching from its exhaust, Ben gazed at the bullet-riddled ruin of his rental Volkswagen and wondered how they were ever going to get back down the mountain in Nico's banger. Somewhere far in the back of his mind he was also wondering whether any rental firm in Europe would ever let him have a car again – he'd lost count of the number he'd wrecked.

But more than anything else, he was wondering where Brooke was at this moment: what she was doing; what might be happening to her. The thought of her trapped in the personal lair of some half-crazy drug lord wouldn't stop whirling around his mind. He was desperately anxious to get off this mountain.

'Sorry about your car,' Nico muttered, then drove the Subaru over the snow to where the fallen tree trunk had blocked Ben's way and made him walk the rest of the distance to the house. Only now did Ben notice that the tree had been deliberately sawn partway through. 'You put that there, didn't you?'

'Now we got to move the fucker,' Nico said from the cab, flinging open his door and pointing at the winch. 'Grab that hook, man.'

Ben looped the thick steel winch cable round the tree and the grinding, creaking motor hauled it across the snow until there was a gap wide enough to drive through. Ben retrieved his bag from the wrecked Volkswagen, climbed into the Subaru and they set off down the track.

Nico was set on making maximum progress despite the conditions. As the car ploughed through snow and slewed from side to side on sheet ice, he used Ben's phone one more time to check on Cabeza. There was still no answer. Nico frowned, shook his head and then began to fill Ben in on the rest of his story.

Chapter Thirty-Five

Back in the day, the Colombian explained, he'd been part of the special detective team assigned to catch the notorious 'Stingray' and bring him to justice. In the beginning they'd scored some minor victories against the elusive drug baron's operations, rounding up a number of his associates, shutting down several of his key supply routes and accompanying paramilitary units to outlying areas to locate and destroy his cocaine plants. At one point, Nico told Ben, they'd had no fewer than thirty-two of Serrato's goons locked up in the Policía Nacional headquarters in Bogotá.

But snaring the man himself was like trying to catch a lizard – grab his tail and it would just come away in your hand, and it would quickly grow back afterwards. For every drug dealer they brought in, Serrato would employ two more; every cocaine plant they burned down would simply be rebuilt elsewhere, only larger and more productive.

In retaliation Serrato declared war on the police, mounting a blitzkrieg campaign of bribery, intimidation and murder. Two of Nico's unit were blown up by car bombs in their own driveways; a third was abducted from a Bogotá nightspot, castrated and crucified on a tree; several more succumbed to payoffs and corrupted the investigation beyond measure by stealing or tampering with evidence, as well as by passing false intelligence to the department.

Within a year, the unit was falling to pieces and the investigation's run of hard-won little victories against the Stingray's drug empire dried up. In the meantime Serrato was forging ever closer networks with his buddies in government, men as influential as they were corrupt. He used prostitutes to entrap members of the police top brass, then blackmailed them into his power.

In the end, the investigation had been hopelessly whittled down to just two men and a woman: Nico, his partner Felipe Morales and a female detective named Laura Garcia. All had been approached with offers of bribery, then threatened when they refused. Even when mysteriously ordered by their superiors to call off the investigation they'd persisted in their off-duty time, convinced that a breakthrough in the case might be just round the corner.

The breakthrough had finally arrived in the shape of Enrico Gomez, a former Serrato employee turned snitch, who promised to provide information that would get Serrato and the whole upper circle of his empire, several notable politicians included, indicted and jailed for the rest of time. The snitch was demanding an extortionate price in return, but in their enthusiasm Nico, Felipe and Laura had figured that the Colombian authorities would be willing to negotiate.

Their enthusiasm had been their downfall. Within twenty-four hours of the revelation of their hot new lead to their superiors, Detective Garcia had been kidnapped from her apartment, gang-raped and shot in the face. The cops had had to identify the body using her fingerprints. The same day, Detective Morales narrowly escaped death and was left with terrible scars and an amputated left arm after his home was engulfed by an incendiary bomb.

Meanwhile, Nico Ramirez had had a call from his distraught wife Valentina to say the children had gone missing from their school.

The mutilated bodies of Carlos, eight, and Daniela, ten, had been dumped in the street outside Police Headquarters shortly afterwards.

The triple hammer blow had ended the operation at a stroke.

'That was the end of everything,' Nico said, gripping the steering wheel tightly as he sped down the mountain road towards Granada. Montefrio was still a long way off, and the leaden sky was threatening snow again. 'It was over. I couldn't stay in the police anymore. Couldn't stay in Colombia anymore. First chance we could, we emigrated to Texas.'

'What about your wife?' Ben asked.

Nico sighed. 'We didn't even speak to one another for a year after it happened. I was flat down on the ground, drinking myself to death. Valentina didn't do much of anything at all, except sleep most of the time. One day it was like I woke up out of a coma or something. I threw away the bottle. Started with the weights and the fitness training, knew what I had to do. But Valentina's spirit was just too broken. She kept getting worse until I couldn't look after her on my own any more. The doctors have all these fancy names for the thing that's wrong with her. She's in a sanatorium in El Paso now. The folks there are wonderful, you know, and they say that one day . . .' Nico sniffed and quickly darted his hand to his eye to wipe away a tear before it rolled down his cheek. 'That one day Valentina might recover and become herself again. They say there's a chance.'

'Is there?'

'I don't know. Maybe. Maybe not. Seven years, I keep going back to see her and I don't see any change. On a good day, she just lies there and I don't know what she's thinking or feeling. On a bad day . . . well, bad days are bad. They can't let her have anything metal because she'll try to cut herself. Sometimes she's like she wants to die.'

'I'm sorry,' Ben said.

'I'm sorry too, man. It was because of me this all happened, because of my job, because I was so driven to catch that piece of shit that I exposed my family to danger. I just have to pray she gets better. She's all I have left in the world. I guess that if she ever recovers, I'll be all she has too.' Nico glanced across at Ben. 'That's why I can't lose my life doing this, you understand? If it wasn't for Valentina I wouldn't give a damn. But I just can't leave her all alone like that.'

Ben took out his cigarettes and offered one to Nico. 'Don't you ever think,' he said as they lit up, 'that maybe you should quit this vendetta and just go home to take care of her? What if something does happen to you?'

Nico looked at him sharply. 'Is that what you'd do, man? Give it up and go home?'

Ben blew out a stream of Gauloise smoke. 'No,' he replied. 'I'd feel exactly the same way you do. I'd want Serrato dead. Him and every man who stands with him. And I'd roll over the top of anyone who tried to stop me.'

'He's gonna die, all right,' Nico said in a tight voice. 'Apart from trying to be there for Valentina, I've had nothing else to do for the last seven years except prepare myself for snuffing out that *hijo de puta*.' He lapsed into a stream of Spanish profanities.

'Seven years is a long time to spend hunting one man,' Ben said.

'Yeah, well, Ramon Serrato ain't someone you can just walk up to and catch like a butterfly. I went back to Colombia a few times, tried to re-establish a few old

225

contacts, asked around. I was wasting my time. It was like he'd just disappeared. Word was that he'd gone legit, like the fucker could just decide he didn't want to be a drug lord any more and take up a new career. But nobody even knew where he was, or if they knew then they wouldn't talk. So I went back to El Paso. Felipe and I kept in touch. The police didn't have any use for a one-armed detective and nobody else would employ him on account of his face being all scarred from the firebomb. He was living on his disability pension in a shitty apartment, spending all his time online searching for anything he could find on Serrato.

'Then three years ago, Felipe calls me and says he's heard that Serrato's left Colombia and moved a thousand miles south, to Peru. Way out in the asshole of nowhere, in the northern Amazonas region bordering Ecuador. We're talking major rainforest, about as far from Serrato's big-city turf as you can get. All Felipe knew was what he'd had to bribe some pissed-off ex-associate of Serrato's to cough up, and even then the information was sketchy. Me, I didn't care why, just wanted to find the fucker. I got on the next plane to Lima, then from there to this backwater called Chachapoyas, bought the cheapest car I could find and drove out to look for him.

'The first nine days I spent driving from town to town, village to village. Some of these places don't even have roads. Finally I get talking to a guy, Miguel, delivery driver for a food company, who tells me about the rich Colombian they say's built himself this big house right out in the forest, a regular palace, he said, a few miles from a village called San Tomás. Tells me the best way to get out there is by river.

'So I found a local floatplane pilot who could take me there. We touched down at San Tomás and then started looking for Serrato's place. Just when I was beginning to think Miguel was full of shit, suddenly there it was in the middle of the jungle, not a house but a compound, like a fucking military base with guards everywhere and high walls all around it. We were able to make a couple of passes overhead before we got too noticed. I could see how well this "law abiding citizen" was protected, and how damn well impossible it'd be to get to him. You'd only have to get within range of the gates and you'd be shot down like a dog.'

Nico shrugged his shoulders. 'That's when I figured that instead of trying to get inside, I'd wait for him on the outside. Back in San Tomás, I hung around for a few days, got talking to a few folks and soon found out that nobody wanted to know about Serrato's place, like it didn't exist. Except Roberto, this local mechanic I met in a bar. He must've sussed out what my business was there. Warned me that if I kept going around asking questions the local cops would bury me. Serrato owns half of them. Then he told me about this crazy old hunter dude who lived in a hut in the woods half a mile outside the village. Said he always had a load of guns to sell, but to be careful of him 'cause he was dangerous. So I go out there and I find the place. Next thing I'm staring down the barrel of a shotgun with this wild-looking old Indian guy on the other end of it, spaced out on Christ knows what. When I showed him American dollars he calmed down some, then after a whole lot of haggling he finally agreed to sell me one of his rifles.

'Then I was ready to start hunting Serrato. I traded in my car for a beat-up Winnebago. Drove out as near to the compound as the road could take me, camped up by day and cut through the forest on foot by night. You can hardly move without stepping on a fucking snake or getting eaten alive by bugs. Couple of times I was nearly caught by the armed patrols Serrato has combing the perimeter around the clock.'

'But you never managed to get inside,' Ben said.

Nico shook his head. 'It can't be done, man. Not by one guy on his own. I couldn't even get to the wall. Hey, let me have the phone again. I want to try Cabeza.'

Ben handed the phone over. A couple of moments later Nico shook his head with a sigh. 'Still no reply. Where'd that asshole wander off to?'

'Keep going,' Ben said.

'This goes on for about a week, then I ran out of supplies and had to drive back to San Tomás for more. I was depressed as hell, thinking, two more days, then I give this up, it's useless. But as I'm driving the RV back to my stakeout, suddenly I see this convoy of vehicles coming the other way – Jeeps and trucks, all tailing a black Mercedes with a man and woman in the back. As the Merc comes past the guy turns towards the window and I get a real good look at his face. It was him. Serrato. By then I knew the roads pretty well and I knew that by doubling back on myself I could pick up this track leading onto high ground where I could get a clear shot at the convoy.

'So I rush up there and lay down in the rocks with the .30-06 bolt-action I got from the old hunter, and there's the convoy coming round my flank about four hundred yards away. I thought I could make the shot. But my heart was beating so fast and my hands were shaking, I could hardly hold the rifle still. Plus the convoy's throwing up a ton of dust and the sun's glaring off the windows. When I thought I had him in the sights I pulled the trigger. Saw the car swerve over the road, slow right down and then take off again. I grabbed that aught-six and jumped back in the RV and got the fuck away from there, hollering and yelling like a crazy man cause I was so sure I'd got him. It was only later on that I found out I hadn't. Alicia caught the bullet in the throat. She must've died right there in the back seat of the car. Shit.'

Nico flicked his cigarette stub out of the window and was quiet for a while, looking pensive. By now they'd descended to the level of the lower foothills, heading fast in the direction of the village of Montefrio. Ben was silent too, waiting for Nico to resume his story while trying to contain the impatience that was gnawing at his guts.

'After Alicia's death, Serrato just withdrew deeper into his compound. He stopped travelling by road and trebled his security. Couple of times I saw his chopper flying over the jungle, and I had this idea to get hold of an RPG to shoot him down with. But it never happened and the crooks I had to deal with tried to turn me in to the local cops, who seized my RV with all my stuff, rifle, everything. I was on the run again. Next time I tried to cross the forest to get close to Serrato's compound I found he'd tripled the guard on the gates and the patrols too. Anyone found hanging around there would get themselves killed, or maybe taken back to Serrato and tortured to death. It was a fucking suicide mission, man.

'What could I do? I went home and started figuring out a new plan. Instead of trying to attack him on his home ground, I'd devote my life to figuring out ways that I could pick his people off one by one. I didn't care if it took me thirty years. If I could just get enough of them, then maybe one day, some way, I'd be able to draw Serrato out of his hole and kill him, too.

'Back in El Paso, nothing's happening. Time goes by, then more time. I had to take a job in a store to earn some money, and I was fucked up over Valentina and losing heart, thinking maybe I'd just have to forget about Serrato and move on, try and get my life back together somehow. Then a couple of weeks ago my buddy Felipe calls to say he's hooked up with this other ex-cop who's got connections we can use to set up wire taps. We still had a list of all Serrato's old associates, the ones who were still alive or not in jail. So I head back to Bogotá and we start tapping phones, all totally illegal, but hey, this is Colombia, right? Top of our list was a guy in Bogotá called César Cristo, vicious sisterfucking crackhead of a contract killer who back in the day was the Stingray's favourite assassin for hire. So we're listening in on all these calls, hours and hours of useless bullshit, when suddenly we're hearing something unbelievable. This guy's called Cristo in the middle of the night saying he wants him to go to Spain to do a job on one Juan Fernando Cabeza. When we heard the voice on the line, we all just fucking stared at each other, we just couldn't believe what we were hearing. It was Serrato himself. The sonofabitch's got balls so big, he didn't even try to code what he was saying. It was all there: the hit, the money, the directions to the target's home, the works. Recorded the whole thing on a hard drive.'

Nico shook his head in amazement at the memory, then went on. 'Felipe wanted to turn it over to the authorities. I told him no way. One, the evidence was obtained illegally and was inadmissible. Two, we'd be dead by dawn if we breathed a word of this to anyone. Three, even if by some fucking miracle Serrato went down, after a year, tops, of drinking champagne and eating lobster with the prison officials, he'd walk free again. That's how the system works. And anyhow I had my own ideas about what to do.'

'You came to Spain to intercept the hitman,' Ben said.

Nico nodded. 'I didn't know why Serrato was gunning for Cabeza, didn't care. But for Serrato to give the order himself, I knew it had to be important. Maybe so important, that if I took out Cristo and anyone else who came after, there was a chance the Stingray himself might even show up. So I borrowed money from Felipe and flew out to Spain in a hurry. An ex-cop always knows where he can find a hot gun. I paid three hundred euros to this dope dealer in a backstreet in Granada for a forty-four and a speedloader full of hollow-points. Then I bought this junk car and drove out to Cabeza's place. I got there just in time. Cristo was about to kill Cabeza with that SIG, but I blew his ugly head off before he could pull the trigger. Found the sonofabitch's Beemer up the road a ways and pitched it over the side of the mountain along with his body. That was last Saturday.'

The same day Brooke was taken, Ben thought. 'How did Cabeza handle it?'

'Let's just say that after that, he didn't need a whole lot of persuading to hide someplace safe. I drove him to the safe house in Montefrio and then came back to hang around here, set my trap and wait for the next guy to show up. Turned out the next guy was you.' Nico shrugged.

'Nice dummy, by the way,' Ben said. 'Pumpkin was a stroke of genius.'

'Had you fooled, you gringo motherfucker.'

Ben ignored the jibe. 'And you're certain this safe house of yours is secure?'

'You're worried about walking into another trap, right?'

'I'd be surprised if Serrato wasn't onto you. Who else knows about the place?'

'Felipe, nobody else. Trust me, it's safe. I left the handgun with Cabeza, just in case; not that the fucker knows how to use it. He's kind of a strange guy. Wears this goddamn silly pork pie hat all the time, like the one Gene Hackman wore in *The French Connection*? Drives me nuts. I wish he'd answer the damn phone, too.'

'Why does Serrato want Cabeza dead?' Ben asked. 'Does Cabeza even know the reason?'

231

'Sure he knows,' Nico said. 'And he's told me what it's all about. The English guy, Forsyte, he knew too. They were going to meet to talk about a bunch of papers that came out of this sunken Spanish warship. That's what it's all about, some bits of paper that must be, like, five hundred years old.'

Ben remembered what Simon Butler had said about the foreign-sounding man calling himself 'Smith' who'd contacted him soon after the discovery of the mysterious casket and bribed him to arrange the snatch in Ireland. Had Smith been working for Ramon Serrato? It seemed the only answer. 'What else did Cabeza say?' he asked Nico.

'He said a lot of these papers were written in some kind of code.'

'Code?'

'You know, spy stuff. Forsyte needed a history guy with the right knowledge to decode that shit because he was pretty sure there was some big old secret there. He was bringing them to show him. Cabeza says the guy was holding onto it real tight.'

The attaché case, Ben thought. Now it was clear to him what Forsyte had been carrying around with him and protecting so carefully. 'So Forsyte died the night before they were due to meet. And the fact that Serrato sent a killer to take out Cabeza at the same time means he was very anxious to cover up whatever was in those papers.'

Nico nodded. 'Anxious as hell. Though killing don't exactly come hard to Ramon Serrato, believe me.'

Ben's mind churned. He knew enough about the history of espionage to know that spies, covert missions and encrypted intelligence had been around for as long as warfare, which was about as long as humans had walked the earth. But what he couldn't understand was what a former

Colombian drug-lord-turned-businessman might possibly want with a bunch of old codes dug up from a sunken ship.

Nico interrupted his thoughts. 'There's more. Cabeza said that not all the papers were written in code. One of them was a letter from the King of Spain.'

Ben looked at him. 'A letter from the King of Spain.'

'You heard me, man. You know how the whole of South America belonged to Spain once? So, back in those days the King of Spain, I guess because he owned everything, he used to parcel up bits of land and hand them out as rewards to folks, ten thousand acres here, fifty thousand there, just like that. The bigger the service to the crown, the bigger the piece of land they were awarded. Whole parts of Texas and California are still owned by those people's descendants. At least, that's what Cabeza says. What the fuck do I know?'

'Get to the point,' Ben said impatiently. None of this was bringing him any closer to Brooke, and he hadn't come to Spain for a history lesson.

'Well, Cabeza said this letter Forsyte was going to show him—'

'The letter that he'd got from the wreck of the Armada warship.'

Nico nodded. '—was more than just a letter. It was a royal warrant, bearing the King's seal. A land grant to some guy he wanted to reward back then in fifteen-something.'

'What's that got to do with coded documents?' Ben said, confused.

'Well, Cabeza says that the guy being rewarded with all this land was a Spanish spy operating in England back then. Must've been one hell of a good agent, because we're talking about five hundred thousand acres.' Nico gave a low whistle. 'I can't even imagine what half a million acres looks like, can you? Except this wasn't exactly prime pasture land. It was

233

half a million acres of jungle. *Peruvian* jungle. The Spanish took Peru from the Incas, right? They fucking owned the place. Peru? Think about it.'

'Serrato lives in Peru.'

'Right. And we know that Serrato'll wipe out anyone who gets between him and that letter, anyone who even knows about it. Which means . . .'

'Serrato's after the land,' Ben said.

'That's my guess too. He must've been planning this for a long time. Bet your ass that's why he moved there in the first place. Somehow those documents are connected to him and he's gonna use them to stake a claim.'

Nico looked at Ben. 'Now you tell me. What does an evil motherfucker like Ramon Serrato want with half a million acres of Peruvian jungle?'

Chapter Thirty-Six

The HM-1 Panteras chopper whipped up a wide circle of dust with its downdraught as it took off from the compound, then climbed rapidly upwards into the early morning sky.

It was one of two light assault aircraft that had once belonged to the Brazilian army and were now owned by Ramon Serrato. Nobody had questioned why a perfectly respectable businessman would need a pair of armoured military helicopters still equipped with their cabin-mounted 20mm cannon.

But then, a man with Serrato's connections didn't tend to come in for too much official scrutiny these days, especially not in these parts. As he knew very well, the praise that the Peruvian government had garnered from the US authorities back in the nineties for their efforts against organised crime and the drug trade was ancient history; in more recent years the country's rulers had chalked up one of the worst reputations for corruption and human rights abuses in South America. It was Serrato's kind of place, all right.

He gazed calmly through his dark glasses at the endless expanse of lush rainforest below. Next to him sat his men Vertíz and Bracca, nursing their weapons. Vertíz was silently, mechanically unloading rounds from the long, curved magazine of his Colt M4 carbine, rubbing the brass casings to a polish against the sleeve of his combat jacket and slotting them back in. Bracca was equally quiet, deeply absorbed in testing the sharpness of the huge bone-handled Bowie knife he always carried with him by shaving hairs off his muscled forearm. He kept the knife's twelve-inch fullered blade so shiny that nobody could ever have guessed the amount of blood it had spilled in its time.

Nobody spoke at all during the hour-long journey as the almost unbroken green canopy rushed past under the chopper. Now and then the trees parted to reveal a twisting stretch of murky river; making its slow way up one of them was an ancient flat-bottomed riverboat whose wizened brown pilot craned his neck up at the passing helicopter and for a brief instant met Serrato's mirrored gaze.

The next break in the jungle canopy was a few miles on: a man-made clearing some five hundred metres in diameter that had only very recently been created. Not a tree was left standing on the broad patch of razed earth. From the air it was almost perfectly circular, and dotted with vehicles and tiny figures. Logging crews in orange overalls and hard hats were still hard at work round its edges as a giant Tigercat machine on caterpillar tracks wrenched trees out by the roots and stacked them in a huge heap for the massive circular saws to cut up. There was no danger of the logging crews reporting to the author-ities what they might have witnessed down there that day – they all worked for Serrato and they all knew the cost of a wagging tongue. In any case, he controlled a good many of the authorities too. He'd soon be making a number of them extremely rich.

Parked in a ring closer to the centre of the clearing was a cluster of open-topped Jeeps and a truck, around which

236

stood a team of twenty or so heavily-armed men, all looking up intently at the chopper coming in to land.

The helicopter touched down. Serrato waited for the rotors to slow and the dust to settle, then stepped from the aircraft and straightened his suit. The immaculate beige silk struck a contrast against the jungle clothing of the men who walked across from the vehicles to greet him. Bracca sheathed his Bowie knife, grabbed his rifle from the floor of the chopper, and he and Vertíz jumped down after their boss to flank him, one either side, as they'd been doing for years.

'Where's Vargas?' Serrato asked the ground team leader, Raoul.

'They're on their way, boss. Radioed in five minutes ago.'

Serrato nodded. 'And so everything went as planned?'

'Sure, boss.' Raoul motioned behind him at the thick forest beyond the edge of the clearing. 'All taken care of, just like you ordered.'

'Was there any resistance?'

Raoul grinned. 'Nothing we couldn't handle.'

'I want to see,' Serrato said.

'Sure, boss,' Raoul repeated, but his words were drowned out by the buzzing approach of the second helicopter. They looked up, shading their eyes from the dazzling sun, as the bright red JetRanger appeared over the forest. Its pilot brought it carefully down to land thirty metres away across the clearing. The aircraft's side hatch opened and a short, stocky, olive-skinned man in a rumpled white suit clambered down with some help from his aides, clutching at the rim of his Panama hat to keep it from flying off in the hurricane from the rotors. He waved to Serrato and crossed the razed earth towards him.

The man was in his fifties, with a cheerful round face that sported a carefully trimmed moustache and belied the fact that he was almost as calculating and ruthless as Serrato himself.

Almost, but not quite. His name was Aníbal Vargas, and he was a senior member of the Peruvian government's Ministry of Housing, Construction and Sanitation, the department concerned, among other loosely defined matters, with the registration and administration of rural land deeds. He was also one of several men in the country who knew exactly with whom he was dealing in Ramon Serrato, and had no problem doing business as long as it was well away from the prying eyes of the press and the political reform activists who made his life far harder than he felt he deserved.

Vargas had amassed himself a small fortune during the last twenty years, massively augmenting his government salary by quietly and illegally offering concessions to oil, gas and logging operations willing to pay a premium kickback for the chance to sneak in and devastate great swathes of rainforest that were supposed to be protected in the interests of indigenous people. He'd always operated comfortably under the radar, shielded by the fact that Peru's regulatory framework was weak, the infrastructure rotten, and the whole system generally so beleaguered by inefficiency and incompetence that neither the bureaucrats nor most of the public even cared any more.

As for the rainforest Indians themselves, aside from the occasional uprising against outsiders coming to plunder their ancient territories, their rights were as easily squashed in modern times as they'd been throughout history, going right back to the Conquistadors.

It was the same story in Peru as in Paraguay, Colombia, the whole tropical Amazon basin. In their time the Indians had been bribed, cheated, shot at, burned out of their homes, murdered wholesale, and their numbers ravaged by diseases contracted accidentally from outsiders – or sometimes introduced on purpose. The Natural Protected Areas Law of 1997 had made little real difference to their plight, although the steady growth of welfare organisations such as MATSES, the Movement in the Amazon for Tribal Subsistence and Economic Sustainability, was a pain in the butt for men like Aníbal Vargas and his colleagues, whose unofficial purpose it was to undo any progress they achieved.

'You're late,' Serrato said.

Vargas was more at home in an air-conditioned office than in the middle of the jungle. He was already perspiring heavily as he stammered his apology, beating away the insects that swarmed around his face, drawn to the scent of fresh sweat. The heat didn't bother Serrato. He was cool and calm. He said to Vargas, 'Now let me show you what your department should have been doing.'

'Are we going in there?' Vargas asked, pointing at the jungle and thinking of venomous snakes and spiders as large as his hand that could scuttle up a trouser leg and sink their fangs into soft flesh. Serrato only nodded. Vargas lifted his hat to wipe the sweat from his balding scalp.

It was cooler under the trees. The jungle was strangely quiet, deserted by the hordes of howler monkeys and the many, many birds whose calls would normally fill the air. It was the silence of death.

The team leader went first with a couple of his men. Serrato followed, still closely flanked by Vertíz and Bracca who were eyeing every leaf and frond with suspicion, their loaded, cocked weapons at the ready. Vargas stumbled along in their wake, cracking twigs with every step and swatting at flies, and the rest of the ground team brought up the rear. Eighty yards into the dense, lush thicket, Serrato paused to peer at the shaft of an arrow embedded in the knotty bark of a tree.

'Tricky little bastards,' the team leader said with a knowing smile. 'Handy with those fucking darts, too.' He showed Serrato the hole above his breast pocket and tapped the lightweight Kevlar body armour underneath that was capable of turning a high-powered handgun bullet at point-blank range. 'Lucky for us we came equipped.'

Serrato plucked the arrow out of the tree bark. A black, glutinous substance was still trickling from its barbed head. Poisons had always fascinated him. He wondered what rainforest plant or creature – a fish? A frog? – the Indians had concocted this from, and what its effects were. Maybe he'd experiment with it. He tucked the arrow under his arm like a swagger stick.

'Remind me of the name of this tribe?' Vargas said as they trudged through the heavy undergrowth.

'Who gives a shit?' Bracca rumbled, and the politician went quiet.

It was another thirty yards farther up the narrow machete-hacked path that they came to the first of the bodies. The corpse lying twisted across the path belonged to an older Indian male, maybe in his late thirties. He was short and stockily built with a shock of glossy black hair, almost naked except for a tiny loincloth and an arrow quiver. He was still clutching the shaft of his bow and the arrow he'd been about to loose when most of his head had been blown away by a bullet. Next to him lay the curled-up body of a teenage boy. White ribs were exposed where a shot had torn away the muscle and flesh of his side. His torso was slick with blood.

'That one's not dead,' Vargas said, pointing. They all looked and saw that Vargas was right. The boy was moving weakly, trying to claw his way forwards over the bloody ground.

The team leader issued a short command. One of his men

walked up to the dying teenager, unsnapped his belt holster and drew out a 9mm Beretta.

Serrato held up his hand. 'No!'

The soldier lowered his pistol uncertainly.

Serrato took a couple of deliberate steps away. 'The silk is so hard to clean,' he explained to Vargas. Once he was out of range of any blood spray he nodded to the soldier and walked on. A moment later the flat report of the pistol cracked out. Serrato didn't so much as glance back.

'Dead now, all right,' Vertíz chuckled, exchanging grins with the others. The government minister was looking pale.

The rest of the Indians lay scattered among the devastated remnants of their village a little way farther on. The bodies and the dark patches of blood soaked into the forest floor were already crawling with huge black hairy flies whose buzzing filled the air. What was left of the primitive village dwellings and store huts would soon be flattened into nothing by the massive machines when the deforestation operation moved in.

'This surely can't be all of them,' Serrato said to the team leader, pointing at the corpses.

'Twenty-seven,' the team leader replied. 'Out of an estimated population of fifty or sixty. Looks like they knew we were coming and got the women and children out just in time. Only the male warriors stayed behind to defend the place. But we'll catch up with the rest pretty soon if we can find some tracks to follow. These fuckers move through the jungle like ghosts.'

'Find them,' Serrato said. 'Before they can make contact with other tribes and word starts to spread. I want this situation contained and resolved as soon as possible.'

Away from the men he said sternly to Vargas, 'This is more trouble than I should have to deal with.' Before the politician could launch into an apologetic reply he demanded, 'The land is mine, is it not?'

'Yes, technically, but . . .'

'Technically? I've presented all the necessary document-ation. I've demonstrated sufficient proof of entitlement. The *escrituras* were transferred to my name as of yesterday.'

The property deeds Serrato was referring to normally took up to thirty-three days to register under the Peruvian legal system. He hadn't been prepared to wait anything like that long and had spent a great deal of time on the phone whip-ping his lawyers to get the complex paperwork through the necessary channels as fast as possible. A five-hundred-year-old land title signed by Philip II of Spain might not have been a document that the clerks saw every day, but with land ownership laws in the state of confusion that they were and Vargas and his people greasing the wheels to ensure that Serrato's claim was rubber-stamped, the deal had gone through as smoothly as he could have wished. Bribes had been paid to all the right people; all the right arms twisted; all the right veiled threats made.

It had mattered very little to anyone concerned that the land in question was a protected native community reserve. God bless Peru.

'The land is mine,' Serrato repeated emphatically. 'I shouldn't even have to go to the trouble of clearing out these Indians. They're meant to be your department.'

'It's a delicate business, Señor Serrato,' Vargas protested. 'What am I supposed to do, with these interfering do-gooder bastards from MATSES and Fenamad breathing down my neck the whole time?' He glanced nervously at the soldiers, who were wandering among the ruins of the Indian village out of earshot. 'It is not just I who has to be careful. If certain people got wind that government officials were colluding 'with . . . with . . .' from the look in Serrato's eye Vargas knew he had to choose his words with extreme care, 'with a private individual such as yourself, to clear half a million acres of protected virgin rainforest without the proper authorisation and set up the biggest unofficial oil drilling operation Peru has ever seen . . .'

'The oil is there,' Serrato said. 'You have seen the test results.'

'The tests conducted illegally . . .'

'But conclusive nonetheless. And you also know how much you stand to gain if the wells yield even half of my consultants' estimate.'

'. . . not to mention this.' Vargas waved a finger at the grisly corpses and wrecked dwellings, and shook his head.

'We agreed on what would have to be done to vacate the land.'

'I did not agree to such a slaughter,' Vargas replied in a raspy whisper. It was the first time he'd ever seen so much blood and death, and the large breakfast he'd wolfed down before getting on the chopper was threatening to make a reappearance every time he looked at the bodies or caught a whiff of their smell. 'There are limits, Señor Serrato. Even here in Peru there are limits. Things are not the way they used to be. This new president we have now may be an idiot, but he is an idealistic idiot who believes in progress and reform. You have no idea how things are at my end.'

Serrato gave a smile. 'My dear Aníbal, you are beginning to sound somewhat less enthusiastic about our project than you were at the outset. Which I must say disappoints me, after so much planning, so many meetings and discussions. I believe I made it very clear to you from the start exactly how I intended to proceed once I had secured the necessary document.' He took the poisoned arrow out from under his arm and waved its tip casually through the air as he spoke. 'However, if you no longer wish to remain involved in the project, please say the word. It will be taken care of immediately.'

Vargas looked at the poisoned arrow and swallowed. If he said the word, he was a dead man. He'd be buried here in the rainforest with these poor bastard Indians. Then he thought about his share of the cash once the oil started pumping. Who cared if it wasn't legal – what was? His days of skimming off the top, chasing after kickbacks, worrying about getting caught, would be over forever. He'd be able to afford more Italian suits, younger hotter mistresses, the black Porsche he coveted to go with his gold one, and that luxury beach house he'd had his eye on for a while. The shopping list stretched tantalisingly out in his imagination.

'Please forgive me, Señor Serrato. You can rely on my complete support. There will be no problems from me, I guarantee it.'

Serrato was about to deliver a cuttingly sarcastic reply when his mobile phone started ringing. He plucked it from his suit pocket and saw that the call was from one of his subordinates in Bogotá. It was one he'd been expecting.

'We got Morales,' the voice on the other end told him.

Serrato had done this kind of thing too often to feel any pleasure or excitement from it. Ordering the kidnap and torture of a fellow Colombian, in this case an ex-cop in league with others standing in the way of his plans, was as routine to him as ordering a gallon of milk.

'Did he talk?' Serrato asked. If the answer to the question was no, it would mean that the men had managed to let Felipe Morales die before they'd got the information out of him. That, in turn, would mean further deaths as punishment for the error.

'Oh, he talked all right, boss. He was a tough one, though.

Had to show him the chainsaw before he cracked, and that was after we'd already taken off his fingers . . .'

Serrato wasn't concerned with the trivial details. 'Where's Ramirez, where's Cabeza?'

'Spain. Place called Montefrio. We have people on the way there.'

'Good. I want all trace of them erased.' Serrato put away his phone. He glanced archly at the piles of dead Indians by the ruined huts. 'This place stinks,' he said. 'Let's go.'

Chapter Thirty-Seven

It was coming on for five in the afternoon and the winter evening was drawing near by the time the battered Subaru rolled up outside the holiday rental cottage in the sleepy village of Montefrio near the Cordoba border, a sprawl of white houses and terracotta roofs surrounded by the hills and olive groves of Granada and dominated by an ancient fortress-like church perched high on a rock.

Ben could understand why Nico had chosen such an out-of-the-way spot to hide Cabeza, though it wasn't a choice he personally agreed with. He'd always preferred safe houses in crowded cities, where a targeted individual could disappear far more easily. In cities, nobody gave a shit about anybody – whereas small communities were always conscious of strangers in their midst, and the presence of strangers tended to generate loose talk.

But then, Nico was a cop, and cops couldn't always know these things.

La Catalina was a modestly-sized former granary on the edge of the village, with thick stone walls painted white like all the other homes in Montefrio. Nico parked the car round the back and led Ben inside, carrying the machine carbine wrapped in his jacket.

It was warm inside the house. The Colombian hung the

SIG from its sling over the banister post in the hallway. 'Professor Cabeza!' he called out; then again, more loudly, 'Hey, Cabeza, where the hell did you go, man?' No response.

Left alone for a few moments while Nico went off to search the house, Ben wandered into the main room and glanced around. The furnishings were simple and rustic: a pitted slab table; an old pine dresser; some canvas chairs. A single large window looked out onto a terrace with a view of the high rocky mound, the church seeming to hang off the side of the lopsided precipice, just waiting to come sliding down to crush the whole village below. The table was littered with history books, papers and a laptop – the kind of things he could imagine a man like Cabeza insisting on bringing with him from home. Next to them was a glass of white wine, half finished and lukewarm to the touch. He walked over to the dresser and pulled open the middle drawer.

He could hear Nico calling Cabeza's name in the background, sounding increasingly irritated.

Stepping back to the table, Ben touched the finger pad of the laptop and the sleeping machine sprang back into life. Whoever had been using it last, presumably Cabeza, had been looking at a website about the history and architecture of Montefrio. The photos on the site looked similar to the view from the window, except that they'd been taken in summer when the high rock was lush with greenery.

Between the images was a piece of text describing the origin of the church. As quickly as Ben learned that it was called the Iglesia de la Villa and had been built in 1486 on the site of a much older Moorish castle following the defeat of the Muslim kingdom of Granada by Christian armies, he shoved that knowledge to the remotest corner of his mind and minimized the webpage to click into the laptop's email program.

'Cabeza! Come on, man! It's okay, it's me!' came Nico's muffled voice from another room. Ben could have called out to him not to bother – Cabeza clearly wasn't there – but he was too busy reading the email exchange he'd just found between the historian and Roger Forsyte. The messages dated back from the discussions arranging their meeting in Spain, all the way back to early December: the time when, according to what Simon Butler had told Ben in Southampton, Forsyte had salvaged the mysterious casket from the wreck of the Armada warship.

There was too much to take in all at once, and both men had been cautious not to give away secret information by email – in places the messages were as heavily coded as the encrypted papers that Forsyte had wanted Cabeza to decipher – but Ben caught veiled references to the land grant from Philip of Spain that Nico had mentioned, as well as to the Spanish secret agent it had been intended for.

'*I certainly would concur with you that revelations of this kind, even after five hundred years, could cause significant ripples,*' Cabeza had written sometime in January. '*If even half the names on this list were truly involved in espionage, it is an incredible discovery.*'

'*Ripples are precisely what I have in mind to cause,*' Forsyte had written back the same day. '*The more significant the better.*'

Ben was scrolling through to read more when Nico came running back into the room, red-faced with annoyance. 'I can't find the fucker anywhere,' he announced.

Ben picked the wineglass up from the table. 'You drink this stuff at room temperature?' he asked.

Nico sipped from the glass and pulled a face. 'No, the bottle's in the refrigerator. What's that got to do with—?'

'It means that your man's been gone for some time.' Ben pointed out of the window at the church in the distance.

248

'And I'd bet that's where you'll find him, taking a little sight-seeing tour.' He clicked back into the website Cabeza had been looking at, and showed Nico.

'Ah, shit. I *told* him to stay here. I *said* not to go wandering about. He knows he's in danger. But he kept talking about that damn church up there, said it was someplace he'd never visited before and wanted to see it. I told you he was kind of an oddball, didn't I?'

Ben hesitated. A voice was screaming inside him to stop wasting time in this place. Brooke was out there somewhere. He couldn't afford the slightest delay in searching for her. But he now knew he couldn't do that without Nico's help. And what if Cabeza knew something?

'Let's go and get him,' he said.

Chapter Thirty-Eight

The tallish, slightly stooped solitary figure making his way through the meandering village streets might have stood out somewhat in a crowd in his suede jacket, bright yellow trousers and rumpled pork pie hat, if there had been any crowds in Montefrio at this time of year. Not that the historian would have taken much notice of them, wrapped up as he was in his own thoughts, as he walked along with half an eye fixed on the Iglesia de la Villa whose bell tower was constantly visible over the rooftops.

Juan Fernando Cabeza was glad to be free again. He couldn't have sat around in that poky La Catalina another minute, with nothing to do except stare at the few books he'd managed to bring from home and helpless against the recurring panic attacks that had been leaving him breathless and shaking every few hours since this whole ordeal had begun.

Every time he shut his eyes he could see the terrifying figure of the hit man César Cristo standing there about to shoot him to pieces with that huge gun. Never before had he come that close to death. It made him realise how profoundly attached he was to living.

But what kind of existence was it for him now, with his world turned inside out, unable to return home because of the threat against him from some obscure enemy, and having to obey the orders of some undereducated, rough-mannered Colombian policeman who'd arrived out of the blue and taken over his life? Admittedly, Nico Ramirez had saved him, and for that he was grateful – but at the same time this situation was just unendurable. What was going to happen to him?

'I'm only a simple historian,' he'd said to himself over and over, often out loud, as he lay wide awake in his bed at night. 'What harm have I ever done to these people? Why can't they just leave me alone?'

But he knew perfectly well what they wanted. For all that he'd led a sheltered, closeted life among his dusty old books, far away from the evils of the modern world, Cabeza was savvy enough about its ways to have been certain, right from the first shocked moments after Nico Ramirez had rescued him from the jaws of death, that this all had to do with the new project of Roger Forsyte's that he'd become involved in. When he'd first heard the stunning news of Forsyte's abduction on the car radio as Nico had been driving him to safety, then learned of the Englishman's death from the TV here in Montefrio, it had only confirmed his certainty. The key to the whole thing lay in those documents, lost for so long at the bottom of the ocean in their watertight casket.

Roger Forsyte had always been secretive about his past life, but he'd dropped enough tiny hints in passing over the years they'd known each other for Cabeza to understand that, long before founding Neptune Marine Exploration, the Englishman had played some kind of role within military intelligence. Cabeza could only suppose that part of Forsyte's training must have been in code-breaking, as by the time he'd first excitedly contacted him about his discovery back in December, he'd already deciphered enough of the documents' hidden meaning to know how important they were.

'Hot stuff', he'd called it. And he hadn't been kidding.

The detached, unemotionally scholarly part of Cabeza's mind that wasn't paralysed with terror regretted that he'd never be able to see the project through. Once Forsyte had let him see the precious documents his job would have been to cast his historian's eye over them, help to break the last bits of code, translate the sixteenth-century Spanish into modern English and generally confirm Forsyte's own initial findings. Once the work was complete, which Cabeza didn't think would have taken very long, it would have been a simple matter of releasing the information to a stunned world. Hidden treasures were ten a penny; earth-shaking scandalous revelations about important historical figures were not. And there were fourteen of them here to expose.

The one document that Forsyte had been willing to show Cabeza a copy of prior to their meeting was the land grant awarded in June 1588 by King Philip of Spain. Age and damp had eaten away at its edges, but otherwise it had been as miraculously preserved as the rest of the papers and was extremely valuable in its own right. Resplendent in crimson and gold, it bore the royal signature clearly at the bottom; above, as legible as the day it had been penned, was inscribed the name of the man the King had seen fit to reward with such a handsome gift. It was a name that Cabeza and every other historian for more than five hundred years had known well: a notorious one at that.

In his day, Sir Christopher Pennick had been a highly influential nobleman whose connections within both Parliament and the Court of Queen Elizabeth I had been virtually second to none. It had been said that he had the Queen's ear on many delicate matters of state policy, and only had to whisper into it to inform some of Her Majesty's most key decisions. But Elizabeth's trusted aide had also been a man with a dark secret.

At a time when the Church of Rome was about as accepted in England as Satan and to be Catholic was a serious impediment to one's prospects, Sir Christopher had wisely revealed his own strong popish leanings to nobody except his wife Anne and a select circle of friends. But his secrecy ran deeper than even Anne knew: when her beloved husband wasn't attending to matters at Court or hunting wild boar on his lands, which stretched from Hambledon to Winchester, he was active in a clandestine movement devoted to the restoration of the Roman Church in England.

When the undeclared Anglo–Spanish War of 1585 began, Sir Christopher and his associates realised that a Spanish victory would make their dream of a Catholic England possible. So, for the next three years, Pennick had used his high-level connections to feed valuable state secrets to the Spanish intelligence network that by the late 1580s had worked its tentacles deep into the British establishment. He quickly became a glittering asset to Spain, cultivating his own stable of dedicated agents within both Court and Parliament. For almost three years his treachery went completely undetected. It was little wonder, in hindsight, that such a valuable and clever agent had been so handsomely rewarded by King Philip.

By the summer of 1588, thanks in part to the efforts of Sir Christopher and his web of spies, the mass invasion of England by Spanish forces was finally ready to launch. But had the Armada managed to reach British shores, let alone achieved its dizzy goal of landing enough Spanish troops to take over the whole country and overthrow Queen Elizabeth's rule, Pennick would still never have received his reward. Even as the massive invasion fleet was setting sail from Lisbon, an anonymous tip-off alerted Elizabeth's notorious and feared spymaster, Sir Francis Walsingham, to Sir Christopher's activities. Pennick was swiftly, secretly arrested for treason and imprisoned in the Tower of London, while Walsingham's counterintelligence disinformation machine spread the temporary rumour that he'd been taken ill with smallpox.

The more gruesome historical accounts showed that Pennick had resisted even the most hideous and barbarous forms of torture devised by Walsingham's men to make him reveal the names of his fellow intelligence agents. Burned, mutilated, his body pierced and broken on the rack, he kept his mouth shut to the end. By the time he died, his wife Anne wouldn't have been able to recognise him. Meanwhile, the Armada was being repelled and soundly defeated by a combination of the Royal Navy and bad weather. It was a near-run thing, as close as England would ever again come to being invaded. When the *Santa Teresa* went down off the northwest coast of Catholic Ireland during that last-ditch attempt to find a safe port so far from home, the land grant Sir Christopher Pennick would never know about went to the bottom with her.

After his death, the traitor was dismembered and his body parts put on public display across London as an example to others. His widow Lady Anne Pennick, according to some historical sources heavily pregnant with their first child, fled England in heartbreak and disgrace, never to be seen again. As for Pennick's network of Spanish agents in England, their names were a secret he carried with him to his grave.

Until now.

As Forsyte had known, and as Cabeza still knew, those very names were listed in code in the secret documents that had been aboard the *Santa Teresa*. It seemed ironic that in doing their bit to scupper the Armada, the Royal Navy had deprived the British Government of the most valuable piece of intelligence they could have hoped for during the war. The staggering line-up of Pennick's treacherous allies in England included seven senior politicians, three high-ranking army officers, one rear admiral and one disgruntled lesser member of the royal family. Fourteen names in all, each of them very well known indeed to modern-day historians, not one of them ever even vaguely suspected of anything less than total allegiance to their country.

Yet there it was, black on white proof of their unspeakable treason, enough to have sent them to the Tower back in 1588 and still enough to cause shockwaves even now. The historical time bomb was set to explode. Forsyte had had it all planned: the media storm, the million-pound book deal, the eight-part TV documentary called 'Hidden Traitors'.

What a splendid coup it would have been, Cabeza reflected wistfully as he ambled through the village. He'd been as impatient as Forsyte, though for slightly purer academic reasons, to witness the impact of their revelations.

But that would never happen now. Was it really possible that someone out there would commit murder to protect the secret of Sir Christopher's treachery? Cabeza couldn't understand it. All he knew was that Forsyte was dead and there were people out to get him, too. It was all a horrible mess and he was frightened and shaken and edgy, unable to sleep at night and with nothing to occupy him all day, sitting around at La Catalina with nothing to do but fret and feel sorry for himself.

So he was extremely relieved to be able to get out and pay a visit to the Iglesia de la Villa. Not his primary area of interest historically – or else he would surely have discovered it years ago, living just a few hours' drive away – but he was convinced that an afternoon spent wandering around the church and the Moorish castle ruins around it would help him forget his troubles, if only for a little while.

He strolled on through the streets of Montefrio, pausing now and then to admire the walled gardens with their palm trees, pretty even in winter, the decorative balconies and street lamps and the old architecture, but never losing sight of the looming church tower which got steadily closer as he threaded his way through the dense maze of narrow streets.

By the time he'd reached the outskirts the houses had thinned out and the terrain had become rougher: rock and scrub on either side of the road, tree-dotted hills all around. Evening was falling, the temperature was dropping. Finding the church was taking much longer than he'd anticipated, and he knew that he faced a long walk home in darkness later. But there was no point in turning back now.

On the road out of the village he met nothing except the occasional car and a brown dog that was ambling along in the opposite direction. Cabeza mistrusted dogs and gave the animal a wide berth. Peering ahead through the falling dusk he thought he could see a sloping path that turned off the road to the left and seemed to lead up through the trees towards the church mound. He'd better hurry, or there'd be no daylight left.

As he walked towards the path his thoughts were interrupted by the sound of an approaching vehicle, and he looked up to see the lights of another car heading into the village. He stepped close to the side of the road to let it by. As it came past he caught a glimpse of the four men inside, all facing their windows as though looking for something. *Must have lost their way*, he thought to himself.

The moment the car had passed him it slowed to a crawl,

its tyres crunching on the rough road. Its four occupants turned simultaneously to give him a lingering stare. Cabeza had often got hopelessly lost himself in strange places, and felt sympathy. He smiled and shrugged apologetically, as if to say 'Sorry, can't help you, I don't live here.'

Nobody smiled back. The car kept on going. Cabeza turned his back on it and resumed his walk towards the path, now just a few yards away on his left. It looked heavy going, all uphill except for a little dip after it left the road. He was glad that he kept himself reasonably fit.

Suddenly aware that he couldn't hear the car any more, he glanced back and saw that it had stopped a little way farther up the road.

Cabeza thought nothing of it.

Not until the car's engine revved hard, its wheels screeched and it came veering back in a tight U-turn, speeding towards him.

Cabeza's heart flipped. For a second too long he stood gaping at the roaring car, then came to his senses and took off at a run. He reached the rocky path and sprinted up it. Heard the rasp of tyres behind him as the car slewed off the road and followed him up the path. There was no way he could outrun it.

Help! Visions of César Cristo loomed up nightmarishly all over again in his mind. It was them again. They'd found him. They were coming to kill him. And there was no Nico Ramirez to save him this time round.

But as he raced down the short dip before the slope rose again more steeply, he saw how narrow the gap between the trees was up ahead. Too narrow for a car. He went dashing between them, his feet pounding on rock and dirt as fast as he could make them go. Casting a frightened glance over his shoulder, he saw the car skid to a halt where the path narrowed.

Yes! There was a chance. The distance between him and his pursuers was widening now.

Then the car doors swung open and the four men burst out of the vehicle. Cabeza saw the dark figures coming after him and let out a strangled moan of panic.

The path was steepening. In the failing light he could see the church bell tower looming through the trees. Just fifty yards, maybe sixty, and he'd reach it. Maybe there'd be somewhere up there to hide. Maybe there'd be people. The men couldn't harm him if there were witnesses, could they? Could they?

He heard a sharp yell from behind and turned to look. One of his pursuers had lost his footing on the loose slope, fallen and gone rolling down several yards. Cabeza saw the man stagger to his feet and clutch his ankle in pain, and he grinned to himself. But his grin quickly dropped as he saw the others moving on determinedly. He turned and stumbled on up the uneven slope, jittery with fear. A sudden gust of wind caught the underside of his hat's brim and flipped it off his head. His precious hat! But he didn't dare go back for it.

Now he was panting hard and shaking all over. Just as the panic was threatening to overwhelm him completely, the ground levelled out under his feet and he realised that he'd made it to the top. The church loomed hugely overhead, surrounded by the craggy remains of the ancient castle walls. But his hope that there might be other people there was dashed. Silence and emptiness all around. It was just him, and four men who wanted to kill him.

Cabeza dashed through the castle ruins towards the Iglesia de la Villa. The fifteenth-century building's blend of Mudéjar, Gothic and Renaissance architectural influences was totally lost on him as he made for the arched entrance, praying that the heavy iron-studded door would be open and crying out with relief when it swung inwards with a shove. He darted through the doorway and blinked in the darkness of the empty church.

Then, his heart in his mouth, Juan Fernando Cabeza searched for a place to hide.

Chapter Thirty-Nine

Nico hammered the Subaru through the darkening streets, scattering pedestrians and sounding his horn at other cars. 'Goddamned historians,' he muttered. 'They're all the same.'

Ben looked at him. 'You've known a lot of historians?'

'Sister married some museum curator. Another real fuckhead. Left her for another guy. You believe that shit?'

'Just drive the car,' Ben said.

The Subaru's suspension bottomed harshly at the base of a jarring cobbled slope, then with a screech of tyres Nico flew round a corner and they were speeding along the quiet road that circled the village. The church bell tower could be seen from anywhere in Montefrio, but as they drove on there seemed to be no road leading to it. 'I can't get close to the damn thing,' Nico said, glancing up from the road at the mound. 'Maybe we need to stop someone and ask, huh?'

'Let's just find Cabeza and get back to the house, all right?' Ben said impatiently. 'We're wasting time here.'

'This is no good. I'm gonna turn ar—'

'No, wait. Pull up there,' Ben said, pointing to the left, where the Subaru's headlamps had picked out a path running up between the trees. Nico swerved across the road and skidded the Subaru to a halt on the dirt. Ben was the first to jump out of the car. He gazed up the path and saw that he'd been right: at the top of the sloping path, some three or four hundred yards distant, the church bell tower stood outlined against the early evening sky. This was the way. But something else about the dirt path perplexed him.

'Cabeza doesn't have a car, does he?' Ben asked Nico, looking at the dark blue Audi that had been left empty, all four doors hanging open, where the trees narrowed on the path ahead.

'Not unless he's gone and borrowed one,' Nico said.

Frowning, Ben walked over to the Audi and laid his palm on the bonnet. It was still warm. He looked down and ran his eye along the scuff marks in the dirt where the wheels had locked under hard braking. He pictured Cabeza on foot. Pictured the car coming after him. Gazed up the path at the church silhouetted in the half-light. His thoughts were disturbing. 'You're sure this place is as safe as you said?' he asked Nico, who was walking over to join him.

Nico looked at the car and shook his head. 'Come on, man, it's a village. People live here.' But Ben made no reply, because he was already heading through the trees and up the slope, his trot quickening to a run.

'Shit, the bastard might be right,' Nico muttered to himself, and followed. 'Shit, shit.'

As Ben climbed the rough slope he could see where some of the stones had been recently dislodged. That hadn't been done by idle walkers. A few yards further up he found a clear shoeprint in the dirt and paused to examine it. It was still fresh and moist to the touch, and deeply indented at the toe by someone moving in a particular hurry. Then a short distance further up the path Ben came across something else. At first it looked like a patch of shadow, or a dark rock. On closer examination it wasn't. He picked it up off the

261

ground and showed it to Nico as the Colombian caught up with him.

'I never saw that movie,' he said, 'but that looks like a pork pie hat to me.'

'That's Cabeza's hat, all right,' Nico breathed. 'Then he did come up here.'

'Not alone,' Ben said, glancing down the hill at the Audi parked near the trees. 'Looks like there are four men after him. Maybe your safe house wasn't so safe after all.'

'But how—?'

'You might want to call your friend Morales in Bogotá,' Ben said. 'Check to see if he's still answering his phone. If he isn't, you'd better hope Serrato's people don't have him.'

Nico suddenly looked anxious. 'I left the SIG back at the house. Think I oughtta go back for it?'

'No time for that now,' Ben said.

They ran on. The last glow of the sun was far below the western hills and the darkness was gathering fast, making it impossible to spot anything more in the way of tracks on the firmer ground approaching the top of the slope. The dark church walls were fully in view now, surrounded by what little of the Moorish castle its Christian conquerors had left standing. Ben led the way through the craggy remains and up to the church entrance. The heavy door lay wide open.

Ben stepped inside. The air felt chill. Only the faintest of light was shining into the church through the doorway and the few small arched windows, just enough to make out the shapes of alcoves and columns and the great curving vaulted ceiling high overhead. Pools of black shadow lay everywhere and seemed to be spreading and deepening with every passing second. He wished he had the mini-Maglite with him, and cursed himself for leaving it in his bag at the house.

He advanced slowly, with Nico behind. Their footsteps rang softly off the stone floor. Ben nudged Nico's arm and put a finger to his lips. Nico nodded. They moved deeper into the shadows, treading lightly. Gradually, as their eyes became used to the darkness, Ben could make out more detail. It had been a long, long time since the church had been used for worship. What looked like a small museum exhibit sat to one side. Other than that, the place was completely empty.

'There's nobody here,' Nico whispered impatiently.

'Shh.' Ben thought he'd heard something moving, but it was hard to pinpoint where the sound had come from in the shadows.

'Come on, man,' Nico said in his normal voice. 'Let's g—'

His words were cut short by an explosion of noise far above their heads, a furious beating sound that echoed dizzyingly all round the walls. 'Jesus!' Nico said, flinching and covering his head with his hands.

But as Ben looked up and saw the flapping shape in the dim light of a high window he realised the noise was a startled pigeon trapped in the dome of the ceiling and trying to find a way out. 'It's just a bird,' he said. But was that all he'd heard a moment ago?

Nico breathed a sigh of relief. 'Scared the crap out of me. Look, we need to get out of— *hey!*'

Ben hadn't lowered his gaze from the ceiling, or he wouldn't have seen the dark shape tumbling down from a great height. It was much larger than a pigeon, and it was plummeting straight towards them. Just in time, he hauled Nico backwards out of the way.

The falling object landed at their feet with a crunch that resounded through the church. Ben had heard the stomach-churning sound of cracking human bones before. The dark gleaming mess that had suddenly covered the floor was blood, and the shapeless heap lying in the middle of it was a corpse.

Ben took out his Zippo lighter, thumbed the flint striker and crouched down to shine the flickering orange flame over the dead man's face.

'Cabeza,' Nico said after a beat.

Chapter Forty

Ben only needed a brief second to tell that the historian's skull was crushed by its impact against the flagstones. In the same instant he also knew that it hadn't been the fall that had killed him. No fall could produce such a razor-straight gash from ear to ear. Someone had sliced his throat, and not long ago.

Ben quickly shut the lighter, snuffing out its telltale flame – but too late, because whoever had killed Cabeza and punted his body off some ledge high above them already knew he and Nico were there.

The proof came with the pistol shot that filled the church like a thunderclap a second later. Ben caught a momentary glimpse of the orange-white muzzle flash overhead: in almost pitch darkness the jet of exploding gases lit up a section of wall and the stone stairway leading up to an arched alcove and what looked like a way through to the bell tower.

Nico let out a yell of pain. Stone chips exploded from the floor between their feet. Ben yanked him close in to the wall, where they were directly below the gunman and out of his field of fire – at least for the moment.

'It's just a graze,' Nico muttered, clutching his arm. 'I'm okay.' Even in the semi-darkness Ben could see how much blood was welling out from between his fingers. He quickly slipped off his belt and wrapped it round Nico's arm. 'Hold it tight. Keep your arm bent.'

Nico drew in a sharp, sudden breath, and Ben thought it was a wince of pain until he realised the Colombian had seen something. Before Ben had time to react, a blinding light was shining on them both. He turned, shielding his eyes from the dazzling glare. He could just about discern a pair of figures behind the light. Two beams shining in his eyes, not one, each from the frame-mounted tactical torch of a pistol.

Above them, the trapped pigeon was still flailing wildly around the dome of the ceiling. A voice snapped out harshly in Spanish, 'Up against the wall and get your hands in the air.'

Ben didn't move. Footsteps were echoing down the bell tower stairway: the men who'd sliced Cabeza's throat and pitched him from the alcove were coming to join their two colleagues on the ground. Three, four. In a matter of seconds the odds were going to double.

'You. I said get against that wall,' said the voice behind the light.

Ben could focus better now on the shapes of the two men in front of him, their outlines visible if not their features. 'What do you reckon, Nico?' he said quietly, not taking his eyes off them.

'I say fuck them,' Nico replied in a savage undertone.

Ben nodded. 'That's what I say too. I'm sick of getting shot at today.' Then in one movement that was too fluid and fast for the men to register, he reached under his jacket, grasped the butt of the revolver that was stuck into his waistband behind the right hip, wrenched it out and squeezed the trigger without aiming.

When he'd come across the handgun in the dresser drawer

back at La Catalina, he'd guessed it was the one Nico had procured from the drug dealer in Granada. Better to have it and not need it than to need it and not have it, he'd thought, and slipped it quietly into his jeans. The short-barrelled .44 Magnum revolver was even scabbier and more beaten-up than the Colt he'd got hold of in Belfast; and if it hadn't been for the scorch marks on the cylinder from the two rounds Nico had already put into Serrato's hired killer, Ben wouldn't have been so sure he could rely on it. But as the hammer dropped on the next chamber in line, the gun went off like a grenade in his hand and the muzzle recoiled high in the air, haloed in white flame.

The bullet caught the nearest man in the chest and cannoned him into his companion. Ben's hearing was suddenly drowned in a high-pitched whine. The man he'd shot dropped his weapon and its light beam flew around to point at the wall. The other was staggering off balance, his gun-torch shining wildly all over the place. Ben pointed the Magnum blindly at a point somewhere above and to the side of the light source, pulled the trigger again and once more the world seemed to erupt in a wall of sound. The hand-filling wooden butt of the revolver kicked back at him like a jab from a heavyweight boxer. Blood flew in the light from the bullet strike. The second man went crashing down on his side and rolled over, his body spread-eagled.

Ben didn't need to check if the two men were dead or not. A handgun capable of knocking down large game at several hundred yards was overkill on a human target at extreme close range. Without a pause, he leaped over to the nearest of the fallen weapons and snatched it up to shine the light towards the stone stairway above him, just in time to see a fast-retreating figure make it to the top of the steps and disappear through the archway.

Four revolver rounds gone, two to go. The gun attached to the torch was a Ruger automatic with a capacity of eight. He picked up the other and was about to toss it to Nico when he saw that the Colombian was slumped against the wall, bent over. With all the blood on the flagstones it was getting hard to tell one man's from another's; Nico's injured arm was dripping with it and he looked pale. 'You're full of fucking surprises, aren't you?' he managed to grunt painfully at Ben, eyeing the .44 Magnum in his hand.

'The things people leave lying around in drawers.' Ben could hardly hear himself speak over the whining tinnitus from the gunshots. 'You'd better stay down here,' he said, flashing his light up the stone steps. 'I don't want you fainting on me.'

'I told you, it's just a graze,' Nico said defensively, then slumped back against the wall. 'Fuck, it hurts.'

'Getting shot's never easy,' Ben said as he headed up the steps. He had the hammer of the .44 cocked in his right hand and was using the Ruger to shine the way ahead. The open-sided staircase climbed some fifty feet up the inside of the wall before it led through the shadowy archway from which Cabeza's body had been dropped. There was more blood there too, a lot more, from where they'd slit his throat. The poor bastard must have tried to hide from them up here, Ben thought. The bloody knife was still lying on the floor.

Ben's hearing was beginning to return again, and he could make out the slap-back echo of the two men's racing footsteps off the stone walls as he gave chase. There was only one way for them to go, and that was up the tower. Another stairway led steeply upward. Ben climbed it at a sprint. Beyond the reach of the Ruger's tactical light he could see his quarry's bobbing torch beams reflected on the stairway walls ahead.

As he ran, one of the light beams suddenly swung round to point at him: there was a crack and a bullet ricocheted off the stonework, stinging his face with flying chips.

Ben levelled both of his pistols and squeezed both triggers at once. The simultaneous crash of the gunshots was numbing in the confined space. The man crumpled and came tumbling down the stairs. Ben jumped aside to let him come rolling and flopping lifelessly past, then raced on upwards after the last man, who had reached the top of the steps and disappeared from sight through another low doorway.

Ben reached the top step a second later, leaped through after him and found himself standing inside the church's bell tower. The cold breeze coming in through its tall open-sided arches ruffled his hair and chilled the sweat on his brow. He looked around him but could see no sign of the man who'd just run in here ahead of him. The church's massive bronze bell and its thick rope hung silhouetted against the sky and the dark hills in the distance. Montefrio was a speckle of lights around the base of the rock far below.

Ben heard a sound from overhead. He looked up to see the man making his way frantically up the iron rungs of the ladder that led to the very top level of the tower: a heavily-built, dark-skinned guy in a black coat. Realising he'd been spotted, the man hung off the rungs with his left hand, aimed his pistol down at Ben and squeezed off two rapid shots.

Ben felt the heat of the first bullet as it punched through the upper sleeve of his leather jacket. The second knocked the Ruger out of his left hand and sent it spinning away through the open arch and into empty space.

He dived for the cover of the bell as the man tracked him in his sights and fired a third shot. The bullet rapped sharply off the bell with an impact that set it swaying heavily on its mountings and filled the air with a quivering, juddering note like a hammer-strike on an iron gong. Ben's left hand was numb from where the Ruger had been shot out of it. He checked his fingers. There was no blood, nothing broken. He took a breath, moved quickly out from underneath the bell, raised the .44 and fired the last deafening round in the cylinder.

The man screamed as the bullet blew open his thigh. He dropped from the iron rungs, hit the swaying bell a glancing blow and went sprawling to the floor so close to the edge of one of the tower's open sides that he would have fallen through it if Ben hadn't grasped his coat and hauled him to safety. Blood was pumping from the ragged hole in his leg. But even with half his quadriceps blown away by the .44 hollowpoint, there was still fight left in the man. Ben saw the knife blade flash in the dim light and moved out of the way of the slash just in time. Repeating out of pure instinct a move he'd drilled and executed hundreds of times in the past, he trapped the blade, knocked it from the man's hand and twisted the wrist to breaking point. The man let out a howl.

'Who are you?' Ben demanded in Spanish. 'Who sent you? Serrato?' He saw the unmistakable flash of recognition in the man's eyes. 'That's right. You know that name, don't you? And what's yours?' Ben rifled through the man's jacket and wasn't surprised to find that he was carrying neither a wallet nor ID. He pointed the .44. 'One round left,' he lied. 'I said, what's your name?'

'Gutiérrez!' the man whimpered, his eyes rolling wildly. 'Armando Gutiérrez!'

'I'll bet you're not from around here, are you, Armando? I'll bet you go travelling all over. Been to Ireland recently?'

'I don't know what you're talking about!'

'No?' Ben thumbed back the revolver's hammer. That tiny metallic *click-clack* of the mechanism cocking and the cylinder snicking round another sixth of a turn was enough to loosen anyone's tongue.

'It wasn't me! I swear!'

'Wasn't me who what?'

'Who cut the English guy's hands off. Bracca did it!'

Seized by a surge of rage, Ben tossed down the revolver, grabbed Gutiérrez by the throat and half-dragged, half-threw him through the arch towards the edge of the drop. 'You're going down, Armando, and it's a long way to the bottom.'

'No! Please!'

'Where's the woman?' Ben demanded through gritted teeth.

'What woman?'

Ben grabbed the collar of Gutiérrez's jacket and shoved him brutally several inches farther over the edge of the drop, dangling the man's whole upper body in space and wedging his own shoulder tight against the side of the arch to prevent them both from falling to their deaths. The wind whistled around them.

'I'm not talking about the poor woman you left to rot in a derelict barn with her head blown off,' Ben said. 'I'm talking about the other one. Her name's Brooke and you're going to tell me where she is. Right now, or else I'm letting you go.'

Armando didn't want to be let go, even though he was probably bleeding to death from the pumping bullet hole in his thigh. 'We took her!' he screamed.

'Took her where?

'*El Capo* – he wanted her.'

'The boss? You mean Serrato?'

'Yes! Serrato wanted her!'

'So you made sure he got her, did you?' Ben rasped. He

271

could feel his eyes bulging. The fury was coursing through him so powerfully that it was hard to breathe.

'I did what I was told!'

'Wanted her for what?'

'I don't know!'

'You've been eating too many burritos, Armando. I can't hold you for much longer.'

'I don't fucking know! Please!'

'Did you kill her when he was done with her? Did you hurt her?'

'She's alive! I swear it!'

'She's alive?' Ben shook him hard from side to side. The material of the black coat began to tear.

'Aagh! Don't drop me! Yeah, she alive! I've seen her!'

'Where? Where is she?'

'At El Capo's place in Peru! Madre de Dios, don't drop me!

'You really believe in God, Armando? Because you know, dirty liars burn in hell for all eternity.'

'It's the truth, I fucking promise on my mother's grave I'm telling the truth!'

'Then your final act in this world was an honest one,' Ben said. 'You can tell that to San Pedro when you meet him in a couple of seconds' time. Make that five seconds. It's quite a drop.'

'No! Please!'

Ben relaxed his grip on the man's coat collar and the material slipped out of his fist. With a last scream of terror, Gutiérrez dropped from the bell tower and went tumbling and cartwheeling downwards into empty air. He'd vanished into the darkness before Ben heard the muffled *crump* from far below. He got to his feet, flexing his sore hand. Turned round and saw Nico standing there looking at him.

'That was pretty fucking harsh, man,' the Colombian said.

'What would you have done with him?' Ben said.

'What would I have done with him? You don't want to know.'

'Then we understand each other.'

Nico gave a pained grin. 'So we're partners now, huh?'

'Till you get yourself killed or I find someone better to team up with,' Ben said. 'How's the arm?'

'Bleeding's slowed down some,' Nico said, looking down at the saturated mess of his sleeve and Ben's belt.

'It's either the local vet for you, or needle and thread back at the house. Think you can handle that?'

'I've been stitched up before,' Nico said gruffly.

'That's fine, because I can't have you pissing blood and flopping about all over the airport.'

'Thanks a fucking million, man. So, we catching a plane?'

Ben nodded. 'How many men did you say Serrato has?'

Nico grunted. 'Plenty enough.'

'You don't have to come all the way. I just need you to point me in the right direction.'

'You'd go in alone? Even after what I told you about that place?'

Ben said nothing.

'Like I said, you're a crazy motherfucker.' Nico paused, chewed his lip. 'Guess that makes two of us.'

'Then let's get moving,' Ben said.

Chapter Forty-One

It was late in the morning when Brooke was awoken by the sound of the lock opening and someone coming into her rooms. One of the worst things about captivity was the way she was slowly becoming used to these invasions, accepting that her space wasn't her own. She sat up in bed, rubbing her eyes. The night had been a long and almost completely sleepless one. She'd spent most of it trying to forget the awful scene of the previous evening.

And thinking. Thinking very carefully about her options.

The emerald and diamond necklace and bracelet Serrato had given her were lying on the bedside table where she'd dumped them. Remembering that she'd left her special little gold neck chain there too, she reached out to pick it up. It wasn't there. She climbed out of the bed, thinking it might have fallen onto the floor, but she couldn't see it anywhere. She was upset about losing it. Right now it was all she had left of her old life. All she had left of Ben.

Brooke could smell the aroma of coffee from beyond the bedroom door. Grabbing a bath towel from the back of a chair to cover the translucent nightdress, for dignity's sake in case her visitor was one of the guards, she ventured out of the bedroom.

It wasn't a guard, but a woman Brooke had never seen

before, hefty and busty with a hatchet face and a severe haircut like a man's. On the table was a breakfast tray laden with warm croissants, steaming coffee and fresh orange juice. 'Isn't it wonderful to be so well catered for,' Brooke said to her in a hostile tone. 'I'll be sure to recommend this place to all my friends that your boss hasn't killed.'

The hatchet-faced woman didn't speak a word, but seemed insistent on watching over her as she picked at the breakfast. Afterwards, she allowed Brooke time alone in the bathroom, but stood like a sentry not far from the door.

After searching again in vain for her gold chain, Brooke took her time in the shower. Afterwards she towelled and brushed her hair in the giant mirror using the cumbersome lapis lazuli hairbrush. She rearranged the bottles of perfume and cans of hairspray on the bathroom shelf, then calmly dressed and emerged wearing the tracksuit bottoms and one of the T-shirts Consuela had brought her. The severe-looking woman was still there, watching her sternly.

Brooke ignored her and wandered back to the bedroom. She lay on the bed and flicked casually through one of the magazines, pretending to read while she went back through her thoughts from overnight.

The plan was coming together in her head now. It was a dangerous game she was undertaking, and what would follow was even more dangerous. It was the only way. She couldn't stay here much longer.

As lunchtime approached, the bedroom door burst open and the hatchet-faced woman strode in. In her coarse, square hands was a hanger with a white cotton dress.

'Don't worry about knocking or anything,' Brooke said.

'I take it that's the latest outfit I'm to be paraded in front of his Lordship in?'

The woman glanced at her, expressionless, removed the dress from the hanger and laid it out carefully on the foot of the bed.

'You wouldn't happen to have laid your piggy little eyes on a gold chain, would you?' Brooke asked her. The woman made no reply. She picked up the green dress that Brooke had left rumpled on the floor, tutted irritably at the creases in it and hung it up in the wardrobe.

Brooke motioned towards the door. 'Thanks, Ugly Mug. Now maybe you'd like to drag your lardy old arse out of my bedroom while I dress myself up for your psychopathic pervert of an employer.'

The woman left. Some time later, when Brooke had finished putting on the white dress, the guards arrived for her routine escort downstairs. One of them was the cigar smoker she'd last seen from her window puffing away surreptitiously, the other a stockily-built man Brooke hadn't seen before. She added him to her headcount of Serrato's thugs. That made twenty-eight now.

As the guards were ushering Brooke down the stairs, she tripped and almost fell. The cigar smoker reached out and caught her. For a moment, his body was pressed tightly against hers and she could smell the cheap, shitty tobacco on him. His strong hands gripped her for slightly longer than necessary; then he grinned at her and let her go.

'I'm sorry,' Brooke mumbled. 'It's these shoes.' He didn't seem to mind at all.

Downstairs, Brooke was shown into an airy room with tall windows that opened onto an outside terrace. Serrato was sitting at a small table in the sunshine. He jumped to his feet to welcome her. 'Good day to you, Brooke,' he said with a smile.

Brooke made the biggest effort she'd ever made in her life. She smiled back. 'Hello, Ramon.'

Serrato appeared delighted. 'You look exquisite. Did you sleep well?'

Brooke replied that she had, and that the headache which had forced her to leave dinner early the night before had soon passed.

'Perhaps the wine didn't agree with you,' he said, 'but the cellar is well stocked with many different varieties. We will find one that suits. Would you care for some lunch? I thought we could eat outside.'

'I was thinking,' Brooke said as he led her out onto the terrace, 'what a beautiful house this is, and how much I'd love to be shown around more of it.' She'd rehearsed that line a hundred different ways during the night. Saying it now, she was suddenly terrified that it was too obvious; that he'd see through it immediately.

But Serrato only seemed even more delighted. 'I designed much of the place myself, you know. Of course it would be my pleasure to show you around. It is your home as much as mine, as I hope you now understand.'

'I do understand,' she replied softly, then paused. 'There was something else I was wondering—'

'Yes, my dear?'

'The piano I saw the other day . . . might I be allowed to play it from time to time?'

'The Steinway? But of course. How you keep your talents hidden from me. I didn't know you could play.'

Why the hell would you, she thought. He was talking as though he'd known her for years. And after last night, she was beginning to understand why that might be.

What had he done to Alicia? The thought chilled her to the core. *You sick, sick bastard.*

But she only smiled and replied, 'Oh, yes, I love music. I had some lessons when I was a little girl and had thought about taking it up again. Maybe you could teach me?'

'Oh, I only tinker a little,' he said, beaming. 'I believe it's important to be immersed in the arts, so I took it up some years ago. Though I would hardly describe myself as anything more than a dilettante.'

'You play beautifully,' she said.

Lunch was served at the little table on the terrace: a light salad with crusty French baguette, along with a crisp white wine. Serrato seemed much more relaxed than she had seen him before, and very pleased with himself, sitting back with his legs stretched out in front of him, pouring glass after glass of wine. It was Brooke's first taste of open air since her kidnapping, and even in the presence of this man she hated so strongly, she savoured every moment; the sun on her face, the warm breeze in her hair. When she'd finished eating she stood up and leaned on the ornate railing, gazing out at the view with her half-empty glass in her hand.

'Magnificent, isn't it?' Serrato said, joining her and topping up her wine.

'Spectacular,' she replied airily. She'd actually been taking careful note of a part of the compound she wasn't able to see from her rooms.

'You're looking at my ancestral heritage,' he laughed, pointing at the distant jungle. 'A gift from the King of Spain.'

She looked at him. 'You're not joking, are you?'

'Not in the least. In all, nearly half a million acres,' he said grandly. 'And one day it will make us two of the richest people in the world.'

Us. She flinched inwardly, but to show her emotions now would be fatal. 'Looks to me like you're already a rich man, Ramon,' she said.

He chuckled. 'I admit, I have not done too badly for a boy from the slums, who grew up fighting for scraps. I was determined to do well in life, and thanks to that determination I have been prosperous. But the wealth you see around you here is nothing in comparison to what we will have once my real plans come to fruition. You see,' he went on, taking another gulp of wine and mistaking her stony silence for curiosity, 'growing up I was never able to forget my grandfather's stories, and his belief that our family had noble Spanish roots. But it was not until seven years ago, when I was already a highly successful businessman at the age of thirty-six, that I finally took it upon myself to travel to Spain to find out more. I spoke to so many scholars: historians, museum curators; I spent countless hours buried in ancient archives, tracing back the name Serrato through the ages.'

He poured the last of the wine into his glass, talking freely now that the alcohol had loosened his reserve. 'That was when I made the four greatest discoveries of my life,' he went on. 'The first, that my grandfather had been telling the truth. The second, that my noble ancestry comprised not only Spanish, but also English aristocratic blood. The third, that my English ancestor, Sir Christopher Pennick, had been awarded a vast tract of land by Philip II for, shall we say, various services to Spain.' Serrato smiled. 'Sadly, it is not until now, five hundred years later, that the King's gift to my family has finally been legitimised and passed to me, the sole surviving heir.' He waved his glass over the distant jungle. 'I drink to Roger Forsyte, who made it all possible. Welcome to my empire. Nobody can stand in my way any longer.'

Now Brooke understood the connection with Forsyte. That was the key to this whole thing: land. Sam had died for the sake of land. 'And what was the fourth discovery,

Ramon?' she asked, trying hard not to let the disgust show on her face.

'Black gold,' he said triumphantly. 'The largest untapped oil field in Peru. For five hundred years it has been sitting waiting for me. And now it is mine.'

For the first time in days, Brooke suddenly knew where she was. It seemed surreal to her that she could be in Peru, a country she'd barely ever even thought about.

Well, I won't be in Peru much longer, she thought to herself, and gazed across the jungle.

After lunch Serrato took her to the salon where the piano was. He graciously pulled out the piano stool for her, fussed over getting it to exactly the correct height, then pressed her to play something for him. Brooke sat down, laid her fingers on the keys and desperately tried to remember the notes of a simple little Bach minuet that she'd played as a twelve-year-old. The piece came back to her, but her fingers were clumsy and her performance was stumbling and filled with mistakes.

Serrato chuckled at the wrong notes. Bending very close over her, he took her hands in his and showed her how to position them on the keyboard. 'The trick is not to stab the notes. You must caress them with a lover's touch. There, that's much better,' he said as she tried again. She felt his hands rest on her shoulders. 'You have such beautiful hair,' he whispered. He bent down even closer and kissed her head. Ran his hands down her arms. She tensed and took her fingers off the keys.

'You are afraid of me,' he said.

'A little.'

'You have nothing to fear, Brooke.'

She looked earnestly up at him. 'You have to understand. All this has been a bit of a shock to me. But I'll try. Just give me time.'

'You make me very happy, Brooke.' He paused. 'You know, you matter to me very much. I will do anything I can to make you comfortable.'

Okay, she thought. *You've softened him up a little and now here's your chance.* 'Some ventilation would be nice,' she said.

'Ventilation?'

'In my room. I always used to have the window open at night at my home in London. In my old life, I mean,' she added.

'The air conditioning displeases you? You would like your windows to open instead?'

'It helps me sleep. And I love to be able to smell the flowers when I wake up in the morning. Can you fix that for me?'

'Anything can be done,' he said with a casual gesture. 'But, my dear, you are unused to life here. The mosquitoes will eat you alive while you sleep. They carry malaria.'

'Then maybe I could have a mosquito net over my bed?' she asked. 'Please, Ramon?'

He frowned, then smiled. 'Bah. What man could refuse such a beguiling lady's wishes? If that is what you wish, I will have it seen to immediately.' He summoned a servant and gave very detailed instructions. The man noted everything down, nodded solemnly and left. 'Now,' Serrato said, turning to Brooke. 'You were saying you would like to be shown around?'

The rest of the long, hot afternoon was spent strolling around the enormous house. Serrato guided her attentively from room to room, opening doors for her and ushering her about in a self-consciously gentlemanlike fashion. He loved to talk proudly about his possessions, and he had a great many to talk about: the antique furniture pieces that had come from such and such a boutique in New York, London or Rome; the history of each painting and its artist;

a detailed account of the design of every architectural feature. He was knowledgeable, even passionate, and despite the hatred that intensified with every minute she had to spend in his company, Brooke had to concede that the man had excellent taste. As the guided tour went on, she took feverish note of as many details of the place's layout as she could cram into her memory. By the time he led her to the stairs to show her the top floor, she knew exactly how to get from her room to the main entrance.

Serrato had saved the best for last. At the top of the stairs he pushed open a door and led her inside a set of rooms that could have passed for the Presidential Suite in the world's most opulent hotel. 'My humble quarters,' he said with a glow in his eye. 'Does the style please you? Be honest with me. I can have the décor remodelled any way you like. After all, one day . . .'

She caught his meaning and wanted to throw up. 'I wouldn't change a thing, Ramon,' she said, extremely careful with her words.

Serrato's smile suddenly disappeared. He stepped closer to her, reached out and clasped her arms to draw her towards him. The urge to back away from him was overwhelming, but she knew that to give in to it would be fatal.

'You are so special to me,' his voice murmured in her ear as he held her tight. 'More special than I could ever explain to you.' He drew back from her so that he could look into her eyes. 'Do you think, Brooke, that you could ever love me?'

Brooke's heart was thumping hard. 'Let's play it by ear, Ramon. All right? See how it goes.'

'But you . . . you like me?'

She could see the dangerous light in his eyes. 'You're a very charming man,' she forced herself to say. 'It's just that I've never been the kind of woman who . . .' She hesitated.

'Who rushes into things. You know what I'm saying, don't you?'

'Yes. You are saying you would refuse me.'

Brooke said nothing.

'I will give you everything, Brooke. Do anything to please you. But you cannot refuse me. I could not bear that.'

She swallowed hard. 'I won't refuse you.'

'Tonight, I regret to say that you must dine without me. I have some business to attend to. Afterwards, when I return . . . will you come to me? Here, in my personal quarters?'

'Tonight?'

'I will send for you,' he said. 'Will you be ready for me then?'

Brooke was suddenly very cold.

'You and I,' he whispered, holding her tightly again. 'You have no idea how much I have longed for it.'

The guards led Brooke back to her room. She leaned against the door, heard the click of the lock sliding home. Footsteps padded away and the guards' voices faded into the distance.

And only then did all the pent-up tension burst out of her in a sobbing gasp. So this was it. Serrato had finally made his move. That night she'd be summoned to him, like the slave girl to the master. To be claimed. To be made his kept whore.

And if she refused, he'd kill her. There was no doubt whatsoever about that.

Slowly, she peeled herself away from the door and crossed the room. That was when she noticed that the windows looked different. Where before they'd been unopenable, now they had latch handles. She tried one. It glided smoothly open as far as the steel bars would allow, letting the breeze into the room.

Brooke nodded to herself. Her plan couldn't have started coming together any later now that the clock was truly ticking. But it wasn't fresh air she was interested in. She went through into the bedroom and saw to her relief that the men who'd fixed the windows had also obeyed their instructions to fit a mosquito net to the four-poster. The translucent micro-netting hung down from the canopy almost to the floor.

Perfect. Now for a small experiment.

In the bathroom, she picked up one of the Chanel perfume bottles. She unscrewed the cap of the spray nozzle and poured a few drops of the liquid into the sink. Then, slipping two fingers into the cup of her bra, she took out the slim lighter she'd stolen from the cigar-smoking guard on the stairs when she'd pretended to stumble. A bra was the only place you could quickly hide anything when you were forced to wear such impractical clothing all the time. As frightened as she'd been that Serrato was going to try to touch her earlier, she'd been even more terrified that he might find the lighter there.

She pressed the little piezo switch and an inch-long tongue of yellow flame darted from the lighter. She lowered it into the sink, touched the flame to the tiny pool of perfume, and drew her hand away quickly as it flared up with a brief but spectacular *whoosh*. That was what just a few drops of the stuff could produce. There was about a litre of it sitting on her bathroom shelf.

She squirted a load more perfume into the air and then sprayed hairspray all over the place to cover up any smell of burning that might have escaped the bathroom. Then, shaking with nerves now that her plan was finally about to become a reality, she started attending to the rest of her arrangements.

Time passed. Dinner was served to her in her room: a

plate of cold meats and salad on a tray together with a half-bottle of chilled wine. She was too anxious to touch any of it. Instead she emptied a pack of cotton makeup-remover pads into the bin in the bathroom and used the empty plastic packaging to wrap up the cold meats.

Then all she could do was wait quietly in the bedroom, going over and over in her mind all that she needed to do. There was no going back any more. The alternative was unthinkable.

It was sometime before midnight when she heard the door unlock. Moments later, Hatchet Face appeared in the bedroom doorway. She was carrying a slim white box like the one Consuela had brought to Brooke's room on the first night.

Hatchet Face laid the box down on the bed. Her lips drew back into a sly smile, revealing the gaps in her teeth. She reached her big, coarse hands into the box and pulled out a silky garment that she held up for Brooke to see.

The negligee was so insubstantial and transparent that it made the nightdress Serrato had given her before look like something a prude would wear. There was something else in the box: Brooke peered inside and saw the flimsy colour-matched stockings and suspenders.

'You put on,' Hatchet Face said. 'Señor Serrato, he wait for you.'

Chapter Forty-Two

The torrid heat of a South American summer wrapped itself around Ben and Nico like a damp towel as they stepped off the overnight Iberia jet that had left wintry Madrid almost exactly twelve hours earlier, and crossed the tarmac at Jorge Chávez International Airport, Lima, Peru. By the time they'd got into arrivals their shirts were already sticking to them, and it was still early morning.

'Two days ago I was worried about fucking frostbite,' Nico muttered, taking off his jacket and rolling up his sleeves, going easy with the left one as the arm was bandaged to the elbow and still tender. Underneath the bandage were the dozen stitches that Ben had put into him back in Montefrio, using the little soldier-repair kit that always rattled around in the bottom of his bag. He winced.

'You'll live,' Ben said.

'You always say that. Question is, how long for?'

They were still a long way from their destination. After long delays in the cloying humidity, during which Ben changed most of his remaining cash for Peruvian nuevo sol, they boarded an internal flight to carry them the four hundred miles northwards to Chachapoyas.

The department of Amazonas was just one of Peru's twenty-five separate regions, itself divided up into seven provinces and eighty-three districts. Chachapoyas was a city in the clouds, over seven thousand feet above sea level and surrounded by mist-shrouded mountains that made the Spanish Sierra Nevada seem like gentle hill country by comparison. Stretching out all around, the subtropical highlands of Amazonas' rainforest looked from the air like an endless undulating blanket of green crisscrossed by tiny blue threads – the vast river system that covered thousands of square miles and fed into the mighty Amazon itself.

It was cooler in Chachapoyas, but the humidity was no less oppressive than it had been in Lima. After collecting Ben's battered old bag, the only luggage the two travellers had between them, they managed to find a taxi to drive them along the desolate single road into the city.

'I told you it was a backwater,' Nico said. 'Now what?'

Every delay, every second that went by without tangible progress was an added torment as Ben kept racing through every aspect and angle of the situation in his mind. More and more, it was a conflict between the human, emotional and very frightened part of him that wanted desperately to keep moving on, and the cool professional who knew that panic and exhaustion were two of the greatest risks facing him right now. If he didn't do this right, it would be Brooke who'd pay the price – if she hadn't already.

He wilfully closed his mind to those kinds of thoughts. 'First we need to make a base here,' he told Nico. 'A cool shower, a hot meal and a bed are our first priority before we make another move.'

All three were available for a handful of nuevo sol at a simple hotel near the centre of the city. As Ben stood under the shower that night, he thought about what was to come. His instinct told him he was entering the final phase of his search, but what lay ahead was still deeply uncertain. He'd stopped caring whether he got out of this in one piece. All that mattered to him was that Brooke did.

Was she really here? Was she still all right? The questions haunted him deep into the night. He wondered whether she had any idea he was looking for her. Or would she be unconscious, drugged by her captors? What, if anything, was he going to find when he got there? After hours of sleepless torment, he got up and went across the dark room to the mini-bar. Only when the floor was littered with empty bottles was he able to crawl back to bed and fall into a fevered sleep.

When he awoke around dawn, he remembered Amal and realised it had been days since he'd made contact. It would be late morning in London. Ben sat on the edge of the bed and dialled the number.

Amal picked up instantly, as if he'd been hovering over the phone the entire time just waiting for Ben to call. His voice sounded croaky and distant, breaking up from the poor reception. 'Where are you? You sound like you're thousands of miles away.'

'I think I know where she is,' Ben said. 'There's a chance she's still alive and I'm going in to find her.'

There was a speechless pause on the other end, followed by the sound of Amal swallowing hard. 'Where? Tell me everyth—' At that point the line went dead. Ben tried dialling once more, but when he couldn't get through he didn't try a third time. There was nothing more to say.

Feeling stiff and weary, Ben took another shower, then pulled on the last of the fresh clothes he had in his bag. He went downstairs, asked the guy in the lobby where he could get a map, and followed his directions to a newsagent's stall down the street.

By the time Ben got back to the hotel, Nico was sitting in the bar waiting for him. He looked sombre. 'I just tried calling Felipe again. That's the sixth time since we left Montefrio. Still no reply.'

Ben said nothing. He was certain Morales was dead.

'I need a coffee,' Nico said. 'Couldn't sleep.' They ordered the biggest pot the kitchen could brew up, and sat at a corner table where they spread the map out between them. Tracing his finger roughly northeast from Chachapoyas, Nico indicated the rough location of the tiny river village of San Tomás, the nearest settlement to Serrato's compound. San Tomás itself was too tiny to feature on the map, but Nico was fairly certain of his bearings and in any case, he assured Ben, the region was filled with expert guides who could take them there.

'We follow the highway out of Chachapoyas sixty, seventy miles,' Nico said, pointing out the directions on the map, 'then turn off and cut across towards the Potro River, right here. There's a river station where you can hire a floatplane pilot to take you the rest of the way to San Tomás. It's a hell of a quicker way than by road, believe me.'

Ben could easily believe it. He nodded. 'That'll do us.'

'Once we get to San Tomás we'll need another set of wheels to get us nearer to Serrato. But unless you're planning on driving right up to his front gates, the final approach has to be on foot, through the jungle. It ain't exactly a walk in the park. You ever been in jungle country before?'

As a young SAS recruit years earlier, Ben had undergone the inhuman endurance test of jungle training in Belize, where he and his patrol had had to learn to move quickly and silently in near-impossible conditions, testing their navigation and survival skills to the limit. Later he'd seen active service in Sierra Leone in West Africa and a dozen other black-ops jungle combat missions in war zones, official and unofficial, across the planet. 'A little,' was all he replied.

'It's another world, man. A green hell filled with everything that crawls and bites. Giant spiders, snakes longer than a Chevy Silverado. If those critters don't get you, the diseases will, and it's got them all. Yellow fever, malaria, dengue, hepatitis, typhoid, tetanus, cholera, fucking rabies. They say you've got to be nuts to go there without inoculations.'

Back in his regiment days the medics had regularly pumped Ben full of more drugs than he cared to count. The proper courses of vaccines took time to administer; anti-typhoid injections alone had to be spaced out over six months for the protection to work. He didn't have six months to waste, or even six more hours. 'Yeah, well, the art of living dangerously is just not to catch anything.'

'Like not catching a bullet, I guess,' Nico said, looking down at his arm.

'I told you, you don't have to come all the way. Just show me where to go.'

'I've come this far, haven't I?' Nico said, stung. 'You think I don't want to finish it?'

'Your choice,' Ben said. 'I'm not going to be responsible for you. Once we're there, you slow me down, I'll walk away. Get lost or hurt, I won't come back for you. I'm there for one thing and one thing only. Understand?'

'That's what I like about you, *Capitano* – you're so full of fucking encouragement.'

'Don't call me that,' Ben said. He drained his coffee and stood up.

'We moving?'

'We're moving.'

'Then let's get fucking moving,' Nico said.

Chapter Forty-Three

The Toyota Hilux they rented from the place around the corner from the hotel was more rust than metal and would have been declared unroadworthy anywhere in Europe, but Ben didn't care as long as it carried them as far as they needed. 'Now we have some shopping to do,' he told Nico.

For the next two hours they drove from store to store, from one end of Chachapoyas to the other gathering together the supplies they needed for jungle travel: bottled water, basic food, thick-soled boots and bush hats, heavy-duty torches and batteries, fire-making equipment, insect repellent, malaria tablets, water purifier tablets, a parang machete for chopping vegetation, and finally a pair of compact but powerful binoculars. Everything was stowed into Ben's bag and a second lightweight rucksack, and cans of spare fuel were thrown into the back of the Toyota.

An hour after that, Chachapoyas was already far behind them as they headed rapidly northeastwards along the highway, passing by landscapes that would have blown anyone's mind but Ben's, totally focused as he was on his goal.

Nico seemed to have remembered the route well. After a long stretch of highway that became progressively less busy the further they got from Chachapoyas, Ben turned off onto a series of unsealed roads so potholed that it was like they had suffered artillery bombardment. On one narrow mountain pass, where nothing but the crumbling edge stood between them and a thousand-foot drop to the forest below, the road had been half swept away by an avalanche. Some way further on, as the road dropped in altitude into a verdant valley, they had to thread their way past a broken-down bus. More people than it seemed possible to cram into the dilapidated vehicle were crowding the roadside, many of them barefoot, some in rags, others in brightly-coloured and heavily embroidered tunics and ponchos. They were surrounded by luggage, children, dogs and a pair of noisily braying goats. A horde of excited nut-brown youngsters chased the Toyota as it passed by, looking as though they'd happily clamber on board and cling to the roof.

Ben drove on. The road continued to drop downwards, the mountain scenery long gone behind a screen of thick jungle. Even with the air conditioning on full blast the humidity was all-pervasive. The occasional glimpse through the endless green canopy overhead showed that the sky was darkening; clouds were gathering ominously. 'Should be getting near the river station,' Nico said, studying the map.

By the time they reached the boat station on the Potro River, the storm that Ben had been expecting for some time had finally been unleashed. The rain was more than torrential. It churned the ground into cascades of mud and lashed the surface of the river and the few sorry-looking craft moored up to the boat station. As they ran along the flimsy boardwalk for the shelter of a row of warped wooden huts, Nico pointed out the red-and-white single-engined float-plane bobbing unsteadily on the water by one of the jetties. 'That's our baby,' he yelled over the downpour, but his words were drowned out by the rolling crash of thunder that made the water-filled air tremble.

They stood under the streaming canvas awning of the boat station and watched as the storm quickly gathered power. A violent lightning display filled the sky. The rain lashed down with ever more incredible force. The brown river water seemed to be rising before their eyes.

'This can't go on,' Nico said.

Ben wasn't so sure. Neither was the flying boat pilot they talked to half an hour later, who shook his head emphatically at the notion of taking his plane out in this weather and told them in rapid-fire Spanish that he'd lived and worked on this river man and boy and seen these storms go on for days at a stretch.

For a wild moment, Ben seriously considered offering to buy the plane so that he could fly the damn thing himself. There had to be some way to get the funds transferred, even out here, and he'd flown all types of light aircraft in the past. But even as the idea was churning over in his mind, another violent streak of lightning knifed through the clouds and struck the tall trees on the opposite bank just a quarter of a mile downriver with terrible force. He gritted his teeth. It seemed there was little choice but to sit it out.

The storm kept on. Ben was pacing the boardwalk when a young guy in worn Levi's and a ZZ Top T-shirt appeared by the huts, apparently unaware of the torrential rain, and came over with a broad grin and an easy swagger to introduce himself in English as Pepe. Despite his youth, Pepe happened to be the proud owner-operator of what he claimed was the fastest boat in the region – and for the right price was only too happy to take them upriver to San Tomás, storm or no storm. This was nothing, he boasted with a dismissive wave at the lashing downpour. If they didn't get hit by lightning they'd be in San Tomás in four or five hours, give or take.

Ben agreed. The deal quickly settled, Pepe ran off to bring his boat round to the boarding point.

'Are you sure about this?' Nico asked. 'I've seen some of these river boats.'

'It's better than wasting time around here,' Ben replied. But when Pepe's vessel came into view a few moments later, he almost opted to wait for the aeroplane instead. The fifty-foot wooden river boat might have been ferrying passengers up and down the Amazonas waterways since the time of the Conquistadors. Its long, flat-bottomed hull was so patched with repairs that little of the original planking remained, and sat so low in the water that the rain streaming through the holes in the makeshift canvas roof seemed quite capable of sinking it entirely before they'd gone a mile. But Pepe's flashing grin as he stood at the helm in the tiny wheelhouse radiated nothing but supreme confidence and he gesticulated at them to board. Ben cursed to himself, grabbed his bag and rucksack and walked out into the deluge.

The storm was still raging violently as the boat station vanished from view round the first bend in the river, and continued unabated for nearly two hours afterwards. By the time the clouds eventually parted and sunlight dappled the choppy waters, it was far too late to turn back.

For most of those long, hot hours they saw little but unbroken jungle. The air was stifling and thick with insects, a situation that was relieved only when the heavens opened for another downpour. At some points the winding river broadened to a vast lake; elsewhere the looming greenery either side of them blotted out the sky and the mud banks constricted their passage so tightly that the boat's hull scraped its sides to get through.

Over the constant chatter and screech of birds and monkeys, the hypnotic burble of the engine, the soft rush of water along the hull, came the sound of Pepe's voice. He talked incessantly in the same cheerful tone as he steered the boat, apparently delighting in regaling his clients with tales of the dangers of the river. He didn't much seem to care whether anyone was listening to him or not. He was a quarter Quechua Indian from his mother's side and had been navigating these waters since the age of eleven. This had been his grandfather's boat, then his father's, until the mean old bastard had fallen overboard eight years ago and been eaten up by a caiman.

The caiman story had Nico glancing nervously at the river banks, where clusters of the reptiles eyed them lazily from the mud, occasionally slipping into the water at their approach and disappearing into the murky depths, or floating like logs with just their eyes and scaly backs above the surface.

Encouraged, Pepe laughed and pressed on with an obviously favourite anecdote of a Dutch missionary he'd once ferried down this stretch of river, who heedless of all warnings had fallen prey to the dreaded willy fish while taking a piss in waist-deep water.

'The willy fish?' Nico asked with a frown. Pepe explained how the tiny fish, a kind of eel called a *candirú* that was invisible underwater, liked to take advantage of careless urinators by swimming counter-current up their urethra and hooking itself inside with its sharp spines so that it could feast, vampire-like, on their blood.

When this fate had befallen the Dutchman they'd been so far upriver from civilization, let alone a doctor, that the only way to prevent fatal infection, shock or a burst bladder was for three fellow passengers to hold the screaming victim down on the deck with his trousers and underpants round his ankles while Pepe himself hacked off the blocked organ with a machete. Pepe chuckled at the memory, and pointed at the deep score-mark the machete's blade had left on the deck planking.

'Holy Mother,' Nico muttered, gazing aghast at the river and all the unseen horrors lurking under its surface.

In the middle of the unlikely tale, Ben had settled into a hammock at the stern and closed his eyes, trying to let the gentle motion of the boat relax his aching, tense muscles. He drifted for a while. When he opened his eyes some time later, Pepe had finally gone silent at the wheel. The river had narrowed again. Foliage was hanging low over the water and almost brushing the wheelhouse as it passed underneath. Suddenly feeling he was being watched, Ben looked up from under the canvas and saw a long-tailed monkey with startlingly thoughtful amber eyes and the face of an old man studying him from a branch.

Recovered now from Pepe's stories, Nico found a battered old guitar in the back of the boat and sat down with it, creaked its tuning pegs for a few moments and began singing quietly to himself in Spanish as he picked out some chords. It was a sad song about lost love. Ben listened to him for a while, surprised by the softness of Nico's voice and the sensitivity of his playing; then his mind began to wander again, lulled by the monotone of the engine and the whisper of the river.

His thoughts lapsed back to a time in France – it seemed like so long ago now – when he and Brooke had been alone in his room on a stormy spring evening at Le Val, just them and a crackling fire and a plate of homemade chocolate cake. It had been just before their relationship had begun; a time when he'd been falling in love with her without even realising it.

'You must eat some of this,' she'd said, holding a forkful of cake to his lips. 'It's a secret family recipe. People round here have gone to war for it. To have it offered to you and not eat it is a sacrilege. An insult to the gods.'

'Okay, you persuaded me,' he'd said. 'It wouldn't do to offend the gods.'

'Definitely not,' she'd murmured, feeding the piece of cake into his open mouth.

'You're right,' he'd said with his mouth full. 'It is pretty damn good.'

'Have another bit,' she'd said. 'It's the ultimate in comfort eating.'

'In that case, maybe just another bit.'

'Let's just chocolate ourselves to death,' she'd said. 'Right here, right now.'

He'd thrown up his hands in a gesture of resignation. 'Fuck it. Why not?'

After eating the rest of the cake they'd sat watching the fire, sharing that comfortable silence that only people who are very close can. Noticing a little fleck of cream at the corner of her mouth, he'd tenderly wiped it away with his fingertip, then carried it back to his own mouth and licked his finger.

He could still taste it, both the cream and the moment. And he could still feel her presence, smell her subtle perfume and the fresh apple scent of shampoo when her hair brushed near his face. It had always made him think of sunshine and summer meadows; pleasant things that seemed to belong in some inaccessible parallel world . . .

Ben's daydream ended abruptly as another rolling peal of thunder crashed above the trees. Pepe grinned back at them from the wheelhouse, as if nothing could make his day more than a violent storm and the imminent prospect of the boat taking a direct lightning hit or being crushed and driven to the bottom of the river by a stricken tree. 'Be in San Tomás in 'bout another thirty minutes, gentlemen,' he called out.

The next thirty or so minutes managed to pass without the boat being destroyed or sunk. Rounding a corner at a point where the river had broadened to its widest point since setting off from the Potro boat station, the wooden quays and jetties and buildings beyond them came into view. 'Looks like this is our stop,' Nico said, standing up.

Pepe expertly steered the boat up to the dock and bumped it gently against its mooring point. 'How are you fixed for work the next few days?' Ben asked him, and Pepe shrugged with a grin as he tethered up the boat. 'You want me to stick around, chief? Anything's possible. How long?'

'I can't say.' Ben pressed an extra few notes into Pepe's hand. 'We good for a while?'

'We good. You doing the tourist thing, huh?'

'Something like that,' Ben replied, grabbing his things and jumping up onto the fragile-looking jetty.

After so long on the boat it felt strange to be walking on solid ground again. Ben and Nico shouldered their heavy packs and walked from the quay into the village of San Tomás. In such heat and humidity even the slightest exertion brought on a full body sweat. Insects filled the air. The streets were made of hard-packed clay that was russety red, almost orange in colour. The thick greenery seemed to encroach on the edges of the village faster than it could be chopped back, as if the jungle had a mind of its own and wanted to claim the land back from the humans.

They walked on. Nearly every building stood off the ground on thick wooden stilts to protect it when the river was at full flood. Many of the houses looked dangerously makeshift, with walls that looked as though they could blow down in the next storm and roofs made of corrugated iron or reed thatch. There were only a few battered, dusty vehicles in the street. People here still used mules for transport and haulage, those who could afford them. Most inhabitants of San Tomás didn't exactly seem affluent, judging by the number of them sitting around morosely on steps and porches as Ben and Nico walked by. Hardly anyone even glanced at them.

A little way further down the street, Nico pointed out a rusty-roofed building with a lopsided sign hanging over the door. 'That's the bar where I met Roberto, right there. You want to grab some food and a beer?'

Roberto wasn't there, and nor was anyone else except for the barman, a big guy in a loose shirt damp with sweat. Nothing moved except for the clattering fans and the flies that buzzed and crawled everywhere. It was almost as unbearably hot in there as it was outside, but by some miracle the beer was ice-cold. They sat at a table by the window to share a large platter of fried beans and rice, gazing through the dusty glass at the still street as they ate. After three chilled beers apiece they could feel the sweat drying on them. They spoke in monosyllables. Ben could sense that the Colombian was thinking the same thing as him. They were close now, walking into extreme danger from which they both knew they might not return.

'Is there anything more you can tell me about Serrato's men?' Ben asked Nico when they'd finished eating, casting a glance at the barman in case the guy might be inclined to listen in. He was more interested in stamping on some bug that was scuttling about behind the bar.

'Like what?'

'Like anything that can give us an edge. Where does he recruit them from, what's their level of training, how loyal are they to him?'

Nico shrugged. 'Back in the day he was always surrounded by the same gang of hardline motherfuckers that he kept real close. Jaime de Soto was one of them, until Laura Garcia put a twelve-gauge Brenneke slug in his ass. He wasn't the worst, though. The worst were Piero Vertíz and Luis Bracca. Both Colombian ex-military. Vertíz is a trained sniper, thousand-yard-plus tack driver. Bracca loves knives, likes to cut people up with a bone-handled Bowie. You remember I told you about the poor bitch they sliced like a kebab? That was his work. He's an animal.'

'It was Bracca who chopped Forsyte's hands off.'

'He'd chop off his own left hand for Serrato. Fucking idolises him. You can bet Bracca's right there with him now, watching over him like a goddamn pit bull. Oh, and the fucker's a cannibal too. At least that's what they said about him back in Bogotá; that he kept human heads in his freezer, ate their brains out with a spoon like ice-cream.'

'You believed that?'

'I'd believe most anything I heard about Luis Bracca. Let me tell you, you go up against either him or Vertíz on his own, you might stand a chance – if you're good, and I mean very, very good. Go up against both at once, forget it. You're a dead man. Which basically means we're dead men.' Nico swilled the dregs of his beer around inside the bottle. 'At least we get a last drink, huh? More than some guys get. We going in there tonight?' he asked after a beat.

Ben nodded.

'So what's the plan – you just gonna walk in there, kill everyone and get your girl back?'

'Something like that.'

'It's what I figured.'

'Does the idea make you nervous?' Ben asked with a thin smile. 'I told you, you don't have to do this.'

'Don't insult me, man. You're not the only one with a reason to be here.'

'I haven't forgotten,' Ben said.

'There's one thing you *are* forgetting, amigo. We ain't armed.' Nico pointed at the handle of the parang that was sticking out of Ben's rucksack. 'Unless you were planning on taking a knife to a gunfight.'

'That's where the crazy old hunter who lives in the forest comes in,' Ben said.

Chapter Forty-Four

Twilight was falling as Ben and Nico made the long trek north from the river to find the hunter's place. Nico led the way. The terrain climbed steadily above the river plateau until the vegetation began to thin out a little and they could see the huge red orb of the sun sinking over the endless tree line. It would be dark soon, and Ben was beginning to wonder where Nico was leading him. He couldn't see any sign of human habitation anywhere, not even the faintest of tracks. 'You're sure about this place?' he asked.

'Sure,' Nico replied over his shoulder. 'Came this way last time.'

They trekked on a while and the shadows around them lengthened. The Colombian suddenly turned with a finger to his lips and whispered, 'Shhh. Real careful. Remember, he is one unhinged kind of dude.' Ben peered through the dark forest in the direction Nico was pointing, and could make out the shape of a wooden cabin nestling among the foliage.

But as they got closer, it looked as though the cabin and the little cluster of plank-built sheds around it were so badly run down that nobody could possibly live there. The place was all in darkness. Nico halted and shook his head, perplexed. 'Damn it, the place looked bad before, but not this bad. Maybe he don't live here any more. Hell, maybe the old fucker died. He was real ancient.'

'I'm not dead, asshole,' said a hoarse voice behind them.

They turned to see an Indian stepping out from the bushes. He was festooned with cartridge belts crisscrossed round his shoulders and a necklace of claws hung from his wrinkly neck. His hair was long and pure white, his skin like brown leather. He was scowling at them furiously from behind the double muzzles of a sawn-off shotgun.

'Shit,' Nico breathed. 'Don't move,' he muttered to Ben.

Ben hadn't been planning on moving, nor was he going to let his hand stray anywhere near the hilt of the parang that hung from his belt. Not many men could have sneaked up on him from behind like that, but the old hunter was as stealthy as a panther after a lifetime of creeping close to all manner of wild jungle quarry – and the mad glint in his eye made it clear that he was perfectly comfortable with the idea of gunning down these two intruders where they stood and leaving them for the jaguars.

'This is my land,' the hunter rasped in his heavily-accented English, stepping towards them through the undergrowth without snapping a twig. 'You walk on my land, I shoot you. That's my law.' With his gnarled right thumb he snicked back one hammer of the old shotgun, then the other.

'Hey, man, don't you remember me?' Nico said, raising his arms in the air.

The hunter squinted at him over the barrels, as if deliberating whether or not to blow him in two. Then a light of recognition appeared in his wrinkled old eyes, and he lowered the gun a fraction. 'You got more money for me, boy?'

'That depends on what else you have to sell,' Ben replied for Nico.

The promise of hard cash was enough to defuse the

situation fairly quickly. The hunter let down the hammers of his shotgun, slung it over his shoulder and jerked his chin with a grunt towards the cabin.

As he and Nico followed, Ben spied a road, little more than a dirt track, snaking away through the trees from the hunter's place. It wasn't difficult to imagine the crazy old man digging the track out himself with his bare hands. But what was most interesting about it were the fresh tyre marks in the dirt – as well as the tarpaulin-covered shape in the shadows of the corrugated iron lean-to where the tyre tracks led. Ben stepped over, discreetly lifted a corner of the tarp and made out a glimmer of rust-speckled chrome.

The old hunter paused to fire up a generator. Lights flickered on in the cabin's windows. He motioned to Ben and Nico to follow.

'Home sweet home,' Nico muttered under his breath as the old man ushered them through a living area filled with furniture he'd carved from forest trees, then into a scullery where skinned monkeys and unidentifiable hacked-up pieces of other animals hung from hooks. Something equally unrecognisable and smelling of glue was boiling up in a cast-iron pot on a stove. Finally he led them into an adjoining room filled with racks of weaponry.

'Enough to fight a goddamn war,' Nico said, eyeing the rows of rifles.

'World War Two, maybe,' Ben replied. Most of the guns looked as if they'd done hard service at Stalingrad. Rattly actions and shot-out bores would be the order of the day. Ben didn't much relish the idea of a weapon that couldn't hit a house-sized target at fifty metres. 'Haven't you got anything a little newer?' he asked the hunter in Spanish.

The old man looked taken aback for a moment that the tall

blond-haired gringo could speak his language, but he shrugged, grunted and opened up a steel locker. Inside stood a row of modern hunting rifles of various types and calibres.

'What about this one?' Ben said, and picked up a scoped bolt-action. It was a Remington Model 700 chambered in .300 Winchester Magnum – delivering up to 4000 foot pounds of muzzle energy and enough knockdown power to kill anything that walked the American continent. The rifle looked new. He drew open the bolt to see clean well-oiled steel, flipped open the protective lids over the scope lenses and peered through, aiming at the furthest spot on the wall. The scope reticle was the illuminated type with a glowing red inner circle and centre dot, offering the shooter that extra edge in limited light conditions. The illumination was strong and clear, showing that there were still a good few hours of battery life left.

That was all Ben needed. The rifle was never going to be more than an initial entry weapon, though as a medium-to-long-distance means of striking at the enemy with the surprise and aggression that they least expected in the dead of the night, it was a pretty good option. The scope wasn't exactly military-grade night-vision optics, but it was far more than he might have dreamed of stumbling across out here in the middle of the Amazon jungle. Once he'd established his method of entry into the compound and neutralised as many targets as it took to get him inside the perimeter, he could improvise, if necessary ditching the rifle in exchange for something more appropriate to the situation.

'I'll take this,' he said.

'No, no,' the hunter protested. That one was his main personal hunting rifle, and it wasn't for sale. Definitely, absolutely not. It wasn't until Ben took out his wallet and started thumbing through notes that he relented and seemed to decide that maybe it was for sale after all, as long as Ben agreed to buy every last round of ammunition he had for it.

'And this one for my friend here,' Ben said, picking out a Savage in .223 calibre. 'You have cartridges for this?'

'I ain't gonna shoot a rifle any more,' Nico insisted with a sour look. 'Not after what happened last time.'

Ben looked at him. 'I don't seem to recall you holding back on emptying a magazine or two at me, just a couple of days ago.'

'That was different,' Nico replied. To the hunter he said, 'You got any kind of handgun? I'd be happier with a handgun.'

The hunter hesitated, then glanced again at Ben's wallet and threw open another cabinet. 'Holy shit, this old timer's got more guns and ammo than Cabela's,' Nico muttered, looking down at an assortment of pistols and hundreds of boxed cartridges. 'Let me see that Colt Python there. Okay,' he said, inspecting the heavy revolver. 'I'm happy.'

'You're going to take a six-shooter into a fight with Serrato's whole army?' Ben asked, staring.

'Way I see it, if I can't get up close and personal enough to use this on him I'm dead anyway,' Nico said.

'Just don't expect me to look out for you all the time.'

'Yeah, and don't cry to me when you have to tote that goddamn shoulder cannon miles through the jungle.'

'As long as I don't have to lug your Colombian arse along behind me, I'll manage fine.' Ben turned to the old hunter, who had been following their exchange with growing confusion. 'Two hundred for the rifle and another hundred for the pistol, ammo included,' he said in Spanish.

'Get the fuck out of here,' the hunter rasped indignantly. 'Four-fifty for the two, plus another fifty for the ammo.'

'Four hundred's nearly all I have,' Ben said, showing him the open wallet. 'It's yours if you throw in the loan of that truck you have out there. That's if it still has an engine in it.'

A loan for how long, the hunter wanted to know. Ben assured him it wouldn't be for more than a couple of days.

'If it don't get all shot to pieces,' Nico muttered.

'I'm not the one who shoots cars to pieces,' Ben said. 'Deal?' he asked the hunter, switching back to Spanish.

It was. The old Indian grabbed his wad of money and counted it suspiciously while Ben and Nico carried their weaponry outside, yanked the tarpaulin off the faded red late seventies Ford F-150 pickup under the lean-to and saw about getting it started. The engine fired up second time with a throaty roar and a cloud of smoke.

'That's good enough.' Ben flicked a switch on the dash and the row of four grille-mounted lamps blazed into life. He let the motor run while he jammed the bags behind the seats, then loaded up his rifle from the munitions supply the hunter had sold him and stowed the weapon in the rack in the back of the cab. 'I'll drive,' he said to Nico. 'You navigate.'

Nico clambered up into the passenger's side with a look of grim determination. 'You ready to go?' Ben said, getting in behind the wheel. He gunned the engine.

'I've been ready to go for seven years,' Nico said.

Chapter Forty-Five

It was night now. The temperature had fallen dramatically. The dark jungle loomed over them and cast menacing shadows everywhere as they jolted and lurched their way through a green tunnel lit by the Ford's powerful grille-mounted lamps. Any obstacle the truck couldn't go roaring over on its oversized wheels and jacked-up suspension, it smashed through like a bulldozer.

The hunter's track was even harder going than it had seemed at the outset. Just as Ben was becoming certain that the twisting, ridiculously uneven path was going to lead nowhere, it widened out and a junction with another road appeared up ahead. The new road was still rough as hell and impossible to navigate at more than thirty miles a hour, but after the endurance test of the track it seemed like a motorway. Nico said he recognised it from when he'd driven around the area in his Winnebago. Now that he'd regained his bearings he gave sporadic directions as Ben drove.

An hour passed. It was rare to meet another motor vehicle. The landscape was variable, sometimes thick forest on all sides, sometimes open country and rocky hills, now and then a lonely farm or a ruin passing by in the night. As they rounded a sweeping bend Ben noticed Nico gazing across towards the high ground on the right. From the Colombian's heavy silence afterwards, Ben understood that he'd been looking at the spot where he'd fired the bullet that had killed Alicia Serrato.

'You know, I never cried for them,' Nico said after a while. 'For Daniela and Carlos. My children. Not a tear.' He gave a bitter chuckle. 'Never told nobody that before.'

Ben didn't reply. There was no reply he could make.

A little while later he heard the soft clicking noises as Nico toyed with his revolver, slipping slender .357 cartridges into the chambers, spinning the cylinder, ejecting them, beginning the process again. Ben had seen a thousand men suffer the same kind of nerves as they faced going into action. He'd suffered them himself enough times. Tonight, though, he felt nothing more than a numb sense of purpose. All that existed was the task ahead, whatever its outcome might be.

Without a word, he held out the crumpled pack containing the last three of his Gauloises. Nico drew one out; he took another, and they smoked in silence, the tips of the cigarettes glowing orange in the darkness of the cab. Ben reached into his pocket for his whisky flask and shook it. There was a little left. He offered it to Nico. Nico shook his head. Ben put the whisky away untouched and drove on.

'Pull into that track there,' Nico said presently, pointing to the left at a gap in the trees. Ben turned the truck and they went jolting and bouncing over rough ground for a couple of miles. 'Okay, pull up,' Nico said. 'This is as close as it's safe to drive. We walk from here. Compound's due west through the jungle.'

'How far?'

'An hour, maybe longer.'

Ben killed the engine and the lights. They climbed down from the truck and grabbed their gear. In the faint moonlight shining through the trees they shrugged on their packs, checked their weapons one more time, turned on their torches and then set off with Nico showing the way.

The jungle came alive at night in all its incredible diversity. The constant chirping and whistling of insects all around them was so loud that it drowned out the soft crunch of their boots on the mossy forest floor. As they walked, Ben felt a sudden, startling impact against his back and whirled round, instinctively raising his rifle halfway up to his shoulder with his hand reaching for the bolt – then saw that what had hit him was a giant flying insect, some kind of winged beetle not much smaller than a bird. He watched it gyrate off in the beam of his torch, then walked on.

The march continued for an hour, as Nico had said. The closer they got to their target the more Ben could see the Colombian's gait stiffening as the tension spread through his body. Ben could feel it too. They both glanced constantly left and right and strained their ears over the din of the insects for any suspicious snap of a twig or rustle of a branch that could signal one of Serrato's patrols approaching.

Then Nico halted and raised a hand to signal before turning off his torch. Ben killed his own. For a few moments they stood immobile, waiting for their eyes to get used to the dark. A few steps onwards, they parted the branches and saw the lights of the compound in the distance. Ben felt his heart heave and uttered an inward prayer that it was all true and that Brooke was here, alive, almost within his reach. If that was so, then all that stood between them now were a cruel, sadistic, power-crazed former drug lord, his murderous personal guard and maybe twenty or thirty heavily-armed troops-for-hire.

And if it wasn't so . . .

If his darkest fears were proved right . . .

Somebody was going to pay a very dear price.

They would anyway.

The perimeter wall stood a hundred metres distant across a stretch of close-cropped stubble. The span of buildings beyond shone creamy-white in the lights from its windows and the strong floodlamps that stood on masts around its edges. To the left, some three hundred metres from where Ben and Nico were hiding in the trees, they could make out the line of the single road that led up to the gates.

They dumped their packs on the ground. Ben unzipped the compartment of his rucksack containing the rifle ammo, and loaded as many rounds as he could comfortably carry into his pockets. While Nico was doing the same for himself, Ben reached for the binoculars, scanned the visible section of road and lingered carefully for a few moments on the compound entrance. 'You said there were how many guards on the gate?' he asked Nico.

'Enough to stop the US Marines from getting through,' Nico muttered. He was breathing heavily as the adrenaline accumulated in his system.

Ben passed him the binocs without saying anything more. Nico put them up to his eyes, and a moment later snatched them away and stared at Ben in bewilderment. 'There's nobody manning the fucking gates,' he said in a hoarse whisper. 'They're just hanging wide open.'

Ben took the binocs back from him, ran his gaze past the top of the perimeter wall and slowly scanned the breadth of the buildings from left to right.

'Well?' Nico whispered tensely.

Ben said nothing. The magnified image showed that the main building was in fact a fine-looking house, large and sprawling on several floors, modern in design with hacienda-style arches and balconies. The rest of the buildings clustered around it were more basic and workmanlike, but painted

311

the same pale colour, which gave the whole the appearance of a little Mediterranean village which had sprung up incongruously in the middle of the endless jungle. Ben was looking for movement in the lit-up windows, but saw none. Then he paused, backtracked a little way and looked again at what he'd just noticed on the upper floor of the main house.

The fact that the three windows were grilled over with thick iron bars bolted to the outside wall would have been enough to get his attention. He'd seen enough remote kidnappers' strongholds in his day to know what a well-appointed captivity room looked like.

But what made his eyes narrow to slits and his breathing stop for a long moment were the black soot marks all over the walls where thick billows of smoke had recently been pouring from the barred windows, as well as two other windows either side and two more above.

There had been a fire inside the house. A serious, major fire – and from what Ben could tell, at its heart had been the room with the barred windows. Even after the flames were extinguished, the gutted rooms would have gone on smoking for a long time. He could see no smoke at all coming from the windows. Which meant the fire had happened many hours ago.

Still not breathing, Ben darted the binoculars' field of vision downwards to where he could make out part of the courtyard between the buildings. He could still see no movement. There wasn't a sound except the chirruping of the insects.

The house and surrounding compound appeared completely deserted.

'Something's wrong here,' he murmured to Nico. 'Something's happened.'

Chapter Forty-Six

No alarm was raised as Ben and Nico crossed the open ground to the compound gates. No guards appeared to challenge them. Up close, they could see that the tall iron gates were buckled and bent, as though they'd been rammed violently open from the inside. There was nothing to stop anyone walking straight in.

Ben worked the bolt on his rifle, but even as he chambered the round he knew he wouldn't be needing it. Not here, not now.

'It's weird,' Nico muttered. 'Last time I was here, this place crawled like a fucking rats' lair. Where'd they all go?'

Ben said nothing. He would almost rather have been shot at. Every step nearer the cluster of buildings deepened his conviction that something terrible had happened here: something that his instincts told him was connected with Brooke.

The acrid stink of the burned-out section of the house wafted across the compound on the warm breeze. He knelt, examining the vehicle tracks on the hard-packed earth. There were dozens of them, made by knobbly all-terrain tyres and dug in hard, leaving furrows, as though one four-wheel drive after another after another had gone speeding out of the gates in such a tearing hurry that nobody had bothered closing the place up behind them, or even leaving anyone to guard it. The tyre tracks all led out of a large square building with doors like those of an aircraft hangar. The doors gaped open. Ben shone his light inside. There wasn't a vehicle in sight. He tried to imagine the kind of emergency situation that would make a high-security fortress like this empty itself so completely. Possibilities filled his head. None of them was reassuring.

Through an archway and along a short path flanked by flowerbeds, and they were at the grand entrance of the main house. It too was hanging open, as unguarded as the front gates. Ben tensed, darting his gaze all around him. Was he walking straight into a trap here? Had Serrato somehow been alerted that they were coming?

But if it was a trap, it was taking a long time to spring. Nico muttered something in Spanish as they walked into the huge marble-floored entrance hall. Ornamental plants and colourful flowers spilled from decorative urns. Paintings adorned the walls. The hallway was surrounded by doors. Ben stepped across to one of them, his rifle ready, and pushed it open. He switched on the light and found himself staring into a large empty salon with a grand piano at the far end.

Across the hallway, Nico called softly, 'I think you need to see this, man.' Ben shut the salon door and stepped over to see what Nico wanted to show him. He was pointing inside another empty room, one that was decked out with wood panels and leather furniture.

'The picture,' Nico said.

Ben looked where he was pointing, and saw with a cold shiver the gilt-framed oil portrait of the woman he'd instantly have taken for Brooke if he hadn't known better by now.

'Alicia,' he murmured.

'I told you, man. She's like a sick fantasy for him.'

And that sick fantasy was the only thing keeping Brooke

314

Marcel alive. But where was she? Ben raced through the ground floor, flinging open door after door, flipping lights on in room after room with his finger on the trigger.

Nothing. Between them they combed methodically through the house as far as the sweeping crimson-carpeted staircase. Nico motioned towards it with a questioning look. Ben nodded. The two of them started making their way upwards, barely breathing, listening hard for any tiny sound and hearing nothing. There seemed to be no sign of life – but Ben would open every door in the whole damn place before he'd be satisfied there was nothing here to find. 'Split up,' he whispered to Nico. 'Yell if you find anything.'

'I find anything, you'll hear more than yells,' Nico said, brandishing the revolver.

'Be careful. Meet you back here in five minutes.'

Alone, Ben followed his nose through the opulent passageways towards the source of the burnt stink, so much stronger up here. Within minutes, he'd found it.

The suite of rooms had clearly been a luxurious one before the fire had ravaged it and turned it into a blackened shell. It had taken several fire extinguishers, their empty canisters discarded about the floor, to quell the blaze. The worst of it seemed to have been concentrated in the bedroom, where he found the charred remains of a four-poster bed. The curtains had been burned away from the open windows. The steel bars bolted to the outside were covered with soot.

Had Brooke been here? Ben's intuition told him so. But his emotions were so badly frayed that he didn't know if he could trust it. He searched through both rooms for some kind of trace of her. Lying on what was left of the bedroom rug was a scorched piece of clothing of some kind. He picked it up. It wasn't anything he recognised as Brooke's. It was the remains of a silky negligee or nightdress, most of the thin material blackened and burned away. Whose had it been? Alicia Serrato had been dead for some time. Had it been intended for some other woman? For Serrato's captive?

As he let the ruined garment slip from his fingers, Ben felt broken glass crunch under his boot. He knelt down, poked around in the ashes and picked up a sliver of glass. He wiped the soot away carefully with his finger. The piece of glass was printed 'HANEL', the C missing. He sniffed it and caught the faint whiff of perfume.

Ben tossed the piece of glass back into the ashes and stood up with death in his heart. He'd come so far, and Brooke was still lost to him. Time was slipping through his fingers like fine sand.

He hurried away from the burnt-out room and tracked back through the corridors in search of Nico. 'I'm in here,' the Colombian called through an open doorway. Ben walked in to find him standing at a broad leather-topped antique desk rifling agitatedly through a sprawl of papers and documents. Behind him was the open door of a high-security wall safe.

'What are you doing?'

'Guess who left here in too much of a hurry to lock up his safe?' Nico said, sifting roughly through more papers and tossing them on the floor. 'For me, this is like being in Satan's den, man.'

'We have to move. Brooke's not here.'

Nico seemed not to have heard him. 'Thought maybe I could figure out where the sonofabitch's gone. Instead I found this shit. You know what this is?' Nico snatched up a glossy transparent folder. Ben saw that inside it was an old manuscript of some kind, heavily ornamented in red and gold and calligraphed in ink, frayed by dampness around the edges but otherwise perfectly preserved.

'It's the land grant from the King of Spain,' Nico said. 'This is what it's all about, what the motherfucker's been working towards all this time. Look at this other stuff. It explains everything.'

Weariness had suddenly gripped hold of Ben's whole body. He flopped in a chair and let the rifle slip out of his fingers to the floor. He felt too weak and drained even to sink his head in his hands and cry for sheer frustration.

'See?' Nico was saying, holding up more papers. 'Old genealogical records, family trees, going back centuries. Serrato's been collecting this stuff for years. It's got the stamp of the National Historical Archives in Madrid, dated seven years ago. You go back to 1588, you see the surname appear for the first time. Serrato, the old Serrato, was a Spanish sympathiser who took care of this Lady Anne Pennick, the wife of the English spy dude, after he'd been executed and she'd run to Spain. Guess the English were still hunting for her, so she entered into this guy's protection and took his name. She was pregnant with her dead husband's son. The kid grew up with the name Serrato.'

'Serrato was the legitimate heir to the land,' Ben muttered, but his mind was far away.

'Right. He must have found out that the lost land grant was aboard the Armada ship that sank near Ireland. Been looking out for years hoping someone would find the wreck. Then along comes this guy Forsyte. Here's all the news clippings that Serrato was keeping. He'd been following the salvage operation right from the start, just waiting to get his hands on the land grant knowing that all he had to do to stake a claim was work on the right government contacts here in Peru. And all the correspondence between his lawyers and some scum-sucking politician called Vargas is right here in this file. But the best part's this.'

Nico snatched up a sheaf of printouts and held them out with a flourish. 'Oil test reports, dating back more than four years. This is why he wanted that land so bad. Half a million of acres of worthless jungle? I don't think so, man. More like half a million acres of the richest untapped oilfields in the whole Amazon lowlands. No wonder Serrato went to so much trouble getting hold of the land grant. It could make him a fucking billionaire ten times over. Nothing was gonna stop him.'

Oil, Ben thought. It did explain everything. Having already learned what lay underneath his ancestral land, Serrato must have been desperate to obtain from Roger Forsyte the only proof in the world that he was the heir to it. When Forsyte turned him down, believing he could score a better deal elsewhere by using the rediscovered documents to unmask a whole list of unsuspected English traitors from the time of the Spanish Armada, Serrato had then sent his people in to work on Simon Butler and find alternative ways of getting what he wanted.

'Brooke just got in the way,' Ben said out loud.

'And she just happened to be a dead ringer for Serrato's wife,' Nico replied. 'Wrong place, wrong time.' Suddenly he tensed again, half-turned towards the door and then looked sharply at Ben with a frown creasing his brow. 'You hear that?'

'I heard it,' Ben said. Suddenly alert and filled with energy again, he snatched up the rifle and pressed off the safety catch. Nico scooped the Colt Python from the desk. They both moved quickly for the doorway.

Out in the corridor, they heard it again. The distinct sound of voices, whispering furtively in Spanish. Ben and Nico spaced out with their weapons ready and their eyes glued to the corner up ahead from beyond which the voices were getting closer.

Five figures approaching. Ben saw them an instant before Nico did. As he stepped quickly round the corner and levelled the rifle into a close-range aim he could see that he hadn't run into a squad of Ramon Serrato's top goons.

Three men, two women. They must have heard the sound of intruders in the near-deserted house and, with all the guards gone, banded together to confront them. Two of the men were wearing white smocks, like chefs, both in their sixties and armed only with a kitchen knife between them. Tagging along behind them was a young kid of about seventeen, with dazed-looking eyes and the bemused grin of a simpleton. The younger of the two women was a tiny cowering thing who let out a shrill gasp when she saw the two intruders appear in the corridor ahead. The only one Ben might have been concerned about was the brute-featured woman in a maid's uniform. She had hands as meaty and rough as a longshoreman's, and in them was a small-bore shotgun that she had pointed from the hip.

The corridor was suddenly filled with cries and shouts. Ben and Nico yelled 'Drop the weapon!' simultaneously. The hatchet-faced woman might have toyed with the idea of letting blast with her shotgun, but only for an instant as she found herself peering down the muzzles of Ben's .300 Win Mag and Nico's Colt, both steadily and unflinchingly trained on the wide gap between her eyes.

She dropped the shotgun and stepped back from it, raising her hands. The cook with the knife did the same. Ben and Nico advanced, keeping their weapons trained on them. 'In there,' Ben said, motioning with the rifle barrel towards a doorway. For the first time he noticed that the brute-faced woman had a raised weal on her cheekbone that was turning purple, as if she'd recently been in a fight. With a surly look, she followed the rest of the servants through the door into an unused bedroom. Ben and Nico herded them up against the far wall. Ben bolted the door.

'We came here for Serrato,' Nico said in Spanish. 'You fuckers tell us where he is, you walk out of here alive. Or else—' He drew his finger across his throat and stuck his tongue out. It had a remarkable effect. The two cooks exchanged frightened glances. The waiflike servant girl was ready to collapse in a faint. Only the simple-minded young guy, who was grinning as though this were all some kind of game, and the brute-featured woman, who was scowling with hatred at Ben and Nico, didn't look scared.

Ben returned the woman's gaze. Something about her was oddly familiar, but he couldn't place it. It wasn't her face – he'd have remembered exactly where he'd seen a face like that before. It was something else; a strange kind of *déjà vu.*

'Somebody better start talking pretty soon,' Nico warned them, thumbing back the hammer of his Colt. The simple-minded kid was suddenly beginning to understand the situation and his lip had started to quiver.

That was when Ben realised with a shock what it was that was familiar about the woman. It wasn't her. It was what she was wearing. Round her thick neck was a little gold chain, simple and plain and yet distinctive enough to him that he'd have recognised it anywhere, even on this ugly brute. It was the same little neck chain that Brooke had chosen in the jeweller's shop in Paris – the one she always wore.

So Brooke *had* been here after all.

Feeling suddenly weak at the knees he lowered the rifle and reached out with his left hand to grab hold of the neck chain. 'Where did you get this?' The woman protested, tried to wriggle away and snatch the chain out of his fingers.

'That doesn't belong to you,' he said. 'You stole it, didn't you? You took it from the woman who was here. Give it to me.'

The woman hesitated, then reluctantly took off the chain and thrust it into Ben's hand. 'Where is she?' he demanded.

One of the cooks finally found his tongue. '*Desaparecido,*' he said. Gone. *El jefe,* the boss, had gone too. It had been after the fire.

Ben reached into his pocket, flipped open his wallet and took out the photo of Brooke. 'Is this her?' he asked.

The two cooks and the young servant girl all nodded in unison. '*Si, si,*' the simple-minded kid blurted out in his slurred voice. '*La Señora Alicia!*' The young servant woman shook her head wistfully at the mention of the name. '*No, Guillermo, la Señora Alicia está muerta!*'

Under pressure, the servants explained between them that the fire had started the night before last. The rumour was that the woman had stolen a truck and made her escape while the men were putting it out. Not long afterwards, the boss had gone after her, taking everyone with him except a handful of poor staff. How could they cope on their own? The boss had been gone nearly two whole days. What would happen to them if he never returned?

Ben slipped Brooke's photo back in his wallet with a shaking hand. Now he knew for sure. He'd found her, but he'd been too late. Forty-eight hours too late.

Instantly he started blaming himself. Thinking of how he'd wasted time over Cabeza in Montesilo, how he'd need lessly delayed in Chachapoyas, how he could have saved time by waiting for the storm to end and taking the floatplane from the Potro boat station.

'Where did she go?' Nico asked the servants. 'Where'd your boss go after her?'

321

Shrugs, blank expressions. 'Out there,' said one of the cooks, waving at the dark window.

Nico looked at Ben. 'How in hell could she have escaped? These guys are more tooled up than the Peruvian army.'

'I found a smashed perfume bottle in the room where they were keeping her. That stuff's highly flammable.'

'You mean she set the place alight *herself*?'

'That would be just like her.'

'Holy shit.' Nico shook his head. 'Hate to say it, man, but if she's out there all alone in that jungle, she doesn't stand a chance.'

'She wouldn't have escaped without some kind of plan in mind,' Ben said, thinking hard.

'Need to be one hell of a smart plan if she wants to get away from Ramon Serrato and his whole hunting party. It's been forty-eight hours. If he finds her, man, you know what he's gonna do. She's worse than dead.'

Ben felt his resolve tighten like a fist. 'Not if I find her first,' he said.

Chapter Forty-Seven

Forty-eight hours earlier

'Put on,' Hatchet Face said again, holding up the negligee. 'Señor Serrato not wait long. He get *mucho enfadado*.' She shook her head in warning.

Brooke stared at the flimsy garment and at the suspenders and stockings the woman had brought her to wear. She closed her eyes. Heaved a deep, shaky sigh. *This is it*, she thought. *This is the moment.*

'All right,' she said. 'I'll put them on.'

Hatchet Face seemed strangely contented as she returned into the living area to wait as Brooke changed. Brooke shut the bedroom door. Took a couple more deep breaths and then moved quickly. She slipped a CD into the stereo system and turned the volume up high. To the strains of Brahms she tore the drapes of mosquito netting from the bed and grabbed the training shoes from underneath, as well as the bag containing the comfortable clothes Consuela had provided for her. She emptied out the clothing, stripped off her white cotton dress and pulled on the tracksuit bottoms and T-shirt, then quickly laced up the shoes.

Hatchet Face rapped on the door. 'You hurry,' came her stern voice from outside.

'Don't come in,' Brooke yelled. 'I'll be there in a minute, okay?'

She ran into the bathroom. Snatched two towels from the rail and dampened one of them with water. She stuffed the dry one into the clothes bag, along with a tub of talcum powder, the mineral water bottle that she'd refilled from the tap and the packet of cold meats left over from dinner that she'd hidden in the shower cubicle. She grabbed a tall can of hairspray and jammed it into her pocket, then picked up all the perfume bottles and carried them into the bedroom with the damp towel over her shoulder.

Brooke had been aware from the start that if she wanted to escape from this place she wouldn't get very far without money, and she didn't have a penny. But Serrato's jewels were worth countless thousands. If she could trade them for a ride or a night's shelter, even a phone call to the outside world for help, that'd be good enough for her. Chucking all of the perfume bottles on the bed she grabbed the jewellery from the bedside table. She slipped the bracelet over her wrist and put on the heavy necklace underneath her T-shirt.

She was as ready as she'd ever be. She was breathing hard with tension. What would Ben have said in a moment like this?

'Fuck it,' she muttered. Then she picked up one of the Chanel bottles and dashed it as hard as she could against the solid wooden bedpost. It shattered, broken glass and perfume showering everywhere. She grabbed another, and another, smashing them into pieces.

Suddenly the whole room was filled with the choking reek of perfume. The carpet was saturated with the stuff. Any second now, Hatchet Face would be sure to smell it and come storming in to see what was happening. Seconds counted.

Brooke retrieved the stolen cigarette lighter from its hiding place under the mattress. She snatched up the negligee. 'Here's what I think of your pervy outfit, Ramon,' she said as she offered the flame up to the material. It caught light instantly. She threw the burning garment down onto the perfume-saturated carpet.

The fire leaped up instantly and aggressively with a breathy *whumph*. Suddenly everything was ablaze – the floor, the bedclothes, the four-poster's drapes, its canopy. Even sooner than Brooke had expected there was a wall of fire licking its way hungrily to the ceiling and spreading outwards to engulf the whole room. Smoke alarms began to screech.

Brooke leaped back from the fierce heat, grabbed the bulging clothes bag and sprinted for the bathroom door shouting '*Fuego! Fuego!*'

The door flew open. Hatchet Face gaped in bewildered horror at the flames and opened her mouth to yell something. Before she could get the words out, Brooke had thrown all her strength and momentum into a punch that sent the woman crashing down on her back. Hatchet Face looked pretty strong and tough, and Brooke had no desire to get into a blow-for-blow fight with her, not even after the few lessons in unarmed combat she'd had with Jeff Dekker at Le Val. A swift kick to the head knocked her out cold.

'Bitch,' Brooke muttered, then ran into the living area.

Within instants there were two, three, four guards storming into the room. By then, Brooke had already dived out of sight and was hiding behind the sofa nearest the door, clamping her damp towel over her nose and mouth as the smoke began to gather thickly. Alarms were going off all down the corridor now. The men balked at the intensity of the spreading inferno. One of them was carrying a tall extinguisher and aimed the nozzle at the flames. He had to retreat quickly as a surge in the blaze threatened to swallow him.

In the panic of the moment nobody seemed to have thought about Brooke or spotted where she was crouching. She knew she couldn't stay there long. The heat from the blaze was becoming unbearable. Worse, any second now Serrato would come running down here in person. She had no intention of being around when he turned up.

The men were too busy spraying extinguishers at the flames to notice her slip out of the burning room. She held her breath as she darted away down the corridor, turning off every light switch she came to in the hope that semi-darkness could cover her escape. She ducked into a room as several guards came sprinting by, one of them yelling into a radio over the screech of the fire alarms.

Then it was a clear run to the stairs. Nobody had seen her. The layout of the house was so familiar now that she knew almost exactly how many paces it was to the entrance – and that number was diminishing fast as she ran. *Keep moving. Keep moving. You're going to make it.*

Fresh, cool air on her face as she bolted through the main doorway, under the arch and out into the cream-coloured portico that ran alongside the house. Free!

But she still had a long way to go. She kept to the shadows. Running men passed her, too intent on the emergency to look around them. She moved away from the house, leaving behind the din of alarms and yelling voices. The stink of burning was strong in the air. Smoke was pouring from her barred windows, as well as from the windows above and either side – but unless it was so out of control that it destroyed the whole building, the extinguishers would soon tame it. She couldn't count on her diversion working for long.

Running low, she passed the walled yard where Consuela

and her daughter had been executed. Up ahead was the high side of the vehicle hangar. It seemed unattended as she approached – then suddenly a guard stepped out of nowhere and confronted her with a look of surprise that quickly turned to one of suspicion.

'You wouldn't turn me in, would you?' Brooke said to him with a coy smile. 'Look what you'll get if you keep your mouth shut.' She tugged the precious necklace out from the collar of her T-shirt and held it out for him to see. He stared at it, mesmerised, a glow of idiot greed dawning across his face.

'On second thoughts, you're not worth it,' she said. She drew the can of hairspray from her pocket and gave him a good sustained burst of it right in the eyes.

He screamed and clapped his hands over his face, dropping his rifle. Brooke rammed a knee into his groin, grabbed him by the ears as he doubled over and wrenched him headfirst into the side wall of the hangar. She dragged his unconscious bulk into the shadows and picked up his fallen rifle. It didn't look much different from the semi-automatic weapon she'd become familiar with on the firing range at Le Val. She racked the bolt and ran towards the rows of vehicles.

Guile wasn't going to get her through those front gates, but something robust and heavy moving at speed might do the trick. She jumped up into the cab of the nearest four-wheel drive truck. The keys were in the ignition. She dumped the rifle on the passenger seat, fired up the engine and lights and hit the gas.

The truck went skidding out of the building with a roar. Brooke floored the pedal and went speeding right through the heart of the compound. Running groups of men scattered in her headlights. Her escape suddenly wasn't such a secret any more.

Brooke saw the tall iron gates approach in her lights and braced herself for the collision. As she roared towards them at full throttle, four guards emerged from the gatehouse, took one look at the truck and aimed their rifles. Shots punctured the night air. The windscreen shattered. Brooke grabbed the rifle from the passenger seat and poked the barrel one-handed through the broken glass as she drove. A squeeze of the trigger; a massive eruption of noise as the thing let loose half its magazine. Bullets sparked off the iron gates. The guards dived for cover and scurried away just in time to avoid being pulverised by the truck's impact.

The truck crashed into the gates. The huge impact threw Brooke forward against the wheel. Bits of masonry and steel bars and pieces of truck flew everywhere. The windscreen disappeared completely. She was dead.

But she wasn't dead, she was through! The truck surged onwards, rolling over wreckage and debris in a massive cloud of dust. Suddenly she could see the road ahead in the yellow glow of her remaining headlight. Whooping with glee, she floored the throttle again and sawed at the wheel as the bouncing, careering truck sped away from the compound.

Back at the house, Ramon Serrato came tearing down from the top floor to find his men in chaos. He grabbed a fire extinguisher from the nearest one and ran wildly into Brooke's room, spraying foam in all directions at the flames.

'Where is she?' he shouted, his face blackened with smoke, eyes streaming. 'Where is she?' Nobody seemed to know. Blank looks all round, even from Vertíz and Bracca.

Over the din of the alarms came the rattle of rifle fire from across the compound. Serrato beat back the last of the flames licking around one of the living area windows, hurled the empty fire extinguisher to the floor and peered out into the night to see the truck's red taillights disappearing down the road towards the jungle.

Chapter Forty-Eight

In her haste to get away, Brooke hadn't checked the fuel level in the truck. As she headed down the road as fast as the heavy vehicle would take her, wind howling through the smashed windscreen, she cast a worried eye on the diesel gauge. It was less than a quarter full. How far could she get on that?

But her worst problem wasn't running out of diesel. It was not being able to see where the hell she was going. The collision with the gates had torn away her nearside headlight and reduced the other to a candle-glow pointing cock-eyed at the verge. The bonnet was now a twisted piece of scrap that obscured her already compromised visibility with every bounce of the suspension on the badly rutted surface. The road snaked into the trees, leading Christ knew where. All she could do was keep it going as fast as possible and pray that the next violent crash over a pothole wouldn't tear her wheels off.

She let out a cry as the tyres lost traction on a bend and the truck nearly went crunching into a giant tree. Somehow she managed to get it back under control. Slowing down was the only sane option, but she didn't dare slacken the pressure on the accelerator. Tree trunks flashed by her side windows; overhanging branches slapped the twisted bodywork. Brooke just kept driving on and on. This road had to lead somewhere. Somewhere with people, telephones, police . . .

Then suddenly, far sooner than she'd expected, there they were: the lights she'd been dreading to see in the rear-view mirror, growing quickly larger and more dazzling. Four; six; ten of them, or even more: a whole convoy of vehicles in chase. In their faster Jeeps, with their knowledge of the road, they would soon catch up with her.

If Serrato got hold of her now . . .

Brooke's fears dissolved into panic as the road ahead suddenly went totally dark. Her remaining headlight had stopped working.

She stamped on the brakes. The wheels locked up and the truck tilted sideways in a heartstopping series of violent bumps as it veered off the road. A ripping, shearing impact tore the steering wheel out of her hands. She felt the nose of the truck dip alarmingly downwards. Something hit the underside with a terrible crash. She was thrown forwards against the dashboard. Even blind, she could tell that she was falling. Falling, trapped inside a three-ton metal cage.

The nightmare descent seemed to go on forever. Impact after impact shook the truck like a bean can and dashed her this way and that inside. Down and down, until it seemed to her as if she'd fallen through to the centre of the Earth.

Then, as suddenly as it had begun, the truck's careering path down the slope was halted in an explosion of water that sent a wave crashing though the destroyed screen to fill the whole cab.

For a few seconds Brooke was certain she was going to drown. She was completely blind. The brackish water was leaking past her tightly-clenched lips into her mouth. At the last possible moment, her thrashing hand found air. Her fingers gripped onto something – it was the grab-handle above the cab door – and with all her strength she managed to pull herself to the surface and take a gasping breath.

She blinked the water out of her eyes. A powerful swirling current was sweeping the truck down the river. She could feel the vehicle rotating as the water carried it along. The level was rising in the cab. Rising higher.

Groping and splashing about, she managed to retrieve her bag and then clambered up onto the dashboard and out through the hole where the windscreen had been. As she balanced precariously on the crumpled bonnet, the truck lurched. She lost her balance and plunged into deep water.

Brooke had always been a strong swimmer, but the battle against the river current was very nearly the end of her that night. By the time she'd fought her way to the dark bank and found a large rock to climb onto, she was utterly spent. The truck was long gone, probably a kilometre downstream by now, or sunk to the bottom.

But Serrato and his men were nowhere to be seen or heard. That jubilant thought was enough to energise her. Coughing and spluttering, brackish water and mud dripping from her clothes, she made her way through the reeds of the riverbank to more solid ground.

Away from the rush of the current, the jungle was filled with a million night sounds. It was cold, too, and Brooke was soon shivering in her saturated clothes. She found a spot to rest against a fallen tree trunk and emptied out her bag by the pale moonlight that filtered down through the leaves. The pack of cold meats she'd so carefully prepared was full of river water, which she wasn't sure was safe to consume even though she'd swallowed a lot of it. The talcum powder had been meant to keep her skin dry to prevent infections – a tip she'd remembered from flipping through a survival manual once. Now it was useless, sodden into pasty clumps. She stripped off her T-shirt and tracksuit bottoms, wrung them out as best she could along with the wet towels, then rubbed herself to keep warm and put the damp clothes back on.

The air was thick with mosquitoes. At least not all her plans had been ruined by the river. She unfolded the mosquito net and draped it loosely round herself. It was large enough to cover her completely, from head to foot, and once inside it she felt strangely comforted despite the alien sounds all around her, the hooting of night birds and the strange, grating bark that she was certain was the roar of a jaguar or some other nocturnal predator prowling not too far away.

Let it roar, she thought. She was free. Smiling, she closed her eyes and curled up against the tree trunk.

Dawn came not with glorious rays of sunshine peeping through the treetops to bathe her in golden light, but with a cascade of torrential rain that jolted her from her sleep and instantly soaked her through all over again.

There was little point in trying to stay dry in this place, she decided as she packed her things up and set off, following the course of the river. Her legs, arms, shoulders and everywhere else ached badly from the effort of last night's swim – and the truck crash probably hadn't done her muscles much good either. But she was determined to keep moving, no matter what. The trainers weren't going to last forever in this extreme terrain; she was hoping that sooner or later she'd find some kind of human habitation, maybe even a village where she might be able to use Serrato's jewels to secure transport or help. She couldn't be too many miles from people.

She couldn't be too many miles from Serrato's compound either, she thought with a shudder. There was no doubt that he would be hunting for her right now. She wished that the rifle she'd stolen from the guard hadn't gone down with the truck – she felt very defenceless without it.

The rain stopped. Brooke walked. And walked. And walked. Rested a while, drank some of her water, forged onwards through the endless greenery. It was hard to keep track of time. Her clothes didn't seem to dry despite the fierce heat that followed the deluge: they just got more and more cloying and filthy and torn. The water in her bottle was going down too fast. She'd thrown away the tainted meat, thinking of botulism and typhus. All around her were a million varieties of leaf, root and berry, but she had no idea which might sustain her, or which might instead bring on a horrible, slow death.

By the time the sun had begun to go down behind the trees, she was staggering with fatigue, dehydrated and badly in need of more rest. She found a patch of leafy ground that was soft and dry, settled down on her towels and cocooned herself in the mosquito net to shelter from the clouds of insects that swarmed everywhere. Darkness fell over her like a blanket.

In her dreams, Ramon Serrato was running his hands over her. Try as she might, she just couldn't get away from his touch. She could feel the pressure of his fingertips crawling lightly over her skin. He'd pause, then move his hand a little further, one finger at a time, always smiling, always watching her with that look in his eye. 'No,' she murmured, reaching out to slap his hand away. 'Get off. Get off.'

She opened her eyes. The night song of the jungle creatures chirped and cackled all around. Her resting place was softly moonlit, enough to be able to make out the shapes of things on the outside of the mosquito net.

Brooke started.

Something had moved.

Something had moved *inside* the mosquito net. Like in the dream, she felt the light pressure of fingertips on her skin. The pressure shifted slightly, then paused again. She blinked. Was this still part of the dream?

That was when she saw the hand on her shoulder.

Except it wasn't a hand.

Brooke screamed and began thrashing wildly to unravel herself from the net. 'Oh, God, get off me! Get off me!' Kicking out with all her strength she felt the net rip. She extricated her body from the torn material and scrambled to her feet. But she was too dizzy from lack of food, from the long march through the jungle, from stress and disorientation. She fell back among the leaves.

The spider had dropped down from her shoulder and was sitting poised on the ground a few inches away. Its body was silvery brown in the moonlight, and with its bristly legs braced wide apart it was just a little smaller in span than a human hand. Its eight clustered eyes were black and beady and watched her inscrutably.

Brooke scrabbled away from it. 'Shoo!' she yelled, flinging a handful of dirt. 'Shoo!'

The spider sensed that it was under threat. Its innate defence mechanism was a danger warning that made it rear up on its back legs, pawing the air with its forelegs, swaying its hairy body gently from side to side and revealing its venomous fangs. It was a highly aggressive species that would attack with shocking speed if the warning wasn't heeded.

Brooke's fingers found a rotted piece of branch on the

ground. She swung it at the spider. 'Go on, piss off and leave me alone!' she yelled.

And the spider attacked her.

She couldn't have moved out of the way in time. It scuttled straight at her and she felt a sharp pain in her left forearm, like a hornet's sting. She screamed and lashed out again with the branch. The spider crawled unharmed into the shadows to wait for its prey to die. Or to wait for the next victim to come along. It didn't care either way.

Brooke dropped the branch and staggered dizzily to her feet. Was it exhaustion and dehydration making her feel so sick, or was it the spider's bite already taking effect? She whimpered in terror and clutched her forearm. Two puncture marks in the soft flesh of its underside were rapidly swelling and burning terribly.

'Oh no,' she groaned. 'No, please, no.' She managed to gather up her things. She had to keep moving. No choice now.

The jungle seemed to be laughing at her as she staggered away through the night. She was crying from the pain of the bite on her arm. It was dark. Getting darker. She could hardly see any more . . .

Then she could see nothing at all as her knees gave way under her and she collapsed into the foliage. She rolled over on her back, tried to call for Ben. Then the darkness swallowed her up completely.

Some time afterwards – it might have been moments, or weeks – she sensed movement. Consciousness filtered back. Her first panicked thought was that it was the spider. The spider was coming after her again.

But no, it wasn't the spider, she realised; the movement was hers. A gentle swaying motion. She understood. She was being gently carried.

She opened her eyes to the hazy grey light of pre-dawn. The face that looked down at her was like nothing she'd ever seen before. The man's dark skin was adorned with swirls and daubs of colour. Brooke only saw it for an instant before she passed out again.

When she reopened her eyes, the sun was blazing brightly above her. Into the blinding light came another face. A Caucasian face, with blue eyes that gazed down at her with care and concern.

'Ben?' she mumbled, trying to reach out to him. 'Ben, is that . . .'

'Shush, child,' said the man.

Chapter Forty-Nine

The hunt was into its third night now.

The column of open Jeeps and assorted four-wheel drives slowly made its rocking, bouncing way along the track through the dark forest, the growl of their engines reverberating off the dense foliage. The swarming insects drifted like dust particles in the beams of their headlamps. The vehicles were filled with men and weaponry, badly overloaded now that two Jeeps and one of the trucks had run out of fuel miles back and their occupants had had to clamber aboard wherever they could find room, to avoid being left behind in the green wilderness. Ramon Serrato wasn't about to let anyone or anything slow down his hunt for his missing prize.

Sitting in the front passenger seat of the lead Jeep with Luis Bracca driving, Serrato was deathly pale, his hair all awry and pasted to his brow. The silk suit that he hadn't bothered to change out of in his hurry to leave the compound was damp with humidity and sweat, stained with jungle dirt and spray from the wheels of the open Jeep. He'd been withdrawn and morose all day and for most of the previous one, barely speaking to anyone. Those men who knew him best could see the simmering fury in his eyes, even now, more than forty-eight hours since the fire at the compound and the woman's humiliating escape. They could only whistle, shake their heads and muse over the kind of fate he must have in store for her when he caught up with her again.

But after all these interminable hours of searching through rainstorms and murderous heat they'd still found nothing but empty jungle – not since two nights ago, when less than three miles into the chase they'd come across the tyre marks where the truck she'd stolen had come off the road and gone crashing down the steep hillside below. Serrato had halted the convoy and personally led a squad of twelve men, with Vertíz and Bracca, on foot down to the ravaged area of river bank where the vehicle had ploughed into the water. But the truck itself had vanished, along with its driver.

None of the men had dared to voice the thought that passed through most of their minds: the woman was dead, either killed in the crash or drowned in the fast-moving river. Not even Vertíz and Bracca, who enjoyed more leeway from their master than anyone else who'd ever worked for him, had been inclined to question his order that they return to the Jeeps and continue their search by road. 'I know her,' he'd insisted. 'She is smarter than that. This is an obvious feint to throw us off the track. She put that truck over the edge deliberately, but she wasn't in it any longer.'

But if it was true that she was still on the road somewhere ahead, she was almost ghostlike in her ability to elude them. Two whole days of exhaustively scouring every route, down to the smallest boggy, swampy track, were beginning to take their toll on the men. Their only food and water were the scant provisions they'd managed to snatch from their quarters in between helping to put out the last of the fire and being scrambled for action. They'd had no sleep other than the few short breaks they'd been allowed as Serrato drove them mercilessly on, combing an ever-increasing area of jungle to no avail. It was futile.

Still nobody spoke a word of complaint. Many of them knew from experience what Serrato could be like when he was upset – but not one of them had ever seen him in a state like this one before.

It was after two in the morning when Serrato finally signalled the convoy to halt and rest for a while. The weary men left their vehicles and limped and stretched their way over to a small clearing near the narrow track. Weapons were stacked against trees. Sticks were gathered, a fire was lit. A bottle of aguardiente surreptitiously did the rounds, quick slugs of the strong liquor taken with a nervous glance over to where the boss was sitting on a fallen tree away from the group. A few of the men exchanged dark, resentful mutterings. Nobody was very happy with the situation.

Serrato was too wrapped up in his own brooding thoughts to take notice of their mood. He looked up sharply as Vertíz and two others, Alva and the new guy Santos, approached. 'What is it?'

Vertíz showed him the small GPS navigation device he was holding. 'Boss, we're going round in circles. We've come all this way and we're still only a few miles from base. The jungle's playing tricks on us.'

'It's impossible,' Serrato snapped – but when he snatched the GPS from Vertíz and looked at the small lit-up screen, he could see it was true. They weren't even that far from the road. He clenched his teeth and sat with his face cupped in his hands.

Santos, encouraged now that Vertíz had finally spoken up, stepped forward and said, 'Señor Serrato, many of us believe that the woman was inside the truck when it went into the river. Some of the men are saying . . .'

Serrato turned to look at him. 'Yes?'

Santos should have heard the dangerous edge in his boss's

voice, but he made the mistake of going on. 'They are saying we should give up this search and go back to base. Most likely, she is dead.'

'I don't know you,' Serrato said. 'You haven't been working long for me, have you?'

'No, boss. Carlo Santos.'

'Do you also take that view, Carlo?' Serrato asked with a tight smile.

Shut up, Santos, Vertíz was thinking.

Santos shrugged. 'Even if she did not die in the river, how could a white woman survive alone in the jungle? Forgive me, Señor, but the bitch is dead. We should forget about her.'

'Forget about her,' Serrato echoed. He remained very still for a few moments. Then he reached inside his jacket. His hand came out holding a Glock. He jabbed the pistol up towards Santos and fired once.

Santos instantly collapsed to the ground with a neat round hole in the centre of his forehead.

The rest of the men had turned to stare at the sound of the shot. The bottle of spirits disappeared very quickly. Serrato stood up to face them. 'So everyone thinks the woman is dead, is that right?' he yelled in livid rage. So you're all experts now, yes? You: what does a dead person look like?'

The man Serrato had singled out backed nervously away. 'Boss, I—'

'It's a simple enough question,' Serrato shouted. 'What does a dead person look like? Does it look like that?' He waved his gun towards the empty jungle. 'Like a lot of trees and bushes?'

Nobody spoke.

'No,' Serrato screamed. 'It doesn't. It looks' – pointing at the dead man oozing blood at his feet – 'like this!' As if to make his point, he fired four more shots into the corpse, which bucked and jolted from the bullet strikes. 'You see? Everyone come around and see what a dead person looks like. You see him lying there?'

'We see him, boss,' Vertíz said quietly.

'Good,' Serrato yelled. 'Now, until I see the woman dead like this in front of me, she is alive. And while she is alive, we keep searching. Any man who refuses to follow me, I will personally execute on the spot. Understood? Now, we move. Leave the Jeeps. We keep going on foot. We will search every leaf and twig of this jungle until we find her.'

It was a long, weary trek through the jungle. Serrato headed the march, the line of men weaving through the trees behind him with their weapons ready. Torch beams scanned all around as they walked. Now and then a jungle animal would take fright and go crackling through the undergrowth at their approach. There were no more secretive looks or mutinous grumbles among the men. Nobody wanted to end up like Santos. They all knew his body would be picked to the bare bones by morning.

Luis Bracca, who could slip fast and silently through the thick of the forest, scouted on in advance, looking for tracks. They'd been marching for nearly two hours and dawn was approaching when Bracca returned to report that he'd come across something up ahead – not a sign of the missing woman, but a small Indian village. 'Maybe fifteen, twenty huts,' Bracca told Serrato.

'She may have taken refuge there,' Serrato said. Bracca privately didn't think it likely that any tribal community would offer shelter to a member of the white race that had persecuted and victimised them for centuries. He said nothing, partly because the boss was in no mood to be contradicted, and partly because he knew what would come next.

Slaughtering Indians was as much fun for him as squirrel hunting was for a young boy with his first rifle.

The armed troop advanced stealthily on the village, communicating only using hand signals. The primitive huts came into view through the trees in the first glow of the morning light.

They were forty yards from the outermost dwelling when the first Indian appeared: a young girl carrying a bundle of sticks she'd been gathering from the forest floor. Her dark, lithe little form was naked except for a cloth round her middle. Her eyes flew wide open and she let out a gasp as she saw the men creeping towards the huts – a gasp that would have turned into a shrill cry of alarm, if Bracca's strong hand hadn't clamped over her mouth. As she kicked and struggled, he drew the big Bowie knife from its sheath and slit her throat with a grin. He held her tightly for a moment as the life gushed out of her, then let her limp body drop into the leaves.

There was a shout. An old man with a white beard and a belly that overhung his loincloth darted back behind a hut and began yelling loudly to raise the alarm. Vertíz quickly skirted the hut, found him in his rifle sights and fired. The crack of the shot rang out. The old man fell on his face and lay still.

Now the whole village was alerted. Serrato drew his Glock and began yelling 'Kill them! Kill them all!' as the line of men overtook him and ran among the huts, firing at everything that moved. The terrified screams of women and children were drowned by gunfire. Bodies fell to the ground left and right, bronze skin glistening with blood.

Not all the Indians tried to take flight. Some of the young male warriors put up a spirited resistance and arrows and darts from blowpipes came whistling through the air, forcing the attackers to dive for cover. Serrato heard the *whoosh* as an arrow flew towards him. He ducked behind a tree and the feathered shaft buried itself into the trunk with a judder. He turned to see one of his men who hadn't moved quickly enough rolling on his back with an arrow in his belly.

Serrato shot the Indian who'd loosed the arrow and then ran to the nearest hut. Brooke wasn't inside it. He ran to the next, then the next, his hope of finding her quickly turning sour. As he emerged from the last empty dwelling with a bitter look on his face, he could see the Indians all scattering, their feeble resistance broken by his men's superior firepower.

'Go after them!' Serrato yelled as the warriors turned and disappeared into the jungle. Vertíz dropped to a crouch with his rifle, took careful aim and shot down one of the running Indians, then another.

Bracca took off into the trees, his teeth bared and his bloody knife in one fist, his gun in the other. Ahead of him, a terrified young woman had broken off from the rest of the fleeing tribe and was leaping through the undergrowth like an antelope. Her face was contorted in terror and covered in tears. The powerful Bracca was more than twice her weight, but his bloodlust drove him on with pounding speed.

They were well out of sight of the huts now. A little bit of privacy was just what he wanted. As he bore down on her his mind was filling with what he was going to do to the little bitch. Old enough to—

His thoughts exploded in a blinding white flash of pain as something solid swung out of nowhere and hit him a crashing blow across the face. The knife spun out of his fingers and the rifle went clattering to the ground. He landed hard on his back. Winded, he could taste the salty blood that was pouring from his broken nose. He tried to struggle to his feet. A hard kick to the chest knocked him back down again.

Bracca looked up. Standing over him, framed in the red dawn filtering through the jungle canopy, was the figure of a man. A white man, with blond hair and scuffed leather jacket. There was a bag over his shoulder and a scoped hunting rifle in his hands, ready to club him with the butt a second time.

The man looked down at the bone-handled Bowie knife that lay in the dirt nearby. 'You must be Luis Bracca,' he said.

Chapter Fifty

After leaving the servants secured in a locked room Ben and Nico had cut back to where they'd left the hunter's old Ford and started trying to pick up the trail. They'd no sooner rejoined the road leading from the compound than a downpour even heavier than the storm at the Potro River station had come pummelling down over the jungle. Within a few minutes, any tyre tracks they might have been able to follow, any clues they might have gained as to the direction of Brooke's escape, had been washed away in a sea of mud. A thousand vehicles could have come this way, or turned off any of the scores of side roads and tracks branching off through the forest, and there wouldn't have been a trace left of their passing.

'This is hopeless,' Nico had yelled over the din of the rain on the truck's roof. 'She could be anywhere, man. It's been two days.'

'I don't care,' Ben had replied. 'I can't stop.' Nico hadn't said another word. He could see the look in Ben's red-rimmed eyes. It was one he could understand.

All through the night they'd searched for any sign of her. The deluge hadn't lasted more than an hour but it had left the road impassable in places. Refusing to give up, Ben had started exploring any little track he could find. No sign. Once he ran out of those he'd continue on foot. Nothing else mattered. He drove on, clenching the wheel. He wanted to get out of the pickup and scream her name until his lungs burst.

Come the first glow of dawn, Ben had had no idea how many miles of jungle track they'd covered. There was nothing. No sign. Nico was asleep next to him.

But then, through the fog of exhaustion that was threatening to make him drop at the wheel, he'd suddenly heard a sound he knew too well. It was the sporadic crackle of rifle fire. 'Listen,' he'd said, rousing Nico.

'Something's happening in there,' the Colombian said when he heard it. 'It ain't so far away, either.'

Ben ploughed the truck into the trees, put his foot down and went crashing on blindly until the vehicle couldn't go any further. He grabbed his rifle and continued at a run through the dense vegetation with Nico close behind. Soon afterwards, they'd seen village huts and running figures among the trees. Heard the last few shots being fired in the wake of what they were beginning to realise had been a massacre of innocent native tribespeople.

'Serrato,' Nico muttered.

Ben had been deliberating what to do when the fleeing young Indian woman had suddenly appeared. She passed within a few feet of where he stood screened behind the foliage. Moments later he'd heard the crackling approach of a much larger, much heavier human. A swing of the .300 Win Mag's solid wooden buttstock had been plenty enough to arrest the pursuer in mid-stride.

Ben stood over the man, who stared up at him with savage hatred. Bracca looked exactly the way Nico had described him: a remorseless killer. His black hair was drawn back in a ponytail. Where his face wasn't covered in blood it was smeared in the same dirt he'd used to cover his muscular arms, like the camouflage cream Special Forces soldiers used. The effect made him look even less human. Ben guessed that the blood spattered across his sleeveless combat vest had come from the same poor victim he must have butchered using the huge red-stained knife that was lying on the ground.

'That's him, all right,' Nico said, stepping out of the bushes to stand at Ben's shoulder. 'That's Bracca.'

'Who the fuck are you?' Bracca growled. He tried again to get up. Ben kicked him back down.

Thirty yards away, the young Indian woman gave one last look back over her shoulder, then slipped away into the forest. Ben watched her go. He glanced back in the direction of the village. He could hear the distant voices of Serrato's men as they regrouped. It wouldn't be long before Bracca was missed.

'You're gonna die now, you murdering piece of shit.' Nico aimed his revolver at Bracca's head.

'I remember you, asshole,' Bracca chuckled. 'You're the cop, right? I remember that little girl of yours, too. Sweet kid. It was my pleasure to take care of her.'

Nico's lips were drawn back from his teeth. The Colt began to tremble in his hand.

Bracca laughed. 'S'matter? You too pussy?'

Ben reached out, gripped the Colt by the barrel and lowered it. 'No.'

'This is the guy who carved up my kids, Ben,' Nico breathed shakily.

'I know that. But I need him alive.' Ben turned to Bracca. 'You can make this easy on yourself by telling me where Brooke Marcel is.'

Bracca spat blood. 'Who's fucking asking?'

Ben planted the sole of his boot hard against Bracca's

chest and shoved the barrel of the .300 in his face. 'Someone who's got no problem turning your skull into a jam doughnut. Where is she?'

'Talking about that little redheaded cooze? We banged that bitch good, every last one of us. I went twice. Then I sawed her fucking head off.'

'You really want to die? Because that's the answer that'll do it.'

'You haven't got the cojones, fuckhead. Just like your pussy amigo there.'

'Three seconds, you'll find out,' Ben said. ' One . . .'

Bracca glowered. Ben could feel the coiled-up power in him, like a wild animal ready to go berserk. 'Two . . .' Ben said. 'I'm waiting.'

'Fuck you,' Bracca snarled.

'Three.'

Something in Bracca's eyes changed. The look of crazed ferocity was suddenly one of terror. It was the look of a bloodthirsty sadist who'd just realised his luck was out; the look of a man who genuinely couldn't answer the one question that might save his life. He opened his mouth and roared out in Spanish at the top of his lungs. 'Help! Over here!'

The distant voices began shouting back. Ben knew they didn't have a lot of time before Serrato's men would be all over them. He stepped away from Bracca, nodded to Nico and said, 'All yours.'

Nico's eyes gleamed. He stepped up to where Bracca lay and raised the Colt again.

'Make it quick. We don't have a lot of time.' Ben could hear the voices getting closer, and the sound of men moving through the foliage towards them: forty yards, maybe less. He slung the hunting rifle back over his shoulder and snatched up Bracca's fallen military assault weapon. The M4 carbine's curved black magazine was almost full.

Bracca's eyes were wide open in fear. Nico cocked his revolver and squeezed the trigger.

Nothing happened. The tiny click of the dropping hammer was almost inaudible.

Serrato's men were getting closer. Someone yelled Bracca's name.

For an instant, Nico stared at the gun in his hand. It was an instant too long. In one fast and violent sweep of his arm Bracca reached for his knife and brought it up and round to stab the blade deep into Nico's thigh.

Nico let out a cry. He dropped his gun and fell.

Bracca was half on his feet, roaring in rage and ready to yank the knife out of Nico's leg and stab him again, when Ben fired the M4. The bullet tore straight through Bracca's skull, blowing off the back of his head.

At the same instant that Bracca's lifeless body hit the ground, Ben saw movement in the foliage. Serrato's men were on them. He flipped the M4's fire selector to full auto, braced himself and sprayed bullets into the foliage. There was a short scream, but there were more men coming, from everywhere. Muzzle flashes erupted from the dark forest. A man burst out of the bushes to the left, firing. Bark exploded from the tree right next to Ben. He felt a hard impact through his shoulder and knew the hunting rifle had taken a hit. He rolled. Fired. Saw the man fall back into the greenery.

'Come on!' he yelled at Nico. The Colombian staggered to his feet. Bracca's knife was still stuck deep in his leg and he was bleeding badly. Ben grabbed him and hauled him into the bushes. One glance at his hunting rifle showed him the terminal damage to the bolt from the bullet hit. He tossed the dead weight away.

Bursts of gunfire came thick and fast as he half dragged, half carried the Colombian in the direction of the track and the Ford pickup. Nico screamed out in pain at every step. Bullets whipped all around them, trembling the foliage as they ran.

Ben knew the M4's magazine was half depleted by now, but if he didn't drive their attackers back under cover there was no way to outpace them. He turned to let off another short burst. An instant before he squeezed the trigger, he caught a glimpse of one of them. The lean-faced, dark-haired man didn't look like the others. The suit he was wearing was stained with sweat and dirt, but it was an expensive tailor-made item that nobody would wear in the jungle. In the fraction of a second that Ben locked eyes with the man, he knew he was looking at Ramon Serrato.

He fired. The man dived for cover behind a tree as Ben's bullets ripped up the greenery. Then it was Ben who had to duck down as a sustained blast of fire came back at him in reply.

Ben's gun was just about empty. But peering ahead through the trees, he could make out a splash of red behind the green. He realised they'd almost made it to the pickup truck. 'Come on,' he grunted, yanking Nico on a few yards more.

'Leave me,' Nico gasped.

'Forget it,' Ben said. He turned and let off another short burst behind them. The gun chattered and jolted in his hand, and then suddenly stopped. The bolt had locked back: empty magazine.

Ben tossed the weapon away. He grasped Nico with both hands and hauled him the rest of the way to the truck. He ripped open the passenger door. As he bundled Nico inside, the passenger window exploded in a shower of glass fragments.

Another bullet punched a silver-edged hole into the red steel of the Ford's wing.

Ben leaped behind the wheel. He twisted the ignition and prayed the bullet hadn't penetrated the truck's vitals. It hadn't. The engine burst into life and Ben slammed it into drive. The windscreen blew apart, stinging him with glass.

He stamped on the gas and the Ford's wheels threw up a fountain of dirt as he hurled it into a tight U-turn to head back up the track the way they'd come. Bullets punched through the doors and scored the roof and blew off a side mirror. Ben kept his head down and his foot on the pedal, and the figures of the men bursting out of the trees in their wake and firing at them shrank smaller and smaller in the mirror. He threw the pickup round a bend and the bullets stopped.

Nico was bent double in the passenger seat, crying out in agony at every lurch of the truck over the ruts, clutching at his leg where the bone hilt of Bracca's knife was protruding from the wound. Even in the dim light of the cab Ben could tell it was a serious one, well beyond his ability to stitch up himself. Blood was all over the seats. Nico's face was ghostly pale and covered in sweat. 'The gun didn't go off,' he groaned over the engine noise and the crashing of the suspension.

'You had a duff primer,' Ben said. 'It happens.'

'You should've let me kill him, man. He was mine.'

'He's dead. That's what matters.'

'You ain't gonna do that to me with Serrato,' Nico said in a tortured moan. 'I gotta kill Serrato myself. Gotta! Understand?'

'Not with that knife in you,' Ben told him. 'You'll be dead yourself pretty fast if we don't get you to a doctor.'

Nico gasped in pain. 'Fuck the knife. You promise me, hear?'

'Fine,' Ben muttered as the pickup truck hit another rut

and the suspension bottomed out with a crash. When he glanced at Nico again, he saw that he'd passed out.

Ben kept driving. He felt the supercharged adrenaline rush of the skirmish with Serrato's men slowly subside. It left him with nothing but a dead, despairing feeling.

Brooke was still out there somewhere. Lost, frightened, defenceless; totally vulnerable. All alone in the vastness of a jungle it would take a man the rest of his life to search.

There was no way he could possibly find her.

Chapter Fifty-One

The day was already more than half gone. Dark clouds hung over San Tomás. As Ben wandered aimlessly through the town, the first patter of rain quickly ramped up to become another of the region's unimaginable deluges, until mud rivers ran through the streets and everyone but the blond-haired stranger was driven under cover.

For the last several hours Nico had been under the care of the kindly Dr Rocha, who operated the struggling one-roomed clinic in San Tomás, the only medical facility for miles up and down the river, with his sister Graça. By the time Ben had delivered him into their hands, Nico had lost a great deal of blood and was in a virtual coma. The doctor had found the knife blade's razor-sharp edge pressing right up against Nico's femoral artery. Another millimetre of pressure and it could have ruptured. Nico would have bled to death in minutes.

Removing the knife and patching up the deep wound had been a long job that had used up most of the clinic's medical supplies and left Dr Rocha looking almost as spent as his patient. Graça had changed the dressing on Nico's arm, frowning a little at Ben's stitching job but asking no questions. Ben had sat with Nico a while as he slept, then wandered outside to try to get some air and pull his thoughts together.

He ambled through the streets, soaked to the skin by the hammering rain. There were a few drops left in his whisky flask. He gulped them down and barely even felt them.

Never before in his career rescuing kidnap victims had he resorted to calling in help from the authorities. It went against all his experience and judgement – but this time he couldn't see any other way. It was going to take a large-scale operation, both on the ground and in the air, to comb an area of the size he was dealing with.

But then there was Ramon Serrato to consider. If half the things Nico had told Ben were true, the former drug lord had connections at the highest levels of government here. What if a well-organised mass search did succeed in finding Brooke alive? Ben had seen corruption in action plenty of times before, and South America was even more notorious for it than the most volatile and dangerous parts of Africa and the Middle East. He knew how easy it would be for a man of Serrato's influence to arrange for someone to put a bullet in her head before she ever left the jungle. And Ben's, too, if he tried to stand in the way. There was a decent chance that if he called in the authorities, he was signing her death warrant. He had to balance that against the virtual certainty that if he didn't, the end result would be the same. A lose-lose situation.

And all that was assuming she wasn't dead already.

The rain was pounding more heavily than ever. Ben slowed his pace and came to a standstill in four inches of muddy water. It was the sight of the corrugated-iron shed, San Tomás's only bar just across the street, that had stopped him. He paused briefly, then headed towards it. He needed something more than those last few drops from his flask to blunt the edge of his anxiety.

The place was almost as empty as it had been before.

The same barman was cleaning up using the same dirty cloth. Two drunks were talking loudly in Spanish at a table in the corner. Ben didn't glance at them as he walked up to the bar and ordered whatever was the strongest drink they had. The barman served him up a fingerprint-covered glass of something that looked like vodka but was about twice as fiery. Ben drained it and asked for another. A double this time.

'Hey!' one of the drunks called from across the room. 'Chief, it's you! Thought maybe you'd got ate up by a croc.'

Ben turned from the bar and realised that it was Pepe, the riverboat pilot. He and his drinking companion, who looked to be a full-blooded Indian, had been there long enough to amass a large collection of empty beer bottles. Both seemed pretty far gone. Ben was intent on going the same route, and he could do it in a quarter of the time with whatever this clear stuff was in his glass.

'Come on over, chief,' Pepe slurred. 'Have a drink with me and my cousin Cayo here.'

Ben didn't feel like company. Besides, he could see that both Cayo and Pepe were plainly upset about something. He just smiled and raised his glass, then turned his back and returned to his own thoughts. Talking to the British Embassy in Lima might not be easy with the limited communications from San Tomás. The best way might be to call Jeff Dekker, fill him in on the situation and get him to liaise with them. Amal would have to be told, too . . .

As Ben struggled with his plans, the inebriated Spanish conversation between Pepe and Cayo went on in the background.

'This is fucking bad,' Pepe muttered.

'Like I said,' Cayo slurred in between gulps of beer, 'I'm

only telling you what my buddy Angel told me. Word's spreading up and down the river since this morning.'

Pepe shook his head. 'Fuck. How many dead they reckon?'

'Angel says twenty, maybe more. Reckons they were Sapaki people.'

'Angel's Murunahua, ain't he? Then how'd he figure that?'

Cayo shrugged. ''Cause a bunch of Sapaki people turned up at his village this morning talking about their relations that'd been killed. Warned the Murunahuas about what's happening. Whole region's shit scared.'

'Fuck,' Pepe said again. 'Someone's got to act, man.'

Cayo gave a snort. 'Yeah, sure. But who? Cops? Ministry? Forget it, man. Just the way it is. Been going on forever, keep going on forever. Who gonna give a shit about a buncha dead Indians? We ain't nothing to nobody.'

Pepe stabbed his finger on the table. 'Fuck that shit, man, there's gotta be something someone can do. Can't just take it up the ass like that, it ain't right.'

'Indians been taking it up the ass for generations, man,' Cayo said morosely. 'What else is there to do, start a war?'

'They got shotguns, don't they?'

'Not these guys, they don't. Sapaki don't have nothing to do with that shit. All they got is bows and arrows and blowpipes and shit.'

'No wonder they got fucked over, man,' Pepe insisted. 'Some marauding asshole walks into a faceful of buckshot, he's gonna think twice before he comes onto your patch again. Darts and arrows? Ain't gonna cut it. This isn't the fucking Inca Kingdom no more. You gotta get with the times.'

His cousin made a resigned gesture. 'So what's changed? Same old, same old. Oil guys gonna take it all away in the end, just like the Spanish did back in the day. And if it ain't the oil guys it gonna be the loggers, the beefburger ranchers, whatever. Can't stop the tide, cuz.'

'That's fucked,' Pepe said, shaking his head. There was a pause as they both reached for their beers. 'So what're the Sapaki doing calling on the Murunahuas, anyhow? My father knew some of 'em, said they didn't like to mix with no-one. I ain't never heard of them coming that far down the river.'

'Came to get serum. That's what Angel told me, leastways.'

'Snakebite?'

'No, man, spider. The white preacher, he sent 'em for it in his boat. They's in a real hurry, too, Angel said.'

'The preacher? That dried-up old fart still alive?' Pepe chuckled, and they shared a brief laugh. 'Since when the Sapaki need serum for a bite? Their own cures don't work no more?'

'Sure they work,' Cayo said. 'They just don't reckon on they work for a white person, is all. Goes against their beliefs.'

'You saying it was the preacher got bit?'

'Nah, man, nothing bite that old iron-butt motherfucker and live. White woman got bit.'

'Preacher got a woman now? You kidding me, right?'

'Nah, man, preacher ain't got no woman. Talking about the woman they found.'

'Like a tourist?'

Cayo shrugged. 'I never asked, Angel never said. All I know is, they found her.'

'She dead?'

'Wasn't dead this morning when they came for the serum, I guess.'

Pepe nodded solemnly. 'Guess that figures.'

Both of them turned and looked up, suddenly aware of the presence by their table. Neither had noticed Ben leave the bar and cross the room. He was standing there, staring at them.

'Hey, chief,' Pepe said with a beaming smile. 'You come to join us after all?

Chapter Fifty-Two

Nico was awake, propped up against his pillow in the tiny ward at the San Tomás medical clinic, when Ben burst in. 'Hey,' Nico greeted him in a faint voice.

'How's the leg?' Ben asked.

'Hurts like a sonofabitch. Doc says I'll be okay, though. Guess I have you to thank for that.'

'Yeah, well, I came to say goodbye. I'm leaving.'

'Leaving?'

'I know where she is.'

Nico sat up in bed, blinking. 'Whoa. Say *what?*'

Ben quickly explained what he'd found out from Pepe and his cousin about the Sapaki tribe's discovery of a white woman in the jungle. 'You think it's her?' Nico asked in amazement. 'Is she all right?'

'I won't know anything for sure until I get there,' Ben replied. 'Pepe's getting the boat ready right now. We're setting off in a few minutes.'

'Where are these Sap—?'

'Sapaki. Deep in the forest, two or three hours upriver. They keep themselves to themselves.'

'You know what *that* means. Better pray they don't stick your gringo ass in a cauldron and boil you up for their dinner.'

'I don't think so,' Ben said. 'Seems they're related to the tribe we came across. Those people didn't look too hostile to me.'

'True enough. Maybe if they'd been a little *more* hostile, they wouldn't have got wiped out.'

'Only half wiped out,' Ben said. 'From what Pepe's cousin says, the survivors are spreading the word all over the region. Serrato may just have a tribal uprising on his hands. What are you doing?'

Nico had thrown the sheet back and was struggling out of bed with his heavily-bandaged leg. 'Whaddaya think I'm doing?' he retorted. 'I'm coming the hell with you.'

'Serrato's not my concern any longer, Nico. I'm only interested in one thing.'

'Yeah, and that one thing is exactly what Serrato's interested in too. You say word's spreading – that works both ways, man. He finds out there's this white woman been rescued by a bunch of Indians in the jungle, you don't think he'll come for her? Your Brooke is gonna draw that fucker like a magnet. And I intend to be there waiting.' Nico hobbled towards the chair where the doctor's sister Graça had neatly folded his clothes, freshly laundered in the only washing machine in San Tomás. His leg gave way under him and he grabbed at the chair to steady himself.

'You're in no state for this, my friend,' Ben said. 'There isn't wheelchair access where I'm going.'

'Oh, nice. You worried about me, or just worried I'll hold you back?' Glowering, Nico grabbed a bottle of Dr Rocha's strong painkillers from the side table and swallowed three of them down dry. 'Don't even think about trying to stop me, man,' he growled. 'You made me a promise.'

'Fine. I'm not stopping you.'

'What about guns?' Nico said. 'I lost my Colt.'

'I don't have time to go scouring the jungle for more arms dealers right now,' Ben said. 'I'll see you back at the boat. You've got twenty minutes to get your act together.'

Nineteen minutes and forty-nine seconds later, Ben looked up from unmooring the river boat and saw Nico stumping along the wooden jetty as fast as his bandaged leg would carry him, struggling with his pack. He looked pale but determined. 'You got room for one more?' he yelled.

Ben slipped the moorings, Pepe gunned the throttle with an irrepressible grin and the boat burbled away from the San Tomás quay. The late afternoon sun glinted gold on the river, a heart-lifting sight if Ben hadn't been so fraught with worry. 'Let me get that,' he said, helping Nico to store his rucksack aft.

Nico pointed at Ben's belt. 'What's this?'

'It's a knife,' Ben said.

'I can see it's a knife. Where'd you get it?'

'Out of your leg, if I remember rightly.' Dr Rocha had had no particular use for the brutal weapon and Ben, having lost his rifle in the skirmish with Serrato's men, had asked if he could have it.

'Kinda ghoulish,' Nico said, peering uncomfortably at the knife and rubbing his thigh.

'Kind of practical,' Ben replied.

The boat chugged on. As San Tomás disappeared behind them the jungle closed in again, the animal chorus from the treetops louder than ever. 'I'm gonna stink of fucking bug repellent the rest of my life,' Nico complained, swatting at clouds of insects.

Ben left him at the stern and went forward to talk to Pepe in the wheelhouse. Pepe reckoned on a three-hour trip, give or take, admitting that he'd never personally ventured so far upriver. He described how his late father had been one of the few river traders to pay visits to the Sapaki and other largely uncontacted tribes, such as the Mashco-Piro, along the further reaches. He'd even learned some of the Sapaki language, an obscure and ancient form of Quechua that dated all the way back to the Inca Empire. Pepe had picked up a few words of it from his father as a kid, but, as he explained to Ben: 'I never reckoned on getting close enough to use it. Like I said before, they don't exactly welcome outsiders. Pop said that's what their tribal name means in Quechua: "alone". That's how they've been for centuries; it's how they want to stay forever.'

'What about the white preacher who lives with them?' Ben asked. 'Is he a Christian missionary?'

Pepe nodded. 'Been with the Sapaki so long I guess they regard him as one of them. Kind of a legend around these parts. My father talked about how he met him once, said he didn't look like any preacher he'd ever seen. Some people say he's crazy. German. Or maybe Canadian. Come to think of it, I don't think anyone knows where he's from.'

The boat chugged on towards the unfamiliar reaches of the river. The first hour dragged past, then the next. Evening was falling and the clouds of insects were thickening even more, until it was almost impossible to draw a breath without choking on a lungful of them.

The atmosphere on board the boat was solemn and silent. Ben gazed down at the passing water, his mind full of anxiety about Brooke. He knew all too well from his SAS jungle training that the bites from certain spider species could be lethal, and South America had some of the worst. He could only pray that the preacher, German or Canadian or whatever he was, had managed to get hold of the serum in time – and that he wasn't so crazy that he didn't know what he was doing with it.

A tiny movement on the far river bank caught Ben's eye and he looked up. Standing in the lengthening shadows among the reeds thirty yards away across the water was an Indian. He and Ben watched one another as the boat glided by. The Indian had patterns of dots tattooed all over his face. He was naked except for a strip of cloth round his middle, and clutched a tall spear. His eyes were piercing and intense.

Ben was distracted for an instant by the splash of a caiman slipping into the water further up the bank. When he looked back at the clump of reeds, the Indian had vanished into the forest, as if he'd never been there.

Ben saw no more signs of human life as evening closed in. When it grew too dark to see, Pepe turned on the lamps mounted on the wheelhouse roof, beaming a yellow glow over the water and the overhanging vegetation. Some time later he announced, 'I think we're close.' He didn't sound too sure at first, but then after a few more minutes he cut the engine and used a long boat hook to pull them into the bank.

'You're certain?' Ben asked him.

Pepe nodded. 'This is where my pop used to meet them. He described it to me. See that dead tree there? That was his landmark.'

As far as Ben could tell, there had been a thousand like it all the way upriver. But he had to trust Pepe's judgement. They disembarked and moored the boat to the dead tree. Pepe shone his flashlight through the greenery, where an earth track barely wide enough for a person disappeared into the trees. 'This way,' he whispered softly, as though people might be listening. 'And watch out for snakes,' he warned. 'You step on the wrong one, you're history.'

They followed Pepe into the darkness. 'You all right?' Ben asked Nico.

'Don't sweat it, man. I'm so full of painkillers, you could stick blades in me wherever you want and I wouldn't even feel 'em.'

'Let's hope we don't get to put that to the test,' Ben muttered as he went on following Pepe along the dark track. It was overgrown in places: Ben used Luis Bracca's knife to slash away the foliage while Pepe chopped and swung with the machete from the boat. The track wound gradually upwards. The jungle seemed even more filled with life than it had on the approach to Serrato's compound. It was as though they'd discovered a completely virgin world where no human being had ever set foot.

That was something that would change dramatically if Serrato's designs on the jungle's hidden oil reserves ever became a reality. Half a million acres of ancient forest would be shorn away as the heavy machinery moved in, and the ancient peoples whose way of life had remained unchanged and untouched since the dawn of history would be eradicated like vermin.

Ben wondered whether the Indians realised just how fragile their existence might really be; just how much of a threat the totally alien outside world was to their green haven.

Pepe suddenly stopped. 'This is definitely it,' he whispered, looking nervously ahead. Two spears, their shafts planted in the earth and their points crossing, barred the way. 'It's a warning,' Pepe explained. 'Telling strangers to steer clear, or else. You sure you want to keep going?'

'I have to keep going,' Ben told him. 'You can turn back if you like.'

Pepe hesitated, then shook his head. 'Ah, what the hell.'

They skirted round the side of the crossed spears and kept going, their torch beams bobbing ahead. Nobody said a word. There was just the whine of the insects and the soft crackle of their footfalls on the jungle floor.

The Indians appeared around them so suddenly and in such total, eerie silence that Ben could have believed they'd materialised out of nowhere.

There were a dozen of them. Fifteen. The torch beams shone off hostile faces and lean bodies painted red and black. A circle quickly closed in around the three trespassers. Spear points were raised; bows were drawn.

Nico froze. Pepe breathed, 'Oh, shit.'

'Don't move a muscle,' Ben said.

Chapter Fifty-Three

The circle tightened round Ben, Nico and Pepe, pressing them close together with jabbing spearheads and threatening arrows. Strong hands whipped out and snatched away their torches, one of which was passed to the warriors' leader. He examined the device, shining it all around him. He was an older man, flabby round the middle. His whole body was stained red with some kind of vegetable dye and he wore a string of decorative beads over the tops of his ears and around his face, attached to his nose by a large ring. He was obviously a man of senior rank – not a chief, maybe, but their equivalent of a squad commander at least.

The commander pointed the torch at his three captives and yelled something to his warriors. Ben didn't need to understand Quechua to catch the tone of his words. Nor did Nico. 'They're pretty pissed off,' he observed.

Ben tucked the bone-handled knife into his belt and raised his hands. 'Talk to them, Pepe. Tell them we don't mean any harm.'

Pepe stammered a few hesitant words to the leader, who just went on glaring and pointing at them.

'I don't think they care either way, man,' Nico muttered. 'Whoa, easy with that, brother,' he said to the Indian jabbing him with a spear. 'Ben, you have any ideas on how to deal with this?'

Before Ben could come up with any, he saw the commander's gaze drop down to his belt. There was a lot more gesticulating and yelling.

'What's he saying?' Ben asked Pepe.

'I think he's asking where you got that knife.'

Ben glanced down at the handle of Bracca's Bowie sticking out of his belt. 'Tell him I took it from one of the men who wish harm to his people. And that I offer it to him as a gift.'

'I don't know if I can say all that, but I'll try.' Pepe addressed the commander again. This time he seemed able to get a few more words out, and they seemed to have a greater effect. The man looked long and hard at Ben from under beetled brows. After a drawn-out pause he signalled to one of his warriors, who darted forward, plucked the knife out from Ben's belt and ran over to hand it to him. Another long pause while the commander inspected the knife with extreme gravity. He shone the light on Ben again, scrutinised him very carefully, spent a few more moments in deliberation and then grunted an order at the warriors.

The spears were lowered. Bowstrings were slackened. The circle drew back. Nico let out a sigh.

'Think we're meant to wait here,' Pepe said as the commander gave further orders and then led a group of the men away with him. As squat and ungainly as he looked, the Indian slipped through the trees with the grace of a deer.

'Wait for what?' Nico said.

'Guess we'll soon see,' Pepe replied.

The remaining warriors were all watching intently by the light of the torches, though Ben would have bet they could see pretty well in the dark. Now that the immediate crisis had eased slightly, he was able to study them. All but one or two had long, thick black hair. Tattoos and other facial adornments appeared standard, and their bodies were dyed either red, like the commander's, or black. Their weapons were beautifully crafted from wood, hide, twine, feathers and stone. The Indians didn't seem much affected by the fact that the Iron Age hadn't reached their part of the world yet. A sharpened flint arrowhead could still penetrate the same vital organs that a steel one could.

Silent minutes passed. Then, with only the faintest rustle of leaves, the commander and his men returned. He was no longer holding the Bowie knife. Pepe listened hard to what he was saying, then turned to Ben. 'Sounds like we're being let into the village.'

'And I thought US immigration control was tough,' Nico joked nervously as the warriors escorted them through the dark jungle. Ben saw a glow of firelight between the trees up ahead, then the shapes of huts came into view. Figures clustered among the shadows, chattering worriedly among themselves as the three strange captives were led into the heart of the village. A crowd of men, women and children quickly formed in their wake, becoming braver and more inquisitive with each step.

Ben, Nico and Pepe were led to the largest of the huts. As they were shown in through the low entrance, Ben saw he'd been right about the commander's rank in the community hierarchy. The most important dignitary of the village was seated on a carved stool facing the doorway, surrounded by a group of other men and women. While everyone else was as unselfconsciously semi-naked as the warriors, the chief was cloaked in a colourful robe that together with the adornments on his face and body were obviously the marks of his office. The hut was filled with the flickering light of the fire at its heart and the scent of the woodsmoke that rose up through a hole in the roof.

The squad commander obviously felt that the lowly captives must be made to grovel in front of the chief. Ben obeyed his barked orders and knelt cautiously on the earth floor by the fire, keeping his head lowered. Nico and Pepe did the same. More villagers were filtering in through the entrance, gathering round to stare at the three strangers, some apparently keen to witness their slow dismemberment, others just gaping in fascination.

Peering up, Ben recognised a face: the young woman he'd saved from Luis Bracca in the wake of the previous day's massacre was standing at the chief's shoulder, talking fast and gesticulating in his direction as if recounting the story to the others of how this man had rescued her from being raped and killed. Like many of the other women she was wearing a kind of sarong around her waist, made from cotton that had been dyed into colourful patterns. Every so often she'd glance across at Ben with bright eyes. The chief was listening quietly to every word. In his hands was the Bowie knife. For some reason, the knife was terribly important to them.

Then the chief made a gesture and the hut fell into hushed silence. After surveying the three prisoners for a moment or two with an air of imperious contempt, he pointed the knife at Ben and shot him a look that said, 'Let's hear it, matey – and it better be good.'

All eyes were suddenly on Ben. As carefully as he could, he explained in Spanish that he and his friends meant no harm or threat to the Sapaki people. He thanked the chief for his great kindness in letting them enter his village. He'd come a long way to find a loved one who was missing, and his search had led him here.

'I can't translate all that,' Pepe muttered. 'I said I knew a few words, not the whole damn language.'

'Let me interpret for you, son,' a voice said – to Ben's astonishment, in a County Cork accent. He turned towards the hut entrance to see a tall, gnarly and slightly bent-over white man in his sixties standing in the doorway. His hair was silver and shaggy, his eyes a vivid blue. The khaki shirt and shorts he wore were probably older than Ben's son Jude.

'You must be the preacher,' Ben said.

'That I am, indeed,' the Irishman replied. 'Father Padraig Scally, at your service. By God, it's been a long time since I last spoke English, let me tell you.' He nodded with a smile to the chief. 'Now, then. Tupaq's a mean old bugger but I think he'll change his tune once he understands.'

Father Scally translated Ben's words into the Sapaki language, which he seemed to speak as fluently as any of the Indians. The chief's expression changed gradually from one of suspicion to one of satisfaction as he listened. When the priest had finished, Tupaq spoke for a long time, and the hut began to fill with chatter.

'Well, that's better,' Father Scally said, turning to Ben. 'Tupaq accepts that you are not the evil murderer they call White Knife, who slew the daughter of his brother. Thanks also to the testimony of K'antu there' – the Irishman motioned towards the young woman Ben had saved, who was repeating her story in an unbroken stream to a group of others and pointing at Ben with a smile – 'he accepts that you are not an enemy of the Sapaki people, and are therefore free to come and go as you please.'

'Please express my thanks to the chief,' Ben said. 'And I'm grateful to you, too, father.'

'So they're not gonna chop us up or shoot us full of arrows,' Pepe ventured.

'The Sapaki are not exactly what one might call a blood-thirsty people,' Father Scally replied with a note of irritation. 'Though there's no telling what unspeakable torments they might have seen fit to inflict on you young fellows if I hadn't been here to moderate their more bellicose impulses.' He turned to Ben. 'Now, I'm not going to ask the nature of your business in Amazonas, or how or why it is you were able to rescue K'antu from those wicked people. But I am curious to know what brings you to this village. You said something about a missing loved one?'

The words were ready to burst out of Ben. 'A woman was found in the jungle. Her name's Dr Marcel. Is she here?'

Father Scally frowned. 'Dr Marcel?'

'Brooke Marcel. I have a picture.' Ben's heart began to plunge towards his boots. Surely, after all this, he hadn't come to the wrong place?

But the priest's next words almost made him collapse with relief:

'You wouldn't happen to be Ben, would you?'

Several stunned moments passed before Ben could reply. 'Yes, I'm him. I mean, I'm Ben.'

Father Scally's wizened face broke into a smile. 'When the fever was at its worst, she must have asked for you a hundred times. So you came looking for her, did you?'

'Is she all right?' Ben asked dizzily.

'She is now,' Father Scally said. 'Why don't you come and see for yourself?'

They left the hut and the tall, long-striding Irishman led Ben through the village, followed by a crowd of excited, clamouring Sapaki people who, now that Ben was officially a hero and not some evil invader come to murder them, all seemed to want to touch his strange blond hair. 'You'll have to forgive them,' Father Scally explained. 'I'm the only white bloke most

372

of them have ever seen. Which I've always regarded as generally a good thing.'

At the far side of the village was a long, low hut with a wooden door. 'This is what I use for a sick bay,' the priest explained to Ben. 'Not exactly the Royal City of Dublin Hospital, but it does us all right. Tica and Kusi, two of the tribe girls, help me run the place. We currently have just one patient.' After a pause he added, 'She won't talk about what she was doing wandering the jungle alone, and I haven't pressed her for answers. To be honest I prefer to remain ignorant.' He knocked gently at the door. 'Brooke? Are you awake, my child? You have a *visitor*.'

Ben felt as if he was dreaming.

Father Scally opened the door of the sick bay.

And there, sitting by the light of a candle on a low bed made of wood and rattan, wrapped in a blanket, her hair tousled, her face turned towards the doorway with a look of rapt bewilderment, was Brooke.

Chapter Fifty-Four

Ben rushed into the hut. 'Brooke—' he began. He couldn't believe it. It was really her. She was wearing a cotton skirt like K'antu's, and a torn T-shirt that had been carefully darned with coarse thread.

'Ben! You're *here?*' Her voice sounded faint.

'You two have a lot to talk about,' Father Scally said with a smile. 'I'll leave you alone.' He slipped away.

Brooke burst into tears. Ben stepped closer to her, welling up with emotion, then dropped to his knees by the low bed, took her in his arms and held her tightly for the longest time.

'I thought I was never going to see you again,' he murmured, rocking her gently back and forth. 'I thought I'd lost you.' She clung to him, weeping. He had to struggle to hold back his own tears. 'I love you, Brooke. I'm so, so sorry that we fought the way we did.'

'So am I,' she sobbed.

'I'm never going to leave you alone again. Never, not for a minute. I swear it.'

Brooke went on crying in his arms. His own face was wet now. He stroked her back, her shoulders, her hair. She felt thin and frail. As she drew away from him to gaze into his eyes he could see her face was drawn and pale in the candlelight.

'You're sick,' he murmured.

'I was,' she said through her tears. 'I'm so much better now, thanks to Padraig.' She touched his cheek. 'Oh, Ben, I can't believe it's you,' she whispered. 'I can't believe you found me. How did you know where I was?'

'It's a long story. Don't worry about it for now. What matters is that I did, and that you're all right.'

She burst out sobbing again at the memory of her captivity. 'It was terrible, Ben. He was holding me prisoner. He's insane. He thinks I'm someone else. I had to get away.'

'I know all about the compound, and the fire,' he said. 'About Ramon Serrato, too. And about his dead wife Alicia.'

'She was his wife? Oh God! *He* killed her, didn't he?'

'Let's not talk about it. Serrato can't touch you now. I'm here. You're safe.'

'Sam's dead,' she sniffed.

He nodded. 'I was in Donegal with Amal. I'm sorry.'

'Amal! Is he here too?'

'He's back in London. He's been worried sick about you. Thinks none of this would have happened if it hadn't been for him and his play.'

Brooke smiled weakly. 'Poor Amal. It's not his fault.'

'That's what I told him. But he needs to hear it from you. And he will, soon, because I'm taking you home.'

'Yes, take me home, Ben,' Brooke said softly. Her voice faded away. Her eyelids fluttered shut and he felt her go limp in his arms. For a moment he was ready to panic and yell for Father Scally – but then he realised she'd just passed out from sheer weakness and fatigue.

He laid her down gently on the bed, brushed the auburn tangles away from her face and kissed her brow. 'You rest now,' he whispered. 'We'll leave in the morning.'

*

'That's completely out of the question,' Father Scally said a few minutes later. Ben had left Brooke asleep in the sick bay and found the priest near the chief's hut, from which the sounds of chatter and laughter were still drifting out into the night.

'No disrespect, Father, but there are places she can be better cared for than out here.'

The priest shook his head firmly. 'The Brazilian wandering spider's bite is no joke – I've seen strong men die from it within half an hour. Thankfully, I can only suppose that she didn't get the full dose of venom, or it'd have been a corpse we found in the forest. She's responded better to treatment than ever I dared hope, but she's still very weak. There's absolutely no way I can allow her to be moved, let alone take a long trip downriver. She needs at least several days' complete rest, maybe a week, before I can permit you to take her away.'

Ben said nothing. The Irishman was making sense, and he knew it.

'You look fairly worn out yourself,' Scally said, his tone softening. 'I'll bet you haven't had a scrap to eat for days. Come with me and I'll sort you out.'

'I'd better find Nico and Pepe,' Ben said. 'They must be hungry too.'

Scally nodded towards the chief's hut. 'Don't you worry about them. They're being well taken care of. This way.'

Ben followed the priest along a compacted dirt path that led round the outskirts of the village to a little hut slightly apart from the others. The dwelling was built from earth and reeds like the rest, but unlike them it featured a little lean-to extension and a flower garden surrounded by white-painted stones.

'This is my abode,' Father Scally said, showing Ben inside.

The furnishings were virtually non-existent, just a raised mat for a bed and a couple of stools carved from sections of tree trunks. In one corner was a tiny, primitive kitchen area that amounted to an open fire and a hook for hanging a pot. A battered wooden chest served as a cupboard.

The priest ladled something that looked like stew from a large dish into a smaller bowl and handed it to Ben with a homemade spoon to eat with. 'It's not bad, actually,' he reassured him. 'And here's a little something to wash it down with.'

He reached into the cupboard and brought out two clay beakers and a bottle of colourless liquid. Pouring a generous measure into one of the beakers for Ben and then one for himself, he said, 'It's not quite the way we used to make it back home, but it'll warm the cockles just the same, sure. And something tells me you could do with a drink. It's been quite a day for you, hasn't it?'

'It has.' Ben took a sip. 'Wow. I haven't tasted poteen since I left Galway.'

Scally chuckled. 'I get the potatoes from a fellow in San Tomás. Got me old still set up in the shed outside. So you lived in Galway, did you?'

'Half Irish,' Ben said.

'Thought there was something good about you. Or half good, at least.' Scally laughed. 'Here, drink that up and I'll pour you another. It's not often I get to share a drink with a fellow countryman.'

'Don't you ever go back?' Ben asked him.

Scally shook his head. 'Last time was almost twenty-seven years ago. But who's counting? Not me.'

'You've been living here all that time?'

'Just about. Doing God's work is all I ever want to do with meself.'

'How well do the Sapaki take to having a missionary in their midst?' Ben asked, genuinely curious.

'For the first fifteen years or so they tolerated me; since then I don't suppose they even notice me. I don't interfere with their ways, and Heaven forbid I should ever go about preaching the Gospel at them. My work isn't about foisting a foreign religion on these fine people. God wouldn't want that, and neither would the Sapaki. They have their own gods – the spirits of the forest, of the animals and the river. No, I'm simply here to serve them as I'd serve all God's children, not to brainwash them.'

Ben looked around him at the primitive hut. 'You gave up everything for this life.'

Scally smiled. 'It all seems very distant to me now. I can barely remember the Padraig Scally who served with the Royal Irish all those years ago.'

'The Royal Irish Regiment?' Ben asked in surprise.

'Medical Corps, First Battalion, part of 16 Air Assault Brigade.'

'I know it is,' Ben said. 'I was a soldier, too.'

'Well, there you are. Two Irish squaddies sitting in the jungle.'

'A long way from home,' Ben said.

'For you, maybe. For me, this is home.'

'I admire you for having left it all behind,' Ben said. He was being sincere.

'To be honest, there wasn't much holding me there any more. You get used to all the high living and Ferraris after a while, you know?' Scally chuckled, then looked serious. 'When the Lord called me to a better purpose, how could I refuse Him?'

'I thought about it once,' Ben admitted. 'About the church. As a career, I mean. In fact I still think about it sometimes. Life just always seemed to have other plans for me.'

'It's never too late to let God into your life, son. He's just waiting for the chance.'

'I think even God would lose patience in my case,' Ben said.

'He never loses patience,' Scally replied. 'He loves us all. We just need to reach out to him. Here, have another drop of this.'

'I could get used to it,' Ben said. He took another sip. 'Father, I can't thank you enough for what you've done for Brooke.'

'I'm just glad she's so much better. The fever was so strong at one point I was scared to leave her bedside. I get the impression you've been through a lot to find her.'

'You might say that,' Ben said. 'She was in a lot of trouble.'

'I won't ask. Whatever it was, she's safe here. And now she's on the road to recovery, I'll be taking me little boat down to San Tomás in the morning for supplies. I'll be back the following day. Give you and our patient a chance to catch up, as long as you promise not to tire her.'

'I'll take good care of her,' Ben said. 'You can be sure of that.'

Chapter Fifty-Five

Ben was sitting with Brooke in the sick bay the next morning, clasping her hand, when Father Scally knocked at the door and stepped inside.

'Good morning, Padraig,' Brooke said.

'You look stronger,' the priest noted with pleasure. 'The colour's back in your cheeks.'

'I feel it,' she said, and squeezed Ben's hand. It was as if they'd never been apart.

'Came to say I'm off,' Father Scally told them cheerfully. 'For what it's worth. What cash there's left for supplies would barely weigh down a butterfly.'

Without hesitation, Brooke reached to the side of her bed and picked up the glittering necklace and bracelet she'd taken from Serrato. 'Here. These are worth a lot of money.'

'Now, child—'

'Take them,' she insisted. 'Let them be used for something good. It's the least I can do.'

The priest gazed at the glittering jewels and whistled. 'Then on behalf of the Sapaki people, I thank you kindly. Jesus, Mary and Joseph, what diamonds. I wouldn't trust meself not to go dropping them in the river, clumsy old fool that I am. But Uchu, Rumi and his girl Chaska are coming with me and they'll guard these baubles with their lives.'

Minutes later, Father Scally set off down the path towards the river, accompanied by the two tribesmen Uchu and Rumi, along with Rumi's twelve-year-old daughter. A whole crowd of Sapaki went to see them off; Ben and Brooke could hear their clamouring from the sick bay.

'They love him. He's a wonderful man, isn't he?' Brooke said.

Ben nodded. 'Yes, he is.'

All through that day, he could see Brooke getting stronger. By the afternoon she was able to take a few steps outside. He walked with her, holding her hand, and they gently explored the village. It was far more extensive than it had seemed at first. There were cultivated gardens filled with fruit and vegetables, and even a small cotton plantation from which the tribe produced their clothing. 'It's so beautiful,' Brooke said.

It was during those peaceful, happy hours that Ben toyed on and off with the idea of telling her about Jude. He still wasn't sure how she'd take the news; and in the end he decided now was the wrong moment. He resolved to break it to her another time, maybe once he got her home to London.

And anyway, there were other things he was burning to say to her first.

The evening saw them joining the rest of the tribe for a communal feast of spit-roasted tapir, grilled fish and a kind of sweet potato mash that tasted far better than it looked. Ben introduced Brooke to Nico and Pepe and they all sat together to eat. Even with the pall of the recent massacre hanging over them, the atmosphere among the tribespeople was buoyant and upbeat. Only Tupaq, the chief, seemed preoccupied.

'No problemo,' Pepe replied through a mouthful of fish

when Ben told him that the priest had said Brooke needed a few more days in the village to recuperate. 'I'm in no hurry to go back,' Pepe added mysteriously. Ben didn't quite understand what he meant, until he noticed the covert glances and smiles that the young guy was exchanging with K'antu throughout the meal.

When everyone was full of meat and fish, some Sapaki girls brought out beautifully spun baskets filled with bananas and papaya. By then, Ben thought Brooke was looking weary again, and insisted on walking her back to the sick bay to rest. 'I feel so much better,' she kept protesting.

'I promised Father Scally I wouldn't tire you out.' He made her lie down, and used his Zippo to light the candle.

'Will you stay with me a while?' she asked, clasping his arm and tugging him down to sit by her on the bed.

'Are you kidding? I told you I wasn't going to let you out of my sight again. And I meant it.' He paused, then added, 'I *really* meant it.'

She smiled. 'What's that mean?'

He took a deep breath and thought, *here goes*. 'It means I want to be *with* you, Brooke. As in . . .'

'As in . . . ?'

'I meant as in, will you have me?' he said.

The candlelight was shining in her eyes. 'Have you?' she repeated, cocking her head to one side.

'Are you teasing me, or has this illness made you slow-witted?'

'Hey, watch it,' she warned him playfully.

'I don't want to be apart from you again,' he said. 'Not ever. Do you understand what I'm saying?'

'Ben Hope; in your own very strange way, are you by any chance proposing marriage to me?'

It was the second time in his life he'd done this. It didn't

382

get any easier with experience. He felt no less bashful and awkward than he had that day years ago near Lake Bled, in Slovenia, when he'd asked Leigh Llewellyn the same question. 'Maybe it's not the right time,' he mumbled.

'Yes,' she said.

'Yes what?' he asked, confused.

'Yes I want to be with you too,' she said. 'Yes, I'll marry you.'

'It's a deal, then,' he said with mock indifference. His heart was thumping. It would have been the worst moment to keel over dead from a cardiac arrest.

'But you have to promise me,' she said. 'No more adventures. No more running off and scaring the shit out of me. I don't think I could handle it again.'

'Look who's talking.'

'I'm serious,' she said.

'I'm serious too,' he replied. 'Serious about wanting to have a life with you. Forever.'

'Then you promise. No matter what happens?'

'No matter what happens,' he said. 'From now on my place is at home, with you. In fact . . .' He hesitated.

'What?'

'I was thinking . . .' He paused again, was about to go on and then thought better of it. 'No, you'll probably just laugh.'

'How do you know I'll laugh? Try me. Tell me what you were thinking.' She ran her hand down his arm. 'Please, Ben.'

'I was thinking about giving up Le Val. Letting Jeff take over, I know he's full of his own ideas for the place. And maybe going back to finish my studies. We could rent a house in Oxfordshire, out in the country somewhere. I wouldn't be in college more than a few hours each day, and the rest of the time we'd be together.'

'You mean finishing your theology degree?'

He nodded. 'I know, you think it's stupid – and maybe it is. But talking to Father Scally brought it all back to me. I can see a future for me there, Brooke.'

'Ben, I think it's wonderful. It's what you always wanted, deep down.'

He grinned ruefully. 'Then again, you can't always have what you want.'

'You have me, don't you?'

'Do I?'

'Oh, Ben, you know you do.'

'What about your place in Richmond? Your career?'

'I'd give them up tomorrow to be with you.'

He looked at her. 'You would?'

'Of course I would, silly. Come here.' She pulled him towards her and they kissed.

'I've just remembered,' he said, gently breaking their embrace. 'I have something of yours.' He took it from his pocket and showed her.

Brooke gasped. 'My little chain! Where did you find it?'

'Just something I picked up along the way,' he said. 'Here, let me put it on you.' He reached round her neck to fasten the clasp. She kissed him again, flung her arms round him and pressed herself up against him. 'Oh, Ben. I still can't believe you're here with me.'

'You can believe it,' he said between smothering kisses.

'Still don't. You're going to have to prove it to me.'

'Stop it. You're not strong enough for this.'

'Try me,' she murmured, pressing him down on the bed.

A soft knock interrupted them and a figure appeared in the doorway.

It was Pepe.

'Shit. Sorry, guys. Ben, they're asking for you over at the big hut.'

384

Chapter Fifty-Six

Tupaq wore a grave expression as Ben walked into the hut. Waskar, the red commander, and a circle of warriors sat around him. Ben could see something was up.

Pepe was worried about his role as interpreter. 'I wish the preacher was here, but it looks like this can't wait.'

'Do your best,' Ben said. He listened as Tupaq began to speak, then waited for Pepe's hesitant translation.

'Uh, he says his people are being killed. Says pretty soon they'll all be gone.'

'Ask him why he's telling me this,' Ben said.

Pepe interpreted. Tupaq looked earnestly at Ben and said a few more words. A glow of excitement appeared in Pepe's eyes. 'He says you killed White Knife. Says you can understand this enemy. You can help the Sapaki fight them.'

Ben was silent for a moment, then shook his head. 'Tell him I understand his problems. But this isn't my fight. I have other responsibilities. Tell him I'm sorry. That's just how it is.'

'That's fucked up, man,' Pepe said. 'That doesn't come from him, it comes from me. These people, they need help. They're all gonna die if someone doesn't—'

'Just tell him what I said,' Ben said flatly.

Tupaq listened to Pepe without a flicker of expression. His reply was brief.

'What did he say?' Ben asked.

'So be it. You can go.'

Ben left Tupaq's hut feeling bad. He hadn't walked five paces when Nico appeared from the shadows of a neighbouring hut. 'Hey. So I hear you're leaving, huh?'

Ben nodded. 'Just as soon as Brooke's able to travel.'

'I'm happy for you, man. You got what you wanted.'

Ben could see the bitterness in Nico's smile. 'I haven't forgotten why you're here,' he said. 'I did my best to help you. I'm sorry.'

'It's okay,' Nico said.

'So what are you going to do now?'

'Serrato's still out there,' Nico said. 'I told you I ain't going to give up. I meant what I said.'

'You take care.'

'Sure. You too, amigo.'

They shook hands.

And that was when they heard the cries of distress from the edge of the village.

'What the hell?' Nico said.

'Something's happening.' Ben took off at a run through the village. Nico hobbled after him. 'Whoa, wait!'

The commotion grew louder as Ben reached the little winding track that led towards the river. He saw a group of Sapaki armed with bows and arrows. It looked as though they'd been out night-hunting, but they hadn't come home bearing quarry for the village.

Staggering up the path in their midst, leaning heavily on them for support, was the bloodied and torn figure of Padraig Scally.

Ben and Nico helped the Sapaki men to carry him back

towards the village. By now, the word had spread and more people were coming running. Ben and the others lowered him gently onto a bed of blankets that some of the women brought for him to lie on. The priest was so spent with exhaustion that he could barely speak. His clothes were filthy and soaking wet, his legs and torso running with blood where thorns had lacerated him.

'What happened?' Ben asked. 'Where are the others?'

'We were attacked on the way to San Tomás,' Scally croaked. 'On the river. Armed men in fast boats. They shot Uchu. He's . . . he's *dead*.'

There was a cry from the growing crowd of distressed Sapaki people. A tribeswoman burst into tears as the meaning of the words 'Uchu' and 'dead' hit home. Uchu's mother, Ben guessed. A number of other women led her away, howling.

'Take it easy,' Ben said as the priest burst into a fit of coughing. 'Fetch some water,' he told Pepe, who'd appeared at his side with Nico. Brooke had heard the commotion and was hovering at the back of the crowd, trying to hear over the Indians' wails of anguish and shouts of anger.

'Our boat overturned,' Father Scally gasped when he'd sipped some water from a cup. 'I managed to swim to the bank, hid in the reeds. I looked back and saw the bastards pulling Rumi and Chaska up out of the water. They were both alive. I climbed up on the bank. Nobody saw me. I just ran and ran.' He screwed his eyes shut in torment. 'I should have tried to save them. I should have *done* something . . .'

'They'd have caught you, or shot you too,' Ben said. 'You did the only thing you could. How many of them were there?'

'I don't know,' the priest groaned. 'Dozens. They weren't

regular troops. Maybe a drug gang, though the Lord knows what they were doing so far upriver. Their leader was—'

'A man in a suit?' Nico growled. 'Black hair, early forties?' Scally nodded.

'Serrato,' Nico said.

Chapter Fifty-Seven

Rumi screamed and writhed on the bare patch of earth among the trees. Half blinded by the agony and the bright lights shining in his face he clutched his shattered, bloody kneecap with both hands.

The man who'd fired the shot stood over the young Indian, lining the pistol up to blow away the other kneecap on his boss's command.

'That may refresh his memory,' Serrato said. 'Now ask him again.'

Raoul Bujanda was one of several of the hired guns who could speak Quechua. He kicked Rumi savagely in the stomach. 'Where's your village?' he yelled. 'Tell us, you filthy fucking savage.'

Rumi's wide, desperate eyes locked on those of his daughter Chaska, in the strong grip of one of the men with a pistol to her head and his hand over her mouth. Her face was streaming with tears. Powerless to help her, he stared around him at the rest of the men standing on the river bank. There were so many of them. More were sitting in the strange boats bobbing on the water a few metres away. There was no possible chance of escape. Nobody was coming to save them.

Serrato opened his clenched fist. The gems of the necklace

and bracelet that they'd taken from this Indian sparkled in the torchlight. 'Tell him we only want the white woman who is being harboured by his tribe. If he helps us, he and his little girl can go free, and he has my word that none of his people will be harmed. But if he refuses, he'll watch her die before he does.'

Rumi listened in stark horror as the grinning Bujanda translated. Chaska struggled and tried to scream, but the man holding her wouldn't let her budge an inch.

'Don't hurt her,' Rumi sobbed. 'Please!' There was only one thing he could do. 'I'll tell you how to get there. It's not very far.'

'You believe a lying Indian, boss?' Vertíz asked Serrato.

'I believe any father who wishes to protect his child,' Serrato replied. 'Get him to point out the exact location of the village on the map,' he ordered Bujanda. 'Then kill them both.'

A few minutes later, two shots rang out over the river. Rumi's last scream was cut short. Serrato watched as the bodies were dumped in the bushes, then ordered his men back to their boats.

The long search was finally over. 'Check your weapons,' he commanded. 'Full magazines. Whatever we find there, we kill.'

'The woman too?' Vertíz asked.

'Her most especially,' Serrato said. 'But nobody touches her except me. Is that understood?'

The outboard motors revved. White foam churned from the propellers. The speedboats pulled away from the bank and took off in formation up the river.

Chapter Fifty-Eight

'It was Rumi who had the jewellery,' Brooke was saying. 'If Serrato found it when he captured him, you can be sure he's on his way here to find me.'

'These people are tough as old boots,' Ben said. 'You don't know that Rumi would have told them anything.'

'I do know Serrato,' Brooke answered. 'Better than you, Ben. I've seen the things he's capable of.'

'She's right, man,' Nico said. 'If Serrato got him, he talked. No question. Forget all your interrogation resistance bullshit. Nobody holds out. Not even the toughest.'

The three of them were grouped together with Pepe at the far end of the sick bay. At the other end, Father Scally was lying on the bed that had been Brooke's. He was asleep, completely worn out from his sprint through the jungle. Tica and Kusi were sitting with him. Tica was sobbing quietly in mourning for Uchu and her missing friend Chaska. It wasn't generally expected that she or her father would ever return.

'And that means he's on his way,' Brooke said. 'In fast boats, with all his men. I counted about thirty of them. Could be more. And they could be here any minute.'

Pepe shook his head. 'Maybe not that soon. I know this river. Look.' He crouched down and used the tip of his machete to trace a curving line on the earth floor. 'See how the river bends? This is us' – marking the spot with his finger –'and this is more or less where the preacher said the attack happened. Get what I'm saying?'

'It's a lot farther round by river than by land,' Ben said.

'Miles and miles farther. And these guys don't know the terrain the way the preacher does,' Pepe added. 'By cutting cross-country he gained a whole lot of time on them. I'd say that even if it didn't take the fuckers long to get Rumi to talk, we still have at least an hour before they get here. Maybe two. The landing place ain't exactly easy to find.'

'You'd better move your boat upriver a way and make sure it's well hidden,' Ben advised him.

'An hour or two still ain't long,' Nico said. 'And time isn't all we don't have. What are we supposed to fight with, bows and arrows?'

Ben thought for a moment. 'I need to go and see Tupaq.'

The chief was alone in his hut when Ben was shown inside by the surly Waskar. Pepe, Nico, Brooke and a crowd of other tribespeople filtered in behind him until the hut was teeming with bodies. The Sapaki people were all looking to Ben and Pepe in hushed anticipation.

'War is coming,' Ben said to Tupaq. 'You asked for my help against these men. Now you have it. But without weapons, there's little we can do to resist them. You understand?'

'We have weapons,' was Tupaq's response after Pepe had translated for him.

Ben shook his head. He pointed at an ornate blowpipe that hung from the hut wall. 'I respect your traditions. But these things your people have used for centuries, they're useless against automatic rifles.'

'I don't think they have a word for "automatic rifles",' Pepe said.

'That kind of sums up the whole fucking problem we're facing here,' Nico grunted.

'Ask him if he has any other weapons in the village,' Ben told Pepe. 'Any kind of gun at all.'

Tupaq reflected solemnly with his lips pursed. After some deliberation he pressed his hands to his knees, slowly rose from his seat and motioned for them to follow him out into the night. A few steps away was another hut, longer and narrower than the normal tribal dwellings. As the chief led them inside, Ben saw that that was because the hut wasn't for habitation, but a private storeroom for the village's head man.

Tupaq spent a few moments bustling about, shifting things from place to place. Then he gave a grunt and beckoned Ben over to his side. He was standing over a wooden box, battered and aged, over five feet from end to end, less than a foot deep or wide.

Pepe translated as Tupaq talked: 'Uh, he says it was his father's, and his father's before him, going back and back.'

The box was decorated in tribal style, but Ben could instantly tell that it hadn't been made here in Peru, or anywhere else in South America. It was a British Royal Navy ordnance crate dating back some two centuries.

Tupaq lifted the box's lid. Inside was a five-foot-long slender object wrapped in cloth. He lifted it out and set one end of it on the ground with a heavy 'clunk'. It was almost as tall as he was. He looked at Ben, then unwrapped the cloth and handed it to him.

Ben blinked. He remembered something he'd once read: how during the struggle for Peruvian independence in the era of the Napoleonic Wars, British military and naval intelligence had been involved in a complex web of intrigue aimed at helping to loosen the ages-old grip of the Spanish on the country. Royal Navy frigates had landed on the east coast of South America around 1815 – and what he was holding in his hands was one of the relics left over from that time. God alone knew how it had found its way out here into the jungle, but it had.

It was a flintlock musket. The flint was sharp, the action was tight, with the date 1801 engraved on its pitted lockplate; a weapon that in its day had been the standard-issue longarm of soldiers and sailors throughout the whole British Empire, known as the Brown Bess. It fired a one-ounce lead ball that could take off a man's leg at two hundred yards. In volley fire, the Brown Bess could mow down an infantry division like weeds. Rudyard Kipling had even written a poem about it.

But . . .

Ben was lost for words.

Nico found them for him. 'You've got to be kidding me. What're we supposed to do with that piece of antique crap? Throw it at the fuckers?'

'This is no good to us,' Ben said with a sinking heart. 'Maybe if we had fifty more of these, with enough powder and ball and the time to train up a militia of Sapaki men to use them, it would help even the odds a little. But this is hopeless.'

Tupaq's look of pride had faded to a frown as he sensed the negativity of their reaction. He made an impatient gesture and snapped a few words at Pepe.

'Uh, he says to come and look over here,' Pepe said. Ben handed him the musket and followed Tupaq to the back of the hut, where layers of old blankets and animal hides were draped over something stacked against the wall. By the light of a burning torch held by one of the warriors Tupaq wrenched one of the hides aside. Ben peered underneath, and his eyes opened wide when he saw the rows upon rows of open kegs. 'Jesus Christ,' he muttered.

He was mightily glad he hadn't chosen that moment to light up his one and only remaining Gauloise. Because if he had, the whole hut – the entire village – might have blown sky-high, leaving nothing but a giant crater in the jungle. 'Get that flame away from here,' he said quickly.

He dipped his hand into one of the kegs and let the fistful of coarse black powder trickle through his fingers. The grains were as dry as the day they'd been made. 'You know what this is, Tupaq?'

Tupaq replied, miming the action of tossing a pinch of the stuff. 'He says it makes the fire go well,' Pepe translated.

'I'll bet it does,' Ben said. 'This is gunpowder. *Boom*. Explosive.'

Tupaq drew aside another few blankets to reveal barrels filled with shiny grey-black balls. Ben picked one out and rolled it between his fingers. The loose ammunition for the Brown Bess. Pure lead. Three quarters of an inch in diameter. There were thousands and thousands of them.

And now he was thinking. Thinking hard and fast.

'Nico,' he said. 'Listen to me.' Away from the others, he spoke quietly in the Colombian's ear.

Brooke pushed forward through the crowd of Sapaki people, trying to hear. 'What is it, Ben?'

Nico shook his head and grinned. 'Oh, boy. You really are one crazy motherfucker. But yeah. It might work. It might just work, if there's still time.'

'Then we have none to lose,' Ben said.

Chapter Fifty-Nine

It was the dead of night. There was a stillness in the surrounding jungle that Ben had never known before. It was as if the creatures of the forest somehow sensed what was coming and had retreated to a safe distance, waiting for the storm to do its worst and pass on by.

Meanwhile, the Sapaki village was anything but still. There was a great deal to prepare, and the seconds were ticking by. The tribespeople who weren't actively helping watched in bewilderment as Ben and Nico worked fast by torchlight to get things ready. Most of the Sapaki still had little idea of what the blond-haired stranger was planning to do with the kegs of black grainy stuff that he had the warriors carrying out of the storage hut by the dozen and placing all around the village perimeter along with bundles of twine and other odd items. But they knew that both the white preacher and their chief had placed their trust in Ben, and that was good enough for them.

Pepe had gone to move his boat, under strict orders from Ben to steer well clear of the village at the slightest sign of anything suspicious. Father Scally, woken by the activity, had emerged from the sick bay to see what was happening. When Ben hurriedly explained to him what they were expecting to happen, possibly within the next hour or two, the priest was adamant that he wanted to be a part of it. He disappeared into his hut and reappeared a moment later with a hunting bow and a clutch of arrows.

'You just tell me where to position myself,' he said to Ben. 'I'm ready for those bastards.'

'I thought you were a man of peace.'

'Shame on the shepherd who runs and hides when wolves are coming to harm his flock,' the Irishman said, sticking out his chin.

'There's something else you can do for me, Father,' Ben told him. 'Once we're done preparing everything, the village needs to be evacuated, and fast. I want every woman, child and noncombatant man outside a zone at least three hundred metres wide, so that they're well clear when things kick off. It's best that Tupaq hears it from you.'

Scally hurried off to talk to the chief. Within minutes, the Sapaki women and children, along with the elder men, were slipping out of the village and disappearing into the dark forest. 'Tupaq insists on staying,' Scally told Ben on his return, 'along with Waskar and his best warriors. They've been making as many arrows as they can.'

'How many arrowheads do we have?' Ben asked.

'You mean just the loose heads? A group of the women go about finding stones most days and shaping them for the hunters to fit to their shafts. I'd say we have hundreds, if not more. Why'd you ask?'

'Gather up as many as you can find,' Ben told him.

Scally thought for a moment, then raised an eyebrow. 'Jesus, Mary and Joseph. I know what it is you're up to. M18A1?'

'Something like that,' Ben said.

'It's diabolical.'

'It's worse,' Ben said. 'Oh, and Father, bring me all the empty poteen bottles you've got, too.'

The work party intensified to a frenzy until everything was finally in place. By then, Pepe had returned safely. Ben found him with Nico and a group of the warriors snatching a moment's rest near the dying fire in the centre of the village. Nico was clutching a weapon borrowed from Waskar, a knobbly wooden club embedded with jaguar claws. Waskar himself, the chief and the rest of the fifty or so warriors were turned out nearby in full fighting trim, their quivers bristling with sharp-tipped arrows.

Ben could smell their tension. He glanced at the luminous dial of his watch. They surely didn't have long to wait now. 'Everyone okay?' he asked.

'Ready to rock and roll, man,' Nico said.

'Me too,' said a tall black figure, stepping out from behind a hut. It was a couple of moments before Ben recognised Father Scally. The priest had daubed himself all over with the vegetable dye the Indians used to colour their skin. He barely looked human. 'War paint,' he explained.

'You'll scare them to death,' Ben said. 'Where's Brooke?'

'She's helping get the last of the women and children into the safe zone.'

'That's where she's going, too,' Ben said.

'Oh no, she isn't,' said a voice. Ben turned. Brooke was standing there with her hands on her hips. 'I'm staying right here with you men.'

'Don't do this to me, Brooke.'

'These people saved my life,' Brooke said firmly.

He shook his head. 'How's this marriage going to work if you don't do what I say?'

'You watch yourself, Ben Hope.'

At that moment, the sound of tinkling bottles came from beyond the huts.

The first tripwire alarm. Something – or someone – was approaching through the trees from the direction of the river.

'They're here,' Nico said.

Chapter Sixty

Nobody moved or breathed. In the unnatural silence they heard the crackle of a footstep through the trees. A man, moving stealthily, slowly, towards the edge of the village.

Then another, a few degrees to the east. The attackers had seen the glow of the village fire. They were splitting up and approaching from all angles.

A twig snapped. A branch rustled.

The length of twine leading to the second tripwire alarm gave a soft twang, and two more glass bottles jangled together.

'Ben?' Brooke whispered. Her eyes were wide and shining in the darkness.

Ben said nothing. Calmly, slowly, he walked towards the huts. Paused near a gap and then felt in his jacket pocket for the Zippo lighter and the wrinkled pack containing his last Gauloise.

'Ben . . .'

He put the cigarette to his lips. Thumbed the striker wheel of the lighter, played the flickering flame against the end of the Gauloise. Clanged the Zippo shut and took a deep draw. The cigarette tip glowed brightly orange. He couldn't remember the last time one had tasted so good, or the last time he'd felt more alive and alert.

He was ready.

'Fuck it,' he murmured. With a final puff, he took the cigarette from his lips and flicked it to the ground in a tiny shower of sparks. The burning tobacco and paper landed at his feet.

And ignited the primary powder trail that led off between the huts. The white flame snaked rapidly away towards the trees, sputtering and spitting like a living thing.

Ben turned to the others and spoke fast. 'Stay near to me, Brooke. Whatever happens. Everyone else – you know what to do.'

The burning powder trail raced away through the trees, where it instantly set off the secondary trails that Ben and the others had carefully laid along little dug-out tracks branching out all around the periphery of the village. Each secondary trail split up several more ways. Within seconds, the dark vegetation everywhere was lit with the bright glow of the flaring gunpowder.

And then the hush of the jungle was shattered by the first series of gigantic explosions. They detonated in such quick succession that they sounded like one continuous ear-splitting roll of thunder.

M18A1, Scally had said. The old soldier had guessed correctly. That was the US military's designation for their Claymore anti-personnel mine, a weapon so fearsomely effective that armies all over the world had devised their own versions of it.

And Ben had copied it too, here deep in the heart of the Peruvian rainforest with nothing at his disposal but a few primitive tools, a few metres of homespun twine, some hollowed-out branches and a cache of ancient black powder passed down through generations of Sapaki and hidden for centuries.

Each blazing powder trail terminated at a tree. Lashed at

chest height with twine to each trunk, connected to the ground via a hollow branch filled with more powder, was a keg of the stuff mixed with hundreds of big lead musket balls and razor-sharp arrowheads. And there were over eighty of Ben's improvised Claymores scattered at key tactical points all round the village, with carefully-hacked paths through the foliage to lure the unwary into their range.

Their combined effect rocked the jungle. Rolling fireballs mushroomed upwards amid clouds of white smoke that blotted out the stars. Trees were severed in half by the storm of missiles blowing outwards in a sixty-degree arc covering everything between the huts and the river.

A moment earlier, Serrato's men had been making their stealthy, confident approach on an Indian village that looked for all the world as though it was asleep and unsuspecting – now suddenly the shocking wave of violence cut a swathe right through them. Body parts flew. Blood showered the foliage like rain. Many of those who weren't instantly chopped to pieces were terribly maimed. Others fell back in terror. But before they could recover their wits, a second rolling detonation filled the air and a dozen more intersecting fields of fire levelled the jungle around them.

Then, silence, apart from the screams of the dying. Flames flickered through the smoke. The stench of sulphur was choking.

Ramon Serrato stood up shakily from behind the fallen tree where he'd taken cover. His face was spattered with the blood of the man next to him, who'd been too slow to duck at the sound of the first explosion and had been cut almost in half.

Serrato couldn't believe what he was seeing. Indians didn't *do* this. They didn't fight back. It was unthinkable. He snatched up the fallen man's rifle and spare magazine.

The time for stealth was over. Screaming at his few remaining men to follow him, Serrato dashed through the carnage of shattered bodies and torn vegetation towards the village. He could barely see through the gunpowder fog.

Suddenly he was in the midst of the huts. Two of them were on fire from the explosions, flames leaping through the smoke. 'Come on!' he screamed at his men. Piero Vertíz appeared at his side, ready for murder. Two others came up behind them.

Whoosh . . . an arrow whistled through the night air and thudded into the chest of the man behind Vertíz. Dim figures flitted between the huts. Another arrow whizzed past Serrato's ear.

'Kill them!' he yelled. He jammed back the trigger of his rifle and held it there, spraying the huts with bullets until his magazine was empty. He released it, slammed in the spare and went on loosing off rounds in all directions. Vertíz and the others did the same. The firestorm tore through the huts, ripped branches off the trees. One or two of the shadowy figures went down, but most simply vanished away into the night. It was like trying to kill an invisible enemy.

Ben had lost sight of Nico in the confusion. A number of Indians had been shot, including Waskar the red commander, killed while leading a group of his warriors into the attack. Tupaq, Father Scally, Pepe and the other warriors were still firing from the trees. Their volleys of arrows zipped between the huts, taking down more of Serrato's men.

Ben kept an iron grip on Brooke's arm and pulled her to the ground as bullets ripped through the hut next to them, showering them with shredded tufts of thatch. Telling her to stay down, he darted out from behind cover and fitted an arrow to his own bow. From where he was standing he could clearly see Ramon Serrato firing off shots like a madman from the centre of the village. Ben drew the bowstring taut and loosed his arrow.

His target wasn't Serrato, but the big guy next to him. The arrow flew straight and drove deep into the man's heart, knocking him backwards off his feet.

'Come on!' Ben dropped the bow and took Brooke's hand. They started running back to where he'd hidden the loaded musket.

Serrato looked round to see Piero Vertíz lying motionless in the dirt with an arrow sticking up out of his chest. He was suddenly all alone. His rifle was empty. He drew the Glock pistol from his pocket and fired wildly into the darkness, screaming with fury. At the twelfth squeeze of the trigger, the Glock was empty as well.

And at that moment, for the first time since he could recall, Ramon Serrato was afraid. He dashed through the village, searching for the rest of his men. All he could see were arrow-skewered bodies littering the ground.

Then he skidded to a halt. Standing in the glow of the burning huts up ahead was Brooke. *His* Brooke.

Serrato was filled with wild rage at the sight of her – and of the man she was with. It was the blond-haired man whose picture had been in her purse. The man she'd assured him was nobody to her. 'You lied to me!' he seethed.

'You shouldn't have tried to find me, Ramon,' Brooke said.

Serrato raised the Glock, then remembered it was empty with the slide locked back. With his other hand he fumbled in his pocket for another magazine. 'I'll kill you, you bitch!'

'I don't think so,' Ben said. He picked up the Brown Bess from where it was propped against a hut wall. The musket was loaded with eighty grains of powder behind a musket ball wrapped in a small square patch of homespun Sapaki cotton, rammed down tightly inside the three-quarter-inch bore. Ben clicked the hammer back on full cock, hefted the long, heavy weapon and peered down the barrel at the lone figure of Ramon Serrato.

Serrato found the magazine in his pocket.

'Shoot him, Ben!' Brooke urged.

Ben took his finger off the trigger and lowered the musket. He shook his head. 'No. I can't shoot him.'

'Ha! What did you expect, trying to kill me with that thing?' Serrato laughed. In less of a hurry now, he began slotting the magazine into his pistol.

'I can't shoot him, because I made a promise,' Ben said.

Serrato's laughter died. 'What promise?'

'One to a friend,' Ben told him.

Nico had emerged limping from the shadows. His face was covered in blood from where a bullet had creased his scalp. His eyes burned with a hotter fire than the blazing huts in the background.

Ben tossed Nico the Brown Bess.

Nico advanced. Serrato backed away, staring at him. 'You!' He raised his pistol. Too slow.

'Adios, motherfucker,' Nico said. He shouldered the musket and fired. There was a bright flash as the striking flint ignited the powder in the pan. A fraction of a second later the gun erupted with an ear-shattering blast.

Serrato was blown off his feet. He landed on his back with a fist-sized hole gaping in his chest, twitched twice, and then lay still.

Nico dropped the musket and fell to his knees. Now that they were avenged, he was finally able to weep for his dead children, and tears rolled down his bloody face.

It was over. Ben and Brooke left Nico alone and walked away, hand in hand.

'We wrecked their village,' he said sadly, surveying the

devastation. The white pall of smoke was drifting high over the jungle, red-lit by the fires.

'And saved half a million acres of forest from being destroyed forever,' Brooke said, hugging him tightly.

The Sapaki people were re-emerging from the forest. There were cries of grief over the fallen, but before long they were lost in the victory chant of Tupaq and his warriors. Father Scally, Tica and Kusi began attending to the wounded. Come morning, the villagers would commence the task of rebuilding.

Ben stroked Brooke's hair. He kissed her face. 'You ready to go home now?'

She nodded.

'Yes, Ben. I'm ready.'

Read on for an exclusive extract from
Scott Mariani's new novel, coming
from Avon in 2014

Prologue

The Altai Mountains
Bayan-Ölgii Province
Western Mongolia

The biting wind was starting to whip flurries of snow across the barren mountainside. Soon, Chuluun knew, the winter snowfalls would be here in earnest and it might be a long time before he could venture out this far again in search of food.

The argali herd the teenager was tracking had led him almost half a mile across bare rock from where he'd tethered his pony further down the mountain. Wolves were an ever-present concern, but the curly-horned wild sheep could sense the roving packs from a great way off, and they seemed calm enough, having paused on their trek to munch contentedly on a scrubby patch of heather, to reassure Chuluun that his pony was safe.

There was one predator too smart to let himself be noticed by the argali. Chuluun had been hunting over these mountains for six years, since the age of eleven, when his father had become too infirm to ride long distances any more, and he prided himself on his ability to sneak up on anything that lived, walked or flew. His parents and seven younger brothers and sisters depended almost entirely on him for meat, and in the harsh environment of Mongolia, meat meant survival.

Carefully staying downwind of the grazing sheep and moving with stealthy ease over the rocks, Chuluun stalked to within a hundred metres of his quarry before settling himself down at the top of a rise, in a vantage point from which his pick of the herd, a large male he estimated stood a good four feet at the shoulder, was nicely presented side-on.

Very slowly, Chuluun slid the ancient Martini-Henry into aiming position and hunkered down behind it. He opened the rifle's breech, drew one of the long, heavy cartridges from his bandolier and slipped it silently inside. He closed the breech and flipped up the tangent rear sight. At this range he knew exactly how much elevation he needed to compensate for gravity's pull on the trajectory of the heavy bullet.

The argali remained still, munching away, oblivious. Chuluun honoured his prey, as he honoured the spirit of the mountains. He blinked a snowflake from his eyelashes. Gently, purposefully, he curled his finger around the trigger, controlled his breathing and felt his heart slow as his concentration focused on the all-important shot. If he missed, the herd would be off and he couldn't hope to catch up with them again today, nor this week. But Chuluun wasn't going to miss. Tonight, his family were going to eat as they hadn't eaten in a long while.

At the perfect moment, Chuluun squeezed the trigger.

And in that same moment, everything went insane.

The view through the rifle's sights disappeared in a massive blurred explosion. His first confused thought was that his gun had burst on firing. But it wasn't the gun.

Chuluun barely had time to cry out as the ground seemed

to lurch away from under him and then heave him with terrifying violence into the air. He was spinning, tumbling, sliding down the mountain. His head was filled with a deafening roar. Something hit him with a hard blow and he blacked out.

When Chuluun awoke, the sky seemed to have darkened. He blinked and sat up, shivering with cold and beating the snow and dirt from his clothes, then staggered to his feet. His precious rifle lay half-buried in the landslide that had carried him down from the top of the rise. Still half-stunned, he clambered back up the rocky slope and peered, afraid to look, over the edge.

He gasped at the incredible sight below.

Chuluun was standing on the edge of a near perfect circle of utter devastation that stretched as far as his keen young hunter's eyes could see. Nothing remained of the patch of ground where the argali herd had been quietly grazing. The mountainside was levelled. Gigantic rocks pulverised. The pine forests completely obliterated. All gone, swept away by some unimaginable force.

His face, streaked with dirt and tears, contorted into an expression of disbelief. Chuluun gazed up at the strange glow that permeated the sky, like nothing he'd ever seen before. Blades of lightning knifed through the rolling clouds. There was no thunder. Just a heavy, eerie pall of silence.

Suddenly filled with conviction that something unspeakably evil had just happened here, he scrambled away with a terrified moan and started fleeing down the slope towards where he'd left his pony.

Chapter 1

The apartment was all in shadow. It wasn't normal for Claudine Pommier to keep her curtains tightly drawn even on a bright and sunny June afternoon.

But then, it wasn't normal for someone to be stalking her and trying to kill her, either.

Claudine was tense as she padded barefoot down the gloomy, narrow hallway. She prayed the boards wouldn't creak and give her away. A moment ago she'd been certain she could hear footsteps outside the triple-locked door. Now she heard them again. Holding her breath she got to the door and peered through the dirty glass peephole. The aged plasterwork and wrought iron railing of the old apartment building's upper landing looked distorted through the fish-eye lens.

Claudine felt a flood of relief as she recognised the tiny figure of her neighbour Madame Lefort, with whom she shared the top floor. The octogenarian widow locked up her apartment and started heading for the stairs. She was carrying a shopping basket.

Claudine unlatched the security chain, slid back both bolts and the deadlock and rushed out of the door to catch her.

'Madame Lefort? Hang on – wait!'

The old woman was fit and sprightly from decades of negotiating the five flights of winding stairs each day. She was also as deaf as a tree, and Claudine had to repeat her name three more times before she caught her attention.

'Bonjour, Mademoiselle Pommier,' the old woman said with a yellowed smile.

'Madame Lefort, are you going out?' Claudine said loudly.

'To do my shopping. Is something wrong, dear? You don't look well.'

Claudine hadn't slept for two nights. 'Migraine,' she lied. 'Bad one. Would you post a couple of letters for me?'

Madame Lefort looked at her tenderly. 'Of course. You poor dear. Shall I get you some aspirin too?'

'It's okay, thanks. Hold on a moment.' Claudine rushed back into the apartment. The two letters were lying on the table in the salon, sealed and ready but for the stamps. Their contents were identical; their addressees half a world apart. She snatched them up and rushed back to the door to give them to Madame Lefort. 'This one's for Canada,' she explained. 'This one for Sweden.'

'Where?' the old woman asked, screwing up her face.

'Just show the person at the counter,' Claudine said as patiently as she could. 'They'll know. Tell them the letters have to go registered international mail, express delivery. Have you got that?'

'Say again?'

'Registered international mail,' Claudine repeated more firmly. 'It's terribly, terribly important.'

The old woman inspected each letter in turn an inch from her nose. 'Canada? Sweden?' she repeated, as though they were addressed to Jupiter and Saturn.

'That's right.' Claudine held out a handful of euros. 'This

should cover the postage. Keep the change. You won't forget, will you?'

As the old woman headed off down the stairs, Claudine hurried back to her apartment and locked herself in. All she could do now was pray that Madame Lefort wouldn't forget, or manage to lose the letters halfway to the post office. There was no other way to get word out to the only people she could trust. Two allies she knew would come to her aid.

If it wasn't too late already.

Claudine ventured to the window. She reached out nervously and pulled the edge of the curtain back a crack. The afternoon sunlight streamed in, making her blink. Five floors below, the traffic was filtering along the narrow street. But that wasn't what Claudine was watching.

She swallowed. The car was still there, in the same parking space at the kerbside right beneath her windows where it had been sitting since yesterday. She was completely certain it was the same black Audi with dark-tinted glass that had followed her from Laurent's family country home two days ago.

And, before that, the same car that had tried to run her down in the street and only narrowly missed her. It still made her tremble to think of it.

She quickly drew the curtain shut again, hoping that the men inside the car hadn't spotted her at the window. She was pretty sure there were three of them. Her instinct told her they were sitting inside it, just waiting.

After the scare and the realisation she was being followed, on her return from Laurent's place she hadn't intended to remain here in the apartment any longer than it took to pack a few things into a bag and get the hell out. But the car had appeared before she'd been able to escape – and now she was trapped.

Were these the men that Daniel had warned her about? If that was the case, they knew everything. Every detail of her research. And if so, they must know what she'd learned about their terrible plans. If they caught her, they wouldn't let her live. Couldn't let her live. Not after what she'd uncovered.

Under siege in her own apartment. How long could she hold out? She had enough tinned provisions to last about a week, if she rationed her meals. And enough vodka left in the bottle to stop her terror from driving her crazy.

Claudine spent the next half hour pacing anxiously up and down the darkened room, fretting over whether the old lady had sent her letters the way she'd asked. 'I can't stand this,' she said out loud. 'I need a drink.'

Walking into the tiny kitchen she grabbed a tumbler, took the vodka bottle from the freezer compartment and sloshed out a stiff measure. She downed the chilled drink in a couple of gulps and poured another. It wasn't long before the alcohol had combined with her fatigue to make her head swirl. She wandered back through into the salon, lay on the couch and closed her eyes. Almost instantly, she began to drift.

When Claudine awoke with a start and opened her eyes, the room was completely dark. She must have slept for hours. Something had woken her. A sound. Her heart began to race.

That was when the bright flash from outside lit up the narrow gap between the curtains, followed a moment later by another rumble of thunder. She relaxed. It was just a storm. The howling wind was lashing the rain against the windows.

She got up from the couch and groped for the switch of the table lamp nearby. The light came on with a flicker. The ancient wiring of the apartment building threatened to black the place out every time there was a storm. The clock on the mantelpiece read 10.25. Too late to go and ask Madame Lefort if she'd posted the letters, as the old woman was always in bed by half past nine. It would have to wait until morning.

Claudine stepped over to the window and peered out of the crack in the curtains. With a gasp she saw that the car was gone.

Gone! Just an empty pool of light, glistening with rainwater, under the streetlamp where it had been parked.

She blinked. Had she just imagined the whole thing? Was nobody following her after all? Had the near-miss in the street two days ago just been a coincidence, some careless asshole not looking where he was going?

The rush of relief she felt was soon overtaken by a feeling of self-blame. If this whole thing had been just her paranoia getting the better of her, then she should never have sent those letters. She'd made a fool of herself.

Suddenly she was hoping that the old woman hadn't posted them after all.

The storm continued outside. Claudine knew she wouldn't get any more sleep that night. She wandered into her little bedroom, flipped on the side light and picked up her violin. One of the upsides to sharing the top floor with a deaf old woman was that she could play whenever she liked. Madame Lefort wouldn't even have heard the thunder.

Thankful that she had something to occupy her mind, Claudine cradled the instrument under her chin, touched the bow to the strings, and went into the opening bar of the Bach sonata she'd been trying to master for the last couple of months.

Another bright flash outside; and at that moment the lights went out. She cursed and went on playing by the red glow from the neon sign of the hotel across the street.

Then she paused, frowning. There'd been a noise. *Before* the roll of thunder. Like a thump. It seemed to have come from above. There was nothing above her apartment but the roof. Maybe the wind had knocked something down, she thought, or sent a piece of debris bouncing over the tiles. She went on playing.

But she hadn't produced more than a few notes before her bow groaned to a dissonant halt on the strings. She'd heard the noise again.

There was someone inside the apartment. An intruder.

A cold sweat broke out over her brow. Her knees began to shake. She needed to arm herself with something. Thinking of the knife block on the kitchen worktop, she tossed her violin and bow down on the bed and hurried towards the doorway – then skidded to a halt on the bare boards as another violent lightning flash lit up the room and she saw the figure standing in the doorway, blocking her exit.

Too terrified to speak, Claudine retreated into the bedroom.

The intruder stepped into the room after her. She could see him outlined in the red neon glow from the hotel. He was tall and broad. Black boots, black trousers, black jacket and gloves. His hair was silver, cropped to stubble. A hard, angular face. Pale eyes narrowed to slits. Around his waist was some kind of utility belt, like builders and carpenters wore.

For one crazy, irrational moment, Claudine thought he was a workman come to carry out the much-needed repairs to the bathroom. But that idea vanished as he drew the claw hammer from his utility belt and came towards her.

She snatched the violin from the bed. Lashed wildly out with it and caught him across the brow with such force that the instrument broke apart. The splintering wood raked his flesh, drawing blood that looked as dark as treacle in the red light. He barely seemed to have felt the blow. He swung the hammer and knocked the shattered violin from her hand. She cowered away from him. 'Please—'

He struck out again with the hammer. Claudine's vision exploded, and white, blinding pain flashed through her head. She fell onto the bed, dazed.

The man stood over her, clutching the hammer in his fist. Strands of bloody hair dangled from the steel claw. Silently, calmly, he slipped the tool back into his utility belt. From another long pouch he drew out a cylindrical tube with some kind of plunger and transparent plastic nozzle attached.

He bent over her. Through the fog of pain, she saw him smile. His eyes and teeth were red in the hotel neon.

The man spoke in English. 'Now it's time for that pretty mouth of yours to be plugged up.'

A hoarse cry of terror burst from Claudine's lips as she realised what the thing was he was holding. She tried desperately to wriggle away from him but he reached out with a quick and powerful hand, grabbed her hair and pinned her thrashing head to the bed, ignoring the wild blows she flailed out at his face and arms.

With his other hand he jammed the nozzle of the tube into her screaming mouth. She cried out and bit down on the hard plastic and tried to spit it out, gagging as it forced its way deep inside.

The man pressed the plunger. Instantly, something foul-tasting, warm and soft filled her mouth. It was coming out under pressure and there was nothing Claudine could do to stop it flowing down her throat. She tried to cough it out, but all of a sudden no air would come. There was an awful sensation of pressure building up inside her as the substance swelled and expanded, filling every cavity of her throat, her nasal passages.

She couldn't breathe, couldn't scream, couldn't open or shut her jaws a millimetre. She stopped trying to lash out at him, and in a crazed panic she clamped her hands to her mouth and felt the hardening foam bulging out from between her lips like some grotesque tongue.

The man dropped the empty canister on the bed and used both hands to hold her bucking, convulsing body down. After a minute or so, as her brain was becoming starved of oxygen, her movements began to slacken. The man let her go and stood up.

The darkness was rising fast as Claudine's vision faded. For a few seconds longer she could still dimly register the man's shape standing over her in the red-lit room, watching her impassively with his head slightly cocked to one side.

Soon she could see nothing at all.

The man waited a few more moments before he checked her pulse. Once he was satisfied that she was dead, he left the bedroom. He unlocked the apartment door and left it ajar as he made his silent way toward the stairs.

WHERE THERE'S HOPE, THERE'S TROUBLE...

—⟨⟩—

THE ALCHEMIST'S SECRET

A former elite member of the SAS, Ben Hope devotes his life to rescuing kidnapped children. When he is recruited to locate an ancient manuscript which could save a dying child, Ben teams up with American scientist Dr Roberta Ryder. The trail leads them from Paris to the ancient Cathar strongholds of the Languedoc, where an astonishing secret has lain hidden for centuries.

THE MOZART CONSPIRACY

Ben is enlisted by Leigh Llewellyn – opera star and Ben's first love – to investigate her brother's mysterious death. But a shadowy splinter group of the Freemasons will stop at nothing to keep its ancient secrets. From the dreaming spires of Oxford to Venice's labyrinthine canals, Ben and Leigh must race across Europe to discover the truth...

THE DOOMSDAY PROPHECY

Ben is searching for missing biblical archaeologist Zoë Bradbury. What is the ancient biblical secret that Zoë uncovered? As Ben moves from Greece to the American Deep South and the holy city of Jerusalem, he discovers the stakes are terrifyingly high. Ben must prevent a disaster that could kick-start the Apocalypse...

THE HERETIC'S TREASURE

Egyptologist Morgan Paxton has been brutally murdered in Cairo and Colonel Harry Paxton – the man who once saved Ben's life – wants Ben to find his son's killer. Ben is plunged into one double-cross after another. His mission leads him from Europe to the banks of the Nile, climaxing in a terrifying showdown in the Sudanese desert.

THE SHADOW PROJECT

Ben is forced to provide protection for Swiss billionaire Maximilian Steiner. Steiner believes that a sinister neo-Nazi cell is targeting him to seize a historic document that supports claims that the Holocaust never happened. The stakes are global – and this time Ben is fighting to protect those closest to him...

THE LOST RELIC

Visiting a former SAS comrade in Italy, Ben witnessed a violent heist at a gallery that leaves many dead. A seemingly worthless Goya sketch was the target. Wrongly accused of murder and forced to go on the run, he must get to the heart of the conspiracy while he still has the chance.

THE SACRED SWORD

Returning to the UK to sort out his stormy personal life, Ben runs into two university friends, Simeon and Michaela. Ben senses that Simeon is troubled but before the truth can emerge about his secretive research project, both he and Michaela are killed in a road crash. Convinced it was no accident, Ben is propelled on a global quest while a ruthless organisation pursues him at every step...